Robert Edric's previous novels include *Winter Garden*, *A New Ice Age*, *Elysium*, *In Desolate Heaven*, *The Sword Cabinet* and *The Book of the Heathen*, which was shortlisted for the 2001 WHSmith Literary Award. His latest novel, *Cradle Song*, is now available from Doubleday. He lives in East Yorkshire.

PEACETIME

Robert Edric

BLACK SWAN

PEACETIME
A BLACK SWAN BOOK : 0 552 77206 2

Originally published in Great Britain by Doubleday,
a division of Transworld Publisheers

PRINTING HISTORY
Doubleday edition published 2002
Black Swan edition published 2003

1 3 5 7 9 10 8 6 4 2

The publisher has made every effort to obtain permission from
the estate of Edna St Vincent Millay to reproduce lines from an
untitled poem by Edna St Vincent Millay in *Make Bright the Arrows*,
published in 1940 by Harper & Row. They invite the estate
to contact them direct and shall be pleased to make the
appropriate acknowledgements in any future edition.

Set in 11/13pt Melior by
Falcon Oast Graphic Art Ltd.

Black Swan Books are published by Transworld Publishers,
61–63 Uxbridge Road, London W5 5SA,
a division of The Random House Group Ltd,
in Australia by Random House Australia (Pty) Ltd,
20 Alfred Street, Milsons Point, Sydney, NSW 2061, Australia,
in New Zealand by Random House New Zealand Ltd,
18 Poland Road, Glenfield, Auckland 10, New Zealand
and in South Africa by Random House (Pty) Ltd,
Endulini, 5a Jubilee Road, Parktown 2193, South Africa.

Printed and bound in Great Britain by
Clays Ltd, St Ives plc.

for Lauren and Nathalie

We think – although of course, now, we
very seldom
Clearly think –
That the other side of War is Peace.

EDNA ST VINCENT MILLAY

Summer, 1946

Part I

1

The girl came slowly towards him, and James Mercer watched her through his binoculars, convinced that he could not be seen by her. He adjusted his lenses and brought her more sharply into focus, his elbows sinking deeper into the fine sand which was already beneath his shirt and in his boots.

It had not been his intention to spy on her. He had been watching for the lorries carrying the labourers, already an hour late, when she had come unexpectedly into view. In the week since his arrival, this was only the second time he had seen her. She walked with no apparent purpose or destination, frequently pausing to look around her. And watching her, even at that distance, Mercer sensed that she gained some small pleasure from being so alone and so aimless. The road was narrow and badly worn, and led only to the houses and abandoned buildings at its end.

The sun was high, and in the opposite direction the line of the road was molten in the haze, its boundaries lost to the drifting sand which came and went from its margins.

The dunes in which Mercer lay provided the only natural vantage point for miles in any direction, and he had gone there to watch for the approaching vehicles so that he might be ready for the men upon their arrival. They were an unwilling workforce and delayed each day's start for as long as possible. It was his intention that particular morning to watch for them coming and then to start up the generators before they arrived, filling the still air with their pall of blue smoke, and hopefully suggesting some degree of urgency about the work ahead.

He looked beyond the girl along the line of the road, marked to the horizon by telegraph poles, but saw nothing. Little other traffic used the road. His own convoys – seldom more than ten or twelve lorries – were often held up by the narrow bridges, and by vehicles coming in the opposite direction. The open expanse of land, sea and sky joined seamlessly all around him.

He lowered the glasses until the girl was once again in focus. She had stopped walking and was now leaning against a post. She brushed the sand from her feet and calves. She wore no shoes. She shielded her eyes and looked around her, pausing briefly – or so it seemed to Mercer – when facing in his direction. He knew she would have seen no light reflected from his glasses because he had gauged the position of the sun before settling himself into the dunes. The act of checking, and then of ensuring that he broke no skyline, had become second nature to him, and realizing what he was doing made him smile.

He raised his head slowly. The girl no longer stood against the post. He scanned the road on either side of this, but saw nothing. He searched the levels beyond, but there was still no sign of her. He raised himself further to take in the wider view, and only then did he see her rise from where she had been sitting a short distance from the post. She straightened the simple dress she wore and resumed walking. It occurred to him that she had been deliberately hiding from him, letting him know that she knew he was watching her, but he saw by the same casual manner in which she resumed her walking that this was unlikely. He let himself sink back into the sand, feeling its warmth against his arms.

He lay with his eyes closed for several minutes, knowing how easily he might succumb to this comfort and warmth and allow himself to fall asleep, but even as he considered this he heard the distant rasp of an engine as the first of the approaching lorries negotiated a bend in the road. He raised his head and saw them coming, relieved that he might now continue with the work he was there to undertake, and at the same time disappointed that his time alone was at an end.

The path behind him, at the landward side of the dunes, would take him quickly back to the excavations, where he might start his preparations in advance of the others.

He rose to leave, and as he did so he saw that the girl was now on the road directly beneath him and that she was watching him. Her eyes were lost to him in the shadow of her hands, only her mouth remained visible, and he knew that she must have run to have come so far from the post in such a short time.

'I was waiting for the lorries,' he said. He indicated the vehicles, still distant and slow-moving, their exhaust smoke hanging like dust behind them.

The girl made no acknowledgement of this.

He felt uncomfortable, imagining he was about to be accused by her.

'We're working on the new Station,' he called down to her.

She said something he did not hear.

'I can't hear you,' he said.

'I said we know who you are.' She took several paces towards him, her bare feet sinking into the sand of the dunes.

'I ought to be getting back there for when they arrive.'

She waited where she stood.

'Nice meeting you,' he said.

She repeated the words, but in a low voice.

Watching her at a distance, he had guessed her to be twelve or thirteen, a child, but seeing her beneath him, seeing her height and her outline beneath the thin dress, he knew that this guess had been wrong, and that she was three, perhaps four years older.

'You have no shoes,' he said, not knowing why he'd said this, and immediately regretting the words.

She looked down at her buried feet.

'Is that what you were looking at through your binoculars?' she said. She shook the sand from her feet until they were uncovered.

'Like I said, I was watching for the lorries.'

'You were watching me,' she said. There was more amusement than threat in the remark.

'I saw you,' he said. 'That's all.' He started down the slope towards her.

'I thought you had to get back.' She lowered her hand, revealing herself fully to him.

'Present or absent, they take little enough notice of me.'

'I know,' she said.

18

The remark surprised him. 'Oh?'

'Only what we hear. You think anything gets said, anything happens round here that everybody doesn't get to know about one way or another?'

There was something conciliatory in the remark and he continued down the loose sand until he stood beside her.

He held out his hand to her. 'I'm—'

'Mercer,' she said. 'From the Authority.'

'James,' he said. 'The Authority?'

'The lifeboat people.'

'You seem to know a lot.'

'Like I said . . .' She turned to look around her.

'And you are?'

She considered the question, as though a choice existed, as though she might either reveal nothing at all or create herself completely anew for him.

Her hesitation made him smile.

'What?' she said.

'Nothing. I asked you your name, that's all.'

'Mary Lynch.' She turned away from him as she spoke.

'I wasn't spying on you,' he said.

'Yes you were.'

'How did you know I was up there?'

'You've been there every morning for the past week, ever since you came. You spy on us all. That's why you're here. You're knocking down all the stuff from the war, and when that's done you'll knock down the houses and we'll all have to leave.'

He was caught off-balance by how swiftly and directly their simple pleasantries had moved into the unrevealed future. There was some truth in everything she said, though none of it could have been known for certain by her, and he was responsible for only a small

19

part of what she had suggested. Equally, he knew that nothing would be served by his denial of what she had said.

'You seem to know a lot about it.'

'And you think I'm stupid and that you can treat me like the rest of them.'

'Rest of who? You mean the other' – he stopped himself from saying 'children' – 'people living up there?' He indicated the distant row of houses.

'Forget it,' she told him.

In the short time they had been standing together, the lorries had come much closer, and the first of these was already approaching them. They were seen, and the driver of the leading vehicle sounded his horn. Three men sat in the cab, and all of them called out as they came close. Mercer hoped they might keep going, but knew this was unlikely. The driver and his companions, along with the dozen or so others in the covered back, were perhaps only four or five years older than the girl. They would be unable to resist talking to her, propositioning her, making some remark about the two of them being together in such an isolated place. He had heard the lascivious remarks they made whenever any of the women from the houses came close to where they were working; heard, too, their conversations regarding wives and girl-friends during their long breaks; he had seen the magazines and postcards they occasionally brought with them.

He wished now that he had not gone down to her. The other lorries drew up behind the first. He told the leading driver to carry on to the site, but the man was reluctant to leave.

'What about you and her?' he said.

'What do you mean?'

'I mean, you coming with us?' He grinned broadly at the girl. 'Plenty of room up here for you,' he said directly to her.

'We can make our own way back,' Mercer told him.

But even as he spoke, the girl approached the cab and raised her foot onto its high metal step, causing her dress to rise and reveal her knee and thigh. The driver and his companions appreciated this, and all three men leaned towards the open window. Everything Mercer now said was ignored by them. The drivers of the other lorries sounded their horns.

He withdrew until he was back in the sand.

The girl did not enter the cab, but stood on the step with her arm looped around the mirror. He was reluctant to say anything more to her in front of these others. She turned to look down at him and he avoided her gaze. Then she said something to the driver which caused him to laugh aloud and then to push the engine noisily into gear. The heavy tyres spun briefly on the road and the lorry moved away. The others followed it.

As they passed him, the men called out to Mercer from the shadowy interiors. He ignored them and looked back to where the girl still clung to the door of the leading vehicle. He saw how her dress was pressed more tightly to her as the lorry gained speed. He saw the hand of the driver hanging loosely beside her, casually brushing her bare arm, as though he was preparing to grab her in case she lost her footing and fell.

2

Later, waiting until the last of the men had left the site, he made a survey of the day's work. Even a cursory glance over the workings showed him that the preparations were behind schedule: a great deal remained to be demolished, and not enough of the new foundations had yet been excavated.

He had made his temporary home in what had been the perimeter watchtower of the nearby airfield. The boundary of this lay across the broadest of three converging drains, and the tower had been used to look out for the returning aircraft as they approached the runway and the body of the airfield half a mile distant. This, too, was in the process of being demolished and returned to farmland. The place had ceased to be operational almost a year earlier, since which time it had fallen quickly into disrepair. A second airfield lay five miles further inland, at Walsham, and this remained in limited use, largely as the test base for the jet-engine planes being developed and flown there.

Upon discovering that he would be required to

remain at Fleet Point, Mercer had enquired about using the abandoned tower and had been told to go ahead, that it was unlikely to be demolished. In all likelihood, he guessed, its crude and unrendered brickwork would quickly succumb to the salt air and it would soon collapse and be lost.

The building consisted of two rooms, one above the other. The lower space was damp and derelict, possessed no windows and had been stripped of its flooring and anything else it might once have contained. The upper room, reached by a simple wooden staircase rising through a central trapdoor, was dry and reasonably weatherproof, at least during those summer months, and it was here that he had set out his few possessions. He slept on a campaign bed, and one of the Trinity House quartermasters had provided him with paraffin lamps and a supply of food and water.

He left the tower and walked around the perimeter of the workings. He made notes and sketches of what had been done and what remained to be completed. He imposed order where, as yet, little existed. He mapped out a plan of works in which he alone possessed faith. His masters and the planners elsewhere remained distant and faceless to him.

He crossed from the site towards the open sea. The tide was out and the water shone in the distance. Several miles of marsh and exposed mud lay between him and the far low-water mark. When the water was high and the marsh covered, the broad drains were filled and running, and all too often work at the edge of the site had to be abandoned until the water fell. In places, the diggers had already undermined the banked drains and had caused further short-lived flooding. The last time this had happened he had accused the men concerned of negligence and the whole of the six-man crew had refused to resume work until the accusation was withdrawn. He had apologized to them, but had made it clear that his understanding of what had happened remained intact. There was no doubt in the minds of any of those involved that the drain had been deliberately breached. The flooding had lasted three days until the water had finally soaked away and the gap filled.

Coming again in sight of the road, he was about to cross it and climb the opposite bank when he heard the sound of collapsing rubble behind him. He paused, listening as the bricks and shattered concrete fell and settled. But this did not fade as usual, and instead there was the sound of further movement, as though someone were moving across the unsteady surface. Signs had been posted warning the locals against trespassing on the site, and they were especially warned against letting their children roam the place. But he knew that little attention was paid to these warnings, and he knew, too, that he and his workers would for ever remain intruders, and that the people living there resented this intrusion onto land they considered they had every right to wander over.

He climbed the embankment and searched the site, knowing that whoever had made the noise would now be hiding somewhere, and would, in all likelihood, be watching him where he stood.

He searched as he had been taught to search, scanning the land beneath him from left to right at a steady pace, starting with the spaces closest to him and then broadening his scope to include the wider area. He saw nothing. A flock of crows rose from the rubble beside the tower. A fire burned on the distant airfield and a column of smoke rose unbroken into the air.

He was about to resume his inspection, knowing that it would serve no purpose to confront whoever might have been there, when a movement caught his eye, and he looked more closely to see a man he did not recognize emerge from amid several pieces of sheeted machinery and walk to the road.

He called out and the man turned and searched for him. Whoever this was, he made no attempt to run or hide, and instead he came further out into the open and waited beside the road as Mercer went to him.

The two men stood several yards apart for a moment, until the stranger extended his hand and went forward. He walked with a slight limp, Mercer noticed, or, if not a limp, then with a certain weakness or injury which would not allow him to make a full and rigid stride. He carried a satchel over his shoulder, but this held no weight.

'What are you doing?' Mercer asked him.

'Searching for buried treasure,' the man said disarmingly.

'Did you find any?'

'Oh, bits and pieces.' He patted his bag. It was immediately apparent from his accent that he was foreign. He spoke English well enough, but with the intonation and emphasis of a foreigner. 'Jacob Haas,' he said, introducing himself, and pronouncing the name 'Ya-cob'.

Mercer took his hand. It felt thin and insubstantial in his own, and the man withdrew it at the slightest pressure. He wore his frayed cuffs buttoned tight across his wrists, and the sleeves of his jacket were too long for his arms.

'You're Dutch?' Mercer said.

'I won't congratulate you on your guess,' the man said. He squinted against the sun, and Mercer indicated that they might both turn their backs to it.

'Would you mind if I sat down?' Jacob said, and the two of them sat against the embankment.

'Are you working on the airfield?' Mercer asked him. He knew that among the men tearing up the runways there were some foreign labourers, and a party of German prisoners of war – those who had even then, fifteen months after the war's end, not yet been repatriated for one bureaucratic reason or other, and those who showed no inclination to leave. During the hostilities they had been imprisoned elsewhere, many of them in Scotland, and some in Canada, and at the war's end they had been returned here to work prior to their release. Some among them had found even these spartan conditions preferable to what awaited them in Germany and so had requested to remain. Many had formed relationships with the farming families to whom they had been allocated, and some had courted local women and were hoping to make new lives here for themselves.

'The airfield?'

'I thought you might be working there. The demolition.'

The man turned in the direction of the rising smoke. He considered this for a moment and then bowed his head. 'I live here,' he said. He indicated along the line of the road towards the town. 'I came here a year ago. Before that I was in London and then Cambridge.'

'A displaced person.'

'That was my title.'

'Are you here with your family?'

Jacob shook his head. 'Only me. I promise you, I have been well vetted by all the various authorities and boards of examiners.' He continued to look down at the ground as he spoke, and Mercer sensed that he had said it all a hundred times before, and to inquisitors far more hostile and suspicious than himself.

'I didn't mean to pry,' he said. 'Forgive me.'

'And you, I guess, are English,' Jacob said. 'Through and through.'

Mercer laughed.

'I did once work at the airfield,' Jacob said. 'But I wasn't up to the mark. What is the expression? Oh, yes – I was found "wanting".'

Then, and afterwards, Mercer noticed, Jacob took great pleasure in using such phrases, as though he alone truly understood them and gained some advantage by this.

'I tried to work there, but it was too much for me. I was told to go away and get strong. I returned several times more, but on each occasion I was unsuccessful. I know men who work there. They keep me informed each time more labour is required. I persist – I fail, but I persist.'

'Is that why you came here?' Mercer said. 'Were you hoping for work?'

'No. I came because the work here intrigues me. And because I have time on my hands. It is summer now, but that will soon pass, and, believe me, winter in this place is a very different proposition, a different world entirely.'

It struck Mercer as the kind of melodramatic, portentous remark only a foreigner would make, but he said nothing.

'So how do you live?'

'By which you mean how do I feed and clothe myself.' He plucked at his shabby sleeve as he spoke. 'I manage. As you can see, I set my sights low. I may not yet possess the strength for the demolition work, but I pick up odd jobs here and there. At present I am liming the walls of a pigsty, and after that there will be fruit-picking in the orchards. I manage. I make do with what I have. And I live alone, completely alone. You would be surprised how much easier life is that way. Please, don't concern yourself. If there is ever anything I need of you, I shall ask it.' He then quizzed Mercer on what was being undertaken at the site.

Afterwards, they sat together in silence for several minutes. A dazzling light now shone on the distant water.

'My father was a glass-maker,' Jacob said eventually. 'And his father and grandfather before him. All my uncles were involved in the trade. It was a family business. And those who were not directly involved with the furnaces and the manufacture and the finishing-work were employed in the warehouses we owned, in the offices which dealt with the accounts and sales, and in the wholesaling and retailing of what all these other men produced. My mother, her sisters . . .'

He stopped speaking after that, and it seemed to Mercer that he had been caught off-guard by how much he had said, and how easily these memories had returned to him. He sensed, too, that a great and unbearable weight lay behind what little he had revealed, and Mercer made his own unspoken guesses as to what this might involve.

'We smash glass by the lorry-load,' he said eventually.

'Everyone does,' Jacob said. 'What else is there to do with glass, but to smash it?'

Mercer did not respond to this, uncertain how the remark was meant.

'I should like very much to return and visit you here, Mr Mercer,' Jacob said.

'I'd appreciate that.'

'I shall, of course, wait until your workers have departed.'

'There's no need.'

'Oh? Last week, I came along the road and several of them, presumably because they mistook me for a German, took it upon themselves to throw bricks at me. I still have the bruises.'

'I can only apologize on—'

'There's no need. They made their point.'

'Hardly any of them saw active service. They had no right.'

'I agree, but they made their judgement of me, judged it right to throw their bricks, and so they threw their bricks. To them, it made perfect sense. Talk to some of the Germans – I'll introduce you, if you like – I doubt you'll find a single one of them who won't have something similar to tell you.'

Mercer knew that it was not an argument that might ever find its two sides converging to agreement, and so he acceded to the remark in silence.

He was about to rise and return to the tower when they were both distracted by the same sound of unsettled bricks on the land opposite.

Jacob was the first to stand up.

'Wait,' Mercer told him. He, too, rose to search the site.

'Over there,' Jacob said. He pointed to where rubble spilled onto the road.

Mercer looked and saw Mary Lynch emerge from the mounds and come out into the open.

'She lives here,' Jacob said.

'Do you know her?'

'Vaguely.' He watched the girl intently as she moved across the loose bricks.

'I spoke to her for the first time this morning,'

Mercer said. It was clear to him that something about her sudden appearance, and so close to them, had unsettled the other man.

'Has she seen us?' Jacob moved to stand closer to him.

'I imagine so.'

The girl stood at the centre of the road and looked at them.

Mercer started to raise his arm to her, but Jacob grabbed it and held it down.

'Please,' he said. He released his grip.

The girl made no attempt to come any closer to them. She wore the same dress she had worn earlier, and stood with her arms by her sides.

After several moments of this, she turned at a noise behind her, and both Mercer and Jacob watched as several other children emerged from the rubble to join her. They were all much younger, indistinguishable as boys or girls at that distance, and they gathered around her, as though waiting to be told what to do by her.

'They shouldn't be there,' Mercer said quietly.

'They go where they please,' Jacob said.

The two men watched as Mary spoke to these others, and then as she pushed them away from her. They left her reluctantly and walked single-file towards their homes.

'How old, do you think?' Jacob said.

'The younger ones? Five, eight, ten.'

'I meant the girl.' But before Mercer could answer him, he picked up his bag and started walking away.

Mercer watched him go. The man neither turned nor paused. At the first bend in the road he left it and followed his path across the open ground, his course marked by the posts of the abandoned airfield.

When he was no longer visible, Mercer turned his

attention back to Mary Lynch. He wondered what it was about her sudden appearance that had unsettled the Dutchman. He waved to her, but she made no sign in return. He called for her to wait for him, but as he left the embankment and started towards her, she, too, turned and walked away from him. He was at a loss to understand this behaviour, but guessed it was some game or other childish indulgence, and so instead of pursuing her, he crossed the road and entered again the wasteland surrounding the tower.

3

The following morning, she was waiting for him as he went outside. He ignored her, but she ran to join him. He turned to confront her.

'You were talking to the Jew,' she said.

'His name's Jacob, and he's a Dutchman.'

'He's a *Jew*. Everybody knows that.'

'Then perhaps they should learn some more about him.'

'Like you have, you mean?'

'No, not like I have; because I haven't – not yet.'

'He's still a Jew,' she said, but the vehemence in her voice had faded.

'So tell me what you understand by that.' He knew she was repeating what others had already said, and that any true prejudice was not her own.

'That he's a Jew, a Jew-boy.'

'And?'

'And that he's here to steal a job – to steal a soldier's job.'

'And which soldier would that be?'

'I don't know. It could be any of them.'

'Do you see him doing that?'

'Doing what?'

'Working. Dispossessing one of these welcomed-back heroes of his well-earned livelihood?' He regretted the facetious remark, the easy advantage he had gained over her.

She stood without speaking.

He scrolled through the chart he carried, searching for the line of the drain he hoped to examine.

'You could give him work here,' she said.

'I don't have the authority. Besides, he wasn't looking for work.'

'He comes to the houses. Last time he was here he was trying to sell things made out of glass. Bowls and small plates, things for candles. My mother bought one, but the others told him to get lost. They told her it wasn't a real bowl, that it was old glass he'd made into something. They told her she'd catch things from it.'

'And what's your father's opinion of all this?' He guessed that this was where her confused resentment originated.

'My father's not here. He's in the Army, and won't be home until next month.'

'Home for good?'

'We don't know. What is there here for him now, she says. What is there for any of us any more?' She looked around her as they spoke.

The news of her father surprised Mercer. He imagined he had seen the man walking with her mother, seen them together amid the others at the houses.

'And what about you?' he said, lowering his voice.

'Living here, you mean?'

33

'Is there work?'

'Not really. And whatever there was, I wouldn't want it. Farm work that pays nothing and has you out in the fields in all weathers.'

'Is there nothing in the town?'

'I suppose.'

'But no means of getting there and back each day?'

'I'd live there,' she said, brightening at the prospect, and then falling silent at her better understanding of the situation. 'Is that a map?' she said, indicating the rolled chart he carried.

He showed her the plans, explaining what he was searching for. He appreciated the effort of her feigned interest.

'They thought they might make some money by having the workers come to stay here,' she said.

'Who did?'

'My mother. The other women.'

'Not much chance of that, I'm afraid. They have a construction camp the other side of town.' An old barracks, surplus to requirements, and being allowed to collapse around the men it now briefly housed. Leaking and unheated, and with the occupants constantly being forced to move from one hut to another as the buildings became uninhabitable. They were employed on a three-month contract. Some time during October, the work would be completed, the men dispersed or sent elsewhere, and the barracks finally abandoned.

He showed her the course of the new drain he hoped to excavate.

'There's already drains everywhere,' she said. 'But they all flood.'

'Hopefully, the work here will prevent that.'

'It won't matter if there's nobody living here, will it?'

'A minute ago you said you couldn't wait to leave.'

'I know.'

He saw then the trap in which she was caught – the distance between her childhood and the enclosing past, and womanhood and the opening future she had yet to span.

He indicated that they might continue walking as they spoke.

'You should have come and introduced yourself yesterday,' he said. 'To the Jew.'

'We've been told to stay away from him.'

'Of course you have.'

'We watch him sometimes when he comes across the sand or the marsh. He spends hours on the airfield. He's always looking for things, picking things up, collecting things.'

'Is he the only Jew you know?'

'Of course he is. Mrs Armstrong said she thought they'd all been killed. She said that if one bit of good had come out of the war, then that was it.'

It shocked him to hear her say these things. 'She sounds very enlightened,' he said.

'She wasn't born here. She came from Birmingham. Her husband died a long time ago. She says the Jews there cheated him out of his business and then threw her out of her home.'

'Jacob is from Holland. Perhaps it was one of his relatives who did it.'

She laughed at this. 'I don't believe everything she says,' she said. 'She lies about most other things, gives herself airs and graces.'

'I'm pleased to hear it.'

'Ya-cob,' she said. 'Ya-cob.'

'Careful. Don't let the others hear you speaking a foreign language. They might turn against you, too.'

'I daresay I never met more than twenty outsiders in my entire life before the war started,' she said. 'Never even heard a foreign accent until the Americans arrived at the airfield.'

'Were you born here?'

'In the town. Lived here ever since, though.'

They continued across the workings. At one point, he stood on a slab of loose concrete and it rocked beneath him, prompting her to reach out her arm to steady him. He dropped the coiled measuring tape he was carrying into the space beneath the slab. Waiting until he was back on solid ground and the concrete had settled back into place, she slid down to retrieve this for him.

'Be careful,' he told her.

Only her legs protruded from the hole. He heard her amplified breathing. She crawled into the space, and for a moment she was lost to him. He was about to peer into the cavity and insist that she come back out when her head reappeared, followed by her arms. She held the tape out to him and he took it. He watched anxiously as she pushed herself back out over the rim of the hole. He knelt and held her upper arms, pulling her as she kicked herself back to the surface. There was dirt and crumbled concrete on her dress, arms and legs.

'Thank you,' he said.

'We go in and out of places like that all the time,' she said.

He was about to warn her against this, but saw how ungrateful this would sound.

'I ought to reward you,' he said.

'With what?' she said immediately.

'I don't know. I don't know what I've got that you might possibly want.'

'I could come to the tower and have a look,' she said, and the remark made him smile.

'I suppose you could. There must be something.'

But his reluctance had offended her and she again regarded him coldly.

'You were the one who offered,' she said. 'I didn't do it because there was a reward.'

He saw what the gift – however small it might prove to be – now meant to her. He imagined her presenting it to her mother; he imagined her recounting the story of how it had been earned.

'I know,' he said. 'Sorry.'

'You could give me some cigarettes,' she said.

'For your mother, presumably.'

'Presumably.' She looked hard at the outline of the pack in his shirt pocket. He took it out. It was half-empty.

'I couldn't give you these,' he said. 'That wouldn't be much of a reward. Besides, she might think *you'd* smoked those already gone.'

'Presumably,' she repeated.

'I meant it,' he said. 'Come to the tower when I'm there. I'll find something more appropriate.'

'I'll choose something.' She brushed the last of the powder from her dress.

They arrived at the site of the new drain. He showed her where it would be dug and what purpose it would serve, and again she feigned interest.

They stood together above one of the sunken, mud-filled channels which emptied into the sea. It was difficult to tell whether the channel was a natural one, or one that had been excavated and left undredged. It ran true enough, but its lip was overgrown and cushioned with turf. Filled with silt, it carried little water, and had grown useless with neglect. He searched his chart for an indication of its origin.

'They lost a small boy in this,' she said. She dropped stones into the water beneath them.

'Oh?'

'Just went missing one day, and then a week later they found him down there. Must have just fallen in and been sucked under by the mud.'

'There are some deep holes,' he said.

'I know. Mrs Armstrong was once watching the – watching Jacob coming across the levels, getting herself all excited because he was walking close to a place like this without realizing it.'

'He seems to know his way round well enough. But then again, if he's forever prowling around looking for things to steal, he ought to.'

'Mrs Armstrong would say you were exactly right.'

'I look forward to meeting her. She probably thinks much the same of me.'

'No, she calls you a desk-soldier who's only good for telling others what to do and who never gets his own hands dirty.'

The remark caught him unawares.

The girl, too, became suddenly conscious of what she had said.

'Right, well . . .' he said.

'That's what *she* said.' She held out her hand, as though to hold his again, but then took it back.

'Don't worry,' he told her. 'I could probably have guessed as much.'

'She's the kind of woman, a minute after you've met her you know everything there is to know about her. She's been good to my mother while he was away.'

'Your father?'

She nodded, and then changed the subject back to the drowned boy. 'They brought him back to the houses for a day and a night and then someone came to take him away. They had to cut him open to see how he'd died.'

'I daresay that seemed unnecessary and unfair.'

'It did. His mother never got over it. She was only young. She used to go and stand where he was found.'

'Here,' he said.

'Here. It was in the war. She was living by herself. Her husband never came back to her. She went away herself after that. The house has been empty ever since.'

Several of the houses stood with their doors and windows boarded up.

He saw what tragedy and blighted lives this one breathless rush contained. He saw how history lived and was simplified there, and how it was contained there. He saw how the bone of fact and the flesh of conjecture came together and were kept alive there.

'Do you have a date for your father's return?' he asked her, hoping to make the remark sound casual following her earlier reluctance to speak on the subject.

'*She* does. She crosses days off on a calendar. It isn't even this year's calendar, but she says the dates are still the same.'

'It'll be a big occasion for you. For all of you.'

But again she was reluctant to be drawn. She resumed throwing her stones into the drain.

She held the tape for him while he measured the ground into which the pipe would be sunk. She collected reeds for him to be pushed into the mud as markers. He could already imagine the complaints of the workers at being told to come so far from the road to undertake the work.

When he was finished, they walked together back to

the tower. On the level ground, she slid her arm through his, and though surprised by the gesture, he was careful not to rebuff her. She pointed out the various landmarks to him – the Old Light, the new, automatic beacon, the distant road bridge and church spire – and though he knew of these already, he was happy to let her tell him of them and what small part they all played in her own life.

Approaching the road, they encountered a group of the younger children. A small boy called to her, and she took her arm from his.

'That's my brother,' she said. 'Peter. Just me and him.'

Mercer looked to the houses beyond and saw the women gathered there.

'She'll want me for something or other,' Mary said, meaning her mother, and she drew away from him.

He wanted to say something to let her know how much he had appreciated her company and her help, but because he could not think of exactly what to say – the words she would not misconstrue – and because she was already moving away from him, and because anything he said would be overheard by the other children, he remained silent and watched her go.

4

He saw her frequently during the following days, but never to speak to, only at a distance, and always in the company of either the other women or the children. It occurred to Mercer that she had been warned to stay away from the workings and the men there. Perhaps she had told her mother what she knew of him, and this had been misunderstood by the woman and she had been told not to speak to him. He regretted this. Now that he had gained her confidence, he had hoped to introduce himself to the others living there, and thus perhaps alleviate his own lack of society in that isolated place.

On the fifth day after their encounter, waiting until the site was again abandoned, he washed himself, put on the cleanest of his shirts, and went from the tower to the houses.

He saw from a distance that a group of women had already congregated, most of them sitting along a low wall which separated the land behind their homes from the encroaching sand and shingle of the shore.

They gathered together like this most days, driven indoors only when it became either too dark or too cold.

He was quickly spotted and they all turned to watch him as he approached.

A younger woman at the edge of the group was the closest to him and she stood her ground until he was only a few feet from her before turning her back on him and walking ahead of him.

He was relieved finally to see Mary Lynch among the women. Other children played nearby. She stood with her mother at the centre of the others. Most of the women smoked, and stood with their arms folded loosely across their chests or stomachs.

They returned his greeting and turned to face him in a half-circle as he finally arrived among them. Some looked at the package he carried and not his face.

'We thought you might have been going on to the Light,' one of them said. She indicated the abandoned lighthouse, its reduced stump now painted grey, further along the shingle.

'I came to see Mary,' he said. 'To bring her this.' He held up the package. He had used delivering her 'reward' as the pretext for approaching them.

'What for?' her mother said suspiciously.

'I'm James Mercer,' he said.

'We know who you are,' the older woman now standing beside him said. 'And *what* you are. And why you're here.'

Mrs Armstrong, he thought. The words were meant to challenge him, each remark a jab in his chest, but he affected to be unconcerned by them.

'Good,' he said.

The woman who had spoken to him first smiled at him.

His lack of response angered the older woman. 'You'll want to deny it all, no doubt,' she said. 'You'll be another of these officials telling us that everything happening here is being done for our own good.'

'Not really,' he said, causing her to fall silent. He regretted that she had so easily created this most predictable of barriers. 'I brought you this,' he said directly to Mary, holding out the package to her.

'What is it?' her mother said.

Mary came forward and took it from him.

'It's a reward for rescuing my tape.'

'*Rescuing?*' one of them said. 'Rescuing what? *Men* are rescued.'

'He dropped his tape,' Mary said. She took the package and bowed her arms to accommodate its weight.

'Open it, child,' one of them said.

But Mary was reluctant to do this, and Mercer saw in her reluctance that he had been wrong to give her the package in front of these others.

'She never said anything to me about a *rescue*,' her mother said, causing several of the others to exchange glances and smiles.

'Whatever, it would have cost me a lot to replace it,' he said, hoping to regain the balance of the exchange. 'Five pounds.' It would have cost him nothing; he possessed many others.

The package contained a dozen tins of food, including those things he knew were still difficult to acquire, on or off ration, and a tin of tobacco. He meant the gift both to impress – perhaps to raise the status of the girl – and to ingratiate himself. It was not to be regarded merely as an obligation fulfilled.

'Open it, child,' the older woman repeated.

He saw Mary flinch at this command, and at the word.

'She never said anything,' her mother repeated, and she nodded her own uncertain thanks to him.

'Give it here,' the insistent woman said.

'Leave her,' Mary's mother said.

Mercer guessed that his presence prevented them from saying a great deal more. He guessed, too, that any unexpected windfall at the houses, whatever its origin, would be claimed and shared by them all.

'She ought not to be taking gifts from complete strangers,' Mrs Armstrong said.

'I dropped the tape down a gap and she was able to retrieve it for me,' Mercer explained.

' "Retrieve" is it now? First it was "rescue" and now it's "retrieve".'

Several of the younger women shook their heads at this unnecessary remark.

'What?' she said. 'What?' feigning aggrieved surprise.

'Let him say what he has to say,' Mary's mother said. Her name was Elizabeth.

Seizing this smallest of concessions, Mercer took out his cigarettes and offered them to everyone, starting with Mrs Armstrong. 'Take two,' he told her, and she did. The others waited for the same offer before doing the same. The packet was quickly emptied and he opened another.

'I didn't mean anything by the remark,' Mrs Armstrong said. 'But a child ought to tell its mother what happens. Especially a child who's practically a woman.'

He guessed her to be fifty or fifty-five years old, though he knew by the look of all the women beyond their youth that she might be ten years younger. The salt air and wind of the place was bred into their faces. They all had dark eyes, and in the older ones these were tightened, as though in constant expectation of that wind.

'She's not a woman,' Elizabeth Lynch said, and she drew her daughter towards her and stood with an arm across her, a hand holding her shoulder. There was only an inch or so difference in their heights.

'It's nothing special,' Mercer said. 'A few bits and pieces.' He hoped Mary might lay the package on the wall and reveal its contents. She put it down, but that was all, and whether they looked at it or not, it remained the focus of all their attention.

'I ought to get back,' Mrs Armstrong said eventually, still nursing her censure.

Several of the women nodded their concurrence, disappointing her further. Mercer saw what a constraint she imposed on them all. Hoping perhaps to be urged to reconsider, the woman remained where she stood and searched her pockets for a key. She further prolonged her departure by issuing a succession of remarks and reminders to most of the women there. Mercer saw how they all tolerated her in this. He saw, too, how greatly extended was the credit of the woman.

He stood with the others for an hour longer. They answered his every question about the place at great length, in minute and frequently contradictory detail. He tried to draw out Mary, but she remained reluctant to speak to him in the company of these others. And when she did have something to say, the women either corrected her or confirmed for him what she said. He saw how uncomfortable this made her and so he turned his attention to those more willing to receive it.

After that hour, a breeze blew up and this signalled the end of their socializing. The same breeze came most evenings, and with it the sky over the sea quickly darkened.

He waited with Mary and Elizabeth Lynch until the last of the others had returned to their homes.

'Are the men out?' he asked the woman.

'Somewhere,' she said. She looked around her.

It had become apparent to him upon his arrival that two societies existed here, that the men and women formed naturally separate groups, even when they congregated together. Until the war there had been a manned Light and a small fleet of inshore boats at the place, but now the Light had been replaced by the automatic beacon, and the few small boats that remained, though used occasionally, were largely in a state of disrepair, and no longer provided even the precarious living upon which the men had once depended. The channel through the shingle upon which these vessels were launched was filling with silt and the boats were pulled out of the water and left where they lay on the beach. He looked now and counted four of them there. Beside them lay a sand-filled tangle of broken and discarded crab- and lobster-pots.

Elizabeth Lynch indicated to him that it was time for them to return indoors.

Mary picked up the package from the wall, but as she did so she caught a metal rod which protruded from the brick and the box tore, spilling the tins to the ground. One of these fractured along its seam and a pale green liquid began to bubble out.

'I'll give you a hand to carry them,' Mercer said. He sensed the woman's reluctance to accept, and rather than be rejected by her, he started gathering the cans into his folded arm. Mary copied him, until between them they held them all.

Elizabeth Lynch led the way to the house. Once inside, she cleared a space on the table for the cans.

He was surprised by the cramped, sparse nature of the room, but was careful to give no indication of this. A threadbare carpet covered only half the floor, and a pile of driftwood and broken casing lay piled on either side of the hearth. The latter had been scavenged from the workings. A wireless set played softly on a sideboard. And beside it stood a photograph of a man in uniform.

Still sensing the woman's unease at finding him so suddenly in her home, he picked up the photograph and said, 'Your husband? Mary told me he was still in the Army.'

The woman looked immediately at the girl, who looked away.

'He wanted to know,' Mary said. 'He asked me. I didn't just tell him.'

Mercer was at a loss to understand this sudden alarm. The woman looked hard at the photograph he held, willing him to return it to the sideboard, which he did.

'I didn't mean to appear—'

'Nosy?' she said. 'As though you were any different from any of the others they sent to see us?' She stopped abruptly. Her eyes moved all around him.

'I'm sorry,' he said. He imagined that the man expected shortly to return was not in fact coming home, that something had happened between the two of them during his absence, and that the talk of his return was now a fiction maintained only for the sake of his children or the others.

He could think of nothing to say to her that would not upset her further.

'I'll leave,' he said.

47

Mary, who had been standing between him and the open door during all this, stepped aside. It seemed suddenly much cooler inside the small room. A scratchy violin played on the wireless; a woman sang in a deep and melancholic foreign language. The last light of the falling sun in the doorway blinded him.

He made a final gesture towards the woman.

'She told me only that he was still away in the Army and that he was soon to return,' he said.

'In twenty-four days,' Elizabeth Lynch said, surprising him by this concision, and convincing him even further that it was a fiction.

There was nothing more he could say.

Mary went ahead of him through the open doorway and called for her brother.

Mercer followed her out.

'I'm sorry if I said anything I shouldn't have done,' he said to her.

'If you were really worried about something like that round here, you'd never open your mouth.'

'I meant about your father.'

'I know what you meant,' she said.

He passed her and walked in the direction of the abandoned Light.

'Listen,' she called to him when he was twenty feet away from her.

'What?'

'Listen,' she repeated. She cupped a hand to her ear.

He turned to face in the same direction. He could hear nothing.

'You can hear the tide coming up through the shingle.'

He listened more intently, and finally he heard the rattle of the shingle beach as it was infiltrated by the rising water.

After that, she returned indoors.

He continued walking to the Light, and as he did so a group of the younger children marched past him. The boy leading them saluted him, and he returned the gesture without thinking, waiting until the last of them had passed him before dropping his hand and continuing his own journey along the shore.

5

He next encountered Jacob Haas two days later. He was inspecting foundations laid earlier in the day when the man emerged from the land beyond the diggings and came directly to him. He carried something, and as he came closer, Mercer saw that this was an instrument dial. Far behind him, towards the abandoned hangars and workshops of the airfield, several dozen giant silver bombers still sat on their wings or stood lopsidedly on their collapsed undercarriages. These were the aircraft which had either crashed there or been taken there towards the end of the war, and which had then been discarded, unrepaired and unwanted as the heavy daylight raids drew to an end. All the serviceable aircraft had been flown from the field in March of that final year.

Jacob held up his prize for Mercer to see. 'Altimeter,' he said.

'What will you do with it?'

Jacob looked puzzled for a moment and then

shrugged. 'It just seemed to be something worth saving, something worth having.'

Mercer guessed then that the man had come to England with considerably less than the shabby clothes on his back.

They walked together to an iron chest half-hidden in the tall grass. The box was padlocked, and the lock rusted solid to the knotted chain it had once secured.

'Is this your hidden treasure?' Mercer asked him, tapping the top of the chest.

'Flares to signal to the returning aircraft. Any plane without its undercarriage properly lowered, or which looked as though it might crash on landing, was warned off, diverted elsewhere so as not to block the runway for the others. What a decision for someone to have to make.'

Only then did it occur to Mercer that Jacob could have seen none of this at the time, that he had arrived long after the airfield had been decommissioned. Then, and later, as he learned more of the man, he saw how he put down these shallow roots into this past that was not his own.

A drain ran nearby, pipes protruding from a clay bank out of which water flowed. They talked about the building work. Jacob told him about the demolition of the runway. There was a gang of men there now, and the noise of their pneumatic drills and steam hammers carried on the still air.

'Do they mind you taking stuff from the planes?'

'They don't see me. I know as well as anyone how the military mind works. You know what would happen. They would rather everything lay there and rotted to rust and dirt than that parts of it should ever be retrieved and put to some use again.'

Mercer nodded. He could not conceive to what

possible use the altimeter might now be put.

'I met the girl's mother,' he said.

'Oh?'

'The other night. I introduced myself.'

'And they welcomed you with open arms?'

'You scare them, that's all,' Mercer said. 'You're an unknown quantity.'

'I know exactly what I am to them.'

'They don't all think the same,' Mercer said, hoping he sounded more convincing than he felt.

'They don't *think* at all, that's the problem.'

'Perhaps if you were able to talk to them,' Mercer said. 'Explain to them.'

'Explain what?' Jacob turned to look directly at him.

'I meant explain how you came to be here, what you have endured, how you—'

'*Endured? Endured?*' He started to say more, but was racked by a bout of coughing, which left him bent double, holding a hand to his chest and gasping for breath.

Mercer held his arm, supporting him as he straightened.

Jacob wiped his mouth with a cloth. His shirt and jacket were buttoned to their collars.

'Perhaps if you loosened . . .' Mercer suggested, but Jacob shook his head.

He sat upright and took several deep breaths. After a few minutes, he was recovered.

'Are you unwell?' Mercer asked him.

'My chest is weak, that's all.'

Mercer knew it was more than this, but said nothing. He watched the trickling water and wished there was some way he might collect this and give it to Jacob.

'Were you in a camp?' he asked after a further minute of silence between them.

Jacob nodded. 'Please, not now.'

Is that why you create this other past?

'I didn't mean to offend you, or to pry,' Mercer said.

'I know.' Jacob wiped his mouth for a final time. 'So, tell me about the women. Was the old one there?'

'You could always avoid them. There are plenty of other places for you to—'

'To hide myself away. I know. The first time she saw me, before she even knew who I was or why I was there, she chased me with a stick. She saw me at the road's end, told me to stay where I was, and then went indoors. I thought at first that she was fetching me something to eat or drink, but instead she came back out with a stick. She came striding towards me and shouting at me like I was a stray dog. As you can imagine, neither of us is much of a runner. She soon exhausted herself, and I'd barely moved from where I stood.'

'You should have gone towards her – she'd have run back indoors.'

'I know. But by then she'd attracted the usual crowd of onlookers. You'll have realized by now – everything that happens here usually draws its own small crowd. Nothing goes unnoticed or unwatched. You'd do well to remember that.'

'What happened?'

'She went on waving her stick and shouting her abuse at me.'

'Did no one come to your defence?'

'The girl's mother told her to stop making a fool of herself, but the woman screamed some abuse at her, too. One or two of the younger ones seemed more intrigued and amused than threatened by the situation, but none of them intervened.'

'How long ago was this?'

'Nine months, less.'

'And yet you still return to haunt and unsettle them.'

Jacob grinned. 'I still return.'

And you use your appearance like she uses her stick.

'They seem to know you well enough,' Mercer said.

'They only know what they want to know. What else did you talk about with them?'

'About their lives here, about the coming changes with the new Station.'

'Did the girl's mother tell you about her husband?'

'The soldier?'

'The soldier in Colchester Military Prison.'

'Prison?'

'He deserted a few days before he was due to be shipped to North Africa, Egypt. He went missing for almost a month. Came back here. Someone tipped the Military Police off and they turned up and arrested him. Four years. He's being released early under some sort of amnesty for Hostilities-Only men. He qualifies, apparently, because although he went absent, he didn't do it while on active service. It gets him off the hook.'

Mercer struggled to remember what either Mary or Elizabeth Lynch had told him or implied about the man. 'Do you think the girl knows all this?'

Jacob shrugged. 'You can understand how much more convenient it would be for him to return as some kind of hero rather than a jail-bird.'

'But surely everyone else must know.'

'Of course they know, but I imagine they'll keep up some kind of pretence while it makes any sense to do so.'

Mercer tried again to remember precisely what Mary had told him, to understand what she herself truly believed.

'Why did he go absent?' he said.

'Who knows.' Jacob started coughing again, but this time the bout was neither so severe nor so prolonged.

'She has a release date,' Mercer said.

'I know. I wonder what she expects. According to a man at the airfield, she never once went to see him in Colchester. The boy, his youngest, was little more than a baby when they took him off. Apparently, him and the girl were close, so perhaps that's why they're keeping up the pretence.'

'She'll soon know,' Mercer said.

'Of course she will.'

'Perhaps the others believe you'll be the one to tell her. Perhaps that's why they drive you off with sticks.'

'Look at me,' Jacob said. 'They don't need any good reason to do that.' He stared absently across the grass and distant runway for several seconds, and then said, 'My sister was her age. Anna. She reminds me very much of her.' His voice was even and low, and Mercer knew not to interrupt him. Then Jacob drew a ball of phlegm to his lips and spat it at his feet with a grunt. In the distance, the drills and hammers finally fell silent. A cloud of flies drifted back and forth above the drain.

Jacob turned to look at Mercer. 'They'll run rings around you,' he said.

'It might serve my purpose to let them do it.'

'And supposing the girl already knows about her father. What kind of homecoming would that be?'

'I don't think she does,' Mercer said.

'Apparently, he had a temper. It wasn't the best of marriages even before all this.'

A klaxon sounded on the airfield, and a group of men, tiny figures at that distance, ran towards one of the buildings. In places, tractors had already started ploughing up the land beneath the recently removed concrete.

'Do you think the man will stay here?' Mercer said.

'I daresay there will be terms and conditions attached to his release. I doubt if it's what *he* would want, but I doubt he'll have much say in the matter.'

'And his wife and children even less.'

'Who cares?' Jacob said. He rose from the chest and wiped the flakes of rust from his trousers.

'Why do you imagine he came back here in the first place?' Mercer said. 'Surely, this was the most obvious place for them to come looking for him.'

'The man who told me all this said he came back because he'd heard his wife was messing around with another man here. She wasn't, but that's what he believed. He came back to sort her out. When they arrested him, they took one look at her and the results of this sorting-out and tried to persuade her to press further charges.'

'What did he do to her?'

'Use your imagination.'

Mercer rose and they walked together along the road.

'Was Anna your only sister?' Mercer said eventually.

'She was.'

They parted where the road turned inland.

'I'd like to come and visit you,' Mercer said.

'There's nothing to see. I live in a room above a warehouse on the edge of town.'

'I'd still like to come,' Mercer said.

6

Mary Lynch returned to see him the following morning. Knowing what he now knew, he felt uneasy in her presence, conscious of what he might inadvertently reveal to her. She, too, seemed wary of him, and it occurred to him that they were both circling the same forbidden subject.

He invited her into the tower. At first, she declined, but he knew that she would allow herself to be persuaded.

Once inside, in the upper room, she went first to the desk upon which his charts and plans lay, and from there to one of the windows which afforded the tower an all-round view. Part of the airfield was also visible from the room, and she stood for several minutes looking out over this.

'Is this your first time in here?' He knew by the ease with which she moved from window to window that it was not.

'We used to come in here all the time.' She meant herself and the other children. 'Until you arrived.'

He began to explain to her why he had chosen the

tower as the base for his work, but she showed little interest in what he said. She went to look over the houses and the sea beyond. There were men on the beach. A solitary woman hung washing on a line. It was a still day and the water was calm, its waves barely breaking against the shore.

'Is that your mother?' he asked her, indicating the distant woman.

She nodded once, watching the woman intently.

'It was good to meet her at last,' he said.

'Why?' She spoke sharply, causing him to remain silent. 'She said after you'd gone that you thought you were better than us and that we could do without your charity.'

The remark surprised him. He could not believe it was what Elizabeth Lynch truly thought of him. 'She didn't say either of those things,' he said.

Her averted glance confirmed his guess, and he wondered what pleasure she had gained from the lie, why she had insisted on telling it knowing he would not believe her.

'No, but *she* said them.'

'Mrs Armstrong?'

'Who else?'

'So what was the point of your lie?'

'Why does it matter who said it?'

'Of course it matters. I'm going to be here for the next two months.' He paused. 'I need to know who my friends are.'

She crossed the room to stand beside him.

'In that case, my mother said I was to come and thank you for what you brought us. She said I was ill-mannered when you came.'

'I should have given the things to you when you were alone. They were yours.'

'My reward,' she said, adding a cold emphasis to the word.

'Is that why you're here?' he said. 'To thank me?'

'Is that what you want?'

He filled a kettle from one of the canisters of water and offered her a drink. She accepted and they sat together at the table.

It was warm in the room. He had tried to open the windows, but most of the panes no longer moved, their winding mechanism seized fast through corrosion and disuse.

'Are these the houses?' she asked him, indicating the dwellings on his chart.

He glanced quickly at the map to ensure that no indication of their future destruction was marked across them.

She turned the sheet to face her, genuinely excited, it seemed to Mercer, at each of the surrounding features she was able to identify. She aligned the chart to the horizon outside and then set about naming everything she saw. He left her to make the tea.

When he returned with the cups and saucers – there had been a case from the quartermaster containing forty-eight of each of these – he found her peering closely at the configuration of the drains and sluices flowing beneath the road in the direction of the town.

'They've all got names,' she said disbelievingly.

'Most features have.'

'Not out here. They usually get called by the last thing that happened there.'

'It's a common enough way of doing things.' He rattled the cup at her and she took it from him, holding the saucer in both hands.

'Sorry there's nothing more practical,' he said.

She studied the two pieces of cheap crockery and the spoon he had laid beside the cup.

'Why did the all-knowing Mrs Armstrong think I was being high-handed?'

'Who cares? She would have said the same whatever you'd done. She reckons that whatever you say, you're here to knock down the houses and kick us all out.'

It was not part of his work to destroy the dwellings, but he could not deny that their demolition was included in the future plans for the site. The houses had originally been built for the lighthouse-keepers and the crew of the earlier lifeboat that had once, briefly, been stationed there. Now neither existed, and the houses – costly to maintain and repair in such an isolated place – were surplus to all practical requirements.

'She worries where she'll go.'

'Where would any of you go?' he said.

'You say that as though it would be a problem,' she said. She set her cup down.

'Would you move into town?'

'I'd keep going until I reached somewhere worth living,' she said. 'It can't all have been bombed to rubble.'

'A lot of it was,' he said. 'It's going to be a long time before a lot of people get back on their feet.'

'But they *are* building it all again?'

'Of course they are.' A month earlier, he had been in London, living in the home of his dead parents.

She considered this for a moment. 'So what you're saying is that it's the people like us who are at the bottom of the list for getting new houses.'

'Not necessarily. It's just that—'

'Just that nobody cared much about us before the war and nobody cares much about us now.'

There was nothing he could say to her. The crockery

rattled in her hand and she separated the two pieces to stop this.

'I probably know as little as the rest of you,' he said. He slapped his hand on the charts. 'All I know for certain is that the new Coastguard Station has to be built. Beyond that . . .'

After several minutes, she said, 'I know,' and nothing more.

They listened to the machinery and the shouting of the men beneath them.

'The house is going to be crowded when your father comes home,' he said eventually, watching closely for her response.

She considered this before answering him. 'No more crowded than it was before,' she said.

It occurred to him that the house contained only two bedrooms, and that she shared one of these with her small brother, that she had shared it as a girl upon her father's departure, and that she shared it with him still.

He considered all this without speaking, and when he next looked at her, she was watching him closely.

'What?' he said.

She said nothing, and he thought for a moment that she had seen something through the window behind him which had attracted her attention.

'You don't have to pretend,' she said eventually.

'Pretend about what?'

'About him.' She meant her father.

'What am I pretending?' he said.

'That he isn't in an Army prison and that he wasn't sent there because he tried to run away.'

'How long have you known?' he said.

She shrugged.

'Who told you?'

'Nobody *told* me. They didn't need to. You only have to listen to what they say to each other. You can hear people whispering through those walls. I've known for about a year. I was there when they came for him. *She* said they'd just come to give him a lift back to his camp, but I saw how they held him and watched him. She said it was nothing, and at first I believed her. I went on believing her because it seemed the best thing to do.'

'And afterwards?'

'It stopped making sense. I looked on a map to find out where he was. She never went to see him.'

'Perhaps it wasn't allowed.'

'What, not even after the war was over?'

'She has no idea,' he said.

'That I worked it all out? I sometimes even think that she's convinced herself he's still off serving like an ordinary soldier somewhere.'

'It can't have been easy for you,' he said.

The remark surprised her, as though her own feelings on the matter had never before been thought worthy of consideration or even remark.

'Why don't you tell her that you know?'

She pursed her lips and feigned indifference, but he saw by her eyes that this pretence only masked her uncertainty.

'She might appreciate knowing that you know. You might be able to share—'

'I don't want to share anything with her. She's had years to tell me. It was up to her. She's the one who went on pretending.'

Mercer remained silent, allowing this sudden and uncontainable outburst to clear the room. She sat shaking in her seat.

'And besides,' she said. 'It's too late. He'll be back in

a few weeks. She's had years to tell me. How is she going to do it now? What would be the point of it all?'

He sensed then, in those few remarks, that this unwillingness to enter her mother's confidence, or to take the woman into hers, was some uncertain form of punishment: she was deliberately keeping herself apart from the woman; deliberately withholding from her the support and reassurance her confession and confidences might bring. This understanding was quick in coming, and he was careful to keep it from her.

'You and your father always got on well together,' he said.

'She tell you that, did she?'

He could not tell her that he had heard it from Jacob Haas.

'I think so. Or perhaps it's just an impression I got from you.'

'He used to take me places with him when I was a girl. She was bad after Peter was born, never the same. She was in hospital for a long time. Peter came home, but she stayed. He said she was staying away deliberately, that there was nothing wrong with her, that everything was on his shoulders. And when she did finally come back to us, it was different. He said Peter was a mistake, an accident, and that everything had been ruined. Peter was sick a lot, in and out of hospital. We had visitors, a nurse or something, who used to come and take him away with her. He kicked up a fuss at that and told her once that if she ever let Peter out of her sight again he'd kill her. He didn't mean it – it was just what he used to say.'

'Were the other women able to help her?'

'Some of them. It was me, mostly. She told me to look after him. I was nine when he was born.'

'You must have resented the intrusion.'

She looked at him as though he had spoken to her in another language. 'Is that what I did?'

'Is that why you want to punish her now – by pretending not to know about your father?'

She locked her hands and smiled. 'I'd never thought of it like that,' she said, but she made it clear to him that even if this were true – which he doubted – then she was thinking of it now, and savouring all she imagined.

'I don't believe you could be so deliberately cruel,' he said. He held her gaze to convince her that he meant this, and to allow her a course out of her forced and malicious reverie.

The smile fell from her face. 'A plus b plus c,' she said. 'It's never really that simple, is it?'

'Not in my experience.' He ran his hand over the charts. 'To read all the books, you'd imagine that the fastest, shortest route between two fixed points was always a straight line.'

He sensed that she appreciated this deeper understanding between them, and the opportunity to explore further her own imperfect assessment of the situation and how she felt.

He refilled their cups, but by then the tea was lukewarm and neither of them drank it.

They were interrupted several minutes later by the voices of two men shouting up the stairs demanding to see him. He told her to wait where she sat while he went down to them.

There was a problem with an excavator. A buried concrete platform had been uncovered where none was marked on the charts. He asked them to explain where this was, what work it held up, and then told them to smash through it. They complained at the extra work. They wanted him to accompany them to the site and see for himself, but he refused, telling them he was busy in the tower.

The men left and he went back up to her. She told him she had to leave.

'You can always come back,' he told her.

'I know,' she said. 'I was sent to ask you if you wanted to come and have something to eat with us one night.'

'I'd like that.'

'I told her you'd make an excuse, or that if you did come, it would only be because you felt obliged.'

'Tell your mother I accept with pleasure.'

'I knew that's what you'd say.'

'Then you were right, weren't you.' He saw immediately how he had been manipulated by her, and how this simple invitation had been made to stand for so much more.

'I'll tell her you'll come in a few days, shall I? You'll need to check your social diary.' She held out her hand to him and he took it. Grasping his, she said, 'You don't have any spare cigarettes, do you?'

'For your mother?'

She made it clear to him that this was not her intention. 'Of course for my mother. You didn't think I'd want them for myself, did you?' She released her hold on him.

A pack on the table contained only two or three and he gave this to her. 'I'm giving you these for her.'

'Of course. There, you've said it now.' She took them from him. And then she picked up the box of matches which lay beside them and loudly counted three from it.

She descended the stairs, and he followed her down.

At the door, she paused and looked outside before leaving.

7

The gun platforms had been installed at Fleet Point during the spring and summer of 1940, when the threat of invasion, albeit elsewhere, had seemed most likely. The blueprints for this work, and the plans and documents accompanying these, were forwarded to Mercer several months prior to his own arrival. He was surprised to see how substantial the structures were, and how much additional work had been undertaken to protect them from the sea. No one can have truly believed that this part of The Wash coast was ever under threat of invasion, but one of the documents suggested that a diversionary assault might be launched here precisely because it would be considered so unlikely. Additionally, this same anonymous report suggested, coastal shipping in the North Sea, increasingly valuable now that the Atlantic was blockaded, might be protected by the guns from any marauding craft this far north. Mercer considered this a far more valid reason for the guns being sited there, but saw, too, how instrumental this deceit of invasion was in getting the work carried out. There was no mention in the report of how that same endangered and unarmed shipping might be protected to the north of the guns' range, where they would be exposed and unprotected for at least a further hundred miles until reaching the mouth of the Humber.

He had studied these charts closely and had based his own plan of work upon them. The underlying map was sixty years old – old enough to show everything that existed at Fleet Point long before the necessity for the guns arose. The houses were marked, as was the abandoned Light. Where the airfield now stood there had been only open pasture, and where the road followed the line of the coast only a track was marked.

There had been some earlier construction work there during the previous war, but this had been abandoned before it was completed. Several large, circular platforms had been built, and the track of a small-gauge railway laid outwards from them, but the former had never been complemented by any artillery, and the sleepers and rails of the railway – presumably to supply ammunition to the guns – had never been added to the reinforced line of their base. It was clear to Mercer that these earlier foundations, long since buried and lost, were a considerable distance from where he was currently working, and so he was able to ignore them.

The tower, of course, was not marked on this earlier map, and it was not until he arrived to inspect the site in the company of the Trinity House men that he saw the structure and understood how useful it might be to him. His original intention had been to occupy one of the empty houses, but someone quickly pointed out to him that this would place him too closely among the people living there. The tower, on the other hand, would afford him both the proximity and the distance he required.

The Army planners had drawn up their blueprints quickly and crudely. The forms and dimensions of their platforms, defences and ancillary buildings were uniform and easily duplicated, using local contractors under military supervision wherever the Ministry of Works men were in short supply. The reinforced concrete beneath the guns had been poured to a depth of six feet, those beneath the other buildings to half that depth. The buttresses, connecting walkways and sea-defences had been constructed less solidly. Someone, Mercer guessed, knew the place well and so knew how short-lived these were likely to be, especially where the walls were built close to the tide line.

The guns themselves had been stripped down and taken away in the autumn of 1944. They had seen little action. A log of their deployment was contained in Mercer's files. They had saved little shipping and sunk no enemy vessels. Every single page of the logs showed up the tedium and emptiness of the lives of the men stationed there.

The block-house built for these crews was the most substantial of the ancillary structures, but the bulk of this had already been demolished prior to Mercer's arrival, the work having been carried out at the same time as the guns were removed. Its sand-filled foundations stood several hundred yards to the landward side of the tower. On the map, a road had been projected between this and the gun platforms, but there was no indication of this on the ground, and again Mercer guessed that it had been omitted from the work by someone who knew the place better than the planners.

In addition to the guns, a number of winch platforms were constructed to the north of the site, from which barrage balloons were once intended to be deployed.

It had been immediately clear to Mercer how much of this earlier work he himself might now completely disregard, turning his attention only to those few structures which lay within the boundary of the new Station and its surrounding yards. The past here was either quickly buried by the sand or drawn away by the sea, and the previous works of man were never mistaken for anything other than the temporary marks and blemishes they were.

Following his first visit to the place, Mercer had returned alone several days later to walk the ground and to assess better what lay ahead of him. The expectations of the Trinity House men were not unreasonable, but everything they now demanded of him was founded upon their preparations for the distant future, rather than any close understanding of the recent past within which the work was about to start.

The men accompanying him on that first occasion had seemed surprised by how many people had gathered to watch their arrival and departure, keeping their distance for the duration of the visit.

In the summer of 1943, a bomber returning to the airfield had crash-landed close to one of the gun emplacements, cracking its revetments and putting the gun out of action for eight weeks, during which time there was no call upon it. The revetment was repaired, but the work seemed a waste to Mercer. Two months later, a distant vessel was fired upon and hit at the mouth of the Freeman Channel. The boat was not sunk, but was driven away and never again seen. It was referred to in the gun's log as a probable E-boat, but the tone of the accompanying report made it clear to anyone who read it that a great deal of uncertainty surrounded the episode. Too much was made of the isolated incident. The same empty, horizon-scanning days stretched away on either side of it; the arrival of every lorry and every aircraft droning distantly overhead was still meticulously noted.

8

Approaching the tower, he saw two men waiting there for him. Imagining that they might have been two of the men of the place, his first instinct was to conceal himself from them, but as he came closer he saw that the man standing closest to the tower door was Jacob Haas.

Mercer watched them for a moment.

The man waiting further back seemed anxious. He constantly looked around him as he waited, and he particularly watched in the direction of the houses. He called to Jacob and gestured to him to leave the tower, but Jacob ignored these entreaties and went on knocking and shouting for Mercer.

Mercer eventually called to attract his attention. Jacob saw him and came towards him. The second man followed close behind. He was almost a foot taller than Jacob, and with close-cropped blond hair.

'We came to see you,' Jacob said simply. He took several of the charts Mercer carried.

The three men turned back towards the tower.

'This is Mathias Weisz,' Jacob said, introducing the second man, who immediately put out his hand.

Once inside the tower, each man put down what he carried and they climbed to the upper room unencumbered.

Mathias, Jacob told Mercer, was one of the German prisoners of war employed at the airfield. 'He expressed a desire to remain, and because, before the war, he worked as a horticulturalist, they found him work breaking up concrete.'

'My father was the true horticulturalist – fruit and roses – I merely copied what he did and then waited far too long to get away from him and his gardens and greenhouses,' Mathias said.

'Are you still, officially, a prisoner?' Mercer asked him.

Jacob laughed. 'Tell him.'

'Until a year ago I lodged with a local farmer, a tenant. He died and the farm went to another man who did not want me working there – he had lost a son in Belgium – and so I went back, voluntarily, to the camp I had been in before the farm.'

'I told him he should have seduced the farmer's daughter and then applied for the farm himself,' Jacob said.

The remark clearly embarrassed Mathias. 'And then be forced to explain myself to the tens of thousands of men who were coming home and looking for work? I don't think so.'

'Tell him the rest,' Jacob said.

'And then the Authorities came looking for somewhere to house their – your – workers and so once again I found myself homeless. There were fewer than a hundred of us remaining by then, each of us tied up in the bureaucracy that moved us slowly towards our release. Most of us were sent to Southampton to await our repatriation there. Those of us who expressed an interest in staying and who were prepared to work were again investigated and questioned. There are eighteen of us at the airfield. Most, like myself, were already living with or working for an English family prepared to vouch for them.'

'He goes twice a week to the police station,' Jacob said.

'Usually, it's closed. I go to the constable's house. He, too, grows roses.'

'And will this arrangement continue until whatever verification you're waiting for comes through?' Mercer said.

'Until I am free of these chains and leg-irons, yes.' Mathias held out his fists and laughed, but Jacob turned away at this. Mathias saw this and immediately lowered his hands.

'And the work at the airfield?' Mercer said, sensing the sudden tension between the two men.

'I went to work there when the farm changed hands. Jacob here thought it would be wise to keep myself in useful employment while I waited.'

'And somewhere, sometime,' Jacob said, 'a Board of Assessors – good, upstanding, hard-working and decent men and women themselves – will bang a rubber stamp over his name and the war will finally be over.'

Neither Mercer nor Mathias himself were prepared for the bitterness of this remark. Jacob, too, seemed surprised by what he had said, and he waved to signal his apology.

'Are you making an application for citizenship?' Mercer asked Mathias.

'Not in the first instance. Merely an application to stay here. Full citizenship might come later.'

'Is that what you want?'

Mathias shrugged. 'I think so.'

'What about your family?'

Mathias and Jacob looked at each other.

'We are peas in a pod, Mathias and I,' Jacob said. 'Strangers on an alien shore.'

'They were killed,' Mathias said. 'Only my mother and father, and an uncle, with whom my father worked.'

'Hamburg,' Jacob said to Mercer.

'I see,' Mercer said, grasping sufficient of what he was being told not to pursue the matter further.

'He could have been sifting through the ruins a year ago if he hadn't applied to stay,' Jacob said.

Again, Mathias seemed embarrassed by the remark. 'But that would have meant abandoning you,' he said to Jacob.

'I would have managed.'

'Of course you would.' Mathias turned to Mercer. 'He came to the farm looking for work. The farmer took him on, but it was soon apparent to everyone that he was capable of doing very little. He lasted two days.'

'During which time I pulled at least three turnips out of the ground,' Jacob said.

'Small ones. He needed – he still *needs* – to rest, not work.'

'And so this good Samaritan took it upon himself to feed and clothe me,' Jacob said.

'I did no such thing,' Mathias said, again directly to Mercer. 'Most of what I was able to give him, I was forced to steal. Nothing was missed.'

'Except by the pigs, eh?'

'Perhaps. He was ill. He suffered many ailments that first winter. I did only what any one man might have done for another.'

74

'Not for a Jew,' Jacob said.

'Yes, for a Jew,' Mathias told him firmly, and Jacob conceded the point in silence.

Mercer left them briefly to retrieve his charts from below.

When he returned with these, Mathias asked to look at them and showed him where he was likely to encounter further unmarked buried concrete; a feeder runway had been laid and then abandoned long before the war's end. It was valuable information to Mercer and the two men sat together at the table so that he might make the necessary corrections to his plans.

'My father grew roses, too,' Mercer said as the last of the amendments was made. 'But I myself was never much of a gardener.'

'Me, neither, if the truth be known,' Mathias said. 'I was twenty-three when the war started. I saw it as my opportunity to get away from all that. My intentions were always clear to him. He tried to persuade me to stay, but they were not proper arguments and he knew I would not be persuaded by them. His brother wanted them to sell the business to a firm of agricultural chemists who were interested in buying it, but who never offered my father enough to tempt him to sell. When the war came, so the chemists came back and increased their offer. My uncle accepted. The nursery covered six acres in the suburbs of Hamburg. The city had grown around them. In my grandfather's time, they were on the edge of the country. And then the air-raids came and they lost everything. Nothing had been formally agreed. My father, mother and uncle were all killed. The chemists bought the land a year later at a fraction of its original value and everything was paid immediately back out to our creditors.'

'Was nothing left for you?'

Mathias shook his head. 'Nothing.'

'Was that why you decided to stay here?'

'Partly.'

They left the table and went to where Jacob now sat at the window looking out over the houses. Mercer sensed that he resented having been excluded by the two men while they worked on the charts.

It was early evening and lights already showed in some of the houses. Smoke rose from several chimneys.

Mercer announced that he was hungry and invited the two men to share his meal. Neither refused. Jacob asked him where he kept his food and then insisted that he would do the cooking. He took a bottle from his satchel and put it on his empty seat. 'Whisky,' he said. 'English whisky, but whisky.'

Mathias picked this up and waited for Mercer to set out three cups.

Mercer drank his and then coughed as the raw spirit burned his throat.

Both Jacob and Mathias laughed at him.

'It's made from those three turnips,' Mathias said. 'They drink it all day at the airfield.' He and Jacob drained their own cups and closed their eyes.

'And yet you seem to be making good progress there,' Mercer said when his voice returned.

'Not really,' Mathias said. 'Like most undervalued workers, they do as little as possible. When I and the other prisoners were first sent there, the local men warned us against doing too much and showing them up for what they were. We were given all the dirty jobs.'

'Where were you captured?' Mercer asked him.

'Normandy,' Mathias said, adding immediately that he could see one of the small boats approaching the shingle.

'They're like you,' Mercer said, watching the boats. 'They do it because it was what their fathers did. There's no living in it for any of them.'

'A dying breed,' Mathias said.

'A dead breed,' Jacob added. 'It's just that they don't know it yet.' He stood at the field oven with steam from the pan rising directly into his face.

Neither Mercer nor Mathias spoke.

The small boat eventually reached the shore and was grounded there. The three men on board jumped into the shallow water and waded ashore. One of them carried a basket that might have held fish. The other two secured the boat to a line in the dunes and then the three of them passed out of sight behind the houses.

'They say you spy on them,' Mathias said to Mercer.

'Their idea of themselves is a long way from the reality of the situation,' Mercer said.

'I know. But it still matters to them. They still speak and behave as though they were in control of their lives.'

'They cling to what they know,' Jacob said, approaching them with plates and the pan. 'Everything else terrifies them. They cling to what they know because, in their minds, everything else has the power to harm them. They still believe that they can hold onto everything, that they can protect it, keep it safe and prevent all change.'

'And you resent them that belief?' Mercer said.

'Resent? I *envy* them it. I envy them it, but I know how deluded they all are by it. I know how easily, when the time comes, you will take everything away from them and destroy it.'

'Me? Not me.'

'You, men like you, it is the same thing. As far as

they are concerned, you are the instrument of that change.'

'Then they're wrong,' Mercer said. '*You're* wrong.' He poured himself a second drink. He had rarely participated in conversations like this, where such grand and intangible concepts were passed so easily back and forth, and which gained some new and human shape in the hands of the men who dealt with them.

'He has offended you,' Mathias said. 'I shall apologize on his behalf. The stupid Jew with his own history smashed to the ground and destroyed. The stupid Jew who still does not see that it is the actions of individuals that count and not these great plans, these uncaring hands swept blindly across charts and maps.'

'You're wrong,' Jacob said to him. 'But I, too, apologize.'

Mercer was uncertain whether this apology was meant for him or for Mathias.

They ate, and afterwards, as darkness fell, Mathias said they should leave. He told Mercer that the long walk home would weaken Jacob considerably.

Mercer invited them both to stay, but they refused the offer and left soon afterwards.

'If I find out anything more that might be of use to you, I'll let you know,' Mathias told Mercer.

Jacob was the first to walk into the darkness, and Mathias went to catch up with him. The two men were quickly out of sight. It was a cloudless, moonlit night, and Mercer imagined the route they would follow back to the town. At Jacob's pace, it would take them well over an hour.

He stood for a moment to let the night air clear his head.

9

He did not see Mary again until the start of the following week. She approached him where he waited beside the water.

He saw her first in the dunes, with the other children, and then shortly afterwards, when she came to him alone. It was a thing he remembered long afterwards, these arrivals and departures of hers, the small dramas she made of her otherwise uneventful comings and goings.

She was carrying something, and it was only as she reached him that he saw that what she held was a dead tern.

'We found it up there,' she said, indicating the grass-topped ridge. The voices of the other children could occasionally still be heard. He said nothing about having seen her with them earlier.

She held the tern out for him to inspect. It was a young adult, smaller than most of the birds that constantly hovered and dived, though its first full and vividly white plumage was already formed. Its head swung limply between her fingers. He pulled out one of its wings and felt the delicate bones and tendons tense at its full span. It appeared to have lost none of its feathers.

'What killed it, I wonder?' he said. He touched the tip of the bird's beak.

'One of the boys,' she said.

'One of the boys? Why?'

'Why not?' she said. 'There's thousands of them. It's what boys do. Are you saying they shouldn't?'

'It just seems pointless, that's all. They're such beautiful things.'

'If you say so,' she said.

'How did they do it?'

'They –' she made a wringing motion with her hands. 'It doesn't take anything.'

'Here.' He handed it back to her.

She took it, folded its wings flat to its weightless body and pushed it head-first into her pocket.

'Will you bury it?' he asked her.

'Is that what *you'd* do?'

'I've never killed one,' he said.

'You're a soldier,' she said. 'It's not birds that you kill.'

'*Was* a soldier,' he said. 'I was an engineer in the Army, and now I'm an engineer—'

'Here,' she said.

He turned away from her. He had come to that far end of the dune ridge in the hope of locating the remains of the unfinished railway, but had found nothing of it.

He was about to ask her if she knew of the line when she said, 'She said to ask you to come tomorrow night.' She waited for him to turn back to her.

'Tomorrow?'

'To eat with us.' Her disapproval of the invitation remained clear to him. In the confines of the house she would be a child again, her mother's daughter, her brother's watcher.

'You could always tell her I said I was busy,' he said.

She considered this. 'She'll make a big thing of it, that's all. She always does. It's embarrassing. She'll spend all day worrying about it, make a mess of it when it happens, and then spend all night worrying about what the others might say. Apart from which, you'd be bored.'

'She might just want a practice run for when your father gets home,' he said, wondering how cruel he intended the remark to sound.

She saw what he had done. 'You wouldn't want to be a practice for that,' she said.

He still had no idea of the man other than what he had heard from others.

'It was a stupid thing to say,' he said. 'I apologize.'

'It was. But not for the reason you think.'

'All this will still be happening' – he swung his arm to encompass the distant workings – 'for a long time after he's back.'

'So? He probably won't even stay.'

'It might be a condition of his parole.'

'His what?'

'They sometimes insist on knowing where recently released people are living, and then on them staying put.'

She considered this for a moment, leaving him uncertain how she regarded the possibility. 'He never listened to anybody before,' she said. 'Tell him to do one thing, and he'll do the opposite. Way he is. That's what *she* says, what they all say. No one's looking forward to him being back here.'

Except you, he wanted to say, but didn't.

'Except me,' she said absently. 'I'm his favourite, see.' She spoke now in a childish, mocking voice. She picked up a handful of pebbles and threw them one at a time towards the water.

'Have things changed?' he said. He knew how all-encompassing and revealing her answer might be.

But all she said was, 'Not really.' She turned back to him. 'What do you want me to say?' she said.

'Say?'

'To her.'

'Tell her I shall be honoured and delighted to accept your gracious invitation.'

'*Her* gracious invitation. I'll tell her you said yes.' She slid her hand into the pocket which held the dead bird, turned and walked back into the dunes. 'Six o'clock,' she shouted to him.

'Should I bring anything?'

But if she heard him, she gave no sign.

At the crest of the rise, she fell to her knees briefly and then struggled back to her feet. He watched as she took out the dead bird, held it close to her face for a moment, and then threw it into the tall grass beside her.

10

The following morning, taking a break from the site, he crossed the road to the sea and waded in the shallows. The water felt bitterly cold after the warmth of the sand. He shielded his eyes to watch the vessels crossing the horizon, their distant outlines molten in the light and the heat, only their slowly unravelling ribbons of black marking their passage. He was distracted from this by a nearby noise and turned to see a man coming towards him along the water's edge. He recognized him only as a man who lived alone there, and as he came closer, Mercer saw that he carried a bundle of driftwood under each arm. He had dropped some of this, and this was what had alerted Mercer to his otherwise silent approach.

Mercer stepped out of the water and retrieved his boots. The man came to him and dropped everything he held to the ground.

'Firewood,' he said. 'Half of it still saturated and all of it full of salt.'

'Will it burn?' Mercer asked him.

'Eventually.' The man held out his hand. 'Daniels.'

'James Mercer,' Mercer said.

'Don't worry, I'm not going to ask you for work,' Daniels said.

'You live in one of the houses,' Mercer said.

'Not for much longer.'

The remark put Mercer on his guard. 'Are you leaving?'

Daniels smiled. 'You tell me,' he said, and then, seeing the unease he had caused Mercer, added, 'Don't worry. I doubt there's a single person here who hadn't worked everything out long in advance of your arrival. Not that they'll ever say anything to you directly. It's that kind of place – say nothing and it might not happen.'

'You weren't born here, then?'

'Copenhagen. My father was a sailor. Thirty years ago his ship docked at King's Lynn and sank there. He was stranded. He met my mother, who lived in the town, and took her home with him. I was born; she didn't settle. She brought me back here with her. He was killed two years later in Cape Town. I came and went between Denmark and here. Not here, specifically, but this part of the coast.'

'Were you in the Army?'

'Merchant Marine.'

'The Atlantic?'

'And the Arctic. My marrow is frozen. Hence all this gathering of firewood at the height of summer. To listen to some of them, you might imagine that winter was never going to come back.'

Mercer saw how he set himself apart from the others by these remarks. He remembered seeing the man with the men at the boats; he had seldom come out to be in the company of the women. It was then that Mercer remembered that this was the man he had seen with

Elizabeth Lynch during his first few days there, the man he had mistaken for her husband.

'You know Elizabeth Lynch,' he said.

'Elizabeth? Of course I know her.'

'I met her daughter,' Mercer said.

'I daresay.'

'It can't be easy for her.'

'Being without her husband, you mean? Don't fool yourself.'

'Did you know him?'

Daniels turned to look out over the horizon. 'Everyone knows Lynch,' he said, as though to say more would be betraying a confidence.

'I shouldn't have asked,' Mercer said. 'So how did you end up here?' It was a clumsy change of direction and he thought for a moment that their conversation was at an end.

'My wife's parents lived here. They both died and she took over their house. We had nowhere else, especially once the war started. Like my own father, I was away more than I was at home with her. We lived in Peterborough before coming here. She hated every minute of it. Here, I mean; not there. We, too, had a son. When the war started and they came to put in the guns, everyone was evacuated for three months. She went to stay with friends in London and our son died there. He was seven.'

'I'm sorry. In a raid?'

'Cerebral meningitis. A week after they arrived. I was away at sea when it happened and unable to return for almost two months. When I finally got back to her she was a changed woman. Everyone else had come back here by then, and she had come with them. She stayed here for a further year. Everyone spoke about her grief and about the balance of her mind being affected. I came home as often as was possible, but it was too little. After the death of our son, nothing was ever the same. She blamed herself for having taken him to London, and she blamed me for having forced her into making that decision because of my absence. I loved her. I loved her before and I loved her afterwards. Unfortunately, I fooled myself into believing that this love would be enough, that it would matter to her, and that it would continue to bind us together. I daresay if the war had ended sooner and I'd been able to come back permanently to her ... There was a coroner's inquest on our son. It wasn't until he was dead that they finally decided on what had killed him. It was ten days before I learned. Radio silence.'

'Is he buried in the town?' Mercer asked him.

'London. His name was Lars. I doubt she had much say in the matter. I last saw her ten months ago. We visited his grave together.'

'Did she move back there?'

'I think she would have gone anywhere to get away from here. I tried to persuade her to return to Peterborough, but she spoke so disparagingly of the place, and of our past there together. And just as I didn't learn of my son's death until long after the event, so, too, I had no idea that she was actually leaving me until long after she had gone.'

'Could you not have gone with her?'

'She told me not to. For several months I had no idea where she was staying. She sent a note telling me she was fine and that I was not to look for her. And so I stayed where I was, with no way of contacting her. *This* was where she would contact *me*.' He dug his heel into the sand. 'I even kept alive the hope that she might one day return here. You must have realized by now that those people born here are tethered to the place.'

'Like Elizabeth Lynch?'

'Like Elizabeth Lynch.'

'And so you stayed and waited.'

'I'm waiting still.'

'When did you last hear from her?'

Daniels shrugged, then said, 'Forgive my disingenuousness. Four months ago. The end of April. The second anniversary of our son's death. She wrote to ask me why I hadn't gone again to his grave with her. There was no return address in the note. No indication of how she felt other than to let me know that she was angry and disappointed in me. I wrote to everyone we had known in London, but no one knew where she was. Either that, or she had warned them against telling me. It is hard to persist under such circumstances.'

The two men walked a short distance back from the encroaching water. Mercer helped Daniels carry the wood he had gathered. Several small pieces were left behind and lost to the waves. Daniels held Mercer back from attempting to retrieve them.

'What do you do here?' Mercer asked him.

'The same as the rest of them.'

'Which is?'

'Gather driftwood, watch the horizon.'

Mercer understood precisely what he was being told and signalled to Daniels that he would ask no more questions on the subject.

They both looked back to the horizon, where nothing but the faintest of smudges marked where the vessels had been.

'Will you go back to her if she writes and asks you to?'

Daniels shook his head. 'I fool no one but myself that that is likely to happen. I'm still waiting, but I can't honestly say that I know what I'm waiting *for* any longer. Perhaps by waiting I merely maintain a state of grace, or something equally fanciful. Perhaps there is nothing else I can do and I am not yet prepared to admit that, not even to total strangers like yourself. She won't write, Mr Mercer. Our son died, and whichever one of us she truly holds responsible for that, she can no longer bear the thought of us being together.'

'So you make provision for winter, and yet you prepare to leave before it arrives.'

'I daresay there isn't a man, woman or child here that doesn't suffer some similar delusion.'

'You don't delude yourself,' Mercer said.

Daniels considered this for a moment and then continued walking.

Mercer followed him. It was beyond him now to ask him his wife's name.

'If I don't burn it, someone else will,' Daniels said as they rounded the final slope of the dunes and the line of houses came into view.

They paused briefly to look over the site and the men working there.

'Surprising how quickly you forget what it all so recently looked like,' Daniels said. 'Another delusion. We believe in permanence and yet it exists nowhere.'

'Perhaps if the world were re-made in the smallest of pieces and at long intervals.'

Daniels was about to respond to this, when he saw Elizabeth Lynch standing in her open doorway and watching them approach. She returned indoors as they drew close.

'Will you leave before her husband returns?' Mercer asked him, knowing immediately how Daniels might misinterpret the question.

'Lynch? I doubt it.' He led Mercer to where a mound of wood lay piled against the wall of a derelict out-building, and through which grew a mound of nettles. A short distance away lay the rotted keel of a shallow boat, its few remaining spars rising above the grass.

'I doubt the place would provide a single man with an honest living these days,' Daniels said. He dropped the wood he carried and went to the remains of the boat. Several gulls rose at his approach, flapping urgently to get airborne ahead of him.

11

The same few women watched him cross from the tower to the houses. It was clear to him that they all knew what was happening, and that they had each already formed their own understanding of the situation. He wished Mary or Elizabeth Lynch had been among them to greet him and to guide him through this gamut of undiverted glances and unspoken thoughts. He wished, too, that he had been able to find something to take to Elizabeth Lynch other than the few tins of food he again had with him. As before, it seemed more like a payment than a token. It was not a large package, but nor was it one he could hide from the watching women, or one he might carry beneath his arm as though scarcely aware he had it with him.

He reached the road's end and raised his hand to those gathered there. They responded immediately, and two of the younger women came towards him.

'What's she cooking for you, then?' one asked him.

He told her he didn't know.

'Not exactly renowned for her *dinner parties*,' the other said.

'It was still kind of her to offer,' he said.

'Why? Get all lonely, do you, sitting in there night after night by yourself?' She patted the arm of the other woman behind his back. 'You should have said. We could have done something about that.' They burst into laughter and he did his best to laugh with them.

They came to where the others stood and the two women detached themselves from him. Someone asked him about the work and he told them what he could. A good deal of what he said, he imagined, would be repeated later to husbands and brothers.

The door to Elizabeth Lynch's house opened and Mary appeared. She beckoned to him. Mercer excused himself and went to her.

Elizabeth Lynch waited inside for him. 'You'll be used to them by now,' she said nervously.

'I suppose me being here and the work must be a constant source of conversation.' He looked for Mary, but she had left the room.

She nodded, avoiding his eyes. 'I'm no different,' she said.

The door at the bottom of the stairs opened and Mary came back in to them.

It was immediately clear to Mercer that she had made a great effort with her appearance. She no longer wore her threadbare dress, but one which had obviously been her mother's, and which had been altered to fit her. Her hair was fastened back from her face, revealing more of her tanned forehead and her ears. The dress was cut higher on her neck and she wore a silver chain around her throat.

Her mother, too, seemed surprised by her changed appearance. She herself wore the clothes she had worn

91

all day, and she looked down at herself and then at her reflection in the mirror above the mantel at this unexpected appearance of her daughter.

'You look very . . . very—' Mercer began.

'Sophisticated?' Mary said. 'I look sophisticated. Perhaps even elegant.' She pretended to draw on a cigarette and then to blow out the smoke through the *o* of her lips.

'You're wearing lipstick,' her mother said.

'Hardly,' Mary said, but without conviction, and then with pleading in her eyes for her mother to say no more.

'I was going to say you looked very smart,' Mercer said. 'But "sophisticated" and "elegant" would be more appropriate.'

The predictability of this remark disappointed her. 'You might as well have said "grown-up",' she said.

'I didn't know she'd gone upstairs to change,' Elizabeth Lynch said. 'I didn't know you were changing. I suppose I ought to do the same.' She looked anxiously from the cooker to the already laid table.

'You ought,' Mary said. 'I can watch this.'

'I wish I'd had something better to bring,' Mercer said. 'Wine, perhaps.'

'Wine?'

'Or flowers. Something less . . .'

'Ordinary?' Mary said, drawing a sharp glance from her mother.

'And predictable,' Mercer said.

She came into the centre of the room and her mother told her what to watch on the cooker.

'She's never had wine,' Mary said to him when her mother had left the room.

'Whereas you, presumably, drink it all the time.'

'Most nights,' she said. She sipped from an invisible glass.

92

They heard the woman's footsteps above them.

'That lot outside will all now be wondering what she's doing drawing the bedroom curtains. Perhaps you ought to go and stand in the doorway to let them know where you are.'

Believing her concern to be serious, he took a step towards the door, but she held his arm and told him to stay where he was.

'Where's your brother?' he asked her.

'He's staying along the row. She thought it would be too much, what with all this fine cuisine and everything.' She went to the cooker, raised the lid of one of the pans there and pulled a face at its contents.

'I *am* aware that you don't want me here,' he said in a sharp whisper.

'But you still came.'

He had expected her denial.

'It would have been ungracious of me to refuse.'

'So you said. She feels beholden to you for the food.' She indicated the package beside him. 'Now she'll probably do it all again and make an even bigger fool of herself.'

'Only you think that,' he said. He regretted not having brought a bottle of whisky from his own small supply, but he knew the woman would have felt even more uncomfortable about taking that from him.

'Perhaps,' Mary said. 'Potatoes and fish. Hardly the Ritz, is it?'

They both laughed.

'And when did you last dine at the Ritz?'

She pretended to think. 'Months ago now. Have *you* ever been there? Seriously.'

'Never.' It was a lie.

'But you've been to other restaurants?'

'Of course I have. I mean, yes, a few.'

She turned her back on the cooker. 'He bought me this chain when I was born. It's supposed to be silver. I was christened wearing it. "Mary" was his choice. His mother was called Mary. He never had two good words to say about her, so God knows why I got landed with it.'

'Don't you like it? It suits you.'

'I don't care one way or the other. Besides, not much I can do about it while I'm stuck round here, is there?'

'So when you leave, will you change it?'

She clicked her fingers. 'Like that.'

Like that, he thought. *You'll walk away, turn a corner, change everything about yourself – your appearance, your past, your name – and become someone new and completely different.* If he'd had a drink in his hand he would have raised a toast to this coming transformation. He saw again how vital this self-belief was to her.

'It makes you look older,' he said. 'The dress.' It was true: she now seemed two or three years older than fifteen instead of the two or three years younger she had seemed to him in the presence of the other children.

'You're just saying that,' she said, but was unable to mask completely the flattery she felt.

'It's true.'

'It's one of hers cut down,' she said.

'So? It suits you.'

'Like my name,' she said. She hooked the silver chain onto her bottom lip, released it, and said, 'She makes me keep it locked away. Not locked, but hidden. They were arguing once and she said he'd never once bought her anything like it.' She lowered her voice.

'I can see that it means a lot to you,' he said.

'I used to think it was really valuable, precious. I used to imagine selling it to a jeweller in one of the bigger towns and getting a fortune for it.'

94

'I have something similar,' he told her. 'From my mother. She gave it to me when I went overseas. A ring that had belonged to her father and his father before him. It had a reputation in the family as a lucky charm.'

She looked at his hands and saw nothing there. 'And then one day, thinking you didn't need it any longer because the war was over, you took it off, and an hour later they sent you here.'

'Something like that.'

They laughed again.

They both looked up at the sound of footsteps above them. Mary returned to the cooker.

'She's coming down,' she said, and as she spoke her mother could be heard descending the stairs.

He knew how self-conscious Elizabeth Lynch might be at making her own entrance, and so he went to stand beside Mary at the cooker and pretended to show an interest in what she was doing. She understood this and raised her voice as the door opened and her mother returned to them. She had changed her clothes, and she, too, had fastened back her hair.

Mercer remarked on her dress.

'I've had it for years,' she said, and the one flat note of unhappy realization in her voice made clear to him the truth of this.

'It's her best dress,' Mary said. 'I told her she should put it on before you got here.'

Elizabeth Lynch nodded. 'She wants everything to be something it isn't,' she said. She looked fondly at her daughter, who looked back at her with an equal affection.

'Now we've both embarrassed him,' Mary said.

But the woman did not properly understand her, and so she smiled and nodded again.

95

12

He was working on his charts the following day when someone entered the room below and called up to him.

He went down and saw Mathias Weisz waiting there, inside the doorway and close against the wall.

Outside, a group of men swung sledgehammers into a tangled mass of wire and brick. Beside them, an even larger group of men tried unsuccessfully to coax a generator into life.

'I think they're having some problems,' Mathias said. He took off his cap and held out his hand to Mercer.

'Have you come alone?'

'Am I under armed escort, do you mean?' Mathias said.

'I meant Jacob.'

'I see. No. I am alone. I've been sent on an errand. One of our own pumps refuses to pump. A worn seal. I've been sent to – what is the word? – scrounge? But I see you have problems of your own.'

'If there isn't a problem they'll create one and then all gather round it for an hour.'

Mathias made a circle with his thumbs and forefingers. 'Six inches.'

'Are you flooding, too?'

'In places. Nothing serious.'

'I'm surprised they didn't follow you in,' Mercer said, indicating the men outside.

'They didn't see me. I came along the shore and up the side of the culvert. If you know where to go, you can walk for miles around here without being observed. Believe me, it was one of the first things I learned to do upon being afforded some degree of freedom.'

'Come up,' Mercer told him. 'I need to clear a few things away.'

Mathias followed him up the open staircase.

'Jacob and I appreciated the other evening,' he said, looking around the familiar room.

'Did he get home all right?'

Mathias fluttered his hand. 'He overestimates his own strength sometimes.'

'Or denies his own weakness.'

'Whatever. He quickly exhausts himself. He imagines himself to be recovered, when, in truth, it will take much longer than he is prepared to allow.'

All of which means you probably carried him the last part of your journey home.

It was warm in the room, and sweat shone on Mathias's face. He took out a white, perfectly folded handkerchief and wiped his brow. He saw Mercer watching him.

'My mother always used to insist that no matter where I was, whatever conditions I was living under, I should always endeavour to have a clean handkerchief

97

with me. She said it would keep me civilized long after all those other civilizing influences had gone or seemed too far away to matter any longer.'

'And were they ever far away?'

Mathias laughed and shook his head. 'What sort of soldier does the son of a rose-grower make? Captain of Procurement. Channel Coast, Division Four, three-five-two infantry division.'

'Normandy?'

'Pas de Calais. We were shifted afterwards, of course, to do our procuring elsewhere, but it never amounted to much in those months after the invasion. I was captured at the beginning of August, exhausted, sleeping in an orchard on the outskirts of a place called Caumont. I think we were heading for Argentan, but I can't be sure. All I can be certain of is that for the past three days we'd been travelling in the opposite direction to a lot of other men, fighting divisions. You?'

'North Africa, Sicily, Italy,' Mercer said.

'Not France?'

'After Italy I was sent home. I was back here for three months, recuperating, then another six months training others. I went to France at the end of July. Bridges, pontoons, anything that meant we didn't have to keep stopping. When did you finally end up here?' He tried to remember if Mathias had already told him this, but could not.

'I was never a particularly high-risk prisoner. It was a great joke to my interrogators that I had spent so long in the Pas de Calais, waiting for you to arrive there, and that all the time I waited I was searching out fruit and vegetables and fodder for horses.'

'Were you serious when you said you got the job because you came from a family of professional gardeners?'

'Never underestimate the blind efficiency of the military mind, of the connections it makes or insists upon. I might have been in the wrong place at the wrong time, but I was never anything less than perfectly suited to the task at hand. Six weeks at an officers' training school and I found myself a captain.'

'I daresay the same work might have been a little more hazardous elsewhere.'

' "A little more hazardous," ' Mathias repeated. 'Yes. The Russian Front, for instance. A thousand other places. Until you arrived, the north of France was never a bad place to be. I farmed there, too. We all did. They laughed at that, also.'

'And because they laughed, you ended up on a farm here.'

'There is a certain undeniable logic to it all, I suppose. It would have been different if I'd been in more of a hurry to get home.'

Or if you had not met Jacob, Mercer thought.

'When I learned my parents had been killed and the nursery destroyed, it scarcely mattered to me where I lived.' He stopped speaking.

'What restrictions are you still under?' Mercer said.

'Restrictions? Not many. I still have a technical classification, of course, and as Jacob told you, I am still required to report to the various Authorities on a regular basis. People have been kind to me here. And where they have been unable to show kindness, they have shown tolerance. It was a surprising thing to me, especially so soon after the war's end, and all that was then revealed.'

'Is that how you learned to speak English so well?'

'I spoke it before. My mother was a great Anglophile. Her own mother was half-English, who met her husband in East Africa. I used to teach it to the others in the camps. Some men were eager to learn; others refused to utter a single word. Some felt betrayed, and others refused to betray themselves in even this smallest of ways. It is hard to think of yourself as an undesirable or dangerous alien when you speak the same language as your accusers and understand perfectly everything they say about you.'

'Have you seen Jacob since the other evening?' Mercer asked him.

'Of course. I see him most days. The road back to our camp runs past where he stays. I find out what he needs – though seldom from Jacob himself – and I try and find it for him.'

'Has he told you what happened to him?'

'Some of it. Not everything. I don't ask.' He came to Mercer at the window, but remained far enough back from it so that he would not be seen by anyone below. 'I know that he was in several of those camps, and that he was finally released from Belsen, if that's what you're asking me.'

'I didn't mean to pry.'

'I know what he tells me he has lost, but I doubt if I shall ever truly understand the weight or the depth or the darkness of that loss. I know he survived and wishes he hadn't. Please—' He held up a hand. 'Ask *him* all this, not me.'

Mercer went back to the table and took the weights from his charts.

Outside, the generator finally spluttered into noisy life.

'Success,' Mathias said.

'I doubt they'll see it like that.'

'We are no different on the airfield. There is a great deal of movement and looking busy, but there are days when very little is actually achieved. Look at me – two hours so far to find a single seal. You think they will all be impatiently awaiting my return?'

'We'll need to go in search of one. I don't know where they're kept. Someone will know. Stay here, if you like. I'll say it's for a pump elsewhere on the site.'

'No need. I am used to it by now.'

They left the tower together several minutes later.

The generator was now running continuously and a pall of smoke drifted above it. A drill had been attached to this and now only a solitary man stood working at the centre of the bricks. Upon seeing Mercer and Mathias, however, a group of others rose from where they had been sitting and came towards them. Someone called for the man with the drill to turn it off. Mercer told them what he was looking for, but none of them knew where he might find the seal. All of them looked hard at Mathias as they spoke to him.

'What's *he* doing here?' one of them said eventually.

'What does it matter?'

'What does it matter?' the man said with forced incredulity. 'What do you mean, "What does it matter?" You know what he is, don't you?'

'He's an ex-prisoner of war working at the airfield,' Mercer said.

'Exactly.'

'So what is it you object to?'

'What I object to is the fact that he shouldn't be here. None of them should be. Behind bars here or behind bars at home, that's where he should be. That's what I *object* to.'

A murmur of concurrence rose around the man.

'Do you know anything about him personally?' Mercer said. 'His name's—' He stopped, suddenly aware that he had forgotten Mathias's surname.

'His name's what?' the man said. He was grinning now, encouraging the more active involvement of those around him.

'It's for him, isn't it,' another man said. 'This seal.'

'It's for the airfield. He's just been sent to fetch it.'

'Then let him come and ask for it. Let *him* look for it.'

'Why are you behaving like this?'

'Why are we behaving like what?'

'With such animosity.'

'"Animosity,"' the man mimicked.

'You know what I mean.'

'Says who?' the second man said.

'He's here because he was sent here,' Mercer said. 'He had no choice in the matter.'

'*He* tell you that, did he?'

He refused to be drawn any further into their impregnable argument, knowing that whatever he said now would only antagonize them further. He looked at each of them for a few seconds and then turned and left them.

'That's right,' he heard one of them say to his back. 'You get back to him.'

'Don't want to keep him waiting, do we?' another added.

The men who had so far said little or nothing underscored these remarks with their laughter. There was no attempt to return to work at Mercer's departure.

Mathias waited for him by the tower door.

'I did try to warn you,' he said as Mercer reached him.

'I know.'

'It must come as a shock to be continually reminded of how little you are to them.'

'Perhaps that's why I insist on living in the tower

102

like someone in a fairy tale, keeping myself above and apart from it all.'

Mercer led the way around the side of the tower until they were out of sight of the men and over-looking the sea. In the distance, an unattended pump performed the barely adequate work of keeping down the water of a blocked drain. A sheeted mound stood beside it. This was mostly fuel, Mercer knew, but might include some spares. He indicated the pump to Mathias and they crossed the broken ground towards it.

Mercer drew back the tarpaulin. Several crates stood beside the drums of fuel. He opened these and told Mathias to search their contents for the seal. He found one immediately, attached to several dozen others.

'Take two or three,' Mercer told him.

Mathias shook his head. 'And deprive myself of further visits?'

Mercer himself took several of the rings and said he would keep them at the tower.

More air than water blew through the hose of the pump, and what little water was raised splashed noisily onto the beach below.

Mathias watched this for several minutes before saying, 'All this flooded last autumn. As far as you can see. You should talk to the people here about it. It happens most years. You could save a lot of time and effort by finding out where it's likely to happen again. This' – he tapped the side of the pump with his foot – 'is not what you need to hold back the water if it decides to come.'

'I'm hoping to be finished here long before the worst of the weather sets in,' Mercer said.

'We all hope to be finished before that,' Mathias said.

'What are they doing with the planes?' Mercer asked him.

'Who knows. Melting them down into saucepans, perhaps? Anything that might have once been made to fly again is long gone. We get visits every few days from someone or other to see how quickly we are progressing. Everyone complains that nothing is being done quickly enough. It sometimes seems as though the whole world is being forced along at a speed it cannot bear.'

'Perhaps it's just a need to keep up the momentum away from what went before.'

'Away from the rose gardens?' Mathias said.

'Away from the rose gardens.'

They left the pump and parted.

Instead of returning to the tower and the waiting men, Mercer walked to the beach. The midday tide was rising and he quickly reached the lapping water.

13

Three days later, Saturday, Mercer walked to the town with the intention of visiting Jacob and discovering where he lived. He knew only what Jacob had told him – that he lived in a room above a warehouse, but he did not know where this was, and he regretted not having asked Mathias for details.

The place called itself a town, but was in reality little more than a large village – the largest for five miles in any direction in that sparsely populated part of the country.

It always surprised Mercer how quickly the sea was out of sight once he had left the workings. A hundred yards inland along the coast road and the water was already gone from view, along with the dunes and the levees of the broader channels.

He went first to the town's only garage, where he hoped to be further directed, but neither of the two men working there had heard of Jacob Haas. Mercer explained who Jacob was, but, similarly, neither of them knew of a Dutchman living in the town. One of them remarked disparagingly that the place was full of foreigners, by which he meant strangers. In all likelihood, Mercer knew, he would encounter some of the men who worked on the site. Their depot lay on the outskirts of the place and they doubtless frequented its public houses.

One of the mechanics suggested asking at the post office, and then directed Mercer to this. The two men sat on the bonnet of the car upon which they were working and watched him go.

At the post office he asked again after Jacob. An old woman stood behind the grille. She was hard of hearing and he repeated the name several times. She considered this for a moment, appeared to make some calculation on her fingers, and then told him she had never heard of the man. Her son was the postmaster, she explained, and he was away, in Spalding, for the day. She made the place sound grand and distant, as though she herself had never been there. She left him to serve a customer, and then returned.

'Perhaps he has his mail addressed here for collection,' Mercer suggested.

She went to a cardboard box and searched its few contents, laboriously reading each label and asking him to repeat the name.

But there was nothing.

Another customer entered, another woman.

'Gentleman's looking for – who is it?'

Mercer repeated the name to this newcomer, and it was immediately clear to him that she knew of Jacob.

She screwed up her face. 'He's the Jew,' she said to the old woman at the counter.

'The Jew?'

'The Jew. You know . . .' She screwed up her face again, as though at a bad smell.

'He's Dutch,' Mercer said.

Both women turned to him.

'Oh, is he?' the customer said. 'Friend of yours, is he? Given him a job out on whatever it is you think you're doing, have you? Given him a job while there's others here not had a day's work since they were demobbed?'

'No,' he said. 'He's not well enough to work.'

The woman raised a hand to her mouth and made a remark he did not catch.

'Do you know where I might find him?' he asked her.

She seemed taken aback at the hostility now in his own voice.

'I know exactly where he lives – stays,' she said, relishing the power she possessed.

'I'd be grateful.' He waited.

Seeing that he would be drawn no further, the woman said, 'Bail's Yard, that's where he *lives*.'

'Can you direct me?'

'He doesn't know Bail's Yard?' the old woman said. She gave him directions, mapping out each part of the short journey with a finger pointed only at the door.

'Thank you,' Mercer said firmly.

'Don't thank me,' she told him.

He left and the two women came to the door to watch him go.

He followed the first of her instructions until he turned from the High Street and was out of sight.

Bail's Yard stood across a bridged drain, and consisted of a large, muddy, fenced-in yard, in which sat dozens of abandoned and useless tractors and other pieces of farm machinery. Beyond these lay a giant, and equally dilapidated, corrugated iron structure, upon the roof of which was crudely painted 'Bail's Yard'.

He moved through the rusting, sagging vehicles and implements, avoiding the worst of the mud and the water. The drain was high and flowing. Weed and flotsam snagged the bars of a weir, collected there briefly, broke loose and floated away in clumps. He tried to imagine where the water entered the sea, where it might cross his own unsettled domain.

He was distracted by the voice of a man who emerged from the vast open doorway, holding a spanner as long as his forearm.

'Help you?'

Somewhere to Mercer's left, dogs barked and rattled the chains which, hopefully, tethered them. Mercer missed his footing at the sound and stepped into a rut which soaked him to his shins. He raised his hand to the man, who remained where he stood.

'I'm looking for Jacob Haas,' Mercer said, preparing himself for further rebuttal or hostility. But instead, the man lowered the spanner he held and came further into the open.

'You Mercer?'

'I am.'

'He has the room over the forge,' the man said.

'Are you Bail?' Mercer asked him.

'One of them. Remaining son of. Last of.'

'So all this is yours?'

'Unfortunately. The old man let it run down while we were away.'

'Overseas?'

'Tank Corps. Recovery and repair. I'd be there still if it wasn't for this.' He held up a stiff, gloved hand.

'I see,' Mercer said.

'I imagine you do.'

'You said "forge".'

'Used to be a blacksmith's. Gas cylinder job. I fire it

up once a week for all the iron-work I still get called on to do. Not much these days. It's mostly salvage, welding, keeping something running that should have been scrapped and replaced ten years ago.'

'How long were you away?' Mercer asked him.

'Four years. Long enough.'

The two men looked around them at the dirty, failed enterprise.

'Has Jacob been here long?' Mercer asked him.

'Eight months, nine. He came wanting the use of the forge. You know about his glasswork. He's a talented man. He should be doing all this somewhere else, somewhere he'd be better appreciated. I live over there.' He indicated a simple brick house and overgrown garden by the drain. 'I offered him a room with me, but he said he preferred not to. Said he wouldn't be much company. Shame. My father died in nineteen forty-two, and my two brothers the following year. There were only ever the four of us.'

They stood without speaking for several minutes. The noise of the flowing water could be heard.

'Is he here?' Mercer said eventually.

'I think so. He doesn't go out much, and hardly anyone ever comes here. Mathias, but that's about all.'

'You know Mathias?'

'Of course. Offered him a job once, but he said he couldn't make any commitments, said he might be sent home at any minute. I suppose we're in much the same boat, me and him,' Bail said. 'All three of us, when you think about it.' He turned to face Mercer. 'I saw what they did, you know.'

'Sorry. Saw what?'

'What they did. Those places. A terrible thing, terrible.'

'Oh, I see.'

'It's not something you can easily take in.'

'Does Jacob ever talk about it?'

'Not to me. We have a kind of understanding. We're both the kind of men who like to be left alone. Chances are, he'll be watching us now, wondering what I'm saying to you about him.'

'Watching us?'

Bail motioned into the dark space behind him. 'Over the forge. There's a window looks down into the workshop. Anybody comes, he hides himself away up there and watches. Not hides, exactly. He just doesn't like surprises. Can't say that I blame him.'

Mercer wondered if this was intended as a veiled warning.

'Will he see me, do you think?'

'I imagine so. He told me he was out at the workings with Mathias. Mathias comes here every other day or so, brings food and whatever.'

'As do you, I imagine,' Mercer said.

'Oh, well, you know – fellow man and all that.' He paused. 'I wish I hadn't seen it, I truly do, but I did and there's nothing I can do about that.' He shook his head and breathed deeply. 'I daresay you saw a few things yourself.'

Mercer peered through the darkness of the vast structure to where Bail had said the window was. He felt reassured by the man's presence.

'Anyhow . . .' Bail said, sensing that Mercer's attention had been diverted. 'Work to do. Go on through, shout for him. He'll hear you. There's a staircase, but watch your footing, it's as ready to collapse as the rest of the place.'

Mercer entered the building and saw that there was almost as much water on the floor inside as there was out. Wooden pallets had been laid as walkways.

More dismantled vehicles and pieces of machinery lay scattered around. Workbenches lay spread with parts and tools. Here and there lay something freshly exposed and shining silver, but the overall impression was one of grime- and oil-encrusted waste. Coils of rope and chain hung from a girder which spanned the roof.

He made his way through the gloom to the rear of the structure, calling for Jacob as he went.

He came to the stairs and saw the cold forge in an annexe beneath these. Broken fire-bricks and mounds of ash and spent coke littered the confined space. Bundles of iron rods lay stacked against the wall.

He called again.

At the top of the stairs a door opened and a light shone out on to the metal platform which ran the length of the high wall. He saw Jacob looking down at him.

'May I come up?' he shouted.

'Of course.' Jacob turned and went back inside, leaving the door open behind him.

Mercer climbed the stairs, feeling them sway beneath him where their fixings had worn loose.

The door led into a room in which a stove had been installed. This heated the room, and the glow of the burning coals provided some further illumination in the dark space. It was not a cold day, but the fire still burned, and looked as though it had been burning for some time. There was a table, crowded with food, crockery and glassware, several chairs, and a worn and much-patched leather sofa facing the room's only external window, which afforded a dull view over the back of the yard and the open land beyond. On a workbench alongside this lay the pieces of Jacob's glassware Bail had mentioned.

Jacob stood at the centre of all this, beckoned Mercer inside and then motioned for him to close the door.

'Bail told me to come up,' Mercer said, feeling the need to explain. He felt like an intruder in the small, crowded space.

Jacob occupied himself briefly by shovelling more coal into the small stove. The room was poorly ventilated, and as makeshift, it occurred to Mercer, as his own accommodation in the tower.

'As you might imagine, I don't get many visitors,' Jacob said.

'More than I receive,' Mercer said.

'And soon the court and all his creditors will declare Bail as bankrupt and as beyond salvation as he already knows himself to be, and all this will be sold from under him, and we will both be once again homeless.'

'Do you think so? Does *he* think that?'

'Look around you. One man. What chance has he got to make a success of the place? You've seen what there is to see; you can easily imagine it.'

Mercer nodded. 'Is it happening already?' he said. 'Bankruptcy, the courts?'

'He refuses to talk about it.'

'Why didn't you take up his offer and move into the house with him?'

Jacob laughed at this. 'What, so that we might spend endless evenings comparing our misery and hopelessness. I think not. I think those two things are best contained and held close.'

'You might be some comfort to each other regardless,' Mercer said. He knew it was the wrong word.

'"Comfort" is not what either of us seeks. Besides, even if it were, I doubt we would seek it here and from each other. Apart from which, I have everything I need here.' He spread his arms.

A world of men alone, thought Mercer.

'May I offer you tea?' Jacob said. 'Or, if you prefer—' He took a bottle of clear liquid from a cabinet beside the sofa. Holding this out to Mercer, he started to cough, and put the bottle down so that he might press both his hands to his chest. The exertion shook him, and he half-sat, half-fell onto the sofa.

'Is there anything I can do?' Mercer said.

Jacob signalled that there was nothing.

Eventually, the coughing subsided and he sat with his head down, panting. He took out a cloth and wiped his mouth and then his whole face with this. 'I'm fine,' he said, making no attempt to conceal the lie. He looked surreptitiously at the cloth before returning it to his pocket. He reached for the bottle beside him and settled it into his lap. He sat shivering for a moment and held his palms to the stove.

Mercer came closer to him and drew up a chair. He examined one of the glass bowls on the bench beside Jacob. It was of the palest blue, with a darker rim and flecked with other colours. 'One of yours?' he said, but the question did not require an answer. It was clear to him that the pieces were the work of an artist, that there was considerably more than expertise or craftsmanship involved. 'Bail told me about the forge,' he said.

'I have constructed a crude kiln there,' Jacob said, his voice dry. 'A primitive and unpredictable thing, largely uncontrollable, but I succeed sufficiently to go on making the effort.'

'You ought to show these to someone. A dealer, perhaps. They're beautiful.'

But it was clear by Jacob's evasive behaviour, his fumbling again for the bottle, his searching around him, that he was not prepared to talk about the glass.

'I mean it,' Mercer insisted.

'I believe you,' Jacob said abruptly. 'And you must believe me when I tell you that I have my own reasons for not wishing to do anything other than to make the pieces and to sell what few I am able to sell to pay for my keep here.'

None of which will last, Mercer thought.

'Besides which, for every ten pieces I attempt to make, nine are destroyed in the process.' He indicated a bucket beneath the bench that was filled to the brim with pieces of the broken, coloured glass.

'You break them yourself?'

'There must be some degree of judgement involved, some control. It might just as easily be dismissed as "artistic temperament", I suppose, but, believe me, nothing could be further from the truth. Just accept that I have my reasons. I have made perhaps forty or fifty pieces since I came here, and that is enough. If I were back in Utrecht right now, I would probably be inspecting sheets of glass waiting to be cut into panes for factory windows. Believe me, this is preferable, far more preferable.'

'Just as Mathias prefers to stand up to his knees in mud and rubble than perfecting the shapes and colours of his roses.'

Jacob smiled at this. 'Hardly,' he said. He handed Mercer the bottle.

Later, Mercer said, 'Bail told me that he'd seen—' only to be immediately interrupted by Jacob, who said:

'He told me, too. It is no true connection between us, no true understanding. It is something in which he, of course, wishes to believe, and perhaps I indulge him in this belief, but it is nothing that truly connects us, I will not allow it to. Do you understand me?' He looked hard at Mercer, waiting for his only answer.

114

'I think so,' Mercer said. 'But I still don't understand why you won't allow him to do what he believes he should do and—'

'For what reason? Guilt? Because it gratifies some uncertain notion of atonement or redemption he may hold?'

'What harm would it do?'

But Jacob refused to answer him. He covered his face briefly with his hand and shook his head. 'He's a good man,' he said eventually. 'I know that. And perhaps that's enough. Perhaps the fault is mine – perhaps I expect too much of people, too much understanding. How am I to explain anything to him – to you, to anyone – when I cannot yet convince myself of the validity or need for that explanation?'

But it was not what he was truly saying, and Mercer understood this. He understood, too, how accomplished the man had become at drawing the sudden tensions out of the room and of diverting their course, of turning a single straight path into a dozen meandering tracks.

Mercer stayed in that overheated room above the cold forge for a further hour. He drank four more small glasses of the spirit, and when he finally rose to leave, he felt himself momentarily unsteady on his feet.

Jacob laughed at this. 'I personally', he said, 'will not be making the effort to rise.' He poured himself another glass. As Mercer opened the door, Jacob said, 'I do appreciate you coming here. I wish I had more to offer you.'

'I'll come again,' Mercer said.

'Mathias will come later. I'll tell him you were here.'

Mercer left the room and waited on the high metal platform until his eyes became accustomed to the darkness beneath him.

14

'Five days,' Mary said to him as he sat on the grass bank beside her.

'Five days what?'

'Until he's coming home.'

The news surprised him. He had seen her on each of the previous few days and there had been no mention then of her father's return.

'She got a telegram this morning. She didn't open it for an hour, just left it sitting there, like somebody had died. I opened it in the end. It just said that he'd already been released and that he'd be here on such and such a date. Five days.'

'And is everything ready for him?'

'What do you mean?'

He had almost asked her if her mother was looking forward to her husband's home-coming.

'I mean is she prepared. The house.'

She looked at him puzzled. 'What about the house? You make it sound as though there was anything she could do about it. He's coming home and that's it.'

'Was the telegram from him?'

'From someone in the Army. He wouldn't write.'

'Something to look forward to,' he said.

She turned away from him and looked along the beach to where the other children played in the distance.

She had sought him out the previous day and offered to do some housework for him in the tower. He had accepted her offer and then paid her for the work. She told him not to tell anyone of their arrangement. 'Is that what it is?' he had asked her, amused by the intrigue she had so easily created around the occasion. She had accused him of making fun of her, and had then left him before he could deny this. It was why he had come to her upon seeing her sitting alone on the bank.

'Will she go to meet him somewhere?' The nearest branch-line station was twelve miles away.

'I doubt it. He'll come here. She said they'll probably bring him.'

'I doubt that very much,' he told her. 'Not if he's already been released.' The man would have been given travel passes.

'I told her they'd probably let him out early because he'd been – I don't know what the word is—'

'A model prisoner? Well-behaved?'

'Something like that.'

'And what did she think?'

'She just laughed. "Him?" she said. "Him?"'

It had been almost four years since she had seen the man. She had been only eleven at his arrest, her young brother little more than a baby. He wondered how much she knew, and how much she now expected of him. There was something guarded about everything she said to Mercer concerning the man: as though she wanted to share her excitement with him, but at the

117

same time was conscious of her own uncertainty in the matter; conscious, too, of not wanting to appear disloyal or dismissive of the man to whom she had been such an ally before his arrest.

'I suppose everybody else knows about his return,' he said.

'Most of them were there when the telegram came. Mrs Armstrong crossed herself and stood as though she was praying all the time the man was looking for it in his bag.'

'Perhaps she thought it was for her.'

'I doubt it. She's had hers. The man asked me where my mother lived. He made her sound like somebody else completely.'

'It's how telegrams work,' he said. 'You're meant to be on your guard before you open them.'

'Mrs Armstrong went and told everyone what had happened and they all gathered outside while she read it.'

A bed of cotton-grass grew along the base of the bank, looking like a line of snow where it stretched towards the houses. A flock of birds sat motionless on the water beneath them.

'I went into town,' he said, not having mentioned this to her previously.

'To see the Jew. I know.'

'I wish you wouldn't call him that,' he said.

She looked at him, half-closing her eyes against the light. 'I know that, too,' she said.

'His name's Jacob.'

She repeated it ten times over.

'I know it's what everybody else here calls him, but I thought you were different,' he said.

She saw through this subterfuge immediately. 'How am I different?'

118

'You know what I mean.'

'If I'm different, tell me *how* I'm different.'

'You have more sense,' he said. 'More compassion.'

She considered this for a moment. 'I doubt it,' she said.

'More ambition, then.'

'And what does that have to do with not calling a Jew a Jew?'

He refused to tolerate this any longer. 'Suit yourself,' he said, and prepared to rise.

She put out her hand and held him back. 'Jacob,' she said. 'And you're wrong about everybody else here calling him a Jew. My mother never does.'

And, presumably, she's already told you not to call him that.

She bowed her head for a moment.

He sat back down beside her.

'It's mostly because I don't have anyone else to talk to. Nobody my own age.'

The oldest of the other girls was at least four years her junior.

'I know that,' he said.

'*She* pretends to do it,' she said, meaning her mother. 'But she doesn't know how to, not really. And besides . . .'

'It's not what you want from your own mother.'

She shook her head. She leaned forward to watch the other children. They were further away than earlier, their voices barely audible.

'What do you remember most about him?' he asked her.

She lay back against the slope, folding her arms across her stomach.

'He used to take me out with him. Fishing. Into

119

town. He used to take me to places I wasn't supposed to go.'

'And your mother disapproved.'

'It sometimes seemed like she disapproved of everything he did. She once told me that his own mother had warned her against marrying him. She said he *used* people and that he'd use me just the same.'

'She loved him, I suppose.'

'Something. I was born six months after they were married.'

'And you think that's why she married him?'

'What else?'

'It wouldn't account for his behaviour afterwards.'

'He always used to complain about feeling trapped. Every time they argued, he'd say it.'

'Trapped by her?'

'I used to think he meant trapped by this place. Who wouldn't feel trapped?'

'But now you think he meant because she was pregnant?'

She nodded.

Nothing he said would relieve her of the uncertain blame she still felt.

'She said that half of everything was her fault, anyway. She used to defend him, especially when she was with the other women. She used to say they didn't know him like she knew him.'

'There must have been something,' he said, wanting to reassure her.

She propped herself up on her elbow. 'You don't have to,' she said.

'Don't have to what?'

'Side with him on my account.'

'I wasn't. I don't know the man. All I know is that you, at least, still have a great deal of affection

120

for him and that his return means a lot to you.'

She acknowledged this in silence.

'Do you think he'll leave?' he asked her. 'Come back here, let the Authorities think he's settled, and then go?'

She shrugged. 'It's what *she* thinks will happen. What is there here for him any more? Farm work? Not even much of that now that the farmers can pick and choose who they take on. He once told her he was going back to the Midlands to work in a car factory. He said he'd be the one to pick and choose if he lived there.'

'Perhaps he'll want you all to go with him,' Mercer suggested, but with little true conviction.

'She wouldn't leave,' she said. 'Not now.'

'And you?'

'You think he'd take *me* with him?'

Her disbelief, he knew, was intended to prompt him into saying more. 'Why not? You could enrol at a college or a—'

'College? *Me?*'

'Why not?'

'Because it's not what people like me do.' She still wanted to be convinced.

'I'm talking about there, not here,' he said. 'The Midlands, anywhere.'

She fell silent, considering all he had just suggested. She had left the local school two months earlier, and it surprised him to realize how little thought she had given to her future, caught in this limbo of her father's absence and the anticipation of his return. He wished he could persuade her not to expect so much of the man or his home-coming. And then he became concerned that he himself might now become the source of further false hope and impossible expectation, and that she might repeat all he had suggested to her mother.

'It must be hard for her,' he said eventually, hoping to distract her from these new thoughts.

'She won't talk about it. Even before the telegram, she said nothing. All *she* wants to do is remember everything good about him. On the one hand, she thinks everything's going to have changed for the better, and on the other, she goes on and on about the way things were as though it was anything worth having in the first place.' She checked herself at this sudden outburst, and he saw again the divides she repeatedly crossed, the opposing directions in which she was constantly being made to face.

'I meant it's going to be hard for her to adjust to having him around,' he said.

'She'll cope,' she said. 'That's what she does – she copes. Copes, and then tells you over and over how well she's coping.' It was the harshest thing yet he had heard her say about the woman, and he regretted even more having raised the subject.

After that, perhaps because she was conscious of having said too much to him, or of having revealed feelings she herself did not yet properly understand, she lay on the bank without speaking. She closed her eyes, and after several minutes of her silence, he wondered if she was sleeping.

He rose to leave her.

'I wasn't asleep,' she said.

'I have things to do.' He gestured towards the site.

'When shall I come and clean for you again?' she said.

He moved so that his shadow ran over her face and the high sun no longer blinded her.

15

'Is there a valid – an *acceptable* – distinction to be made, Captain Mercer, between, on the one hand, actually killing a man, and on the other, allowing a man to die when you remain convinced that some action on your part might have saved his life, or at the very least have improved his chances of survival until someone better able to save his life was able to reach him?' Mathias kicked at a mound of clay-encrusted bottles turned up by one of the airfield diggers.

Beside him, both Mercer and Jacob paused at the remark.

Mercer let the lost rank pass. It occurred to him that Mathias had been so long among military men of one sort or another that he felt more comfortable using it; 'Mister' always sounded too formal in his hard English, derogatory almost.

Jacob shook his head in disbelief at the question.

It was clear to Mercer that Mathias was talking about himself, and that he had long considered asking the question. Until then, in the hour the three of them had been together, he had remained largely silent.

'I suppose it would depend on the men and the circumstances,' Mercer said, knowing how inadequate an answer this was, hoping to prompt Mathias's own further explanation.

He had encountered the pair of them at the end of the runway and they had beckoned him to them. A group of Mathias's fellow prisoners congregated at some distance, kicking a ball against one of the abandoned outer buildings of the airfield.

'Just tell us,' Jacob said, surprising Mercer by this bluntness, knowing that Mathias had hoped for a further degree of understanding and acceptance before being made to explain himself.

'It was during our retreat from Vimont,' he said. 'One of my men, a boy really, was struck by several shell splinters in his face and chest. I put pressure pads on the worst of the wounds. His own field-dressing case was empty, filled with cigarettes. Several others stopped beside me. He'd only been with us a month, since the middle of May.'

'What was his name?' Jacob said. 'Use his name.'

'Kretschmer, his surname was Kretschmer. We all called him "Adolf". For obvious reasons.' He turned to Mercer. 'He was very enthusiastic, you see. Keen to push you back into the Channel and then to chase you home over it. Having been hurriedly sent there, we did nothing but scramble away from the coast for a fortnight. Sleep and run, sleep and run. Through Falaise to the east. You were at our heels all the way. It became a joke to us – waiting for the order to regroup and counter-attack. We all knew it was never going to happen.'

'It wasn't him,' Jacob said.

'Wasn't who?'

124

Jacob pointed to Mercer. 'It wasn't *Captain* Mercer coming at you across the waves.'

Now the word sounded sour in his mouth, and Mercer wondered why he had bothered with this pointless correction.

'No, of course,' Mathias said.

'Go on,' Mercer told him.

'The wound in the boy's neck—'

'In "Adolf's" neck,' Jacob said.

'The wound in his neck wouldn't stop bleeding. Perhaps something vital had been severed, I don't know. I stayed with him while others ran and rode past us. Someone threw me more bandages, but nothing else. I stupidly tried to give him water to drink, but he couldn't swallow it and was forced to spit it out with the blood he was already choking on. He begged me not to leave him. Not to not let him die, just not to leave him. Shells were already falling far ahead of us.'

'Your shells,' Jacob said to Mercer.

'Shut up,' Mercer said, causing Jacob to smile.

'And against his own pleas there were others from the men – men I knew far better – running past us. I shouted to ask if there was anyone else prepared to stop and help him, but few did little more than pause, regain their breath and run on. A shell landed on the road directly ahead of me. I was showered with dirt and stones. Four or five men lay dead. He was yelling by then, insofar as he could form the words through his screams and the splashing of his blood. I tried to stop an empty half-track, but the driver veered off the road to avoid me and carried on going. I remember there was a solitary woman in the back of it looking out at me. Then one of my own sergeants – a man I trusted – knelt beside me and asked to look at the boy's wounds. I showed him. I believed that here, at last, was someone prepared to help me. But instead he said that the boy was already as good as dead, and that I would be too if I didn't run. He pulled me to my feet. I remember I dropped the boy's head and that it hit the surface of the road with a knock. I started running, barely resisting the sergeant, who was pulling my arm.'

'What else could you reasonably do?' Mercer said.

'I could have stayed with him. I could have kept the pads pressed to his bleeding neck. I could have gathered more bandages. Like I said, I could perhaps have kept him alive long enough for someone else to help him.'

Jacob made a dismissive noise at hearing this.

'It's what I believed,' Mathias said to him.

'You still ran. You still saved your own skin. That sergeant wasn't pulling you away. You were doing your own running. If you believe otherwise, then you're fooling nobody but yourself.'

Mathias conceded this in silence.

'And did he die?' Mercer asked him.

Mathias shrugged.

'So, for all you know, he might have been found and cared for and saved.'

'I don't believe it,' Jacob said disbelievingly. 'First *he* tries to deceive himself, but cannot, and now *you* try to do the job for him and make an even bigger mess of it.'

'You did what you could,' Mercer told Mathias.

'No,' Jacob insisted. 'He did as little as his conscience would allow.'

Mercer could still not understand the man's hostility. 'He could have run past without stopping in the first place,' he said.

126

'I agree,' Jacob said. 'And *that* would have been the more honest course of action. It is what you or I might have done under similar circumstances.'

'I doubt it,' Mercer said.

'All this was when?' Jacob asked Mathias.

'The end of June, two years ago.'

'Then it *is* what I would have done,' Jacob said.

'Did you ever try to find out what happened to the boy?' Mercer said, his words intended only to maintain a distance between the two men. Jacob showed no other signs of hostility; nor did Mathias signal his defensiveness by anything other than what he said.

'Impossible. I was taken prisoner two days later. The sergeant, too. He told me to stop worrying about the boy.'

'The soldier,' Jacob said.

'Few others had liked him,' Mathias said. 'He was too earnest, too keen.'

'Because *they* all knew the invasion was coming and that it would prove unstoppable.'

'Perhaps. But they stayed and fought until the time came to withdraw.'

Mercer waited for Jacob to say perhaps 'to run', but he said nothing. Instead, he watched Mathias closely, and seeing this, Mercer better understood the nature and purpose of his testing hostility.

Jacob put a hand on Mathias's arm. 'You were no more responsible for his death than Captain Mercer here, sitting in the Italian sun under a lemon tree.'

'Only for not having tried harder to save him,' Mathias said.

'And do you blame yourself more than all those others who ran straight past you, or does their indifference absolve them of all responsibility? How many other corpses did you run past during those days

127

that might have still been living men? Perhaps they were all alive. Perhaps you might have saved them all.' His hand remained on Mathias's arm.

'He's right,' Mathias said to Mercer, wanting to ensure that no ill-will now existed between Mercer and Jacob, and to suggest to Mercer that he would not have raised the subject in Jacob's company if he had not been prepared for his companion's honest, if scathing, remarks.

A cry went up from the distant footballers, and all three men turned to look. It was unclear, at that distance, what had happened.

'Goal,' Jacob said.

There was no apparent order to the distant game – every man chased the ball in whatever direction it was kicked. A solitary figure stood against the building awaiting their assault on him.

'That's Roland,' Mathias said. 'Conserving his energy.'

'For what?' Jacob said. 'More digging?'

'For his great plan of escape.' He stared at the man.

'Seriously?' Mercer asked him.

'No, not seriously,' Mathias said, but too quickly to sound convincing.

The mob of men raced towards the building and the single figure was lost to view.

'Perhaps when you return home, perhaps then you'll be able to find out what happened to the boy,' Mercer suggested.

'I doubt learning that he survived, that he lived, would make him feel any better about what he did,' Jacob said. He leaned back on his elbows and looked up into the sky.

'Whatever happened, he gave the boy some comfort,' Mercer said.

This thought seemed not to have occurred to Mathias.

'Saint Mathias,' Jacob said, and hearing this, Mercer's first instinct was to shout at him to stop being so deliberately and pointlessly provocative, but before he could speak, Mathias himself said:

'The apostle chosen to replace Judas Iscariot.'

'Saint Mathias the Remorseful,' Jacob added.

'That's me,' Mathias said, and the two men burst into laughter, leaving Mercer feeling excluded by the sudden intimacy of this exchange.

'*Was* there a Saint Mathias?' he asked.

'Apparently,' Jacob said. 'Though some doubt exists in our half-remembered schooling as to the exact circumstances of his beatification.'

'Only that Judas Iscariot was in some way involved,' Mathias said. 'I knew none of this until our mournful friend here pointed it out to me. I doubt my parents had the faintest idea. My uncle Mathias was killed at Verdun. We held his memory sacred, but only at a local monument; his body was never recovered.'

'Remorse is not necessarily the self-indulgent commodity Jacob here would have us believe,' Mercer said.

Jacob lowered himself backwards off his elbows and slowly applauded the remark.

'Ignore him,' Mathias said.

'Impossible,' Mercer said, loud enough for Jacob to hear.

'Bravo,' Jacob said.

In the distance, a further cry went up from the footballers, and immediately afterwards, a siren sounded, calling them back to their work.

'Full-time,' Jacob said.

Mathias rose and brushed the earth and grass from

his legs. 'Go home,' he said to Jacob, who shielded his eyes to look up at him. 'Walk slowly and rest often.'

'Yes, mother,' Jacob said.

'Tell him,' Mathias said to Mercer, but Mercer knew as well as any of them that it was beyond him to tell the man to do anything. He repeated Mathias's words and Jacob rose from where he lay.

The siren sounded again and Mathias started running back to the others. He paused to call to Jacob that he would see him soon. Jacob raised his hand, but said nothing. Mathias resumed running.

'How will I cope when he is finally made to return home?' Jacob said, jokingly, but with genuine concern in his voice – as much, Mercer imagined, for Mathias as for himself.

'I ought to be getting back, too,' Mercer said.

'No man who dies in battle dies well,' Jacob said. '*Henry V.*'

'I know,' Mercer told him. 'And any man who imagines war to be anything but a bloody, dirty business is a fool.'

'The boy probably died in his arms. The sergeant will have seen it, even if Mathias chose not to.'

Mercer doubted this, but said, 'Probably.'

On the runway, Mathias finally reached the others, and he drew them to him as though an invisible cord had been pulled through them.

16

Two days before the anticipated return of Elizabeth Lynch's husband, and as he again awaited the arrival of the lorries, a man arrived on a motorcycle and stood in front of the tower calling up for Mercer.

Mercer went out as the rider was unfastening his helmet and removing his heavy gauntlets. The man saluted him, and Mercer returned the gesture.

'I've been sent from Transport to let you know they won't be coming,' he said. He would clearly have preferred a written message to hand over than to have found the unwelcome words himself.

'Who won't be coming? The workers?'

'Transport wants a full inspection and service of the lorries. Turned up late last night. Got to be done, apparently. No arguments.'

'How long will it take?'

'Day at the most,' the man said. 'Two at the outside.'

Mercer imagined the celebrations as the gathered workers were informed. 'And in the meanwhile?'

'In the meanwhile what?' The rider looked around

131

him at the workings. The site still looked more like one in the process of being demolished than one undergoing reconstruction.

'What am I supposed to do here?'

'Carry on as normal, I suppose, but without them,' the man said, shrugging.

Mercer guessed then that this messenger knew the workers and that he had already seen them prior to his journey from the town.

'Tell Transport that I want them back tomorrow.'

'Not very likely,' the man said. 'Friday.'

Mercer shook his head.

'Look on the bright side,' the man said. 'Anything found wrong with the lorries, it's bound to be fixed by Monday.'

Assuming the mechanics were prepared to work over the weekend, Mercer thought, which was unlikely. 'Are there any instructions for me?' he said. 'For what I might do without a workforce?'

'Nobody said anything to me,' the man said. He lit a cigarette and unfastened the top of his jacket. 'What you building here, anyway?'

Mercer started to explain to him about the new Coastguard Station.

'That the sea, then?' the man said, interrupting him.

'That's the sea,' Mercer said.

And the man, detecting this hostile note, said, 'I was only asking, mate. Only trying to show some interest,' and he flicked away what remained of his cigarette, pulled on his helmet and fastened it, then pushed his hands into the gauntlets, doubling their size. He sat on his bike revving the engine for several minutes, and those few women who had not emerged from the houses at his appearance came out now and stood watching him. He left Mercer and rode zigzagging over the uneven ground towards them.

Mercer watched as the younger women gathered around him. One of these climbed onto the seat behind him and he rode her in a jolting circle. He offered the same to the others, but no one accepted. He sat with them for several minutes longer before finally returning to Mercer and pulling up close in front of him. A cloud of dust settled around the two men.

The rider said something which Mercer did not hear over the noise of the engine – something which, apparently, required no answer, for the instant the man had finished speaking, he turned and left again, raising his hand to the women as he went.

Mercer searched the small group beside the houses. Neither Elizabeth Lynch nor Mary was among them. And only then, as the noise of the bike faded in the distance, did it occur to him that they might have heard the rider upon his arrival and imagined him to come in connection with the returning man. He wished he could have gone to them and explained the messenger's mission without this lingering audience.

17

At midday, he left the deserted site and walked to the airfield. Here, too, it seemed as though little was happening.

He was walking along the centre of the half-demolished runway when someone called to him. A man rose from behind a roofless bunker and called again. He recognized Mathias and went to him.

Upon reaching him, Mercer found Mathias in the company of six others, all of them sitting in the shade of the bunker wall out of the sun, their picks and hammers scattered beside them.

Mathias made a brief introduction. The men were all prisoners of war, some awaiting their repatriation, and some, like Mathias, who had applied for permission to stay, and whose futures had not yet been decided. All of them spoke some English; all of them knew who he was.

'We have our own transport,' one of them told Mercer when he told them about the lorries.

'We will leave early,' Mathias said. 'They told us

there was a day's work in breaking up this section of the runway in readiness for the bulldozers, but we finished it in only a few hours.'

Several of the men drank from their water-bottles, and Mercer saw by the nature of their expressions as they did this that it was not water they were drinking. It was also clear to him that it did not concern them to do this in front of him.

'Today is Roland's birthday,' Mathias said, indicating a man who looked fifty, at least twenty years older than any of the others.

Mercer remembered Mathias's remark about the solitary footballer from several days earlier.

Roland rose and saluted, stood unsteadily for a moment and then sat back down.

'Congratulations,' Mercer said.

Mathias handed him his own flask and he drank from it.

'Fifty-two,' Roland said, as though this new age were a sudden and unexpected weight on his shoulders. He said something else, but in German, which Mercer did not understand.

'He says that if he'd known he was not to be sent home immediately the war ended, then he would have kept his big mouth shut, or only opened it to tell his captors what they wanted to hear,' Mathias said. He paused. 'Party member,' he added in a lower voice.

Mercer looked again at the man. The arms of two of his companions now lay draped around his shoulders.

'He has a wife, seven children and four grand-children,' another of the men said to Mercer. 'And he has heard from none of them in almost a year. They lived in the East, Prenzlau.'

'I see,' Mercer said.

Mathias then announced something to them in

German, at which they cheered. 'I told them to stay where they are for a couple of hours, and then we'll leave.'

All around them, at regular intervals across the ruptured runway, holes had been drilled and the surface loosened in readiness for the bulldozers. In places, the surface lay buckled and torn and the slabs had been stacked in mounds with the dark earth of the old fields encrusted on their undersides. It was hard work, even for men using power tools.

Mathias spoke again to the others and then indicated to Mercer that they should walk.

'I told them I'll be back in two hours.'

'Are you their foreman, then, their supervisor?'

'Unofficially.'

'Meaning you know best how all these dodges work and they are only too happy to comply.'

'They work well,' Mathias said. 'And some of them, like Roland, cannot sleep at night for worrying about what is happening to their families. I do not bear that particular burden, but I can easily imagine what they must be going through.'

'I suppose so,' Mercer said.

They walked towards the airfield perimeter. Mathias led the way to another roofless shelter, into which they descended to sit in the shade. The frames of several beds lay at one end of the cool space, and the litter of recent occupation covered the floor.

'Another of your hiding places?' Mercer said.

'One of many.'

Mercer cleared the paper and empty tins from two chairs and they sat facing each other.

'Is Roland having problems?' he asked.

'None that are not of his own making. As I say, he was a party member, and proud of it. He was captured long before me, when the war was still being won, and did not have the sense to keep his mouth shut.'

'And so now he's being punished for it by being kept here so long.'

'That's how he sees it. He worries for his family.'

'Has he not yet renounced everything?'

'Too late for all that.'

'And you?'

'Me?'

'Have you heard anything yet about your release?' It seemed the wrong word.

'I thought for a moment you meant had *I* renounced everything.'

'Did you ever share Roland's convictions?'

Mathias shook his head. 'But it makes me no less complicit in what happened, in what was done in my name.' He was talking about Jacob.

'You could tell me you had no real choice but to accept what happened,' Mercer said. 'You could tell me you kept your eyes averted and that it was all the work of others.' It was what he wanted to hear Mathias say.

'Life is never so simple. I might just as easily ask *you* what *you* did about it, what *your* armies or air forces did to help them. Where do *you* draw the line between the perpetrator and the onlooker? If you ask me did I know it was happening, then my truthful answer would have to be yes. I knew nothing of the details, of course, or of the true extent of *what* was being done, but I cannot deny that I knew *something* was being done, and that it was being done in my name.' He paused. 'They showed us those films as part of our re-education. There was no doubt *then* what had been happening. There was prejudice and tormenting a long time before the war started.'

'"Tormenting"?' It seemed a strange word to use.

'What else would you call it?' Mathias said.

'And where good men did nothing, so evil triumphed?' Mercer said, regretting the words immediately.

'More glibness; more words masquerading as explanation; more simplicity where the complexity of the situation and of the lives involved will never be understood. You know nothing, nothing at all.' Mathias stopped speaking and looked up. He signalled his apology for what he had said. He raised his hand, and both men saw that it was shaking.

'I don't mean you – not you, personally,' Mathias said.

'Yes, you do,' Mercer said. 'I can't deny any of it.' He, too, had seen the newsreels. He, too, had watched them in a cinema in an audience wanting only to cheer the news that the war was finally over. The man beside him had vomited into his lap and over his legs.

'My father employed men in his nursery. Three of them were Jewish. They had been with him a long time. They worked alongside him as he and his brother built up the place. They were good workers, experts at what they did. It was they who one day approached my father and told him what was happening to them. They told him what restrictions were being placed on them, each month a few more. Soon, they said, it might even be impossible for them to continue working for him. He listened to all this, and he sympathized, but I imagine even he, in those early days, believed that the three men were overreacting. My mother knew their wives, their children, most of them grown, though still living at home. My father did his best to reassure them, but they told him his reassurance would not be enough, and that if he did not himself comply with whatever new regulations or decrees were being issued, or if he tried to defy the police on any of these matters, then he too might be punished alongside them.'

'How did he respond to that?'

'Who knows? I imagine he agreed with them, but that he still believed the situation was not so black as they painted it. You have to remember, the war was still four or five years away, and there was then no real prospect of it. He was working hard, the nursery and his roses were acquiring a reputation. He and his brother looked set to prosper.'

'So he had to weigh all this against what he might stand to lose.'

'I imagine so. And then one morning the men came to him and said it was forbidden for them to work for him any longer. They showed him the documents they had been sent. Their work must be given to an unemployed German man. A man who knew nothing of the work, who, in all likelihood, did not *want* to work. Never imagine for one moment that my father was not aware of his debt to those three men.'

'Did he contest the order?'

'That was his first instinct. But they were frightened men, those three. They knew how dangerous and futile this noble gesture might prove to be. They knew who, ultimately, might be made to pay the price of his bravery, his intransigence. They told him he must comply, otherwise *he* would be punished and the business would suffer anyway.' He laughed then, and rubbed a hand over his face.

'What?' Mercer asked him.

'His largest order at that time was for several thousand of his finest blooms to decorate the stage and aisles of a grand midnight rally.'

'And he complied?'

'Of course he complied. High-ranking party officials visited him personally. They, too, were specialists, men who took a pride in their work. They flattered him: his roses were the best they had ever seen; how many thousands could he produce over the coming months? How long would the blooms last? He was even asked about the creation and the naming of new flowers. He was a man in his element. And when he raised the question of his labour force with these new friends of his they told him not to worry, that there were ways around and through every problem.'

'And were there?'

'Sometimes. A week after the rally, he was visited by the local police chief, who had been sent to compliment him on his displays and who wished to negotiate a regular order with him.'

'And the Jewish workers?'

'My father contrived a scheme whereby the men would continue to work for him without pay. Officially, you see, they could no longer remain on his payroll. Having established with the chief of police that this was a feasible plan, my father then secretly arranged with the three men to pay them in kind. My mother was put in charge of the operation. She bought food and household goods and whatever else they needed and requested, and she ensured it was delivered to their homes without any direct connection being made between them and my father. The new workers, as my father had anticipated, did little and knew even less about what was expected of them. In addition to which, they treated the three Jews badly. My father, of course, was then expected to pay for their silence. He was always careful to agree with them, and never to let his true feelings show when he was in their presence.'

'So he was paying out twice the wages for the same work?'

'Some weeks, much more. One by one, however, the three men were driven from their homes – either because they were no longer able to pay the rent or some new edict or other was issued – and they were forced to move in with relatives. They were then denied medicines and hospital treatment, and so that, too, my father attempted to provide for them when it was needed. And then, of course, the war came, and everything changed. One day, one of the men simply did not turn up for work. My father asked the others what had happened to him, but they were reluctant to tell him what they knew. They told him not to ask. I think he believed they had lost their faith, their trust in him. It angered him, their reluctance to tell him. And then, a few weeks later, the remaining two men were gone. My mother made enquiries, but learned very little. Even the chief of police would say nothing. Months later, all he would admit to when pushed, doubtless drunk at my father's expense, was that the three workers and their families had been relocated and that they were now working elsewhere, though doubtless not for a rose-grower.'

'And you heard nothing more of them?'

'Nothing. A few months before I left home on active service, the police chief was dismissed from his post and another man installed. My father was sent for immediately and told by this new man that not only was there no place for roses in the new world being created, but that evidence had come to light of my father's efforts on behalf of the three men. My father had fought alongside his brother in the Great War. He took his medals and written commendations with him to show this new police chief and the man swept them

141

from his desk and laughed in my father's face. Supplies and equipment, until then regularly delivered to the nursery, failed to appear. Other trusted members of his workforce were called away. What was rose-growing compared to the turn of the tide in Africa, in the East? More useless workers were forced upon him. My mother became ill. The agricultural chemists made their final, derisory offer. I was away during most of this. Every four or five months I returned home for a few days. It was barely conceivable to me what had happened to him, how the nursery was being run down. I tried to persuade the two of them to leave. My mother's sister lived near Stuttgart. I wanted them to go to her. I saw how the war would go. My aunt was willing. Even my mother, I believe, saw that the time had come for them to leave. But she would not go without her husband.'

'What happened?'

'A raid. They were killed and the nursery destroyed. Plane after plane, bomb after bomb, night after night.' He stiffened his palm and passed it back and forth in front of him. 'Who knows, perhaps they even came from here; perhaps this was where they came back to and landed.'

'And you never again returned home after they were killed?'

'I was a prisoner by then. And as understanding as you English like to believe you are, I doubt, under the circumstances, that I would have been granted compassionate leave.'

They sat without speaking for several minutes.

Eventually, Mercer said, 'Does Jacob know all this?'

Mathias shook his head. 'And nor shall I tell him.'

'It might—'

'It might what? Might compare to what *he* has to

tell? I doubt that very much. And besides, perhaps he might imagine I was in some way seeking his forgiveness for what he has suffered in my name. It's the last thing I want.'

'Forgiveness?'

'Forgiveness, understanding, redemption, call it what you will. Absolution, even. I want nothing from him, and he wants nothing from me. And as far as I can see – him, too, I imagine – that is the only way forward. The world can watch its Nurembergs and its Tokyos, but this is where the real work of moving on and making good is done.' He slapped his palm against his chest and then against the wall beside him. Then he looked at his hand and brushed the dust from it. 'You bring out the melodramatic in me,' he said. It was his way of saying he appreciated this opportunity to talk openly, and Mercer understood this.

'The drink and the sun are probably more to blame,' Mercer said.

'If you say so.' Mathias climbed onto his chair, rested his arms on the surface of the wall and looked out over the expanse of land ahead of him.

'You can see why they wanted to cover it with airfields,' Mercer said.

'Were you ever bombed?' Mathias asked him.

'Once, in Forlì, south of Bologna.'

'They came day after day in France,' Mathias said. 'The same planes, the same times. Some of us were even convinced that their bombs fell in exactly the same places. There was little to oppose them. I knew then that, whatever else happened, however long it might take, the war was lost.'

'Did you think you might be killed?'

'Never. What man does?'

Me, I did, thought Mercer, but said nothing.

Later, the two men left the shelter and walked back to where the others awaited them.

The appearance of Mathias signalled to them all that they might now return to their barracks. By then, Roland was drunk and asleep, and it took several of them to rouse him. He woke slowly, reluctantly, uncertain, at first, of where he was or what he was doing there, and then it all returned to him and he swore at the men who had woken him.

18

Jacob sat beside the glowing forge. Bail stood nearby, working the bellows. A powder of ash and sparks blew up from the mounded coke. Jacob showed Mercer the kiln he had constructed at one side of the forge. He held in his hands a small amber-coloured bowl, broken at its rim, and with a crack which threatened to break it in half.

Mercer had come on the day of the firing by arrangement with Jacob, uncertain what arcane or private ritual he might have been invading. He was intrigued by what Jacob was still able to achieve there amid such unlikely surroundings and with such crude and makeshift equipment.

Bail had come out to investigate the barking of his dogs, and had called Mercer into the forge, where Jacob awaited him. Bail himself was engaged in the repair of a piece of machinery Mercer did not recognize. It was beyond him to suggest to either of them that the forge had been fired up under this pretence, and that Bail's sole purpose in doing so was to allow

Jacob to continue with his glass-making. Neither man spoke to him for several minutes after his arrival, their attention focused instead on the changing colour of the coals.

Despite the heat of the day and the room itself, Jacob again stood in his tightly fastened jacket and with cloths wrapped around both hands. Bail, however, was naked from the waist up. His injured hand remained gloved and rigid, though this did not appear to hinder him in his work. His chest and stomach were slick with sweat. Ash from the forge stuck to him and darkened.

'Are you about to make something?' Mercer indicated the kiln.

'This.' Jacob held out the broken bowl and Mercer took it from him. 'Hopefully, this time with success.'

'What happened?' Even chipped and cracked, the bowl was a beautiful thing.

Jacob shrugged. 'That's the nature of glass. Perfect one second, shattered the next. Perhaps it cooled too quickly. Unlike our Vulcan here, who can douse his lumps of molten metal in drums of water, glass needs to be treated more sensitively. I occasionally wish it were otherwise, but . . .'

Beside them, Bail took up an iron rod and settled it into the coals, raking them over it as he continued to work the bellows.

Jacob took back the damaged bowl. 'I made this one last week. It was perfect for a day, and then, within minutes, the piece at the rim broke off and the crack appeared.' He showed Mercer the crucible of broken glass he intended melting. 'When the kiln is up to temperature, I shall set the glass in it to melt, and when it is sufficiently liquid, I shall attempt once more to shape it.'

'Do you use a mould of some sort?'

146

'Some might. I prefer to blow it and then to shape it in my hands. It was the first thing my father taught me to do. He told me it would teach me respect for the glass.'

'Because it would burn you?'

'Because it burned me, yes. It was a simple enough lesson to learn.' He indicated the leather pads on the bench beside him.

Bail withdrew the glowing bar from the forge and started to shape it on his anvil. The bar curled and lost its colour, and he measured it against the piece it was intended to replace. It seemed a simple enough task, dependent more on the man's strength in shaping the metal than any precise measurement or craftsmanship. Jacob, too, watched Bail at work, his eyes rising and falling with Bail's arm and hammer.

After a minute of this, Bail returned the rod to the fire and stood back from the forge.

'Not ready yet?' he asked Jacob, indicating the kiln, the inner bricks of which now glowed white-hot.

Jacob shook his head.

'He's a perfectionist,' Bail said to Mercer. There was respect and envy in his voice. He took a half-smoked cigar from his pocket and lit it with a glowing coal lifted from the forge with his pliers.

'Churchill,' Jacob said.

Bail pretended to make a speech, but stopped abruptly as the dogs outside resumed their barking, and he went to investigate.

'He worries that the bailiffs are coming,' Jacob said as Bail passed him.

'Let them try,' Bail said. He picked up another of his hammers as he went.

'Are you feeling well?' Mercer asked Jacob when they were alone.

'I'm never truly well. You have surely grasped that much by now. But, yes, relatively speaking, I am well. Well enough to do what I have to do.' He motioned to the kiln. 'It gives me some small purpose.'

It gives you all *your purpose*, Mercer thought. He took a handful of broken glass from the cold crucible and rolled it in his palms. Its edges had been ground and it did not cut him. The powder settled into the creases of his hand.

'Alchemy,' Jacob said unexpectedly.

'"Alchemy"?'

'Turning that into this.' He held up the broken bowl. 'True alchemy. To insist that this concerns only the conversion of base metals into gold is to miss the point.'

'I know nothing of it,' Mercer said, alerted and encouraged by Jacob's sudden enthusiasm.

'No? The alchemical tradition tended towards the heretical rather than towards the established church. It was a way of exploring the connections between the terrestrial and the celestial, between the four lower elements of earth, wind, fire and water, and the fifth element.'

'Which was what?'

'The quintessence, Mr Mercer. Pure spirituality.'

'I always imagined it to be something more prosaic, something to do with—'

'Greed?'

'Perhaps.' It was not what Mercer had been about to say.

'I imagine that is what most people think. After all, we live in an age that only recently thought nothing of plundering gold from the mouths of men, women and children.'

The remark shocked Mercer, and there was nothing he could say in reply to it.

Jacob saw this. 'I've offended you,' he said. 'It was not my intention. According to the few true alchemists, every object, every substance in the natural world signifies – has as its counterpart – something metaphysical, something beyond understanding on the basis of natural or scientific laws alone. According to those men, the world is not simply the naturalistic thing the vast majority of mankind considers it to be, but is filled with spirits, with soul and with intelligence – an *anima mundi* – where every object has its own unique and special properties. Do you understand?'

'I think so. And all this is represented for you in your glass-making?'

'Something of it, yes. I do not deceive myself that it is a perfect or all-encompassing explanation, or that it even provides the justification for what I do, but I see in it, in my understanding of it, something untouched by others, by those greedy enough to want only that gold, by those men who possess no wonder, no awe, and who are impressed only by their own worldly achievements and power.'

Mercer understood then how much more he was being told, and how well this imperfect explanation suited Jacob's purpose.

'And is it what your father also believed?' he said.

'It is. And he had the sense to instil the belief in me. Everything else might be stripped away and lost or destroyed, but belief, true belief, belief founded solely on understanding can never – *never* – be taken away from a man.'

'And is that belief sufficient and potent enough to keep a man alive?'

'Of course. More than enough.'

'And your bowls are some kind of justification – a manifestation, almost – of your belief.'

'You surprise me, Mr Mercer. That is precisely my point, though, again, I concede that it is not a perfect understanding, and certainly not one that I would wish to have to explain in any greater detail.'

And is it all that remains to you, this belief? Like a tightrope, and one now so high above the ground that you can no longer see that ground beneath you. And one so long that you cannot see for certain how far into that same black distance it stretches ahead of you.

Jacob held out the crucible so that Mercer might brush the last of the powder from his palms back into it.

'Is the kiln ready?'

'Possibly,' Jacob said.

'Do you have no way of testing it?'

'Like I said, it is not a precise science. I daresay if it were to become one, then it would lose its appeal for me.'

They were joined by Bail, who said that the dogs had been barking at nothing, but whose poorly disguised concern was evident to them both.

'Ready?' Bail said to Jacob, who nodded.

Bail took the crucible in a pair of tongs and slid it into the kiln, closely watched by Jacob, who told him to push it further into the small structure. Bail did this and then returned to the bellows.

Jacob indicated for Mercer to follow him outside.

'What will you do with it – the bowl?' Mercer said.

'Who knows? If it breaks again, I shall destroy it completely, just as I have destroyed its imperfect predecessors; but if by some miracle it emerges intact and perfect, then I shall either keep it and look upon it as some sort of justification for all my belief and hard work, or I may sell it. My existence here is not so spiritual as I might sometimes wish to believe.'

'Or as you would want others to believe.'

Jacob smiled at this. 'Precisely.'

'You sold a bowl to Elizabeth Lynch,' Mercer said.

'Before the others chased me away, yes.'

They walked between the mounds of useless and abandoned machinery towards the drain.

'Can I return with you and watch you shape the bowl?' Mercer said.

Jacob shook his head. 'I'm afraid not. For that, I prefer to be completely alone.'

'For what reason?'

'For no reason other than that I have spent the past few years of my life surrounded by tens of thousands of others without a single moment of true privacy.'

'I understand,' Mercer said.

'I doubt that, but then I would doubt anyone who said the same. Whatever else has happened, you still live in a world where you can choose to believe or not to believe in a great deal. For me, that choice no longer exists. I'm not saying this because I expect your sympathy, or even that I expect you to believe me, but merely to make clear to you the distance between us, you and me. And I say it, too, because I know you will not be offended by the remark, and because I appreciate being able to say it without also having to frame my apology for it. As you might have guessed, I am through with all those old niceties and platitudes.'

They reached the drain and stood looking over it.

'Did you lose everything?' Mercer asked him.

'Everything and everyone. You may believe you can imagine how that feels, but you cannot.'

'My brother was killed at Anzio,' Mercer said. 'He was wounded and died six days later.'

'I'm sorry. Were you close?'

Mercer nodded.

'And your parents?'

'My father died when I was a boy. My mother died ten months after my brother was killed.'

'Then it was no coincidence,' Jacob said.

'No.'

'Look,' Jacob said, and he pointed to where a solitary swan drifted seaward on the drain.

'How long will your glass stay in the kiln?'

'Not too much longer. The temperature rises and falls, unfortunately, but no real harm will come to it once it has become molten. In Utrecht, Anna and I used to take turns at sitting up through the night with our father while he waited for the fire and the heat to build. Even for him, a master craftsman with thirty years' experience, there was still a great deal of uncertainty involved. And perhaps that was what appealed to him, too. He possessed industrial thermometers, of course, but he insisted he could tell more simply by spitting on different parts of the kiln wall than by what they told him. He taught Anna and myself how to do it.'

'Perhaps he just liked spitting,' Mercer said.

'Perhaps. We cooked our meals against those kilns. He owned four, one for each kind of work. In the largest, he could produce sufficient ordinary, clear glass to glaze a hundred windows. And in the smallest, he would make bowls like mine. Anna, too, was taught everything I was taught. It was expected of me that I would follow him in the trade, but she also expressed the same desire. Our mother was angry at hearing this, and she berated him for having put the idea into his daughter's head. She insisted that he dissuade her. He promised her he would try, but then when he was alone with the two of us, he told Anna to do whatever she pleased. She was only nine when the war started, thirteen when we were forced to leave our home and the glassworks.' He paused to watch the swan pass them by.

'What happened?'

'We were driven from our home, and what we left behind, others simply took for themselves. I imagine the kilns were not yet cold from their last firing before their new owner stood before them, rubbing his hands at the thought of all those new and lucrative Army contracts about to arrive.'

'Which Army?'

'I doubt it mattered to him.'

'Were you able to retrieve nothing?'

'We gave and sent what we could to relatives and to our true friends, but we did not know then that the same thing was shortly to happen to them and that they too were to be driven from their own homes and businesses. Jews live with other Jews, Mr Mercer. Our whole society was Jewish. It was what, in the end, made everything so easy, so complete, so *containable*.'

Mercer did not fully understand this last remark, but he said nothing.

The swan drifted further from them, swivelling its head to watch them as it went. There had been rain earlier in the day, and the drain was dark and heavy with silt.

'How is your own work progressing?' Jacob asked.

'Days, weeks pass when nothing seems to be accomplished, and then one morning I look out and the job's done. I doubt if there's a single man working there who cares enough even to wonder what it is they're achieving there, what the finished thing will look like.'

'They disappoint you.'

'Only because I'm stupid enough to expect so much more of them.'

'My father used to say that a genius might make a pane of glass, but only a fool would see nothing but his own reflection in it.'

'Meaning what?'

'I don't know. Perhaps it wasn't meant to mean anything. He was as full of such empty profundities as I am. Perhaps I inherited them from him.' He slid back his sleeve an inch to look at his watch.

'Show me,' Mercer said.

Jacob turned his arm so that Mercer might see his inner arm and then drew back his sleeve to his elbow.

'I'm sorry,' Mercer said. 'I shouldn't have asked.'

'Your curiosity would have got the better of you sooner or later.'

'It was still unthinking of me.'

'It was one of the first things Bail asked me. Mathias, too. Did you not believe it happened?'

Mercer half-shook, half-nodded his head.

'Then now you need have no doubt,' Jacob said. 'For what that's worth.'

'It was still wrong of me to ask,' Mercer said.

'As unthinking as the men who held my arm while another put it there?'

'Can it not be removed?'

'Of course. As easily as one of my bowls might be smashed. Women held my sister's arm, and those same women stripped her naked for the pleasure of looking at her and fondling her while they did it to her. You cause me no offence, Mr Mercer.' He drew down his sleeve. 'I have to return to my glass,' he said. 'And to Bail.'

Mercer wished him luck.

They parted, and Mercer followed the drain in the direction taken by the swan.

19

On the eve of the return of Elizabeth Lynch's husband,
he watched Mary and her mother walking on the
shore. He lay in the dunes where he had first seen
Mary, and he watched the two of them, anxious not to
be seen by them, not to intrude on this final evening
they shared together.

Elizabeth Lynch walked slowly, occasionally looking around her and gesturing to Mary as though she
wanted her daughter to walk closer to her. But Mary
kept her distance and walked back and forth across the
sand ahead of her mother. They were too far from him
for Mercer to hear what they were saying, but even at
that distance he could discern that the woman was
agitated; whereas Mary, he saw, affected the same
uncaring nonchalance she frequently adopted in
his own company. She paused occasionally to
allow her mother to catch up with her, but then
when the woman came close, she resumed her
walking. Elizabeth Lynch seemed not to notice
this game her daughter played and remained

enmeshed within her own anxious thoughts.

It was clear to Mercer that there could have been nothing except the return of the man on both their minds, and that this was why they had come away from the houses and the others. The woman, he imagined, would have suggested the walk, and Mary would have reluctantly agreed to accompany her. Elizabeth Lynch would be listing her concerns for the future, and her daughter would regret being forced to listen to them, probably believing that the woman was making a fool of herself with everything she now insisted on sharing with her.

Mercer watched them until they reached the point where the road came closest to the sea, and where they stood together for a few minutes before turning back. He saw Elizabeth Lynch finally reach out to Mary as though expecting her daughter to go to her and be held by her, but instead Mary continued to keep her distance. After that, the woman stopped gesturing, and she too fell silent, coming more slowly back along the beach behind her daughter. He saw the two sets of footprints they left behind them, the woman's in a near-straight line out and back, and the girl's forever crossing back and forth over this path, as though she were a dog, restless and searching and ceaselessly running around its owner.

Mercer sank lower in the grass as they approached, convinced they had not seen him, and even when they were directly beneath him, neither the woman nor the girl paused or looked up to where he lay.

He waited until they were long past him and out of sight before rising and returning to the tower.

He worked for several hours on the quartermaster's reports he had been asked to submit, but the work involved little true calculation, merely a great deal of guesswork, and it did not satisfy him.

He fell asleep where he sat, and was woken after only an hour of restless sleep by a noise which he believed to have come from close by, either from the room below or somewhere immediately outside. He imagined at first that someone from the houses had come in search of him and had called up to him.

It was dark by then, and he waited in the poor light for whoever had called to call again. After several minutes of silence he went to the hatchway and looked down. He called out to ascertain if there was anyone there, but received no reply. He descended the stairs, unlocked the door and went outside.

With the exception of the waning moon and the few stars around it, the world lay in almost total darkness. He called again to ask if there was anyone there, but this time in a much lower voice, unwilling to reveal himself to anyone who might be watching. It was impossible to see further than twenty or thirty yards in any direction. Across the road, the houses lay in complete darkness. His breath formed in the night air.

He was just about to concede that the voice or noise had been part of a forgotten dream from which he had woken, when he heard the sound of someone walking on the loose rubble close behind the tower. He moved quickly and silently around the building, his eyes growing accustomed to the darkness as he went, and he stood against the corner of the wall to look in the direction of the noise. He heard a further sound a short distance ahead of him and, peering towards this, he saw a shape pass low against the ground from one mound of rubble to another. A dog, perhaps, though he had seen no animals among the people all the time he had been there. Whatever the creature was, it then

158

paused, as though suddenly aware of him. It turned towards where he stood, raised its head for a moment, and then resumed its slow, loping walk across the open ground. He realized then that he was watching a fox – one come out of the fields into the dunes in search of a roosting bird, or perhaps a fish left stranded by the tide. Several of the workers had told him of the tracks they had found in the sand, but these had been ill-defined and easily lost. The animal was briefly out of sight behind the rubble before reappearing on the level ground bordering the road.

Mercer left the corner of the tower the better to follow its progress. The creature seemed convinced that it was in no danger and continued moving at the same even pace. It crossed the road and was again lost to him in the rising sand.

He ran to where it had disappeared, climbed the first low mound, but saw nothing. His own footprints, he realized, had destroyed whatever prints the animal had already left, and the light was too poor to see anything ahead of him.

He stayed in the dunes for several minutes longer, until he heard the strained, coarse bark of the fox, now at some distance from him. It was this which had woken him, and though disappointed not to have observed the animal any more closely, he was pleased to have identified the noise.

He left the dunes and returned to the road. He remembered the desert foxes he had seen in Libya and Egypt, scavenging among the mounds of empty cans, scarcely bigger than cats, and with thin, erect ears the size of small plates. He had seen the animals for sale in the town markets, in cages scarcely large enough to hold them. He had known a man in the Seventh Motor Brigade who had bought one of the creatures for a mascot, and who had then flung it away from him when it had bitten his hand.

A few days later, he had arrived at Sidi Rezegh and had seen the same tanks and support vehicles scattered across the road, all of them smashed and useless, most without either their turrets or their tracks, and some of them still burning, or smoking, two days after they had been caught in the open and destroyed. He had been warned by the men retrieving the bodies not to get too close to the hulks. Unexploded ammunition, they told him. They all wore cloths over their faces against the smell of burning. On the forward horizon lay a second group of tanks, more recently destroyed, and the smoke rising from these was thicker and billowed into the pale blue sky like ink spilled in water. He remembered the line at which it gathered and thickened, and above which it did not rise. He had asked the medical orderlies about the man who had owned the fox, but none of them knew him. It was clear by the way they avoided him that there had been few, if any, survivors of the engagement.

He stopped now at the road and looked out over the water. He knew there was no way of preventing these sudden, powerful and painful memories from returning to him unbidden, and he wondered how long they would remain with him. He waited for a further call from the fox, but nothing came. He identified the solitary bright light of Venus in the western sky.

Returning to the tower, he sat at his desk until three in the morning.

As a boy, he had always had a pet dog, and he surprised himself by remembering and then listing the names of eight of these in the order in which he had owned them. Some of the animals had been shared between himself and his brother, and some had attached themselves to him alone. He chose his favourites. A letter from his mother had reached him in Naples telling him of the death of the last of these pets. She said the dog had died in its sleep, but it had been a young animal, a terrier, and he had guessed otherwise. She had enclosed a photograph of the dog sitting on the arm of a chair. He had remembered every detail of the room in which the chair stood, and this, he now remembered, rather than the death of the animal itself, had left him speechless with sadness.

Part II

20

He was woken again the following night, this time by the sound of a man shouting. He went to the window. It was half past two and a light rain was falling. He could see nothing beyond the land immediately surrounding the tower. A solitary light showed far along the beach. The line of houses stood in darkness.

The man called again. Mercer did not recognize the voice, but knew immediately that this was Elizabeth Lynch's husband finally returned.

He had been expected all through the previous day, but had not showed. No word had come to explain this delay, and both Mary and Elizabeth Lynch had taken turns waiting at the road's end, looking out for him. Mercer had explained to his workers what was expected to happen there at some point during the day, but most already knew this and considered the event of little consequence.

A light came on in one of the windows, followed by another in the adjoining house. A silhouette appeared at an upper window. The man below fell silent briefly, and then called out again to whoever was above him. The silhouette belonged to Elizabeth Lynch. She withdrew and was immediately replaced by the lesser outlines of her children. Mercer saw Mary as she opened the window wider and leaned out. Her brother struggled to push himself into the space beside her.

A further light came on downstairs and the door opened, revealing the man in the darkness. His wife had gone down alone to let him in. Yet another light came on further along the row of houses, its occupants woken by the shouting. It was by then clear to Mercer that the man was drunk, that this had been the cause of his late arrival, and that because he was drunk he felt no compunction to keep his voice low, or to ensure that his long-awaited return was the private occasion his wife had been hoping for. Elizabeth Lynch beckoned him to her, but he remained where he stood and continued calling up to Mary at the window above him. Elizabeth Lynch returned inside. She must have called up the stairs to her daughter, because a moment later Mary withdrew from the window and closed it, leaving only her brother looking down and waving. The man approached the doorway and stood there without entering for several minutes longer.

Mercer studied him now that he was fully revealed in the light, albeit distantly. He was shorter and slighter than Mercer had imagined from the solitary photograph he had seen. He held his arm across the doorway, and though Mercer could not see her, a shadow on the ground indicated to him where Elizabeth Lynch stood immediately inside.

He watched closely, convinced that the man would soon go indoors and that the unwelcome public part of this small drama would soon be over. But rather than enter the house, he then backed away from it to the outer edge of the block of yellow light falling through the doorway, where he resumed his shouting, waving his arms at the boy in the window above. Mercer grew concerned at the extent of the man's drunkenness, and of the humiliating spectacle he seemed intent on creating. Though no more lights showed, others would undoubtedly now be watching in the darkness.

Despite what he had said to Mary, Mercer had anticipated that Lynch might have been brought home by the Military Police, or if not brought, then at least have been met from a train and given a lift over this final, difficult part of his journey. What he now believed was that the man had come by bus to the town, and that he had stayed there, celebrating his release, until it was too late to do anything except walk those final few miles of his journey home through the darkness.

Lynch then left his own home and turned his attention to those other houses showing a light. He left his watching wife and children to walk back and forth in front of these and to shout in at their occupants. No one came out to confront him, though Mercer saw the fleeting shapes of the people inside come and go from their windows.

Eventually, a door towards the end of the row opened and a second man appeared. He carried something which might have been a length of timber, but which might just as easily have been a rifle or a shotgun, and at first Mercer thought that this was Daniels, who had gone out to confront Lynch and to end his noisy provocation. But then the man revealed himself more clearly and Mercer saw that it was one of the others – an older man, to whom he had spoken only once, and then only to be ignored. A woman appeared in the doorway behind him. He said something to Lynch, and Lynch fell silent and approached him. The two men stood a short distance apart and spoke to each other. Then the older man propped the stick or rifle in his doorway and returned to Lynch with his arms extended. His wife followed him out. They both wore coats over their night-clothes. The fine rain showed in flecks against the lights of the houses.

Lynch appeared to calm down, and he and this other man stood together in conversation for several minutes, watched by the man's wife. Further along the row, Mary and her mother now stood together in the doorway of their own home, neither of them making any effort to attract the attention of Lynch or the man to whom he spoke.

Eventually, the two men parted, and the older man and his wife returned indoors.

Mercer watched as Lynch came slowly back along the houses to where the woman and the girl awaited him. Neither left the doorway at his approach. The man stumbled as he came, almost falling. Regaining his balance, he called out to them. They were the first words Mercer heard clearly. Lynch asked them what they were looking at. Neither answered him. Mary, Mercer saw, took a step forward to stand in front of her mother, and in a reciprocal gesture of defiance and defence, Elizabeth Lynch put an arm across her daughter's shoulders. She said something to her husband and he shouted back at her. And then, in the dying echo of his voice, Mary herself spoke to him, and hearing her voice for the first time in all those years, the man fell silent, eventually answering her calmly and quietly. He moved closer to his wife and daughter, and the three of them stood together in a group in the brightly lit doorway for a few moments longer, after which they finally went indoors and the door was closed and the light lost.

Mercer returned to his bed, but could not sleep. He wondered why the man had insisted on announcing his return in this way, and why, even as drunk as he clearly was, all discretion and all consideration of his waiting wife and children had been beyond him.

The wind grew stronger, and the rain blew against the dry panes of his own windows, gathering in lines along the corroded frames.

21

'We were taken first to the camp at Papenburg, just inside Germany, south of Emden.'

Mercer had not heard of the place. He tried to imagine where Emden might be. He saw only the coast running west to east, from the diminishing Dutch islands to the Danish peninsula.

Jacob considered him for a moment. They sat together at the edge of Bail's Yard, the perimeter drain immediately behind them. He picked up a metal rod and drew a simple map in the dirt at their feet. 'That was the start of our journey, although it hardly matters to know where we were.'

'Except, perhaps, that you were still close to Holland,' Mercer said.

'Why do you believe that mattered? Do you think those millions upon millions of journeys ever had anything but a single direction? The only thing to know is that we were all still together then, Anna, my mother and father, myself. Papenburg was basic, cold, but there was still some semblance of order there, still some suggestion that all the lies we had been told over the previous years might have been built around a solitary, and perhaps believable, grain of truth. Do as you are ordered to do, they told us, and you will stay together. Simple as that. There were many other families there, some of whom we knew. Two of my mother's sisters had been taken there with their own husbands and children ten months earlier. We arrived in July, nineteen forty-three.' He scribbled the map between his feet back into dirt.

'Were you there long?' Mercer was distracted. Two days had passed since the night of Lynch's return, and neither he nor anyone else at Fleet Point had seen the man or his wife and children. He regretted this distraction. It had been his intention, upon visiting Jacob, to ask him what he had heard in the town concerning the man's return, but instead Jacob had started unexpectedly on this very different story. 'Forget him,' he had said dismissively, upon Lynch's name being mentioned. 'He'll come to you when he's ready – when he's worked out what use you are to him, what he might get or take from you.' The words and all they implied concerning his understanding of the man had surprised Mercer, but he had not responded to them. Shortly afterwards, Jacob had started his own tale.

'Long? Less than three months. When the place filled, or when word came from dear old Otto, whole rows of barracks were emptied and the trains came and went.'

'Otto?'

'Otto Bene. Consul-General. He lived in a palace in The Hague. It was his job to ensure that Holland was cleared of its Jews. The first deportation had taken place a year earlier. We had been invited to go and wave off all those people who had been only too willing to leave – the ones who believed all the promises. My Aunt Clara had wanted to go then. She thought that by agreeing to go she would gain some benefit. My mother and father persuaded her otherwise; her husband, too. She railed against my mother, saying that we were making things worse for ourselves by delaying, by resisting. Her husband, my Uncle Solomon, worked alongside my father. I imagine the two of them heard a great deal which they repeated to no one. My mother told her sister that we were safe because of the glassworks – even the Germans needed glass, especially with all those newly broken windows. Clara's son – he was three or four when the war started – was also called Otto. We tried not to call him by it, but his mother insisted. After those first deportations, though they were never called that then, things did not go so smoothly for the other Otto. In August of that year, the hottest days of a hot summer, two thousand more were called for, but only two or three hundred turned up ready to leave. I remember reading in a newspaper about how inconvenienced the Germans felt because they had provided so many trains and crews, most of which were no longer required.'

'Had you realized by then what was happening?'

'Some had. Most preferred to believe the contradictory rumours they heard. My aunt showed us the postcards and letters she had received from some of her own long-gone neighbours telling her of the wonderful homes they now lived in, the worthwhile jobs they did.'

'All of which—'

'All of which convinced my father that the glassworks provided our greatest hope. It was where we hid, eleven of us, in an underground room which had

172

once been part of a giant old kiln, but which was long out of use. We were taken there one or two at a time. My father, of course, and his brother, could not hide. He told the authorities that my mother, Anna and I had gone to Rotterdam, and that he had not heard from us since our arrival there. He said he was concerned for our safety.'

'Was he believed?' It seemed a transparent lie.

'I doubt it. But there was no hurry, then – so what if we weren't sent away for a few months longer? I daresay there were a dozen men in the works who would happily have betrayed us all for the price of a bottle of drink.'

'Is that what happened?'

'Eventually. I don't know. Perhaps Otto and the authorities knew we were there all along and thought it best to go looking first for all those others whose whereabouts they did not know of. We stayed from August to the following June in that old kiln, and when the factory worked through the night, which happened frequently in those days, we were stuck in that underground room for days on end. Afterwards, when the place was deserted, we went up into the empty workshops and yards and we were able to wander as freely as we had done before. My father paid for the food and clothes that were brought to us. Almost everything we needed, we were able to get. My cousin Otto was too young to be any real company for me, and my only true companion was Anna. She was eight years my junior. My parents never made any secret of the fact that she had come as something of a surprise to them. Following my own birth, my mother miscarried three times in four years. Her sister came to live with us to help care for her. She never left. I think my mother resented this intrusion,

173

but she was in no position to refuse her help.'

In front of them, Bail crossed from one side of his property to the other on a small tractor which possessed few of its body panels. He waved to them and they returned the gesture.

'What's he doing?' Mercer said.

'What he always does. Trying to appear busy.'

'Was no one able or prepared to speak out for you, to protect you?'

'We were a conquered nation; our Government was in exile. Our ministers issued proclamations, veiled threats of retribution, but there was no sense then that they would ever be in a position to carry these out. Besides, we lived from day to day, week to week. I read once in a newspaper that nine Dutchmen had been imprisoned and then deported for harbouring a single Jewish child. The time had come, I suppose, when the Germans no longer felt the need to hide these things from us. Everything they did trumpeted their invincibility. Too many of us came to believe their lies.'

'But not you?'

'I would be lying if I told you I understood better than anyone else in that cellar what was happening. What I do remember is being told by my mother to be careful what I said or repeated in front of Anna. She saw how close we had become during those months. She told me that my sister looked to me for guidance and reassurance. I doubt that was precisely how Anna saw it, but they were my mother's words, and I never forgot them.'

'And once you arrived in—' Mercer had forgotten the name of the place, remembering only that it was close to Emden.

'Papenburg,' Jacob said. 'Strangely, after all those months of hiding and of uncertainty, and because we had remained together on the train and in the place itself, I felt a perverse sense of relief.'

'Relief?'

'I know. Perhaps that is the wrong word. But we had lived with our fears for so long, our nightmares of what lay ahead of us, that to arrive in Papenburg and to be still living together – I don't know – I suppose I even believed – at least for the weeks we were to remain there – that we had once again gained some control over our – what would you call it? – destiny?'

'Presumably, your father and uncle were replaced.'

'At a day's notice. And, presumably, for having lied about our whereabouts. They had considered themselves so indispensable, as though no other two men in the whole world knew how to make glass like they made it. They were lucky not to have been more severely punished. Behind one of the warehouses there was a pyramid of broken glass ten feet high, breakages, dumped there ready to be melted down when the need arose. Anna and I were warned to stay away from it, of course, and, of course, being so warned we were drawn to it even more. A single stone thrown to the top of that mound would cause a landslide of glass of every colour. We went there in the winter months when the factory was empty. It was our place. We sat at the foot of that glass mountain and made our plans together for the future. She wanted me to tell her what our parents would not. She wanted to know why we were being treated and humiliated like that.'

'What did you say to her?'

Jacob paused before answering. 'Lies,' he said. 'I told her lies. I started then, and I never stopped. Lie after lie after lie.'

'You gave her hope,' Mercer said.

175

'Is that what I did?'

'How could you tell her of things about which you yourself knew so little?'

'I could have prepared her, made her stronger, made her ready for what was to come.'

'She was only thirteen years old.'

'What did that matter? How many other thirteen-year-olds, ten-year-olds, five-year-olds do you think were told those same lies? How many of *them* benefited from being kept from the truth, do you think? I lied to her and I made promises to her, and in the end the lies and the promises became the same thing, and each as worthless as the other.'

'You were surrounded by people who would have denied what you told her if it was what they, too, didn't wish her to hear.'

'What they didn't want to have to confront themselves, you mean.'

'They were your parents.'

'Who ignored all my pleas at least to begin to prepare her for what might lie ahead of her, of us all.'

'So you believed they failed her, just as you failed her?'

Jacob did not answer this, though it was clear to Mercer that it was what he believed. He looked down at his feet and jabbed the metal rod into the ground.

Neither man spoke for several minutes.

'You might imagine it helps me to make sense of all these things by talking about them,' Jacob said eventually, turning away from Mercer as he spoke.

'And doesn't it?'

'Why should the senseless ever make sense?'

'You told Anna what you told her because, under the circumstances, there was nothing else you could tell her. You knew as much and as little as anyone.'

Jacob shook his head at this. '"Under the circum-stances",' he said, and then he rose and started walking to where Bail still passed back and forth on his tractor.

It was clear to Mercer that he did not want to be followed.

Jacob reached Bail, but said nothing to him above the noise of the tractor. Bail left the yard and drove along the road leading into town. Jacob stood for a moment and watched him go. In the silence which followed, he finally turned to look back at Mercer.

Mercer rose and looked for his own path out of the yard onto the surrounding land, and it was only as he followed this, as he finally left the town behind him, that he understood why Jacob had chosen to make this place of dereliction and waste his home.

He came out onto the open land and searched for the simple plank bridge over the first of the drains.

22

On the third day after his return, Mercer saw Lynch and Mary standing together at the edge of the workings. It was early evening and they had waited for the workers to leave before crossing the road to where they now stood. Mary was pointing things out to her father, though the man's gaze wandered to places other than where she pointed.

Mercer took this opportunity to introduce himself to the man. He went out to them, and the instant she saw him, Mary stopped talking.

Lynch turned, and he too watched closely as Mercer approached them over the broken ground.

'I'm Mercer,' Mercer said, not knowing how else to begin.

'She told me.' The man held out his hand. 'Lynch,' he said. 'Me and you sound as though we've got a lot in common.'

Mercer had never visited a military prison, but tales of the places – though doubtless exaggerated – were common among the workers.

'Best thing ever happened to this place, you ask me,' Lynch said. He drew hard on the cigarette he smoked. 'She's been filling me in on all the necessary.'

'I told him what you—' Mary began.

'I've just told him,' her father said sharply. 'It's him and me talking now. Not you.' He winked at Mercer. 'Fifteen and she knows everything there is to know. Look at her. She was a kid when I went away. Look at her now. A kid.' He threw down the last half-inch of his cigarette. His words embarrassed Mary, and though she moved no further away from the pair of them, she half-turned from them in a gesture of separation.

'You must have a great deal of catching up to do,' Mercer said to him.

'Catching up? Me and her, you mean?' He looked at his daughter. 'I don't know if that's what I'd call it. There's a few things I wouldn't mind catching up on, but mostly it's just more of the same. All this might have changed' – he indicated the workings and the rising foundations – 'but not much else. If I hadn't been in Colchester, I doubt any of us would still be here.' He spat heavily and rubbed the phlegm into the sand with his foot. 'Parole requirements, see. Fixed abode, means of support, that sort of thing. A year. Though I doubt they're going to be too keen to check up on me all the way out here.'

'Do you need to report in the town, the police station?' Mercer said, reminded of Mathias's casual arrangements.

Lynch became suddenly defensive. 'You seem to know a lot about it. Been checking up, have you? Worried about all this valuable equipment lying around?'

'All I meant was that the lorries come and go all the time – if ever you need a lift, just ask. I can't guarantee it, but if they're prepared to be flexible about your appearance . . .'

'Flexible? It's the Army, mate. Flexible?' He turned again to Mary. 'Hear that? Flexible. You were spot on about him and his fancy words.' He turned back to Mercer. 'No offence, mate. Just something she said. I was asking her about you. My fault, really; perhaps I shouldn't have done.' He looked pointedly at the cigarettes in Mercer's breast pocket, and Mercer took these out and offered him one.

'Years since I had a decent smoke,' Lynch said. 'You get your tobacco in there, but it's piss-poor stuff. You wouldn't wish it on a Kraut.' He laughed.

'Take them all,' Mercer said, knowing that this was what the man was hoping for. He saw Mary flinch at the language her father used.

'Mary's been a great help to me,' Mercer said.

'Oh? Like how? Doing what?'

Mercer wished he hadn't spoken. Mary looked at him briefly and then turned away again.

'She helped me get my room cleared out,' he said.

'She does sod-all in the house,' Lynch said. 'Watches the other one' – he meant her brother – 'but that's about it.'

Mercer knew how untrue and unfair this was, and he wanted Mary to turn back to him so that he might somehow signal this understanding to her without having to say anything more to the man on the subject.

'What do you mean, she helped you clear your room? Have her in there working for you, do you?'

'Not exactly,' Mercer said.

'What then? Don't think I'm criticizing. It's just that I'm her father, and I won't see her taken advantage of. Her mother lets them get away with murder. But not me.'

'I told you, he paid me,' Mary said to him. She, too, Mercer understood, wanted to say more, but was unwilling to prolong the twisted conversation. They were both being used by Lynch, and the man clearly relished the control he now so easily exerted over them.

'When she says "pay" . . .' Lynch said.

'I gave her what I thought was fair,' Mercer said. 'The place was a dump when I moved in.'

'No need to tell me what it was like. Used to be in and out of it all the time. Bit of peace and quiet away from prying eyes, if you know what I mean.' He laughed again. 'Perhaps I could come in and have a look round some time. For old time's sake. Lived here since I was a boy. You don't just chop a man off from all that and not expect him to want some of it back.'

Mercer didn't understand what he meant by this, but he said nothing to encourage the man any further in his insincere reminiscing.

'That's what I've been trying to get through to her and her mother, but she's too young to know what I'm talking about, and the other one's either too stupid or she doesn't want to know. Her mother was born here, and to hear her talk you know for a fact that she's going to die here and then be proud of it. I keep telling her, what did we fight a war for if it meant that everything was going to be exactly the same as it was before? I lost a lot of good mates over there. I can see what you're thinking, but they were still my mates and they still got killed or knocked about doing what they did. And they were proper soldiers, like I was, like I would have gone on being, given the chance, if my so-called elders and betters hadn't stuck to the rule book like they did. If they'd been a bit more *flexible*.' It pleased him to have been able to repeat the word, and he said it again

181

so that there would be no misunderstanding his true meaning.

It now seemed to Mercer that there was a measure of calculated malice in everything the man said.

'You're welcome to come to the tower any time I'm there,' Mercer said. 'My charts and plans are there and I need to keep the place secure.' He wondered why Mary hadn't attempted to leave them, but guessed that had she done so, her father would have called her back and humiliated her even further. At least while she stood within hearing, she knew what he might say about her.

Lynch took out another cigarette and lit it without offering one to Mercer.

'Will you find work?' Mercer asked him.

'Here? What do you think?'

'I meant in the town.'

The man shrugged. 'There's always something. The Light still pays for the house.'

'The Light?'

'Trinity bloody House. Charitable trust. Pays for the houses. No rent, see, even for ex-jail-birds like me. Charity cases, that's us.'

It had never occurred to Mercer to wonder how Elizabeth Lynch could afford to live in the place.

'Proper charity cases,' Lynch repeated. He called to Mary, though she stood only a few feet from him. 'I was just telling him, proper charity cases, us.'

Mary said nothing.

'She's ashamed,' Lynch said. 'Every time it's mentioned. Probably still thinks money grows on trees.'

In Mercer's blueprints for the new Station, there was a precise timetable for the destruction of the houses. The Old Light, too, was to be reduced even further, to half its present height, and a succession of automatic beacons, some anchored offshore, installed in its place. There were no plans to improve or deepen the few inshore shipping channels, and these fixed lights were intended more as warnings, keeping vessels away from the shallows, than as markers guiding them to old and reliable anchorages.

'Will your return change anything?' he said to Lynch, uncertain of what he was asking. 'Regarding your landlords, I mean.'

'You tell me. They're not happy. Probably hoped I'd be long gone by now. Which I would be if it wasn't for those parole conditions. They can't kick us out, see, not just like that. They wait until each house comes empty and then they board it up and let it fall to ruin.'

'Mary told me you were a fisherman,' Mercer said.

'I told him you sometimes went out on the boats,' Mary said, looking from Mercer to her father.

'Fishing?' the man said. 'That's right. I was a fisherman, though it wasn't necessarily fish we were fishing for, me and all those other fishermen.' He raised and tapped his cigarette. 'Catch my drift?'

'Contraband?' Mercer said.

'Bit of this, bit of that. No harm done, not considering Government taxes. Nothing too big, just enough to keep us all ticking nicely over.'

'And presumably you were never caught.'

'Not *caught* caught. They knew what was going on, but there was never anything they could prove. Worst comes to the worst, you just tip it over the side. You can always put a few fish in the bottom of the boat to make your story good. Too much draught, see, on the coastguard vessels. They could never follow you out of the deeper water. Never learned that particular lesson.'

'Does it still happen?' Mercer recalled the times he

had seen the other men at their boats in the fading light.

'Sometimes,' Lynch said. 'There's others got their greedy hands on it now. It's not a living. Plus, she goes on at me about it.' He meant his wife. 'Reckons we're jeopardizing our chances of staying in the house if I get caught at it. Won't look too good to the Prison Board, either.'

'No.'

But the man was no longer listening to him. 'Look at her,' he said, indicating Mary. 'I'm talking to you,' he called to her. 'At least look at me.'

Mary turned.

'Showing her ignorance,' Lynch said to Mercer. 'You could take her for eighteen in this light,' he said.

Mercer considered this unlikely, especially in view of the shabby clothes she again wore.

'What you think? Eighteen? Or have I just been out of circulation for too long? You should see some of the women in the town on Saturday night. And one or two of them here are no better.'

'Who do you mean?' Mercer said.

'You don't want no names. I'm talking about them forever giving the eye to your lot.'

'My lot?'

'Don't come the idiot. Christ, you know who I mean. Your diggers and labourers. You're not denying that some of them haven't been a bit fast off the mark.'

'There's been a bit of' – Mercer stopped himself from saying 'fraternization' – 'flirting here and there, on both sides, but I doubt it's been anything more than that.'

Lynch laughed. 'A bit of flirting? Shows how much you know. Bloody officers – see what they want to see and the rest gets hidden away.'

'Are you suggesting—'

'I'm not suggesting anything, mate. Forget I ever said anything.' He turned back to his daughter. 'Mary, come here, come and tell your fancy friend what you and her were telling me the other night about what's been going on here behind his back.'

'There's no need,' Mercer said. 'You're probably right. I daresay it's inevitable in a—'

'Mary, I said come here. *Now*. You deaf, or what?'

She came to them. 'What?' she said.

'"What?" she says. You heard me. Tell him.'

'It's right what he says,' Mary said.

'I know,' Mercer told her, hoping again that she would understand everything he intended to convey to her.

But Lynch insisted. 'Tell him,' he said. He raised his hand to her and then lowered it. Mary made no attempt to defend herself, and Mercer saw then, in that simple gesture, how completely the man had reasserted himself after his long absence.

'Some of the others, the women, have been carrying on with the men on the site,' she said. 'That's all.' It was the least she could say to him while fulfilling her father's demands.

'Satisfied now?' Lynch said.

Mercer wondered how he might have responded to this unprovoked and vindictive goading had Mary not been present.

'Come to think of it,' Lynch said, 'she's probably been up to a bit of it herself.'

Mary reddened. Where she now stood between them, it was impossible for her to turn away and hide her face.

'I'm sure she hasn't,' Mercer said. 'Whatever it is you mean to imply.'

185

'"Mean to imply,"' Lynch mimicked. 'You saying she's not up to it, not old enough?'

'I'm saying that if I'd seen anything of the sort, I'd have stopped it. She's fifteen.'

'And some of your lads are what, eighteen, nineteen? It's not that much of a difference. Girls, see, they grow up fast.'

He looked at his daughter, and for the first time since Mercer had come to them, there was something approaching affection in the man's voice. He reached out and held her shoulder, and Mary put her hand on his.

'Sorry, love,' he said to her. 'I know you wouldn't have been up to any of that. Too busy looking forward to me getting back, eh?'

She nodded and kept her head down.

'She'd have told me, see,' Lynch said. 'Just like she told me all about you and what you and her get up to together.' He nodded to the tower. 'Said the place was like a pigsty before she got to work on it.'

'It was,' Mercer said quickly. 'And it still would be if she wasn't able to keep it straight for me.'

'Woman's touch, see,' Lynch said. 'Only, in future when she comes, clear it with me first, OK? Don't want any of the neighbours getting the wrong idea, do we? Don't want them putting two and two together and coming up with—' He motioned to Mary.

'Five,' she said.

'Exactly. Taught her that when she was a little kid. Two and two, five.'

Mercer wondered at the tenuous and unlikely connections the man was insistent on re-establishing.

Lynch drew Mary closer to him and put his arm around her waist. 'We'd better be getting back,' he said to her. 'She'll be wondering where we are. She's a worrier, see,' he said to Mercer. 'Makes herself sick with it. Only happy when she's got something to worry about. Drives you crazy. Still, me and her can keep each other company now.' He kissed Mary on the cheek.

Mercer guessed him to be no older than thirty-three or four, and knew that Mary must have been born when her parents were little more than children themselves.

She did nothing to extricate herself from her father's grip.

'Time I was getting back, too,' Mercer said, and he turned and left them.

'I'll send her round tomorrow or the day after,' Lynch called after him.

'Fine,' Mercer said, unwilling to tolerate the man's remarks any longer.

'She'll see you right.'

The man and girl remained standing at the edge of the site, and they were still there when Mercer reached the tower and finally looked back at them. He regretted how he had allowed Lynch to dominate everything that had happened, and how the man had taken advantage of his own uncertainty and Mary's embarrassment to do this. It had surprised him to see how little Mary had been prepared to stand up for herself, how little of her usual confidence she possessed in her father's presence.

He went inside and climbed to the upper room, avoiding the window so he would not be seen by them.

23

He looked for her the next day, but she did not come to the tower. Following a morning working alone and undisturbed, he left to inspect work close by the Old Light. There were no labourers at the site, but upon his arrival there he saw Jacob and Mathias together in the dunes, Mathias helping Jacob down to the firmer land below. Jacob stumbled frequently on the loose slope, and each time this happened, Mathias helped him back to his feet. It surprised Mercer, following Mathias's recent reception among the workers, to see them so close to where these others still worked.

Mathias saw him watching them and pointed him out to Jacob. The two men did not divert their course towards him, but continued to the beach, where they finally sat together, lost to view, at the foot of the dunes.

Mercer went to them.

Mathias rose and stood between the dune path and where Jacob remained on the ground. Mercer descended with the sun behind him, and it was not until he was below the high skyline that Mathias was finally able to identify him.

'It's Mercer,' Mathias called to Jacob, whose head appeared above a stand of marram grass. He was wiping his eyes with a cloth and still brushing the sand from his clothes.

'We thought you might have been someone else from the site,' Mathias said as Mercer reached him. 'We've been here before. No one comes and no one can see.'

Mercer indicated the two small boats on the calm sea. 'Except them,' he said.

'What do they care? They'll think we're two of your men hiding from you.'

Mercer went to Jacob and crouched beside him. The man looked unwell. His face was pale and his brow and cheeks coated with the sweat of his recent exertions.

'He insisted on coming,' Mathias said in explanation. 'And now he's exhausted.'

Jacob tried to say something, but was defeated by his breathlessness.

'See,' Mathias said. 'The man's an idiot.'

Mercer said nothing, unwilling to concur with this friendly but pointed criticism while Jacob was unable to speak for himself.

Mathias climbed halfway up the path and peered over the rim of the dunes. He was searching to ensure that Mercer had not been followed, but he denied this when Mercer suggested it.

'I wouldn't blame you,' Mercer told him. 'They're unshakeable in their prejudices.'

'I'm not concerned for myself,' Mathias said, flicking his eyes to Jacob, who now sat folded over his raised knees. 'We've encountered them together before. They've lived too long with an enemy to do without one now.'

'The *idea* of an enemy in most cases.'

'Whatever,' Mathias said. 'And supposing I and my fellow countrymen were the only Germans they *had* seen, how do you imagine that would improve the situation?' The question required no answer.

The two men settled themselves in the sand and grass beside Jacob. Mathias took a flask from his knapsack and gave it to Jacob, who took it and fumbled with the stiff cap, unable to open it.

'I always put it on too tight,' Mathias said, taking the flask back and easily loosening the cap. Jacob splashed water over his face and neck, letting it run beneath his shirt.

'Why did you come so far?' Mercer asked them.

'Into hostile territory, you mean? We didn't intend to. He wanted to see the sea. There's no work on the airfield because of the bombs and I—'

'Bombs?'

'The bombs we found. I thought you would have known by now. Everybody who lives here was told. All your workers know. Did no one mention them?'

'Unexploded, presumably.'

'How else would you see them?' Jacob said, and even those few words seemed too much for him.

'Still packed in their crates,' Mathias said. 'They were in an underground store at one of the loading bays. It seems someone locked the door and just forgot about them. We came along, and for the past six months we've been piling broken concrete over them. One of the contractors was taking this away. They broke open the door and there they were. There's been no work there since. Happily, the underground store was deemed to be too close to our own equipment stores for us to continue. Someone from Disposal is coming to take a closer look at them.'

'And meanwhile . . .'

'And meanwhile we all enjoy a few days' break. They were warned to keep the children off the airfield. They were there within minutes of the things being found.'

'Will the Army detonate them?' Mercer asked him.

'Who knows? Who cares?'

Jacob made the shape of an explosion with both hands, throwing up sand which settled over his legs.

'Perhaps if I'd been digging there myself,' Mathias said. 'Perhaps if I'd set them off under me – save everyone a lot of trouble and wasted time, eh?'

'Was it a possibility?' Mercer asked him.

Mathias shrugged. 'Perhaps. I doubt if any of them have had their fuses set.' He brushed the sand from his own legs, and for a moment, or so Mercer imagined, he was reminded of the death of his parents.

Jacob, too, understood the connection that had been so suddenly and so unavoidably made, and he flattened his hands and worked them into the sand at his sides. 'Sorry,' he said.

'Forget it,' Mathias told him.

After that, they sat together in silence, watching the distant figures on the two boats. Remembering all Lynch had told him the previous day, Mercer wondered now which of the men were involved, and what it was they were waiting for. There was no indication of a net, no floats or buoys in the sea around the boats.

'Are they fishing?' Mathias said eventually.

'I expect so,' Mercer said, unwilling to speculate further on all Lynch had half-suggested.

'Waiting for someone or something, more like,' Jacob

said. He lay back and rested his head in the sand. He wheezed with every breath he took. Neither Mercer nor Mathias commented on this. Gulls circled high above them; other birds rode the sea around the boats.

'Did your bowl come out unbroken?' Mercer eventually said to Jacob.

Jacob shook his head. 'Cracked as it cooled. I don't know who was the more disappointed – Bail or myself.'

'I think he appreciates—' Mercer began, before Jacob raised a hand to stop him speaking.

'Whatever he appreciates, I appreciate more the fact that he only fires up his forge to allow me to continue, however misguided or deluded he considers me to be.'

'I don't believe he thinks either of those things,' Mercer said.

'Whatever. We both go through the motions, Bail and I.'

'Not for much longer,' Mathias said.

'Oh?'

'Some local businessmen have submitted a plan – submitted it almost a year ago – to buy the land and build a sugar-beet refinery. The bank is keen to see it happen.'

'He's been forced into a corner,' Jacob said. 'All bow down to the money-men.' He started coughing at the effort of having said so much.

'And if Bail goes, then he goes,' Mathias said quietly to Mercer.

'I know.'

'He needs to be in hospital,' Mathias added loudly, intending Jacob to hear him repeat something he had said a hundred times before. 'A proper hospital with proper treatment and care.' He turned back to Mercer. 'Wait until you've spent a winter in this place. The winds are from the Arctic and the snow from Russia. You'll see.'

'Not me,' Mercer said, but the man did not hear him.

'But, oh no, he knows best, of course. He's a survivor; they all are. What is wind and snow to a Jew?'

As before, Mercer considered the remarks harsh and unwarranted, but he understood Mathias's purpose in making them.

Sweat continued to bead on Jacob's brow and cheeks. Mathias took out his clean handkerchief and wiped this away. This caused Jacob some pain and he gave an involuntary gasp, baring his teeth.

'The girl's father finally came home,' Mercer said.

'We heard. We also heard that he wasn't just imprisoned for going absent, but that he almost killed a man, a new recruit, someone he'd tricked into a rigged game of cards, and who couldn't pay what he owed straight away. He was beaten and kicked half to death. When the man was arrested, apparently, they still weren't certain if the boy would recover.'

'Are you sure?' Mercer said, but knew as he spoke that there must have been more to Lynch's sentencing than a simple matter of absenteeism.

'All of the local men working on the airfield know about him and about what happened,' Mathias said.

'Is he in one of them?' Jacob said, indicating the boats.

'Probably,' Mercer said.

'I imagine you already know everything there is truly to know about him from his wife and daughter, eh?' Mathias said.

Mercer shrugged, uncertain what the remark was intended to reveal.

'And you hope somehow to spare the girl's feelings

193

by not joining in our speculation about her worthless father,' Jacob said.

'Something like that,' Mercer finally conceded.

They remained in the dunes for a further hour. Mathias shared what little food he had brought with him. Mercer declined his offer, insisting he had his own supplies to draw on. Jacob took what he was given, but ate little. The cold meat and fruit attracted sand-flies, and Jacob in particular was constantly engaged in wiping them from his lips and chin. Eventually, the insects became unbearable and Mathias buried what remained of their uneaten meal and poured water onto a cloth for Jacob to wipe his face. Even then the flies congregated on the sand where the food was buried.

24

Later, when the time came for Mathias to return to the airfield, it was clear both to him and to Mercer that Jacob was in no condition to make the journey back to Bail's. Jacob had been sitting in the sun for over two hours, and still every small exertion seemed to exhaust him. Mercer and Mathias walked together to the water's edge to consider what to do.

Jacob, knowing what they were discussing, and accepting that he was now incapable of walking back to town, said nothing.

'He can come back to the tower with me,' Mercer said, knowing no other course remained open to them.

'You'll wait until the others have gone before taking him there?' Mathias said. The drills and hammers could still be heard in the distance.

'I need to go back myself, now,' Mercer said. He looked at his watch. It was almost four. A further hour would pass before the others left.

'Will you return for him?' Mathias asked, increasingly anxious about his own need to leave.

'Of course. Will he be all right here by himself?'

'It's how he spends most of his time. Alone. Waiting. Dependent on the kindness and allowances of others. He lives among strangers. Whatever *we* might like or choose to believe, that is what we are to him.'

It struck Mercer as a strange thing to say, especially considering Mathias's undeniable affection for the man.

'Will that change, do you think?'

Mathias looked at him as though he had completely misunderstood his previous remark. 'Perhaps,' he said, but with no conviction. He, too, looked at his watch.

They returned to Jacob, who appeared to have fallen asleep during their absence, but who opened his eyes at their approach.

Mathias told him what they had decided, and Jacob acquiesced in this by closing his eyes again.

Mercer had anticipated that he might complain, but he did not.

'I should have listened to the wise German and stayed at home,' Jacob said.

Mathias crouched beside him and spoke to him.

Mercer heard little of what he said, but imagined he was reassuring Jacob about what was happening. Even though there was no work on the airfield, Mathias explained, a check would be made on the prisoners at their camp in the town. He dare not be absent at any such roll-call for fear of jeopardizing his application to stay.

Watching the two of them together, Mercer saw again the true nature of the responsibility carried by one man for the other, and saw, too, the fine and shifting line between that responsibility and the dependence it created and sustained. He saw how carefully Mathias explained everything, how the few hours of the immediate future were so precisely and reassuringly plotted. There were times, then and later, when this understanding between the German and the Dutchman was perfectly balanced and accepted by them both, and when it needed nothing but the silence between them to make itself clear.

Mercer stood back until Mathias had finished, after which Mathias gathered together his belongings and ran up the dunes in the direction of the airfield. The comparison between the two men – one so debilitated, the other so full of vigour – could not have been more marked.

Alone with Jacob, Mercer explained again what he himself now needed to do.

'Just go,' Jacob told him, aware of Mercer's concern at leaving him alone. 'What harm can come to me here?'

'The tide might come in and drown you,' Mercer said, both of them aware that, were it not already ebbing, the water would not come within fifty yards of where Jacob lay.

'Or I might be swallowed up by an earthquake. Just go. I promise you, I shall be here when you get back. You already explain yourself too often to Mathias.' He closed his eyes again to preclude any further discussion. The sun was no longer directly above him, though the sand remained warm in the shelter of the slope.

Mercer left him, following a different path from the one taken by Mathias.

As he approached the site, hoping to avoid those few men to whom he might now have to explain his absence, Mary stepped onto the road ahead of him. She walked in the same direction and did not see him behind her. He resisted the urge to call out to her. His first encounter with Lynch remained fresh in his mind, and he hoped now to avoid the man until he was able to speak to her alone about what had happened. It occurred to him that the two of them might have again been together, and that Lynch was nearby and watching. He thought of Jacob in the dunes and let her draw further away from him, until she finally crossed the road and was lost to sight.

He arrived at the tower, collected several of his charts and went in search of the men he needed to see. One of these, a foreman, told him that the girl had been looking for him and that he'd sent her away and told her not to come back. Apparently, she had a message for him from her father, but this, the man suggested, was probably just something she'd made up to account for her presence there.

Probably, Mercer agreed. He asked about the recently discovered bombs on the airfield and the man told him all he knew, which was no more than he had already learned from Mathias. The man said they had enough to worry about with their own work to get too concerned about what happened at the airfield. Again, Mercer avoided all further conversation by agreeing with him.

Waiting a further hour, until the last of the lorries had gone, he went back to the dunes, taking with him a blanket and a bottle of water.

He was crossing beside the abandoned Light when he again saw Mary. She called to him. He waved and called back to her that he was too busy to stop. He searched all around her for Lynch, but saw no one.

'I've been looking for you,' she called.

He cupped his ear as though he could not hear or understand her.

'Earlier. I was looking for you.'

'Tomorrow,' he called back.

She did nothing to hide her disappointment at this response. He pointed away from her, hoping to suggest some urgency, and then resumed walking.

Leaving her behind, he came to where the two small boats he had earlier seen out at sea were now moored in the channel beside the Light. There was little water in this and the boats lay on a bed of shining mud. A simple jetty joined the vessels to the channel's steep bank. There was no sign of the men.

He turned from the open land into the dunes. Mary was no longer visible behind him. Whatever he said to her now, he realized, whatever he confided in her, would find some cold echo in her father.

Reaching Jacob, he found him asleep. It had grown cooler on the shaded slope, and he unfolded the blanket and laid it over the sleeping man's legs. Jacob woke immediately, uncertain at first where he was or what was happening to him.

'It's me,' Mercer said to him. 'Mercer.'

'What?' Jacob struggled to sit up and to look around him.

'Me, Mercer. We were here with Mathias. He had to leave. You're coming back to the tower with me.'

Jacob shook his head and looked down at the lines of sand which had formed against his legs and sides. 'I was dreaming,' he said. He raised his arms to allow Mercer to continue wrapping the blanket around him.

'Are you cold?' Mercer asked him.

He nodded.

Mercer pushed the blanket tighter around his legs.

'Thank you,' Jacob said. He reached out and held Mercer's arm for a moment.

'The site's empty,' Mercer said.

'Still, will it not inconvenience you to have me so close?'

'Not at all. I'll be glad of the company.'

'I doubt that. I sleep very easily. Not well, but easily.'

'Can you stand?'

'I imagine so.' Jacob pushed himself upright. 'How long have they been gone?'

'Long enough. Besides, it's none of their business.'

'Of course.'

'I mean it. They probably resent my own presence more than they resent yours. They expected something better than this, that's all. I actually heard those who had seen active service wondering what it was they'd been fighting for.'

'Whatever it was, they were not fighting for people like me.'

'I doubt any of them had the slightest idea what was happening.'

'Few still do,' Jacob said. 'And most will continue to deny it.'

'Deny it?'

'Of course. To many, it is a source of great shame. Believe me, there was nothing noble or heroic in our – in my – suffering or survival.'

'But *denial*?'

Jacob remained silent for several minutes, then said, 'You have a great deal in common with Mathias, and for that small mercy I am grateful.'

'Meaning you and he have had this same conversation a thousand times already.'

Jacob smiled. 'Perhaps not a thousand.'

'He was telling me—' Mercer began.

'He was explaining to you about the nature of my dependence upon him. This kindness of strangers in which I am steeped. You must not consider me ungrateful, but you must understand that there is an art – what would you call it, a *grace* – to receiving and accepting all these acts of kindness without becoming *too* dependent or too beholden. The act must in some way satisfy the giver just as it fulfils a need in the person to whom it is directed. Sometimes the former is considerably less straightforward and harder to either understand or to accept than the latter.'

'You and Mathias,' Mercer said.

'Me and everyone,' Jacob said. 'But, yes, especially Mathias.'

'I understand,' Mercer said.

'I wouldn't expect that much of you. Nor, I imagine, would I want it. I sometimes think that it is only our imperfect understanding of most other people that makes them tolerable to us.'

'Seeing only what we want to see in them, you mean?'

Jacob held out his hand for Mercer to help him from the slope to the firmer shingle of the beach. They started walking. The blanket was now draped over Jacob's shoulders and he held it with both hands at his chest.

'Mathias is right about the hospital,' Mercer said as they reached the open land of the site, and he looked around them to ensure they had not been seen.

'Of course he is. But he knows only of his own imprisonment.'

'Surely that's not how it would seem to you – a prison.'

Jacob shook his head. 'Nothing so obvious or straightforward. But I prize above all else my solitude and what little true independence I am able to fool myself into believing I still possess.'

'You needn't stay there for long. Just until you were well again.'

201

'And how long do you imagine that might be?' Jacob paused, leaning forward slightly to ease his breathing and to clear his throat. He, too, looked around them. 'I can't imagine how I came this far out,' he said.

They arrived at the tower without being seen and without encountering anyone.

A piece of paper lay beneath the door. Mercer picked this up. *We came looking for you. Not in. Lynch.*

'From one of the foremen,' he said. He waited at the foot of the stairs, helping Jacob as he climbed.

Arriving in the room above, Jacob finally shed the blanket and sat down.

Mercer prepared them tea and something to eat. After which Jacob asked him if he had anything stronger to drink. Mercer took out a bottle of whisky and gave it to him.

'I must seem very abrupt and ungrateful to you,' Jacob said. 'I honestly believed I might have re-educated myself to the ways of civilized men by now.' He filled a glass to the brim, mouthed a silent toast and drank it.

'What did you say?' Mercer asked him.

'I was drinking to my sister. I do it every day because I have so few other ways of keeping her memory alive. I have a single photograph of when she was a girl, eight or nine years old. One solitary picture, that's all. Everything else was lost.'

'You have your memories,' Mercer said, refilling the glass and pouring a drink for himself.

'You would not want the memories I possess, Mr Mercer.'

'I'm sorry. I didn't think.'

'Memories of which I will never be rid or free. This is good drink. Usually, I am forced to toast her in something poor and raw, something which burns my mouth and throat and stomach, and which fills my head with its bitter and lingering fumes; it seems somehow more appropriate, more fitting.'

'This is all I have,' Mercer said.

Jacob drained the second glass and held it out for more.

'Will you tell me about her?' Mercer said.

'About Anna? What is there for me to tell that will make any sense to you. I loved her more than I ever loved anyone in my whole life, including my mother, and she was fourteen when she died. We were not separated, you see, and I was with her or close to her the whole time. You cannot imagine what she was to me, or the loss I suffered when she died.'

'It's painful for you,' Mercer said, hoping to indicate that he regretted having asked so bluntly and that Jacob need not go on.

'Of course. But it is not a pain I would happily or willingly lose. Anna. She was day and night to me, Mr Mercer. She gave me purpose. And, please, don't misunderstand me – I am not one of your Romantic poets struggling for a metaphor or a symbol. Day and night. I was her older brother, see, her protector, her saviour; I was the one who would ensure she would survive; I was the one who would protect and save her; I was the one who told her everything she needed to hear; I – we—' He stopped abruptly, unable to continue, and they sat together in this awkward, unbroken silence for several minutes longer.

'May I have the blanket back?' Jacob said eventually. 'I feel the cold like an empty house feels it.'

Mercer gave him the blanket and fetched him another. He brought this from a cupboard in the room below, and when he returned, Jacob was again sleeping.

Mercer wrapped both blankets around him and took off his shoes. His feet beneath were bare and dirty. He lifted these and folded the blanket beneath them.

It was not yet seven. He himself rarely slept until midnight.

He worked at his charts for several hours, catching up with everything he had neglected during the day.

He watched the lights appear in the houses. He watched Mary's house in particular, but saw nothing of its occupants.

Later, in the darkness, as he prepared for bed, he heard the raised voices of men who must have earlier gone into town. He heard Lynch among these.

Jacob remained undisturbed by the noise. The stiff blanket lay around his face like a shroud.

One of these returning men played a harmonica, and its plaintive, discordant sound came sharply through the darkness. The men kept their distance from the tower, and walked one by one to their homes until silence returned.

25

The following morning he woke to find Jacob gone. The blankets lay on the floor beside the chair, and the half-empty bottle of whisky stood close by. He wondered if Jacob had woken and returned home in the darkness, or if he had waited until dawn and gone then. Mercer himself had woken several times during the night, but had heard nothing.

It was almost time to start work and he made his final preparations in advance of the others. In a few days' time, work would start on the laying of a major culvert, diverting water from the site of the new Station. Preparations for this were already underway, and all the smaller feeder drains, some as far as two miles inland, were being cleared or sealed in readiness for the work. For the few days this would take, the men employed on it – the majority of the workforce – would be forced to work up to their waists in mud and water and silt until the new culvert was operational and the old drain finally abandoned.

It was Mercer's intention that day to walk the course

of the old drain to assess where it might best be briefly blocked and diverted prior to its incorporation in the new scheme. There would be some localized flooding; feeder drains and dykes would overflow; land drainage and outflows would be temporarily affected. In ten days the afternoon tide would be at its lowest for a month, and the work was planned to coincide with this.

It was the contemplation of this, and of that coming day's work, that finally drove all thought of Jacob from his mind. He knew that if he had not reached his room at Bail's Yard, then he would hear about it. In all likelihood, Bail himself would come out on one of his resurrected machines.

He was distracted from his charts by the noise of the approaching lorries and he went outside to await them.

The first arrivals disembarked at some distance from the tower, and they seemed to Mercer to be more subdued than usual. He went to them. The remaining lorries passed him on the road driving towards the houses and the sea, and it was only as he saw the men gathered together that it occurred to him that they had perhaps come upon Jacob, still lying where he might have fallen in the night. Approaching them closer, he was relieved to hear laughter. Several of the men saw him and stood aside, and it was only then that he saw Mary and Lynch at their centre.

The man was holding court, and it was immediately clear to Mercer that he already knew some of these others from their time together in the town. Mercer regretted that he would now be obliged to confront the man not only in the presence of Mary, but in the midst of the labourers, too. He saw what an added advantage their presence offered Lynch, and how they might be made to side with him against Mercer and the unwelcome demands he made on them. He saw what an appreciative audience Lynch now had, what he had so easily gained. He remembered the message beneath the tower door.

The foreman saw him coming and he told the others to pick up their tools and start working. They were reluctant to do this and did nothing to hide their reluctance. The presence of Lynch, Mercer saw, made them brave.

Lynch complained loudly that he hadn't finished talking with 'his mates', and that he didn't appreciate being interrupted. Mercer knew better than to respond to this calculated provocation.

Mary, he saw, was barefoot, and wearing her mother's short skirt and blouse. The blouse was armless and with a low neckline. She had again brushed back her hair and tied it off her face. She was clearly uncomfortable at the centre of the men. She avoided looking at Mercer.

Lynch wore a vest and his Army trousers and boots, looking no different from any of the others. He had tattoos on each of his upper arms, and he was showing these to the men around him as Mercer arrived. One of the designs was of a near-naked woman and Lynch was performing a trick which involved flexing and relaxing the muscle upon which she was drawn. His arms were thin and dark, accentuated by the whiteness of his vest. The sides of his ribs showed. Mary stood close beside him.

He uses her like bait, Mercer thought.

The foreman shouted again for the men to start work, but again few responded to this.

And then Lynch said, 'Come on, lads, do as you're told. Poor bloody infantry, jump to it,' and he saluted

207

the foreman, soliciting even more laughter. He said something to Mary and she moved even closer to him. She watched Mercer as he walked amid the reluctantly dispersing crowd, and then bowed her head as he finally entered the circle of the few remaining men.

'Be fair,' Lynch said loudly. 'They're officers. What can you expect? Never dirtied their hands in their lives. That's what *you're* here for.'

There was a chorus of sour agreement at this. Lynch had turned himself into their unelected and unassailable spokesman: what they felt but were unable to say, he might now say but not necessarily feel; where they felt themselves shackled by the authority of Mercer and the work ahead, Lynch stood uncompromised by all authority.

Mercer waited without speaking as the last of the men finally withdrew and started work.

'Sorry for any delay, Major Mercer, sir. Just me and the lads having a bit of a chinwag. You know what us old soldiers are like. Have to stick together. Me and the girl were just having a look round, didn't even know this lot were due.' It was an obvious lie – the routines of the site were long since familiar to everyone who lived and worked there – but Lynch did nothing to disguise the fact. 'Catch you later, lads,' he called to the departing men. 'Say goodbye,' he said to Mary. 'Where's your manners?'

Mary said goodbye to the men still close enough to hear.

'Don't worry – she'll keep me straight,' Lynch called after them.

It surprised and concerned Mercer to see how readily the workers had accepted Lynch, and how easily he had ingratiated himself by pretending to be one of them. He wondered how many of them knew of the man's past, but then realized that this would not necessarily count against him in their own assessment and acceptance of him.

As he waited, Mercer saw one of the workers approach Lynch and then turn his back to Mercer as something secretive took place between them.

The man said something to Mary and she left them.

'Go and say hello to your friend,' Lynch said loudly, and he pushed her away from him.

'What are they doing?' Mercer asked her when she came to him.

'Selling tobacco,' she said.

'Is that what they were waiting for in the boats yesterday?'

'It's not just him,' she said.

The transaction completed, Lynch came to them.

'My ears are burning,' he said.

Mercer saw the bulges in his pockets and down the front of his vest.

'So?' Lynch said. 'You working for the coastguard now? Customs and Excise?'

'No. But I do have an obligation to warn *them*' – he indicated the departing men – 'against doing anything illegal.'

'Warn them all you like,' Lynch said. 'The stuff sells. The only advantage in selling it to them here as far as I'm concerned is that it saves me a long walk.'

'The less you tell me, the better,' Mercer said. 'And it might be—'

'Came looking for you yesterday,' Lynch said.

'I got your note.'

Lynch pulled a face. 'And?'

'I was busy until late.'

'You were entertaining the Jew-boy,' Lynch said. 'That's not "busy". First of all, you, him and the other

209

one spend all afternoon spying on us from the dunes, and then you and him come back here for your tea together, all nice and cosy.' He turned to Mary. 'What did I tell you? You want to watch yourself around men like that. They might not be after what the rest of them are after, but—'

'He was exhausted. He's sick,' Mercer said, unwilling to tolerate the man's goading any longer. 'Besides, she already knows him. And so, presumably, you know all about him, too.' He looked hard at Mary as he said this, hoping she understood his criticism of her.

'I saw that stupid bit of glass he fobbed off on her mother,' Lynch said. 'One born every minute, you ask me. Still, that's what your average Jew-boy's good at, I suppose. And you're right – she does tell me everything. We're like that, me and her.' He held up his crossed fingers. 'Always were, always will be. Nothing's changed in that department. Anything I want to know, I just have to ask. I know, for instance, that you're forever sniffing around her.'

'He isn't,' Mary said. She looked anxiously from her father to Mercer. 'I never said that.'

'Didn't need to,' Lynch said, encouraged by her sudden alarm. 'I've got eyes in my head. I hear things. And her next door has an opinion or two on most things. Well?'

'Well what?' Mercer said, feigning a composure he did not feel.

'You been taking an interest in her?'

'I only said—' Mary said, but then stopped abruptly.

'Only said what?' Lynch said.

'I only said you'd been considerate to us, to all of us,' Mary said, speaking now directly to Mercer. The revelation embarrassed her.

'"Considerate",' Lynch said. 'That's another big word. Kind of word that covers a multitude of sins.'

'And probably not one that you hear too often in connection with yourself,' Mercer said.

Lynch considered him without speaking for a moment and then slowly applauded him. 'Very clever. She said you were quick on your feet. Next you'll be telling me that we're trespassing. I was going to come by myself and wait for the lorries, but she insisted on coming with me. Wanted to dress herself up, come with her old dad and see him in action. Like a shadow, she is.' He winked at his daughter and then repeated the gesture until she responded.

'She always struck me as being very independent-minded,' Mercer said, conscious that whatever he now said about Mary would later be twisted and used against her. One way or another, he realized, everything he said would only fuel the man's resentment and anger.

'Her mother said I ought to see you about a job on the site. Said it'd look good for me. I told her it wasn't really my speciality, digging holes in the dirt while somebody looked on and told me to dig deeper. Had enough of that sort of thing in Colchester.'

'I can imagine,' Mercer said.

'No you can't. Not your sort. That's what I was trying to get through to her' – he motioned towards Mary – 'what I was trying to get through to the pair of them. There's "them" and there's "us". They think the war's changed it all, but they don't know bugger-all, not really.'

'You could find work in the town if you were serious about it,' Mercer said. 'And, technically, yes, you are trespassing. But then you knew that already, so I won't insist on you leaving. I've told her and the children often enough not to go too close to the workings, but they always do.'

'Like I said,' Lynch said. 'Like father, like daughter.'

Mary pulled up the neck of her blouse and held her hands on her shoulders.

'What do you think of her new clothes?' Lynch said. 'I told her mother that she ought to start buying her something a bit more – what's the word?'

'Fashionable?' Mercer said.

'Something a bit more becoming for her age. Look at her, she's not a kid any more. You've only got to look at the faces of some of this lot to see that.'

Again, the remark embarrassed Mary, and it was difficult for her to hide how she felt.

Seeing this, Lynch smiled and said, 'See – now I've hurt her feelings. Typical woman. What you think?'

'What I think is that I ought to be getting to work,' Mercer said. 'Go and stand over someone digging a hole.'

'Course you should. You're a busy man. Everybody can see that. Expecting him back, are you?'

'Who?'

'The Jew-boy, that's who.'

'You don't even know the man,' Mercer said.

'What is there to know? Him and the Jerry – that's a bit strange, don't you think? One lot spends years trying to get rid of the other lot, and now here they are, living in each other's pockets and looking out for each other like they're the best of friends.'

'They *are* friends,' Mercer said.

'Don't make me laugh. You'll be telling me next that Hitler and his mob weren't serious about what they were up to. Nuremberg – you listening to any of that? Wireless and papers are full of it. You ought to keep yourself up to scratch, mate. Thousands of 'em, still walking round like they own the place. Perhaps – what's his name? – perhaps *Mathias* – perhaps he was tied up in it all, perhaps his hands are still dirty. Perhaps *that's* why he wants to stop here and not get sent back home. Perhaps they're still looking for him, and he knows better than most what's waiting for him when he finally does get sent back.' He pulled an invisible rope round his neck.

'You're being ridiculous,' Mercer told him. He regretted that the unfounded accusation and all it implied had been made in front of Mary.

'You can believe what you like,' Lynch said. 'But there's one or two others round here think the exact same as me.'

'Then they're as ignorant and as blind and as bigoted as you,' Mercer shouted at him, stopping abruptly as the men working by the road turned to look at him.

Lynch applauded again. 'Well done. That wasn't too hard now, was it? At least now we know where we stand, you and me. Perhaps you're right about everything and perhaps I'm wrong about everything, but think about this – in a month you and this lot will be long gone, whereas me and her and her mother will still be here and nothing else will have changed. Not a single thing. Nothing. It's like I was saying to her – you and your sort come here and stir everything up and then you just wander off somewhere else to do the same there and don't give a toss about what you leave behind. You can tell me I'm stupid and blind every single day you're here, but it won't alter facts, not in the long run.'

It occurred to Mercer to wonder if, perhaps through the misunderstanding of his wife and daughter, the man truly believed him still to hold his commission, or if, as he suspected – and unlike Mathias's use of the title – it was merely the easiest and most pointed of Lynch's insults.

Several of the workers approached them carrying coils of heavy hose from one of the pumps. They wanted to know which of the workings needed to be drained first. It was work upon which Mercer believed them to be already engaged and he was angry that it was not yet started. But with Lynch still looking on, he concealed this anger and told the men where to go.

One of them blew out smoke and said, 'Nice stuff,' to Lynch, who raised his thumb and said, 'Plenty more where that came from. You come straight to me or the girl. She knows where the stuff is and what it costs.' He turned back to Mercer. 'Real asset, she's going to be.'

The men laughed and walked away, the hose trailing on the ground behind them.

Waiting for Mary to catch his eye, Mercer said 'Goodbye' to her and followed them.

'That's right – you just walk away,' Lynch said, not loudly, but loudly enough for Mercer to hear and yet pretend not to have heard. 'See?' he said to his daughter.

26

Later in the day, he went to the perimeter of the airfield to see if he could find Mathias and discover what had happened to Jacob, but the place was deserted. He saw where a barrier had been erected around the recently discovered bombs. A sign warned everyone to stay clear. A solitary man crossed the expanse of broken runway alongside the stacked planes. The uneven slabs of the fractured concrete had the appearance now of the waves of a rough sea. The man saw Mercer where he stood, paused for a moment to look at him, and then continued into one of the buildings. A gentle breeze had risen off the sea, and the distant silver bodies creaked and rocked in their stacks.

Mercer felt certain that Mathias would have already learned of Jacob's departure, and he wanted to ask him what he believed they might now do in an effort to alleviate the man's all too obviously worsening illness.

He returned to the tower to find Mary already inside. He asked her how she had broken in – those, deliberately, were his words – and she indicated the window he had left open. He understood how constrained she had been in the presence of her father, but, equally, he regretted how unquestioningly she had allowed the man to say and imply the things he did about her in front of the others, how easily, how *willingly* almost, she allowed herself to be manipulated by him to his own ends.

'He doesn't mean half the things he says,' she said, motioning for him to lock the door.

'He does,' Mercer said flatly. 'And if he doesn't mean the things he says, then why say them?' He saw what a poor argument this was against her own understanding of the man. He went to the open window and secured that, too. 'What do you want?'

She shrugged, uncertain of how to respond to this unexpected hostility.

'Just to say that,' she said.

'No doubt he'll be close outside somewhere. Hiding, perhaps.'

'He went into town with some of the others.'

'Do you do *everything* he tells you to do?'

'It's easier. She tells us not to upset him.'

Because he takes it all out on her, Mercer thought. 'You're his children,' he said. 'You shouldn't have to tolerate all this. He's the one who has to adapt.'

'She says that we're different from how he remembers us and that it's hard for him.'

'It's hard for you all. He doesn't seem to be having too many problems in making his presence felt.'

'She says he's just like he was before he went away. He shouts a lot; they argue. She says that what happened to him wasn't fair. Everything he tells her, she agrees with.'

'I doubt she has much choice,' Mercer said. 'But *you*

216

do.' He waited, hoping she might acknowledge this and agree with him.

'He had to hit Peter because of the noise he was making,' she said.

'Your brother.' He had forgotten the boy's name.

'He told her to shut him up, but she couldn't.'

'The things he sometimes says about you – it's still not right.' He wondered if he had said too much. She no longer wore the blouse or the short skirt.

She saw him looking at her dress. 'He told me to put them on,' she said. 'He said it would be the quickest way of getting rid of the tobacco.'

'And you agreed to do it.'

'You make it sound as though I had a choice.'

'I know,' he said, knowing now that his purpose in trying to make her understand how the man was using her would not be served by confronting her like this.

'He's still my father,' she said, looking away from him.

There were fifty responses to the remark.

'Of course he is,' Mercer said. 'But I'm still glad he's not here now.'

She smiled at this.

Say it, he thought. '*Me, too.*' But she said nothing.

They went together to the upper room. She made tea, and he let her, seeing what simple pleasure she gained from the act. She told him to sit down. She expressed her surprise at his store of sugar.

'Take some,' he told her. 'For your mother. A gift. From me.'

'He wouldn't be too happy about that.'

'You could say it was payment for some work you'd done.'

'He'd like it even less.'

'You could tell him you stole it,' he said, knowing

that this would appeal to the man, and she looked at him sharply.

She put down her cup and rose from her seat.

'I'm sorry,' he said.

'I've never stolen anything,' she said. She sat back down. 'Well, not much. And I wouldn't steal anything from you.'

'I know,' he told her.

'At least not from in here.'

They both laughed at this.

'I just thought it might be a way round you having the sugar,' he said. 'He thinks little enough of me already, especially where you and I are concerned.'

'You and me?'

'Our friendship.'

The remark flattered her and she could not hide this.

'In fact, come to think of it,' he said, 'you're the only friend I've got round here.'

'My mother said you were "decent".'

'He'll have enjoyed hearing her say that.'

'He hit her,' she said. 'Not hard, and only once.'

Again, there was nothing he could say.

The room was filled with the afternoon sun; flies circled the ceiling in a clumsy and restless torpor.

'I'm sorry,' he said eventually.

'What for? It's hardly your fault.'

'No, but I do appear to antagonize him.'

'Everything does that. And if it wasn't you, it'd be someone or something else.'

'Jacob or Mathias, for instance?'

'Them. Or her next door. Or Peter. Or Daniels.' She refilled their cups, paying great and unnecessary attention to the pouring.

'What does your mother think will happen?' He tried to make the remark sound casual.

'Happen?'

'Will he stay? Will he go? Will he find work?'

'Are you saying you think he might leave us again?' The prospect of this genuinely concerned her. 'Is that what *you* think he'll do?'

'I just wondered if he'd said anything, that's all.'

'You probably think it would be best all round if he did go. He's only been back five days.'

'Of course he'll stay,' Mercer said. 'He has no choice.'

'If he wants to go, they won't stop him. Besides, perhaps he'll want to take me with him and I'll get out of this dump at last.'

Now it was Mercer's turn to be alarmed. 'Would you go with him if he suggested it?'

She considered this. 'It'd be something.'

'You can go without him,' he said.

'I'm fifteen,' she said. 'I've got no prospects. Whatever they are.'

'Who told you that?'

'Nobody needs to tell me. He says I'm just like her. Finished before I started.'

'That's not true.'

'You don't know,' she said.

It was clear to him that she did not want him to pursue the matter. She rose again and walked around the room, pausing at his desk and at the blankets still on the floor before returning to sit beside him.

'I don't believe everything he says about Jacob and Mathias,' she said.

'I know you don't.'

'He thinks everyone should believe what he believes. She goes along with him, but only because it's the easiest thing to do.'

'And you?'

'It's mostly best to keep your mouth shut.'

'I'm learning that,' he said.

'It's just that half the time he treats me like I'm still a kid, and the next minute he thinks I'm *her*.'

'I can see that, too,' he said.

'Is that us, then – a friendship?'

'I hope so,' he said.

'In that case, I am delighted to make your acquaintance.' She spoke in a voice not her own. Then she held out her hand to him and he took it and pressed it to his lips.

27

'I have this to show you.' Jacob handed Mercer a folded piece of paper. His hand was steady, but Mercer sensed his uncertainty or reluctance in the gesture. There were occasions when Jacob's hands trembled to the extent that holding a cup or a glass was difficult for him – not so much for the disturbance itself, but for the attention it attracted to the motion. He remarked on this and held his fluttering fingers in front of his face and watched them. He could not account for the affliction, insisted that it did not concern him, and said that he was only forced to consider it when it happened in the presence of others.

Almost a week had passed following the night at the tower, and this was the first time Mercer had seen him since then. Jacob looked a little better than previously – still pale and weak and slow-moving, but less breathless than he had been after his journey, and it occurred to Mercer that he had not left Bail's in all that time, that this was the reason for the small improvement in his health.

Mercer had sent word to him and had then come to see him in the room in which the man's lonely existence was now almost wholly contained.

He took the square of paper Jacob had given him and carefully unfolded it. His first thought was that it might be a letter, written either by or to his dead sister, but as it opened in his hand he saw that it was a flimsy printed leaflet. He held the sheet taut against its tendency to fold back in upon itself. It contained only seven lines:

Protest against the detestable persecution of the
   Jews!!!
Organize self-defence in the factories and districts!!!
Solidarity with the Jewish victims of the working
   people!!!
Snatch the Jewish children from Nazi violence
   – take them into your family!!!
Strike!!! Strike!!! Strike!!!
Solidarity!!! Courage!!!
Fight proudly for the liberation of our country!!!

At the bottom of the leaflet was the date, October 1943, and the words *Dutch Resistance Movement*.

'I took it from the corpse of a woman I knew. She came after us to Papenburg and then to Auschwitz. She was eighteen, or perhaps nineteen. Not a woman, still a girl. She and I had attended the same school. She was in a class two or three years below me. She clearly had no true idea of where she was going or of what was about to happen to her, otherwise she would not still have had anything so dangerous or incriminating in her pocket.'

'How did it incriminate her?'

'She had read it. She had saved it. She was Jewish.'

'Did you see nothing similar yourself before you were sent away?'

'No. We knew, of course, that something calling itself a resistance movement existed, but not that it concerned itself with the Jews. That was the work of individuals.'

'Did it give you some hope, seeing it?'

'In Auschwitz? Hope? No, it gave me no hope. My parents were dead by then, and I was separated from Anna. I was still able to contact her and to see her occasionally, but by then our lives had long since started to unravel. We were pieces of ourselves. Whatever we had once been as individuals, and whatever we had once been to each other, counted for nothing.' Jacob gestured for the leaflet to be given back to him. '"Snatch the Jewish children from Nazi violence",' he read. 'I was no longer a child, but Anna was. No one snatched her from that violence, no one took *her* into the safety of *their* family.'

'Why did you keep it? Surely, it was a risky thing to do under—'

'"Under the circumstances"? I kept it because it made me angry to see everything set down so plainly, so simply. It angered me to see all those exclamation marks, as though the thing were being shouted aloud in some public place and in the faces of our persecutors. It angered me because for so many of us those simple and obvious choices no longer existed. It made everything so black and white with its good and its evil. Of course some people responded to it and did what little they could, but for everyone who helped, there were a thousand others ready to denounce us, and for each of those thousand there were another ten thousand only too willing to look away, to ignore or to tolerate what was happening. "Voor Joden Verboden".'

He carefully refolded the leaflet and slid it back between the pages of the book from which he had taken it upon Mercer's arrival.

'You took it and kept it because that in itself was an act of rebellion,' Mercer said, finally understanding.

Jacob acknowledged this. 'A futile and pathetic act of rebellion.'

'Were you able to show it to Anna?'

Jacob looked up sharply at this. 'No, of course not. For her even to have known of its existence would have put her in jeopardy. There were informants everywhere.'

'It might have given her the same hope, caused the same anger in her from which you yourself drew some strength.'

'In Papenburg, perhaps. But not afterwards, not *there*. You talk of risk, of those risks worth taking, but in that place nothing was calculable; there was no reason, no connection between how one lived and how or why one died. To be in the wrong place at the wrong time was a risk, but who was to know where or when that was? People were chosen at random, the sick and the healthy alike, and they were killed. I'll tell you something.

'Anna had a friend, a girl called Rosa. One day, the woman in charge of Anna's hut called for everyone to go outside and line up. This woman then told Rosa, who was a year older than Anna, and well known in that part of the camp for her good looks, to go to her. Even Rosa's shaved head did little to detract from her looks. She and Anna had arrived together, and so, in the way of the lost and the terrified, they had stayed together as far as possible. Rosa went to the hut leader and then this woman called for another to join them. This time her choice was an old woman who had seemed close to death for several days. She was ancient, at least fifty, and barely able to stand. For weeks, according to Anna, she had made herself inconspicuous. Others had stolen her food and she had refused to complain. The two of them, Rosa and this breathing corpse, stood one on either side of the hut leader, who then called over a German sergeant who had been standing close by, his pistol drawn, keeping an eye on what was happening. He came smiling and stood with the three women. Anna stood as close as she dared to the front of the crowd and her eyes never left Rosa's. The hut leader then announced that today was her birthday and asked everyone to sing to her. The sergeant conducted them with his pistol. Anna said the woman stood with tears in her eyes, as though this demonstration of false affection had been spontaneous, done willingly, with feeling, as though it *meant* something and was not merely another whimsical display of the woman's brutality. Anna said there were at least half a dozen nationalities singing that song, but that despite the conflicting languages there was little discordance in the overall harmony.

'And then, when the singing was done, the hut leader applauded her singers. She put her arms round Rosa's shoulders and round the shoulders of the old woman – as though she were about to have her photograph taken with them. She even told them to smile, to be happy for her. I imagine you never saw such broad smiles. And then this woman released her grip on these other two and announced to the watching crowd that someone new was coming into their hut and that a space needed clearing for this newcomer. They all understood this for the lie it was, of course – the newcomers came in their hundreds, not individually. Just as the huts were cleared wholesale. Someone had to go, the woman repeated, and the choice had to be made between the women on either side of her – Rosa and the old woman. Some in the crowd started shouting the old woman's name, a few even called out for Rosa to be chosen. I suppose there was still envy, jealousy, even in that place. I asked Anna what she had shouted, and at first she denied having called out anything. But then she confessed that she had called out the name of the old woman.

'Eventually, the hut leader called for silence. The sergeant waved his pistol. It was clear, the leader shouted, that the preferred choice was the old woman. She took Rosa's arm and led her to one side of where the old woman stood. The sergeant came forward and said something to her. The old woman bowed her head and covered her face with her hands. The man raised his pistol and held it close to the side of her head. And then, as everyone tensed themselves against the shot, he turned abruptly, aimed the pistol at Rosa, and shot her instead. The hut leader applauded him and the two of them embraced. They had been in it together from the very start. Women in the crowd screamed and called out when they saw what had happened, how they had been used, and the man waved his weapon at them, his other arm still around the hut leader's waist.'

Jacob paused after this, and closed his eyes.

Mercer felt his own throat constrict. Even if he had wanted to speak, the words would have been no more than a hoarse whisper.

'Anna, of course, watched only Rosa,' Jacob said. 'She said she fell first to her knees and then forward onto her face. She, Anna, had been the last thing Rosa had seen before she died.'

Mercer shook his head.

'The old woman, too, fell to the ground. Perhaps she

even imagined that she, and not Rosa, had been shot. The hut leader went to help her to her feet, caressing her face, wiping the dirt from her, holding her and reassuring her that everything was going to be all right, that she would soon be well and strong again. She pointed out the nearby corpse, telling her loudly that Rosa had deserved to die, that she had been vain and conceited, whereas the old woman was kind and wise and well-respected in the hut. Then she led her back into the crowd, among whom were the women who, only a minute earlier, had been calling for her to be killed instead of Rosa. The sergeant shouted for four of them to pick up the corpse and to follow him. There were places throughout the camp where these "incidental" corpses were gathered together ready for collection at the end of each day.'

'Was Anna one of the four?'

'Thankfully, she had more sense. It wasn't unknown for the guards to choose the weak or the sickly to carry the bodies and then for them too to be shot at the collection points. It saved time and unnecessary labour. No – Anna did not volunteer to carry her friend. The sergeant picked the four women nearest to him and then led them away with Rosa swinging between them. They returned a few minutes later.'

'And the old woman?'

'She died later that same night. Perhaps she woke from a nightmare of all those voices calling her name. Who knows? I didn't learn any of this until a week later, when I was next able to see Anna. It occurred to me immediately that she, and not Rosa, might just as easily have been chosen. I warned her against attracting the attention of the hut leader, but she said that the woman had already spoken to her, that she had commiserated with Anna at the unfortunate death of her friend. Anna said she had held her, and that she, Anna, had cried in this woman's arms. She said the last time she had been held like that, it had been by our mother.'

'Did you know for certain that your parents were dead by then?'

'And our aunts and uncles and all our cousins. *I* did.'

'But not Anna?'

'How hard would *you* have tried to convince her of that particular fact if she had been your sister? I told her that it was what I *believed*.'

'But that there was still some doubt?'

'Yes. It would have been too much for her. She was so vulnerable.'

'To the attentions of others?'

'To everything. She needed to have a better understanding of all that was happening to us.'

'And being separated from her, you weren't able to help her see things as clearly as you yourself now saw them?'

'I was in a trap of my own making. Who would want his fourteen-year-old sister to see those things so clearly?'

Jacob picked up the book which contained the leaflet and returned it to a shelf of others, pushing it into them so that its spine was flush with those others, and so that its secret was completely hidden.

He came back to Mercer and asked him how the work at the tower was progressing. Mercer told him, grateful that they had come so swiftly, albeit contrivedly, on to this new course. Grateful, too, that Jacob had been able to tell him this awful story. And even though it was a third-hand telling, the course of the story's progress served once again to emphasize to Mercer the indivisibility between Jacob and his lost sister.

Later, when it was time for Mercer to leave, and as he and Jacob walked slowly towards the town together, Jacob remarked that he did not envy those survivors who now lived into old age with their own memories of what they had seen and what had happened to them.

'Because they will not diminish?' Mercer said.

'No – precisely because they *will* diminish,' Jacob said. 'And because those people will live in a world where everyone else might learn of what happened, and all these others, these onlookers, will have their own ideas and opinions about what happened.'

'You think the tales of the survivors will not be believed?'

'They will swim in a sea of concern and false understanding, and they will drown in that sea. Not at present, of course. Faces are still turned away, but eventually, one way or another.'

Mercer did not agree with this unthinkable prediction, but again he said nothing.

They parted soon afterwards at the first of the houses.

28

The removal of the bombs began the following day. Early in the morning, two hours before the arrival of his own workers, Mercer was approached by the men in charge of the airfield and told that the Disposal Unit considered it necessary to take the bombs away using the coast road, this being now the least irregular way out of the airfield. The use of this route, they explained, would mean that work on the Station and the surrounding land would need to be suspended for the day, and Mercer's own workforce kept as far as possible from the bomb-laden vehicles. They made it clear to him that he had no alternative but to comply with these demands. Bombs with a combined weight of a hundred and eighty tons had been discovered. He asked them if the bombs were armed and they became evasive, convincing him that they were not and that these excessive precautions were unnecessary. They insisted it made no difference. They looked around them at the seeming disarray of the site. Disposal and demolition, two different things entirely, one of them said to Mercer, taking back the documents which proved their authority over him, and causing his companions to smile.

Mercer was angry at being given such short notice of all this activity, but he knew better than to prolong his useless arguments. All the Disposal men continued to serve in the Regular Army. His own lost rank would count for nothing.

He walked with them back to the perimeter and watched the teams preparing for the removal of the bombs. He asked the airfield men what was likely to happen, but none of them knew for certain. The most logical course, one said, would be to detonate the bombs somewhere in the surrounding open land, but none of the others considered this likely. Another man told Mercer that he had served on the airfield when it was operational and that the unarmed bombs were being treated with ten times more caution now than they ever were then. He said he had seen bombs roll from their tractor carriages and that men had simply rolled them back across the concrete. Mercer told the man he had seen the same thing in Italy, at an American base where a squadron of Mitchell light bombers had been stationed.

They separated after that, and later, when his own workforce arrived, Mercer explained to them what was happening. The road would have to be cleared of the lorries; these were to be driven on to the ground between the houses and the Light. He had expected the men to welcome this additional break from their work, but instead they complained that if they had been informed earlier, then they might have stayed away completely, either in the town or in their camp.

Later in the morning, several of the airfield men returned to the site and sought Mercer out. They sat with him in the tower and compared their work. They told him to ignore the man who had insisted on showing Mercer the forms of authorization. He was still missing the war, they said; it was a common enough complaint.

Once the lorries were parked, most of the workers returned to gather in groups close to the houses. The inhabitants went out to them and the removal of the bombs was endlessly discussed.

Later still, more men from the airfield came in a body to stand at the perimeter, and Mercer saw Mathias and his companions among these. They had been sent away while the work of winching the bombs to ground level was carried out.

'Good workers,' one of the longer-serving airfield contractors said to Mercer, indicating where the prisoners congregated apart from the others, and out of sight of Mercer's own men, who remained close to the houses. 'Shame, though,' the man added.

'About what?' Mercer asked him.

'Half of them have applied to stay here,' the man said. 'Word came at the weekend that most of them have been denied and that they're going to be sent home.'

Mercer looked back to where Mathias stood watching the distant work.

'For what reason?'

'Who knows? Some who want to go are staying, and some who want to stay are going. You know how these things work. Think of a perfectly rational, logical answer to a problem, and then work out how to complicate it and how to get as many pen-pushers as possible involved.'

'Like the bombs?'

'Like the bombs.'

'Do you know if Mathias Weisz is being allowed to stay?'

'Mathias? Not sure. Does he want to? The boss has written to whoever sent the order saying that they're all engaged on vital work and that he can't spare any of them until it's finished.'

'Will it work?'

The man shrugged. 'Apparently, there's some kind of appeal process. It takes thirty days, so they'll be here for at least that.'

'And the ones who want to go, and who can?'

'They'll be stuck with the others until it's sorted. They won't be too happy about it, obviously, but what are they going to do?'

'His parents were killed in an air-raid,' Mercer said.

'What difference does that make?' the man beside him said, then pointed and added, 'They've started.'

Mercer looked to where the first of the bombs were being removed.

'This'll be happening all over the country,' the man said. 'They're going to be finding those things for the next fifty years. You mark my words. The guns in half the planes are still stuffed full of live rounds. All supposed to have been stripped out. We caught a little kid playing with a flare the other day.'

'Someone from here?'

'I imagine so. When he saw us he dropped it and ran off. A phosphor flare. I once spent a day trying to get what was left of a wireless-operator out of his hole after one of those things had been set off by a piece of flak. A dozen wet, black pieces of him, that's all we got.'

Looking down, Mercer saw Mary and both her mother and father come out of their home and approach the men gathered outside. Then the three of them, now in the company of some of the others, crossed the road and climbed a raised bank to look out over the airfield. Someone gave Lynch a pair of binoculars, and he used these, first to study the airfield, and then to look all around him, finally spotting where Mathias and the other prisoners stood and watched. He remained focused on the men for several minutes before turning away. There were no other women present, and even at that distance it was clear to Mercer that Lynch had insisted on his wife and daughter accompanying him. He held Elizabeth Lynch by her arm, as though she might fall from the bank. Mary stood several paces from them. Lynch gave his daughter the binoculars, but the man to whom they belonged immediately took them back from her.

'We lose the Germans, it'll set us back two months,' the man beside Mercer said.

It encouraged Mercer to hear this, knowing that if the work was likely to suffer, then everything possible would be done by those in charge of the site to keep them there for as long as possible.

'Bureaucracy versus brawn,' he said to the man.

'Something like that.' The man concentrated now on the distant work, counting aloud the number of bombs that had already been lifted from their forgotten store.

Mercer left the tower and, avoiding Lynch and his family, he made his way to where Mathias and the others now sat amid the rubble. He recognized some of the men from his afternoon among them in the bunker. They greeted him and asked him what he knew about the removal of the bombs. It was their opinion that they ought to be detonated where they were, that this could only speed up the destruction of the runway.

Mercer told them he thought this was unlikely.

'No one tells us anything,' the man called Roland

234

said to him. 'Perhaps they think we might sabotage the work.'

The men around him laughed, but the laughter was short-lived, and Mercer sensed something of the despondency which now lay over them following the news of their applications.

'I heard about the repatriation notices,' he said to Mathias at the first opportunity, and knew immediately from Mathias's response to this that his own request to remain had been denied. 'What will happen?' he said.

Mathias shrugged. 'I imagine there is a right of appeal.'

'There is,' Mercer said.

'And that this appeal process will be fairly, meticulously and rigidly observed.'

'It's worth a try,' Mercer told him, but with little conviction. 'You have nothing to lose.'

'Your Authorities are not renowned for changing a decision once it is made,' Mathias said.

'The contractor in charge at the airfield will appeal on your behalf. He needs you here.'

'We know all about that. Thirty days. The end of September. Roland here has his wife and family waiting for him – though God knows where – and he has been told that at least a further six months will pass before *he* is eligible for reconsideration. He is a field-cook. He cooks stew.'

Mercer remembered the distant footballer from a month earlier.

'I must have done some terrible things,' Roland said, and held up his arm in a rigid salute, a gesture which shocked Mathias as much as it did Mercer. The man's disappointment and anger had made him reckless.

'He was a field-cook,' Mathias repeated, and knocked

the man's arm down. He looked quickly around them. 'He is also, it often occurs to me, his own worst enemy.' No one else beyond the group of prisoners had witnessed the gesture.

Roland signalled his sullen apology to both Mathias and Mercer. 'Perhaps the men in charge here tasted my food,' he said, and those around him laughed again.

Mercer was careful to avoid all mention of Jacob in front of these others. He knew that Mathias was as concerned for Jacob as for himself regarding his enforced repatriation.

'Perhaps, once you've returned home, you'll be able to come back here later.'

Mathias smiled at the suggestion.

Before Mercer could say any more, several men appeared around the side of the tower and came towards them. Mercer recognized them as one of his own crews. These men, a dozen of them, talked among themselves – now clearly enjoying their own unexpected idleness – and then fell silent as they approached where Mercer and the Germans sat together. They stopped a short distance away. One of them carried a length of wood, and seeing the Germans he held it ahead of himself as though it were a rifle. He looked ridiculous and several of the Germans commented on the gesture.

Roland made his hand into a gun, pointed it and said, 'Bang, bang.' There was more laughter.

Mercer rose and stepped forward to ensure that he was seen by these newcomers.

'What do you want?' he called to the men.

'Want? Nothing. It's a free country.'

'"A free country",' Roland repeated. He blew on his fingers and then slowly opened them.

'Join us,' Mercer said.

'Join *them*?' one of the men said.

Mathias came forward to stand beside Mercer.

'They've been sent away from the airfield while the bombs are removed,' Mercer said to the men.

'We know why they're here.'

'Pity the bombs were left there at all,' another of the men said. 'They should have been used and then—' He stopped speaking as several of the other Germans, those who understood what was being said, rose to their feet.

'Go on,' Mathias said.

But the men on the road appeared to lose conviction. They were outnumbered by the Germans by at least two to one. Someone whispered something, and the man who had made the remark about the bombs told Mercer that he was wanted at the lorries.

'That's why we're here,' he said. 'Looking for you. Everybody's telling us what to do, and some of us aren't happy about it. First they want the lorries past the houses, now they want us to park up two hundred yards down the road. We said we'd find you and see what you said.'

Sensing that this was his only way of defusing the situation, Mercer said that he, and he alone, told his own workers what to do.

'That's what we said,' the man said. He, too, seemed relieved that the confrontation had passed its peak.

'Tell them to sit down,' Mercer whispered to Mathias, who translated and relayed this. He was the first to lower himself back to the ground, and the others followed his lead, until only Roland remained standing. Mathias shouted at him and, having made his point, Roland turned and walked away.

Mercer left Mathias and went to the men on the road. Turning to the Germans, he shouted, 'You can stay there; don't come any further on to the site.'

Some began to protest at the remark, but again Mathias spoke to them and explained what Mercer was doing.

Leading his crew away from the tower, Mercer regretted that he had been unable to arrange to meet Mathias later in the day.

Coming out beyond the houses, he saw Lynch, his wife and Mary still standing and watching the airfield. They had been joined by several other local men and women. The children of the place were gathered in a separate group a short distance away.

Mary saw him and he waved to her. She kept her arms by her sides, but quickly flicked open her hand in response. Neither Lynch nor her mother saw him as he passed behind them with the others.

Out on the airfield, the first of the bombs were dragged on trolleys across what remained of the runway. A round of applause rose amid the rubble and the dunes. The children stopped their playing to watch. What they all secretly wanted, these distant watchers, it occurred to Mercer, was for one of the bombs to fall and to explode, and he knew how, for the rest of the day, their unspoken disappointment would be tempered by their endless speculation on the subject.

He followed the men to the lorries, some of which had already been moved, and the rest of which stood with their engines running in readiness, throwing up sand and dust behind them, the drivers wearing goggles and some with handkerchiefs tied across their mouths. The first man he saw with his face covered in this manner reminded Mercer of his brother, and he tapped the pocket holding his wallet, in which there was a photograph of the man with his own weather-beaten face similarly covered. He was unrecognizable

238

in the picture, but it had been the last one taken of him before he was killed, and for that reason alone Mercer had chosen to carry it with him everywhere he went.

29

Mathias came to him at the end of the afternoon.

As Mercer had been warned, the removal of the bombs had lasted all day, and no work had been done on the site. He had ignored the advice of the Disposal men and had sent his own workers back to town early. The passage of the lorries along the sea road had caused no delays at the airfield, and it remained his opinion that the bombs were unarmed and harmless and that work away from the perimeter might have proceeded as usual.

'Won't you be missed?' he asked Mathias as the two of them sat together in the tower.

'Not today. Not with all this going on. They still count us occasionally, but less and less often. We come and go. And today they can have little idea where any of us are. After your departure, they called for volunteers to return to the airfield.'

'What for?'

'The men taking away the bombs called for others to sit beside them in their restraining cradles on the backs of their lorries. Only as far as the town. They still considered the road too uneven and needed someone to ensure the bombs stayed in place. They assured us they were all without fuses and perfectly safe.'

'Still . . .'

'Precisely. So you can imagine how much more appropriate, how much more fitting it must have seemed to some of them to have one of us holding onto the things. I'm being unfair, of course. Their own men sat alongside us. We were just there to help, extra ballast.'

'So no one was blown up?'

'Happily, no. Some of us made several journeys. Once in the town the roads were considered sufficiently improved for the bombs to be rocked and jolted to their final destination unattended.'

'So your men are scattered between here and there.'

'My men? Oh, yes. Some of us here, some of us there, some of us in between. I made sure that I was able to return.'

It was four days since Mercer's visit to see Jacob and hear the story of Anna's friend. He asked Mathias if he had seen him more recently.

'Yesterday,' Mathias said.

'And?'

'And he remains unwell while protesting ever louder otherwise.'

'Does he know about your failed application to stay?'

'Of course. And, like you, he possesses an unwarranted and unfounded faith in the appeal process.'

'He told me about his sister, Anna,' Mercer said, still uncertain of how many of those same tales Jacob had already told Mathias.

241

'I imagined he had.'

'He blames himself for her death.'

'He blames himself for not having ensured her survival. I imagine he believes there is a great difference.'

It seemed to Mercer that Mathias spoke of the girl as though he had long since known and understood everything that had happened to her, and of the ties that still bound her to her brother.

At Mercer's suggestion, they left the tower and walked on the beach. Though August was drawing to a close, it had been a warmer day than usual, and the tower was airless. On the beach, at least, a slight breeze blew in off the water, and both men faced into it as they walked.

'Perhaps if you had someone to sponsor you in your application to remain, then whoever decides these things might look again at your application,' Mercer said. The idea had occurred to him earlier, but despite his initial enthusiasm for the proposal, he quickly realized that he himself was unlikely to be considered as such a sponsor, and that Mathias's employer would be a far better proposition.

'My employer, for instance?' Mathias said, as though reading these thoughts. He shook his head. 'He has been asked too many times. He has written on behalf of others, but to no avail.'

'Perhaps if *I* tried,' Mercer said.

'It is kind of you to offer, and I understand why you might want to do so, but I would rather you did not involve yourself. Besides which, I can do nothing until my preliminary appeal is decided one way or another.'

'And the others? Roland, for instance?'

'Some of them have become desperate men. Roland, idiot that he sometimes pretends to be, has not seen his wife or family for almost four years. His son was killed at Stalingrad. His elderly mother lived with his wife for a short while but the two women argued and his mother left.'

'Does he fear for his marriage?'

'He fears for everything.'

They walked away from the houses until they were beyond all sight of them.

'Will he – will any of them – do anything stupid, do you think?'

'If you are asking me if any of them will try to return home before their appointed time, or if any of them will run away and hide here, then my honest answer is that I cannot say.'

'But you believe it possible?'

'As I said, desperate men.'

It was clear to Mercer that he was being diverted from Mathias's own thoughts on the subject, and it was beyond him to ask any more directly.

'Perhaps immediately after the war's end,' Mathias said. 'Perhaps then, when there was nothing but confusion, and all those men had not returned to their desks and factories, perhaps then it might have been possible to disappear or to invent oneself anew, but not now.'

'Did they give you a reason why some of you were successful in your applications and others not?'

'Nothing very specific. "Suitable", "Unsuitable", not much else.'

'Suppose you were to marry an English girl,' Mercer said, the idea only then occurring to him.

Mathias laughed. 'Where is she? And besides . . .'

'Besides, what?'

'Do you honestly believe me capable of doing that to someone? Marrying them for that reason?'

243

'It would make sense. There need be no true deception involved. You could pay.'

Mathias stopped walking and pulled out the linings of both his pockets. 'She would have to come very cheaply,' he said. 'Who did you have in mind?'

'No one,' Mercer admitted.

'Perhaps someone here,' Mathias said.

They walked in silence for several minutes.

'Thank you for this morning,' Mathias said eventually.

'It wouldn't have come to anything.'

'Perhaps. But whatever happened, it would not have helped matters. In addition to Roland, there are five or six other hotheads who would have happily risen to the bait.'

'I don't really understand why they continue to regard you with such hostility after all this time. The people in the town don't feel the same.'

'Upon meeting him,' Mathias said, 'one of the first things Jacob told me was that while I was here I should do nothing to attract undue attention to myself.'

'I imagine it's how he himself must have learned to live.'

'Him and his sister, yes.'

'Has he told you what happened?'

'Not really. Just that the two of them were together and that she died and he survived. What else can there be to know? I don't imagine he believes there is anything to be gained by endlessly telling the story to whoever might listen. Nothing will change.'

'I don't imagine there are all that many people who want to hear it.'

'No. Everyone now is looking ahead, not to the past.'

But some men, Mercer knew – men like Jacob, and like Lynch – were as tethered to that past as they were bound within their own bodies.

'I learned from my failed application that I am still, officially, a serving soldier,' Mathias said. 'I daresay I will have as many hoops to leap through over there as I have here.'

'Do you think your own Government is insisting on your return?'

Mathias shrugged, but it was clear to Mercer that he, too, had considered this.

They reached a point where the road approached the beach, and where its foundations of rubble, eroded by the sea, lay exposed to them. They sat in the shelter of this, knowing it was where they would part. A large ship crossed the horizon, its smoke trailing unbroken for several miles behind it.

'My cousin served on submarines,' Mathias said. 'My mother's sister's child. He was killed on his fourth voyage. "Voyage" – it sounds so heroic.'

'I can't think of anything worse,' Mercer said.

'He was our first family casualty. His brother died on the Rhine. My father's sister's son was blinded. He, too, was a sailor. He sailed once to the Caribbean. No one believed him when he told us where he had been. We joked about him securing our supply of bananas. He was bombed off Brest. That's where he was blinded.'

'Did he survive the war?'

'He took his own life towards the end. The Russians came two or three days later. He had a sister. She ran away two days after he died. No one has seen her to this day.'

'How awful,' Mercer said.

' "Awful", yes. What I'm trying to say, I imagine, is that the war there, in Germany and Poland and Russia, was a different thing entirely from what it was here, or even in France before the Second Front.'

'I can imagine,' Mercer said.

'I believe you can, but that is what it will be – imagining. I daresay people might consider this imagining to be an understanding of sorts, however imperfect, but it isn't.'

'No,' Mercer said.

'True loss lives only within us, and is made not the least more bearable by being shared with one or a thousand others, or by being imagined by those others.'

'Perhaps not. But perhaps people still feel the need to make the effort to understand, to imagine.'

'Why? Because they consider it to be part of the so-called "healing process" we hear so much about. It is indulgence, nothing more.'

'So are we all so completely alone with the losses we bear?' Mercer was not accustomed to such weighty conversation, and he anticipated Mathias might laugh at what he had said.

But Mathias did not laugh, nor even smile; instead, he turned to Mercer and said, 'Of course we are. Every single one of us. Even you.'

Me? Mercer thought, unprepared for the remark, and unwilling now to prolong this painful dissection by saying it aloud.

Mathias, too, realized that too much had been said, and that they had deceived only themselves in diverting from their course.

The sun fell lower in the sky behind them, and when they finally rose from where they sat, it cast their elongated shadows across the sand.

'I saw the girl's father,' Mathias said as they prepared to part.

'He was watching the airfield.'

'He, too, came to see us after you'd gone. His wife

246

and the girl came with him. There were others. He told the woman and girl to take a good look at us.'

'Neither of them shares his views,' Mercer said.

'And neither of them said anything to contradict or silence him. They both did as he said. He picked up a stone and threw it at Roland. He missed, but only because that was his intention. There were still a dozen of us. He expected the woman and the girl to do the same. He shouted at them. One of the other men told him to forget it. I told everyone to remain sitting on the ground. He reminded me a lot in his appearance of the dirty, exhausted American soldier who took me and all those others prisoner. I thought all day that he was going to grow weary of looking after us and shoot us all. We'd heard stories.'

'What happened?'

'Today? He let himself be persuaded by the man talking him out of it. He turned on his wife instead, said she'd betrayed him and that he should have known better than to depend on her. I think all the others were just as uncomfortable with what he'd done. I thought Roland might rise and throw a stone back at him.'

'Did you warn him against it?'

'I said nothing. Perhaps I wanted him to do it; I know some of the others did.'

'Did he – Lynch – know who you were?'

'Me, personally? I doubt it. Besides, who am I?'

'Mary will have told him about you.'

'The stone was definitely aimed closer to Roland,' Mathias said.

They parted after that, and Mercer walked slowly back along the beach, leaving it before he reached the houses to avoid the few people still gathered there.

It was almost dark by the time he arrived at the tower, and he sat for an hour at his desk without lighting his lamps.

30

He saw nothing of either Lynch or Mary for the next three days.

He did, however, encounter Elizabeth Lynch, once, alone on the beach, but upon his approach she had been reluctant to talk to him. She looked hurriedly around her as he greeted her, as though she believed they were being watched.

'Is he out there somewhere?' he said.

She seemed genuinely surprised by the remark.

'Lynch.'

'Him and her are in town,' she said.

'I heard from Mathias what happened,' he said.

'Who's Mathias?'

'Mathias Weisz. One of the Germans. He told me about Lynch throwing the stone.'

'Oh, that. He didn't mean anything by it.'

'Just his way?'

'That's right,' she said. 'He never threw it to hit anyone.'

'Then why throw it in the first place?'

'Bit of fun.'

'Throwing a stone at a man who he knew was in no position to retaliate or even defend himself.'

'Nothing to stop them from doing either,' she said, and once again it dismayed Mercer to realize how immediate and instinctual her defence of her husband was. He regretted that he had made no real effort to contact her after the meal she had prepared for him. Since her husband's return, she had withdrawn almost completely from the society of the place, venturing out only in his company, or with her children. He remembered her sudden appearance as he had approached her home with Daniels, the way she had waited and then withdrawn upon recognizing him. He knew better than to mention Daniels's name to her now.

'Neither you nor Mary threw stones,' he said eventually.

'We might have done.'

'Mathias said that you were reluctant, that Lynch was angry at something.'

'What would he know? A German. Was he the man who nearly got hit?'

'No.'

'Well, then.' She turned to leave him, and he saw only then the bruise on her cheek. She raised a hand to the mark, knowing he had seen it.

Neither of them spoke.

'Mathias was grateful,' he said after a minute of this awkward silence. 'He thinks your reluctance to throw anything prevented the others from joining in.'

'Then he's wrong. And you can tell him that from me. Mary might not have done anything, but I would.'

'Why?'

'What do you mean "Why?" They're still Germans,

aren't they? If it wasn't for them and the war, Lynch wouldn't have been called up and gone away and got himself into all that bother. And he wouldn't have turned out like this.' It was clearly what Lynch himself had told her. Perhaps when he had struck and bruised her. A line of reasoning in which none of them could ever believe, but which remained unchallenged in its simplicity.

She sensed that she had said too much and fell silent again.

Of the three of them, Mercer realized – father, mother and child – she had deluded herself the most about the man's return and about their future together. He wondered if it would not have been fairer of Trinity House to tell everyone living there of their eventual plans for the place. At least then some cold reality, some rigour, might have informed these hopeless expectations.

Now that he had seen the bruise, she made no further effort to conceal it from him.

'He said he'd asked you for work,' she said.

'Not within my power. You know that. He knows it.'

'He said you'd told him something or other just to get rid of him.'

'I told him the truth.'

'He would have said the same whatever you'd told him.' It was her first concession, and he felt encouraged by it.

'I wouldn't lie to him,' he told her.

'You will eventually,' she said. 'Everybody does. Tell him what he wants to hear, I mean.'

'Not knowing how important his return is to you and Mary,' he said.

'Everything he tells her to do, she does,' she said. 'She won't deny him a single thing.'

251

'I know. I saw her with him the other day, selling the tobacco.'

'He made her pick those clothes from my wardrobe. Told me I had no cause to complain because I hadn't worn them for years. Told me I'd let myself go.'

'He can't know how difficult it's been for you, living here alone with your children to care for.'

'No one's suffered compared to him,' she said.

'That's according to him, I take it.'

'What else,' she said. Her growing confidence – knowing that whatever she said would not be repeated to her husband – had made her momentarily brave.

They walked away from the gently breaking waves.

'How's Jacob?' she said unexpectedly.

'Not well. Have you seen him recently?'

'I know Bail. Everybody does. He used to come out to work on the boats before the war.'

They stopped walking. She picked up a piece of cloth, shook the sand from it, examined it and then threw it back down. 'Habit of living by the sea,' she said. She looked out over the water. 'There was a ship sunk during the war,' she said, pointing to the horizon. 'A coaster, nothing much. We had seven bodies wash up here. All within a few yards of each other. Happened one night, November time. We used to hear the planes often enough, with the airfield so near, but that one small coaster was the closest the war came to us.'

'I suppose the tides and the channels would gather the bodies together.'

'Some of them were laid so close and with their arms over each other, just as though they were holding each other up, trying to help one another out. Boys they were. One or two older men, but mostly boys. Someone from the Ministry came, and then a lorry full of coffins arrived a day later. They told us all to stay away, but we went out and pulled them all clear of the water-line. Instinct, see. She must have been carrying coal, because it all came washing up over the next few weeks. We had a field day. There were four of them never found. Must have gone down with her, I suppose.'

'How was she sunk?'

'We never knew. Most likely to have been a stray mine, they said. Either dropped from a plane or one of our own floated loose.' She paused. 'Does Jacob talk to you much about that place he was in?'

'Not really.' He hid his surprise at this sudden change in direction.

'I saw that newsreel,' she said. 'People got up and walked out, said there should have been some warning. Woman sitting next to me just sat with her hands over her eyes asking me to tell her when it was finished. It was a terrible thing to see. Was it the same place?'

'Possibly, or another like it.'

'That poor man,' she said. 'We none of us know the half of it.'

'Most – all – of his family were killed,' Mercer said.

'And that's why he came here, is it? Some of the things they said had happened, you wouldn't think one man was capable of doing them to another. There can't be much left in him.'

'Sorry?'

'In him. Faith, trust in his – what is it – fellow man, that sort of thing.'

He remembered Bail using the same words. 'I was thinking much the same,' he said, and was about to say more when she suddenly turned away from him.

'Behind you,' she whispered.

He turned, expecting to see Lynch, but saw only another woman coming along the beach at some distance from them.

As she approached, Mercer recognized her as one of the younger women with whom he had spent time during those earlier, warmer evenings, one who had always responded to the calls and encouragement of the men. She was perhaps nineteen or twenty, only four or five years older than Mary, and he saw in her a great deal of what Mary might become were she to remain there.

She stopped only a few feet from them.

'You two look cosy,' she said.

'We were just talking,' Mercer said.

'Did I say otherwise? All I said was you looked cosy.' She turned to Elizabeth Lynch. 'Your loving husband not around, I take it.'

'In town,' Elizabeth Lynch said, her face still half-turned from the woman.

'That's handy.'

'I ought to go,' Elizabeth Lynch said to Mercer.

'Don't worry – I won't say anything,' the woman said.

'Because there's nothing to say,' Mercer said, his voice rising.

'Right. No. Just the two of you miles from anywhere having a nice cosy chat.'

Unable to tolerate this intrusion any longer, and angry that he and Elizabeth Lynch had been interrupted like this when he might have learned so much more from her, Mercer said, 'I'll go. It was nice meeting you. Give your husband and Mary my regards.'

Elizabeth Lynch said nothing, knowing that all this was said solely for the benefit of the watching woman.

'What about me?' the woman said. 'Wasn't it *nice* meeting me? Don't *I* get your regards?'

Mercer looked at her and she smiled coldly at him.

'Don't worry,' she said. 'I know when to keep my big mouth shut.' She reached out and turned Elizabeth Lynch's face with her finger. Elizabeth Lynch did nothing to resist her.

Mercer anticipated that the woman might now regret what she had said and perhaps apologize for her behaviour, but she did nothing other than lower her hand and turn away from the older woman's gaze.

31

Two days after this encounter, he set out from the tower with the intention of finding Daniels. He had not spoken to the man since they had carried wood together. He asked another of the men he encountered if he had seen Daniels, and he indicated the abandoned light-house, where he had spoken to him an hour earlier.

As he came close to the structure, he saw Daniels on the far side of it.

He turned at Mercer's approach and came towards him. He pointed out to Mercer where the silt and shingle had combined to build outwards from the old shoreline, leaving the Light further and further inland as the years progressed.

'Five years ago, the high tides covered its base,' he said. Fifty yards of overgrown foreshore now lay between the building and the water-line. It was early evening, the light was already fading, and with the onset of darkness came the sharp smell of the sea.

Daniels invited him into his home, and Mercer accepted.

The house was as small and as crudely built as all the others. Heavy furniture filled the single ground-floor living room. It was considerably cooler inside the house than outside. Piles of papers, clothes and half-filled cases lay scattered on the floor and on each of the surfaces.

'Have you started packing or not finished unpacking?' Mercer said.

'Both.'

Mercer had intended the remark as a joke, but he knew from Daniels's tone that this was not how he had understood it. Either suggestion, Mercer saw – the twin notions of forced return and unwilling departure – implied more than Daniels was prepared or able to discuss with him.

'Perhaps I thought she'd see the error of her ways and come running back here,' Daniels said.

'Her return must have been highly likely, surely?' Mercer said, knowing how dismissive the remark might have sounded.

'Exciting place, London, especially during wartime,' Daniels said. 'The bombs and rockets might have added an unwelcome note to the proceedings, but apart from them, I'd say it was the place to be. *She* obviously thought so.' He still loved her. He had lost her without understanding why she had gone, and her loss remained unbearable to him.

'Will you leave a forwarding address?'

'Do you mean will I tell Elizabeth Lynch where I'm going?'

It only then occurred to Mercer that if Daniels left the place without letting anyone know where he was going, then there would be no chance whatsoever of his wife ever finding him in the future. He knew with equal conviction that the woman was not coming back, that she had made a new life for herself elsewhere, and he wondered how many more years would pass before Daniels, too, started to move forward. Everything about the untidy, crowded room spoke of the emptiness at its centre.

Mercer picked up a photograph of the three of them together. He recognized the Old Light. He looked hard at the small child in the picture, held between both parents.

Daniels cleared a seat for himself and threw more wood on to the low fire.

'He was five when that was taken,' he said. 'Same age the Lynch boy is now.'

It seemed an unnecessary, though pointed, comparison to make, and Mercer wondered if the child played any part in Daniels's own cold regard of Lynch. Daniels took the photograph from him and stood it back in its place.

Thin curtains hung at the only window. They were holed, and frayed at the edges, and the evening sun bled through them. They were seldom opened.

'This was never how I intended to live,' Daniels said, indicating the room around him.

'Would you have stayed in Denmark if your wife had settled there?'

'Her name was Amelia.' And even saying that much was almost beyond him.

They were interrupted by the noisy passage of two jet-engine aircraft low over the houses and the whole room shook in the turbulence of their passing.

'You get used to it,' Daniels said, smiling as Mercer put out a hand as though to steady himself. It was the first time in all his time there that the aircraft had come so close or flown so low over the place. 'You should have been here a couple of months ago – one of them crashed.'

'Here?'

'Out on the water. Apparently, they'd been putting on a demonstration for some high-ranking visitors. The plane was climbing almost vertically when something went wrong and it started to lose power and to twist and turn. It must have been obvious to everyone watching that something was seriously wrong with it.' He made a clumsy, spiralling motion with his hands.

'Did the pilot get out?'

Daniels shook his head. 'Apparently, he tried to get the plane back under control. And, having gone up, up, up, it flipped over on to its back, hung there for a few seconds, and then came down. I watched it from the dunes. We all did. Like with the bombs, somebody made the mistake of coming to the houses earlier and forbidding us to watch. I doubt the descent, if you can call it that, lasted more than two or three seconds. Straight down, both engines screaming away. It hit the water, but the tide was out. I expected an explosion, but there wasn't one. It just hit the water and disappeared. Someone said afterwards that the canopy-release mechanism had failed and that even if the pilot had tried to get out, he wouldn't have been able to. They had a boat waiting, but it found nothing. The few bits of wreckage didn't surface for hours. The rest of it must have hit the mud and buried itself deep.'

'Was the pilot ever found?' Mercer said, remembering what Elizabeth Lynch had told him about the bodies of the seamen.

'Not so far. There's a marker buoy where they think the bulk of the wreck still lies, but they can't even be certain about that, otherwise they'd have come and retrieved everything by now. They were all over the place for a few days, kept everyone away. I offered my services, but they turned me down. They looked in all the wrong places for stuff to wash up.'

'And since then?'

'The planes still come and go. No fancy aerobatics, though, no shows.'

'There must have been any number of crash-landings over on the airfield,' Mercer suggested.

Discussions were already under way in the town concerning the erection of a memorial to the Americans who had been stationed at the airfield, and to those who had died, either there or on missions.

'There was never any church here,' Daniels said. 'It would have made a big difference. A chapel, even. The town was always too far off. When a boat was lost, or somebody drowned, then someone would come from one of the town churches and hold a ceremony on the shore.'

'But it was never how the people here mourned their losses?'

'They appreciated the gesture, but they knew that's all it was. No, they mourned in their own ways.' He took down a bottle from a shelf beside the hearth.

By then the new wood was burning and the heat and noise of the sudden blaze filled the room. Ash and dust spread from beneath the grate over the boards at Mercer's feet. Sparks flew into the room and died before they landed; occasionally, a burning ember fell from the hearth and added its own distinctive aroma to the room.

Daniels poured them both drinks.

'You're right to think that I resent Lynch his two children when my only son died,' he said.

'You may re-marry and have more,' Mercer said.

Daniels considered this and shook his head. 'He's

four houses away and I can still hear him shouting at her, at them all, through the walls.'

'You can't have believed that he would have changed while he was away.'

'At least not for the better.'

'Did you try to persuade her to leave before he came back? Her and the children?'

'Leave with me, you mean? She wouldn't have done it in a hundred years. Whatever you might choose to believe now, having seen him for yourself, she has never been unfaithful to him, or disloyal. I told her once, drunk and angry, that she was a fool to stay with him and she hit me. I apologized, of course, but I'd said it and it was too late and there was no going back. Perhaps I was hoping she'd learn her lesson the way I learned mine.'

'Whatever happened then, you seem to understand all this clearly enough now.'

Daniels refilled their glasses. 'I've had plenty of time to think about it. She told me from the outset that Amelia would never come back here.'

Your own unfaithful and disloyal wife.

'Most of the others thought they were being kinder in suggesting otherwise, but not her. And when I asked her how she could be so certain, she said she didn't know why – just that she knew Amelia wouldn't come back. She said she didn't ever want to become an excuse between us. There was already enough un-certainty, she said, without us creating more.'

'It was her way of telling you that she would not jeopardize her marriage to Lynch.'

Daniels laughed. 'The boy was only a baby when they arrested him. It was her way of protecting her son – nothing to do with how she felt about Lynch.' He drained his glass.

Mercer was not convinced by this, but he said nothing. Everywhere he looked in the place – in the houses and beyond – he saw the soil in which Daniels's anger lay rooted. It was an open, exposed place, and yet there did not seem to be the smallest part of it which did not possess its secrets.

The last of the falling sun penetrated the shabby curtains, and Daniels moved around the room lighting lamps. The fire cast its own shifting pattern of shadow and light over every surface. The voices of the children could be heard outside.

'They'll erect a memorial to the air-crew who died,' Mercer said.

'Not here, they won't. And they won't put a stone up for that poor bastard who landed nose-first on the bottom of the sea. They'll want something clean and solid and dignified.'

'Unlike the actual deaths of the men they commemorate, you mean?'

'I sailed on a ship that sank forty miles off Cape Wrath. She wasn't torpedoed or bombed; she was just overloaded and too old for the job. She started taking on water the minute we left Liverpool. Forty-seven men and only eleven of us were rescued. We had a corvette with us, but she was too busy running up and down the line to come back and take care of us. Friendly waters. Told us there was a boat coming out from Peterhead for us. Well, whether it was on its way or not, it never got there. Instead, we got two days of storms. I don't hear much talk of *that* particular monument.'

'Perhaps people need time to see all these things in perspective.'

Daniels looked at him in disbelief. 'All they need time for is to forget,' he said.

The clock on the mantel struck eight.

'I ought to be getting back,' Mercer said, and rose to leave.

32

Lynch approached him the following morning, and Mercer's first thought was that the man had heard of his encounter with Elizabeth Lynch two days earlier. He braced himself against the man's assault, relieved that he was alone, and that the men closest to him were at least a hundred yards distant. He saw Lynch coming and started walking away from him, depriving him further of the audience he craved.

He heard the man calling to him as he walked, but pretended not to hear, finally stopping and turning only when it was impossible for him not to have heard.

'I've got work to do,' he said as Lynch finally reached him.

'No need to be so unfriendly,' Lynch said. 'I only wanted to ask a favour.'

'What?'

'I need a lift into town. If any of the drivers was going back there in the next, say, hour.'

'Unlikely,' Mercer told him.

'But you could make it happen, right? If you wanted to. I wouldn't be asking if it wasn't important.'

'I need them all here,' Mercer said. 'The work's behind.'

Lynch held up both his palms. 'Only asking, mate, on the off chance. We'll walk.' He put his finger and thumb in his mouth and whistled loudly.

Behind him, Mary appeared from beside a stack of empty fuel drums.

'Thought it might save her feet,' he said to Mercer. 'That's all. Thin as paper, them shoes.' Lynch himself wore sturdy boots and he stamped his feet several times.

Mary came to them.

'No luck,' Lynch told her. 'You were wrong. Nothing doing.' He turned back to Mercer. 'She was the one who suggested I ask you. The walk there and back a few days ago wore her out. She said you had something coming and going all the time. You did offer, remember?'

'Not today,' Mercer said. He knew Lynch was lying about Mary having made the suggestion. 'But if anything comes up, I'll let you know.' He turned to Mary as he spoke.

'No good,' Lynch said. 'Need it now, mate. Not much point, otherwise.'

'Do you have an appointment?'

' "Appointment"? You could say that.' He pulled out a folded sheet of paper from his shirt pocket. 'Appointment with the Law. Noon, it says, they say. No show and they'll come and take me away again.'

Mercer saw from Mary's reaction to this seemingly casual remark that this was the first time the suggestion had been made in front of her. He saw how swiftly and easily he had again been deceived and outmanoeuvred by the man, and how his daughter had again been used in that deception. Anyone else might have said that Lynch was shameless in this use of the girl, but Mercer understood that shamelessness was the least of the man's faults, and that there was something considerably more calculating and self-serving involved in this manipulation of his daughter, and, through her, Mercer himself.

'Is that likely?' Mercer said. 'I doubt it.'

'Chance I'll have to take,' Lynch said. He stuffed the paper back into his pocket. 'Chance we'll all have to take.'

'You could start walking and see if anything comes along,' Mercer suggested.

'*I* could,' Lynch said. '*She's* the one looking forward to a nice comfortable ride. She's worried that she'll slow me down, aren't you? Worried that her old dad'll miss his appointment.'

Thus prompted, Mary nodded.

'Pity you can't do all this when you're in town on other business,' Mercer said, emphasizing the last word to ensure there was no misunderstanding between them.

But Lynch only considered the remark and smiled. 'Oh, you know what these people are like,' he said. 'Besides, I prefer to keep the two things separate, if you know what I mean.'

'Does Mary need to go with you?' Mercer said.

'Insists on it. First thing she said when I got up. When were we going? How long would we be staying? What would we be doing there? She feels about this place like I used to feel.'

Mercer wondered at the extent of the man's own delusion. He lived in a world entirely of his own making: that which he could alter, he altered; that which he could not, he ignored; and the suggestion of violence continued to underpin everything he did – whether sudden, witnessed and uncontrollable, or distant, unseen and unheard. He wore a mask, continually revealing the unsettling sneer behind the unconvincing smile.

'Perhaps someone will be going from the airfield,' Mercer suggested, knowing this was more likely.

'I wouldn't sit in a lorry with one of *them* if you paid me,' Lynch said.

'They're not all Germans.'

'Good as. And the ones who aren't might just as well be, the way they treat them.'

'Then perhaps you could walk and Mary could get a lift.'

'Very clever,' Lynch said. 'Besides, she wouldn't want to abandon her dad, would you?'

Not like you abandoned her, Mercer thought.

Still Mary said nothing, and Mercer regretted this. As before, there was nothing he could say in her presence for which she or Elizabeth Lynch might not later be made to bear the consequences. He considered suggesting to her that she might return to the tower and clean it again in the near future, but he knew that Lynch would intervene and prevent this, and that this arrangement and all it represented between them would be used and demeaned by the man.

'Time we made a move,' Lynch said suddenly, turning away from Mercer.

'Perhaps you could buy her some new shoes,' Mercer said, regretting the remark immediately.

Lynch stopped walking, his back still turned. 'And perhaps *you* could try keeping your nose out of other people's business,' he said.

Mary stood only a few feet from him, within reach.

'It was a serious suggestion,' Mercer said, anxious now to release this sudden tension between them. 'You presumably have contacts who could find a pair.'

Mary kicked the sand from her feet. She wore no socks beneath her flimsy sandals.

Lynch watched her and shook his head. 'If they're as useless as your friend here thinks they are, then you'd be better off without them.'

Mary stopped kicking. 'What?'

'You heard me. Take them off. I'm obviously incapable of providing for my own family. Take them off.'

'But I—'

'*Take them off.*'

Mercer nodded at Mary to comply.

She reached down and pulled off one of the sandals. Its pale outline remained marked on her foot. She held it towards her father.

'And the other one,' Lynch said.

'I honestly think—' Mercer began.

'And I honestly think you ought to keep out of it. I think you've said enough, don't you?' He turned back to Mary. '*I said the other one.*'

Mary took off the second sandal, and this, too, she held out to him.

'What are you giving them to me for?' he said, acting puzzled. 'I already told you – they're useless, worse than useless. What do I want them for? According to your friend here, all they're good for now is throwing away.'

'I didn't say that,' Mercer said.

'Throwing away?' Mary said.

Mercer had never seen her with anything but the sandals on her feet.

'You heard me.'

'But—'

'Oh, so first it's *him*' – he jerked a thumb over his shoulder – 'telling me what's best for you, and now it's you. Everybody knows what's best except me. I said throw them away. Now. Here. *Do it.*'

Mary looked to the ground on either side of her.

'Do it,' Lynch repeated.

Mercer saw the man's fists open and close at his sides.

Mary threw the first of the sandals into the grass.

Lynch watched where it landed and laughed. 'Further,' he said. 'Anybody would think you were going to go back later and pick them up the minute my back was turned.'

Mary threw the second sandal further. It fell amid the rubble and none of them could see for certain where it landed.

'That's better,' Lynch said. He walked to one side of the road, picked up the first sandal and then threw it with a grunt even further into the site.

Mercer looked hard at where he imagined it had landed, trying to fix the spot in his mind so that he might retrieve it when the two of them had finally gone.

Lynch eventually turned to face him. 'You're right,' he said. 'She deserves better. Sandals are for kids. I'll get her something new in town. Not that there'll be anything in the shops, of course, but I'll see what I can come up with. Shouldn't be too difficult for somebody as resourceful as me, eh? Perhaps you could come with us, help her choose. In fact you might want to choose something yourself for her. Perhaps you might even want to prove to her how concerned you are about all this and buy her a pair yourself.'

Behind him, Mary closed her eyes.

'I'm sorry,' Mercer said to her, ignoring the man between them.

'No, you're not,' Lynch said. 'Your sort never are. Always ready to interfere, mind, always ready to pass judgement on others, but never prepared to put their hands in their own pockets, never prepared to actually *do* anything.'

Mercer felt each of the words like a blow, and again he could not understand how they had come to this, how single-mindedly Lynch had created and then dominated this confrontation, how he had made and then shaped it regardless of the others involved.

'What if there *had* been a lorry?' Mercer said.

'What?'

'What if I'd said straight away that there was a lorry going into town and that you were welcome to a lift on it?'

'I don't get you. You said there wasn't.'

'And by which you understood me to mean that even if there was a lorry, I wouldn't want you on it.'

Lynch considered this for several seconds. 'What did I tell you?' he said to Mary. 'Next thing, he'll be telling one of the drivers to take us into town. He'll be wanting you to think that none of this has anything to do with him, have you believing that you threw your shoes away all on your own accord. Nothing what-soever to do with him. All that's down to me and you, see? Me and you, because we're common and stupid and he isn't. What a shame – poor kid's got no shoes to wear, but what's that got to do with him? What can he do about it? That's all her stupid, ignorant father's fault – man's an idiot.'

Mercer refused to respond to this confused and contradictory reasoning.

'Dad—' Mary said, not knowing how to stop him,

but not wanting to hear whatever he might have been going on to say.

'What?' Lynch said, an aggrieved look on his face, his palms again raised.

'We ought to go,' she said.

It did not even occur to Lynch, Mercer thought, to realize that his daughter was now prepared to start walking barefoot over that rough ground to bring his spiteful accusations to an end and to draw the two men apart.

'See?' Lynch said to Mercer. 'You probably want to believe that this is all *my* doing, but it isn't – it's yours. *She* knows that, and *I* know it. The only one here with his eyes still closed is you.'

But again Mercer refused to be drawn. Whatever he said now would only prolong the girl's agony. Her feet would be quickly cut and bruised on the rough ground. He knew it was impossible for her to walk so far barefoot.

'Don't worry,' Lynch said, rubbing a hand over his face. 'We're going.'

Beyond him, Mary started walking, and if the hard surface caused her any pain, then she did not show it.

'Look at her,' Lynch said. 'Just like me at her age.' He ran to join his daughter and to put his arm around her shoulders. He whispered something to her and kissed her cheek.

Mercer resumed walking in the opposite direction, stopping only when he knew he could not be seen to watch the two distant figures on the road. They remained close together, the man's arm still around his daughter, the girl still matching him step for step.

Later in the day, coming back along the same path, Mercer could not even decide for certain where the three of them had been standing. He searched the ground where the sandals might have been, but found nothing.

33

Jacob handed him a small glass. It stood on his flattened palm and he held its rim between his thumb and forefinger.

'Is it one of yours?'

It was clear by the way Jacob handled the glass that it was precious to him. 'I bought it in the town a few days ago for nothing.'

'And you're obviously delighted by the fact.'

'That I actually found it? Or that I paid nothing for it because the woman who sold it to me had no idea of what it was?'

'Both, probably,' Mercer said. He took the glass and held it to the light. He saw immediately that both the base and rim were uneven, and that slight imperfections in the shape and colour existed elsewhere. He pointed all of this out to Jacob, who watched him and nodded, and said, 'What else?' clearly savouring the exchange.

'Is it hand-made?' Mercer said.

'1760 or 1770 would be my guess.'

'Is it for wine? It seems too small.'

'For good wine, drunk in small quantities.'

'A woman's glass?'

Jacob fluttered his hands, pleased. 'Most would say so, but I doubt it.'

Mercer looked more closely. The surface was etched, and an illegible engraving ran around the rim. He had seldom seen Jacob so animated; not even when making his own pieces had he been this excited.

'Ovoid bowl, bridge-fluted and inscribed,' Jacob said, as though presenting him with a clue.

'What does it say?'

' "Bona Fide", though it's obviously well-worn.'

'Glass?'

'Yes, even glass. It was a common enough inscription. Anything else?'

'It's got—' Mercer tapped where the glass was shaped.

'Facets,' Jacob said. 'A floral cartouche and short vertical flutes on the rim. Diamond-faceted stem and a plain circular foot. Pity about the foot. I imagine the maker might have wanted to ornament that, too, but was frightened of damaging the stem by becoming over-elaborate.'

This was how Jacob's father might have spoken, how he might have relished and displayed his own expertise to his son, Mercer thought. It was what Jacob had grown up imagining he might inherit. It was a muscle, a reflex, like every other, that had been wasted, a dream that no longer returned.

'Do you know who made it?' he said.

'No. It's definitely English. A man called Wilkinson made a lot like it.'

'Locally?'

'Cambridge. So not too far away for it to have found its way here.'

Just as you did, Mercer thought.

'Perhaps even when it was newly made,' Jacob said.

'But just as likely to have come here last week in a box of junk upon someone's death and a house being emptied and fought over by greedy relatives.'

'Who had no idea what they were throwing out. Precisely. You see the varied courses of history, these dull, superficial and untrustworthy provenances. All these beginnings and endings.'

'Then I'm pleased you found it,' Mercer said, handing the glass back to him.

Jacob took it just as carefully as he had given it, and then stood it on the table beside them. He rested his forefinger on the rim and rocked it gently to reveal the unevenness of its base.

'I once did some work in Leiden for a collector. He taught me a great deal. I catalogued his collection for him. He was a wealthy man with several thousand pieces. He knew far more about what he had than I did, of course, but he wanted everything set in order, a record making. He wanted someone else to see and to appreciate what he had, someone who understood as well as he did the true value and meaning of all those pieces.'

'Is that when you knew you would never be content with making glass for windows?'

'Possibly. Yes.'

'What happened?'

'With the collector? What do you imagine happened? Delicate and easily broken glass, Mr Mercer. Not diamonds, not gold, not bundles of tightly wrapped bank-notes.'

'Was it all lost?'

'Most of it. Stolen.'

'Looted, you mean?'

'A piece of glass, whatever its value, is an irresistible thing to an angry man.'

'So was nothing saved?'

'A few dozen pieces, hidden away in a hole in a cellar wall.'

'That's something.'

'Not really. In all likelihood, they are there still. Or the house will have been destroyed and the cellar filled with rubble.'

'You could perhaps return one day to try and retrieve them.'

'Or perhaps they are better left where they are. Perhaps in a hundred years someone who knows nothing of how they came to be there will uncover them and wonder at their history.' He came to sit closer to Mercer.

Outside, in the yard, Bail was busy clearing a new path through the mounds of salvage.

'A lot of noise for a man with nothing to do, don't you think?' Jacob said.

'Perhaps imagining yourself to be busy is as important as actually having something useful to do.'

'For Bail, perhaps.'

'Has he heard any more from the bank or the people wanting the land?'

'Probably. I don't ask and he never tells me.'

Once again, it surprised Mercer to see how all these other small and varied dramas moved inexorably to their own conclusions around his own. He had gone into town with several others to collect a repaired generator. The driver would call for him in an hour. He had suggested to Trinity House that they gave the generator to Bail to repair, but the man to whom he had spoken had laughed at the suggestion and called Bail a joke. Mercer had not persisted.

Jacob had not returned to the tower or the site since his enforced stay there a fortnight earlier. In all likelihood, he was now too weak and too easily exhausted to make the journey on foot, and Mercer regretted this.

'Tell me,' Jacob said suddenly, looking closely at Mercer. 'That night, and since – did my talk of my sister embarrass you?'

'Not at all. It's important for you to be able to talk about what happened, to remember her. She was your sister and you loved her. Why should talk of her embarrass me?'

'Perhaps because I love her no less now than when she was alive,' Jacob said. 'No less now than when we were small children playing in our garden together, safe from the world. No less now than when we were in the camps together and I vowed to protect her.'

'She must have known that you did all you possibly could for her,' Mercer said, uncertain where these remarks were leading.

'Must she? I still failed her, Mr Mercer, and nothing in the world or in the sum and total knowledge of man can alter that particular fact. *She* never absolved me of that promise; *she* never told me it was forfeit to circumstance.'

Neither of them spoke for several minutes. They listened to Bail moving beneath them. His dogs barked at every sound. It was a duller day than usual, with a cloud-filled sky, and cooler.

'Perhaps she wasn't *able* to release you from your promise,' Mercer said eventually. 'Perhaps her belief in it – in you – was the only thing that kept her alive for so long. Perhaps for her to accept your inability in the—'

'What? Perhaps then I might have felt better about myself and my failure?'

'I was going to say that it would involve as great an act of faith for her to release you from that vow as it did for you to make it in the first place. Perhaps she did that without telling you, and perhaps both acts were of equal and vital importance. Yours to her, and hers, unspoken, to you.'

For the first time, it occurred to Mercer, he had suggested something to Jacob which Jacob himself had not already considered a thousand times over.

'You mean she *did* absolve me of that responsibility, my vow to her, but that it was beyond her to say so because she knew how it would make me feel? Because it was not necessary, not after twenty months, to make my failure any more clear or painful to me? Or because by then there was nothing else remaining to bind us together? No humanity, no hope – no idea, even – of the future, only the absolute certainty of our deaths?'

It was a bitter and imperfect explanation, but a perfect understanding, Mercer knew, would remain for ever beyond them.

'Yes,' he said emphatically, hoping the notion that his sister had absolved him of his responsibility towards her might now take root in Jacob's mind and provide some solace, however brief or illusory. 'I won't pretend to understand everything that happened,' Mercer went on, taking advantage of Jacob's momentary uncertainty, 'but I know *you* well enough, I believe, to know that you would have done everything possible for her. And I imagine Anna knew you better than anyone, and so she must certainly have known that you would have done everything in your power – if not to save her in the end, then to make what life remained to her as fulfilling and as hopeful as possible.' It was more than he had intended to say, but he had been encouraged by Jacob's silence to continue. Normally the man would have stopped him by saying something disparaging, but now he sat in his chair, gripping its arms and with his eyes tightly closed. Mercer decided to say no more until he better understood how much or little of what he had suggested Jacob was able to accept.

'It sounds trite and unconvincing to say that I would have sacrificed my own life if it had been possible for her to have lived,' Jacob said eventually, his eyes still closed.

'I daresay that was never an option.'

'No. The true choices still remaining to us towards the end were considerably starker.'

'I can imagine.' Again, it was the kind of remark to which Jacob would normally have reacted angrily, but again he said nothing.

'For ten days before she died, she was in an infirmary. Does that surprise you, that there should be such places? There were several: one for men, one for women, one for children. Even one for those whose sickness meant they needed to be kept in isolation. Everything very efficiently run, real doctors, real nurses, real medicine bottles with real labels on them.'

'Was it all done for show?'

'For the Red Cross. Certainly no one else was fooled. How else could all those deaths be explained if no one was ever ill beforehand? Of course, this was not to consider the vast majority of people who were killed immediately upon entering the place, or who were killed shortly afterwards. I daresay that someone somewhere calculated that so many per cent of all deaths in those places were caused by disease and certifiable illnesses.'

'And the infirmary provided that quota?'

'Anna and the others like her provided that quota.'

'And the books appeared balanced.'

'You cannot imagine what keeping up appearances meant to those people. There was no pretence elsewhere, of course, in other camps, but when they finally understood that the war was lost, then certain concessions were made.' His hands were now white on the arms of the chair. 'Typhus,' he said. 'And if that wasn't enough, scarlet fever. Upon our arrival there we had been asked what childhood illnesses and infections we had already suffered. Neither of us could say for certain. We guessed at what we might or might not have had, what might now provide us with some immunity. I was clever then, I still had my wits about me, and I told them that Anna and I had survived everything on their list. Typhus, of course, was not listed. Nor the dysentery which could reduce the weight of an already sick child by two pounds a day. We lived with children who could bend neither their arms nor their legs because of the abscesses and sores on their elbows and knees; children with holes in their cheeks caused by gangrenous rot; others who could scarcely open their eyes or their mouths because of the pain this caused them. For my own part, I was old enough to remember most of what I had already suffered. They had asked us the same at Papenburg, where my mother had been able to answer in greater and more truthful detail. She had seemed almost proud of all I had suffered, as though my survival had been an achievement for which she alone had been responsible. I doubt it ever occurred to her then to wonder why we were being asked such questions.'

'And Anna?'

'I was not present when they asked her about Anna.'

'So when you were asked later . . .'

'I lied.'

'You guessed.'

'I lied. Of course I lied. I knew then why we were being asked. A child who had already suffered all those ailments was not afterwards going to become a liability. That child would not then grow sick and infect others.'

'You sought to protect her,' Mercer said.

'Of course I did. I sought to protect us both with my lies.'

'And if—'

'And if I'd been less convincing, or if I myself had been less convinced by my lying, then perhaps I would have been better prepared for the scarlet fever when it came and killed her. What good then were all my lies? What single ounce of good or comfort were they to her then?'

It seemed to Mercer that Jacob asked the same painful and unanswerable question of him every time they met. In truth, of course, he asked it only of himself.

Neither man spoke for several minutes.

Jacob wiped his face and kept a hand over his eyes, breathing heavily as he regained his composure.

Mercer picked up the small glass. 'What happened to the collector?'

'He was a wealthy man, so who knows,' Jacob said. 'He lived alone, he had no close family to consider, no children to try and save alongside himself. There were always tales of whole boatloads and trainloads of people being saved by one means or another, so perhaps he escaped and he, too, lives to this day. Perhaps his priceless collection was all he possessed to lose. Who knows?'

'Perhaps he survived and returned to gather together what remained of it,' Mercer said.

'And next you will suggest to me that I myself return to Utrecht and reclaim my own valuable inheritance.'

'Of course you should,' Mercer said. 'One day.' He could not imagine why he had not thought before to ask about the business and what Jacob might now retrieve of it for himself. But even as these thoughts ran through his mind, he saw Jacob slowly shaking his head.

'It would be impossible for me to return,' Jacob said.

'But it would be a way forward for you. Even if you feel you can never return there because of what the place itself means to you, then you at least deserve some acknowledgement of your rights, compensation, perhaps. There must be justice.'

'Justice?' Jacob said abruptly, as though it were the only word he had heard. 'Why? Because without it, or without some fear of it, evil will continue to prosper over good? Too late and too simplistic, Mr Mercer, too late.' He stopped, breathless at having become so agitated. He looked at the glass on the table beside him, and then he picked it up.

Outside, a louder noise than usual suggested where Bail had toppled a mound of scrap.

'Do you ever talk about any of this with him?' Mercer said.

'With Bail?' Jacob smiled. 'Never. You see how I use people to my own ends. Bail, you must understand, serves a different purpose entirely.'

It comforts you to see that there are these other men lost in their own helplessness, rage and despair, Mercer thought.

'Is it humanity, do you think?' Jacob said.

'Sorry?'

'That prevents *me* from smashing it?' He held up the glass. 'Is it my humanity – something even *I* cannot deny?'

'I don't know,' Mercer said honestly. 'But it would be something worth believing.'

'To know that I still possessed it?'

Mercer nodded. It was another lie, another excuse – but one in which both men now needed to confess to believe, because without even that uncertain belief, everything else might become suddenly unbearable.

' "Bona Fide",' Mercer said, indicating the glass.

'The man who inscribed it will have thought nothing of it.'

'You don't know that for certain.'

'No. But, again, I am more easily convinced one way, and you the other.'

A horn sounded in the yard below, sending the barking dogs into a near-frenzy.

'I have to go,' Mercer said. 'Is there anything you need, anything I can do for you?'

Jacob shook his head, and then, unexpectedly, as though he had been saving the remark for this last moment, said, 'She came and watched me, watched over me.'

'Who did?'

'The girl. That day in the dunes. When I was alone, awaiting your return. She knew I was there and she came to me.'

'What did she say?'

'I pretended to be asleep. She stood over me and watched me, and even though she believed me to be asleep, she still spoke to me.'

'Oh.'

'She told me she felt sorry for me.' He paused and looked directly at Mercer. 'A child's pity, Mr Mercer – imagine that.'

'What else?'

'Nothing. She waited a few minutes longer and

then she went. She brushed the sand off my chest.'

'You should have pretended to wake and then spoken to her,' Mercer said.

'I know,' Jacob said. 'But it was beyond me.'

Below, the driver sounded his horn again.

'Tell Mathias you came,' Jacob said, breaking his reverie. 'Tell him to come if he has the time.'

'He has concerns of his own,' Mercer said, uncertain whether or not Jacob had yet heard of Mathias's unsuccessful application.

'I know,' Jacob said. He rose and stood at the centre of the small room as Mercer gathered together his few belongings and then left.

34

Mary came to see him the following day. He had not seen her since the incident with her sandals, and he imagined Lynch had forbidden her to come to the tower. He was still at a loss to understand the man's bitterness and his contempt for almost everyone around him. To accept that this behaviour was merely a consequence of his frustration and resentment at being forced to remain there when he would have preferred to be elsewhere seemed too simplistic to Mercer. He far better understood Mary's loyalty to the man, despite her own growing awareness of how she was being used by him. Her feelings for Lynch remained rooted in her childhood, and in her imaginings and expectations during those long and uncertain years of his absence. Mercer also knew that Lynch alone represented to his daughter her most likely way out of the place, and that, despite his own denials and rebuttals, she had attached herself to him in the equally uncertain hope that this might soon happen.

She came into the lower room and called up to him.

Cautious in case he had again been deceived, and Lynch was about to appear alongside her, he shouted down for her to wait where she was.

He heard her descend the few stairs she had already climbed.

She stood away from the open door and watched him come down to her.

'Close it if you like,' he said. 'Where is he? What errand are you on this time?'

She could hide neither her surprise nor her dismay at the remark.

Mercer, too, had not anticipated sounding so caustic or dismissive.

'I don't know where he is,' she said.

'And I'm supposed to believe you?' he said.

'It's the truth. Is that why you didn't want me to come up – because you thought he might follow me?'

'You sound as though it was the last thing he'd do.'

'So does that mean *I'm* not to come here again?'

'What do you want?' He was still not convinced that Lynch was not about to appear, with or without her contrivance.

'I came to say sorry for the sandal thing,' she said. 'To apologize.'

He looked immediately at her feet. She wore a new pair of shoes. She, too, looked down at these. They were black, with a double strap, and covered little of the tops of her feet or her heels.

'You do realize that he manipulated the whole situation, don't you? He knows he can't do it when it's just me and him, so he uses you – stands you between us – to play his pathetic games.'

'I know all that,' she said. 'I'm not stupid. He got me these.' She turned one foot and then the other towards him.

'Did you walk into town with him?'

'Of course not. Barefoot? Is that really what you think he was going to make me do? You thought he wanted to get at you by making *me* do that?'

'He's more than capable of it,' he said. He saw how inappropriate the flimsy-looking shoes were for the rough ground of the place.

She shook her head – whether in disbelief or disagreement at what he had suggested, he could not be certain.

'I'd have been cut to pieces. He told me to go home and then he went without me. I'd wanted to go with him, get away from here for a few hours at least. He came back with these.'

'Did you look for your old ones?'

'Glad to be rid of them, to be honest. They were rubbish; I'd had them for years. At least these fit me. He told me how much he paid for them.'

'What did your mother say?'

'About what?'

'About losing your old ones. She can't have been too pleased. They would still have fitted your brother.'

'What do you think she said? Anyway, I imagine *you* went looking for them.'

'Oh?'

'It's the kind of thing you'd do.'

'Because of the guilt I'd feel at having caused you to lose them in the first place?'

She considered this. 'It's just the kind of thing you'd do. She went looking for them when she heard what had happened. Waited until he'd gone, of course, and then went looking. She was out for hours.'

'Did you help her? You at least had an idea where they'd landed.'

She shook her head. 'I told you – I didn't want them

back. He told her it was all your fault, told her every-thing that had happened.'

'She wouldn't necessarily have believed him,' Mercer said.

'Why not? He's still her husband, isn't he? *She's* still his wife.'

'Did he—' He stopped abruptly.

'Did he what? Did he hit her?'

'I only meant that it's obvious to everybody here that they're having a few problems.'

'Is that what they are – "a few problems"?' She walked in a circle around the room, pausing to inspect the empty cases and surveying rods which were now stored there. 'I know exactly where the sandals are,' she said eventually. 'And I saw you looking for them after he'd gone. I waited until you'd finished and then I went out and got them. An hour later, she started looking.'

'Where are they?'

'I buried them.'

'And you let her go on looking?'

She clicked her lips. 'She found this. She took some-thing from her dress pocket and gave it to him. It was a cigarette lighter, small and made of brass with a regimental crest on one side. 'It probably belongs to one of the men. She told me to bring it back to you. She never told him she'd found it.'

He took it from her. He flicked the cog against the flint and a small flame appeared. 'I'll ask,' he said.

'She said there might even be a reward. Might mean a lot to a soldier, something like that, she said.' She avoided his eyes as she spoke, indicating to him that the suggestion had come from her and not her mother.

'I'll mention it,' he said.

A group of men congregated outside. They were

uncoiling cable, and the empty wooden spools lay beside them. Everything Mercer and Mary now said would be overheard by them.

'Come up,' he said to her, indicating the open stairs.

She climbed ahead of him, her new shoes close to his face.

'Do you accept it?' she said as he lowered the trapdoor behind them.

'Do I accept what?'

'My apology. The sandals.'

'Of course,' he said. 'I just wish that sometimes you could see more clearly what he's doing. I know he's your father—'

'But sometimes he behaves as though everyone in the world hates him and he hates everyone in the world. That's *her* speaking, by the way.'

'I can imagine.'

'I don't think he hit her over the sandals.'

'So was it something else?'

She shrugged. 'Mostly it doesn't have to be anything specific. If he's that way out, then he doesn't really need a reason.' She walked around the room in the same way she had circled and examined the one below. She had not been there in over a week and the floor and surfaces were cluttered. Unwashed dishes had accumulated; empty glasses stood in clusters. A dozen charts lay unfurled in layers across his desk. She batted her hand at the flies which still circled the room.

'Does he hit you and Peter?' he asked her as she picked up the book he was reading, her free hand across the back of the chair in which Jacob had slept.

She hesitated before answering him. 'We're both still just kids to him. Of course he does.'

'You say it as though you believe he has a right to do it.'

288

'So what am I going to do? And besides—'

He waited, but she refused to continue.

' "Besides" what?'

'He won't be here for that long,' she said. She put down the book and turned to face him.

'Oh?'

'Not according to him.'

'Whatever you tell me, I won't repeat anything,' he said.

'He'll still get to know.'

'Not from me. What about the conditions of his parole?'

'He said he wasn't going to stick it for much longer, that he could do a lot better for himself somewhere else. She begged him not to go, but he said they'd got more important things to do than to come looking for him. He told her she'd lived her life by the book and look where it had got her.'

'They *will* go after him,' Mercer said. 'I know it makes little sense, but it's what they'll do. They'll have no alternative.'

'I know,' she said. 'It's the Army.'

'And are the rest of you included in these plans of his?'

She looked sharply up at him.

'I see,' he said. 'Only you.'

'He told me not to say anything. Especially to her.'

'It won't happen, Mary.'

'Why won't it? Because *you* say so?'

'And you'd go? Just like that? You'd leave your mother and Peter? You've just said you know they'll come looking for him.'

'Exactly – *him*, not me.'

'And your mother would once again be—'

'He said she'd had her chance. She could have gone

289

any time he was away. She could go with him now – we could all go – but she won't.'

'This is all she knows,' Mercer said, realizing how feeble a reason or excuse this was to her.

'And so I'm expected to stop here and rot with her, is that it?'

Once again, he heard Lynch in everything she said. Unwilling to prolong the argument to its predictable conclusion, he indicated the teapot on the table, suggesting to her that he made them a drink, but, as before, she insisted on doing this herself. She stood panting after her outburst.

'Did he say anything more specific?' he asked her when she had regained her composure and as they waited for the kettle to boil.

'I'm not *that* stupid,' she said, her voice now even and low. 'He'd soon get as sick of me as he gets of her. I'd get in his way. I'm *already* in his way.'

'What do you mean?'

'I heard him. I was supposed to be asleep – we both were, but we weren't – and he said he wouldn't even have come back here in the first place if it hadn't been for me. He wanted to see me, he said. He said she was flattering herself if she thought *she* was the reason he'd come back.'

'He came back here because it was part of his release agreement,' he said.

'That's what she said.'

'And?'

'He just laughed at her and said, "Exactly", and that as soon as he was in the clear, he'd go. He told her then that he was thinking of taking me with him. She started screaming at him. He told her he'd asked me and that I'd been desperate for him to take me. She accused him of lying and he said that all she had to do was ask me.'

'And did she?'

She shook her head. 'She won't do it. But I can see it every time she says something to me or looks at me.'

'And what will you tell her if she does ask?'

'She won't.'

'Because for as long as she doesn't ask, then she doesn't have to hear you say you're going.'

'Something like that.' She lifted the steaming kettle from the stove and poured the water into the teapot.

'It would kill her,' he said.

'She'll get over it.'

'That's him talking, not you.'

'He says I've got to start thinking of myself. What else is going to happen to me stuck here?'

In the drawer of the table upon which she set the cups and saucers lay the plans from which the houses and the road's end had already been erased.

'I'm going to be sixteen soon. Millions of girls of that age are already working. And I don't mean on farms or in factories. I told her what you'd said about me going to college.'

'And?'

'At first she said you ought to mind your own business, but I think she could tell that I was taken with the idea. In the end, she seemed quite keen on it. But then she spoilt it by saying there wasn't a college in the town, so where would I go?'

'I take it she mentioned none of this to your father.'

'What do you think? She knows what he'd say.'

'He'd say you were likely to get your head stuffed full of fancy words and ideas.'

'Exactly like you.'

'Exactly like me.'

They sat together at the room's centre, beyond all

sight of anyone looking up from below. She put down her cup and held out her hand to him.

'What?'

'Your hand,' she said, and gestured.

He held out his hand and she clasped it. 'I just wanted to see what it was like,' she said.

'And?'

'That's all you ever say sometimes. "And? And? And?"'

'And?' he said. He felt her fingers settle into his palm.

'I just wanted to see what it was like. I've never held a man's hand. Except his. You think I flirt too much with the others on the site.'

'No, I don't.'

'Yes, you do. You don't say it, but you think it.'

'I just think you ought to be careful, that's all.'

'Why – because they're supposed to be grown men and I'm only a girl?'

He saw again how lightly and easily she moved around him.

'Something like that.'

'Don't worry. It's what they think as well. They're not going to try anything, especially now *he's* back.'

'There's still a lot of room for misunderstanding.'

She gripped him harder. 'You should listen to yourself sometimes. Sometimes you talk round and round in circles because either you don't want to say what you mean or you don't know *how* to say what you mean.'

'Lucky for me that you can read my mind, then.'

'I know. You can let go now.'

He released his slack grip, but her hand stayed where it was for several minutes longer.

'You'll go, won't you?' he said as she finally withdrew from him.

'A minute ago you told me he was lying, that he was using me and that it would never happen.'

'I meant with or without him. He's just the stick come back to stir everything up.'

'More tea?' she said, mimicking a voice she might have heard on the wireless.

'And you understood that all along.' He held out his cup to her, and in that instant she seemed a completely different person to him.

'She even said that *she'd* be better off without him,' she said.

'She might be right.'

'So what have any of us got to lose?' She licked her finger and wiped at a mark on one of her shoes. 'I saw Jacob and Mathias yesterday,' she said, straightening and sitting back in the chair with her cup held on her legs.

'Together?'

'In one of the lanes not far from town.'

'What were they doing?'

'Just standing.'

'Did they see you?'

'I went and said hello to them. I don't think Jacob was very well. He could barely talk. Until I showed up, Mathias was standing with his arm around him. He told me that Bail had had some unwanted visitors and that he'd brought Jacob away from the yard until they'd gone.'

'What visitors?'

'He didn't say. Everybody knows about Bail. Mathias asked me what I was doing. I stayed with them for half an hour. I don't think Jacob wanted me there. I think I make him uncomfortable.'

'Oh?'

'Probably something to do with his sister,' she said,

but with no true understanding of what she was suggesting.

'Perhaps,' Mercer said, unwilling to speculate on what he only half-understood himself, and hoping to divert her from any closer understanding of how Jacob might regard her.

After that, she rose. 'I ought to be going. I only came to bring the lighter.'

'No you didn't,' he said. 'I'll find out who lost it.'

'The reward was my idea,' she said. 'Not hers.'

'It's still a possibility,' he said.

'Besides which, you'd already guessed.'

He followed her down the stairs, but she told him to stay inside as she let herself out.

'You think he'll be watching?' he said.

'He usually is. That or he'll get to hear about it.'

'The new shoes suit you,' he said.

'No, they don't. But I could hardly make my appearance in fashionable society wearing a pair of old sandals, could I?'

It occurred to him then, watching her go, and watching the men uncoiling the cable running to walk alongside her, that she possessed nothing, and that when she finally did leave her home and her childhood behind her, then she would leave them completely, taking nothing with her, and afterwards reinvent herself anew in the eyes of a world which knew nothing of her.

Part III

35

'Among my liberators' – Jacob paused, as though surprised at his own use of the word – 'was a Scottish medical orderly. A Scotsman. Few of us, even those among us who spoke some English, could understand much of what he said. He told us to call him "Jock" and said he was from Glasgow and that this was why we couldn't understand him. I was still suffering from dysentery, a result of the typhus. I shall never forget his first words to us upon opening the door to the barracks in which we awaited him, fearful and disbelieving. He stood there, bathed in the sunlight of the opening, looked in at us all, some of us already stumbling and groping towards him, and he said – I shall spare you his accent – he said, "Oh, my poor bloody boys." Those were his words. "Oh, my poor bloody boys." Even draped in the blankets and overcoats we had been able to gather from the already-emptied huts, we were still all so thin and so small to him. There were men there old enough to be his father, his grandfather even. "Oh, my poor bloody boys." It was all the compassion I needed. That, for me, was the moment when I knew for certain that I alone would continue to live.' He paused again, blinking rapidly at the memory, savouring it, ensuring that not even the tiniest part of it had been lost to him.

'This was in Belsen?'

Jacob nodded.

'How long had you been there?'

'Since the start of that last winter. By train again to a compound outside Braunschweig, and then marched to the camp.'

'And was Anna still with you?'

'Not *with* me, but she was embarked on the same journey. I heard afterwards that a great number of women had been taken to Sachsenhausen – there was a camp there – and from there to Belsen a few weeks later.'

'Fleeing the Russians, presumably.'

'Of course fleeing the Russians. They were animals. What horrors they would commit, what atrocities. Imagine: sixty miles on the other side of the Wieser and I would have been back in Holland. It made no sense to move us, weak and suffering as we were, most of us never likely to be well enough to work again, but the orders were to move us and so they did.

'The barracks in which we awaited our release stank to the heavens. It was a designated typhus barracks. Corpses lay where the life had departed them. There were only makeshift latrines. Even those of us long accustomed to that stench were made to retch by it. Anyone else opening that door would have been knocked over by it. As if the sight of all those skeletons was not enough. But that Scotsman just stood there. "Jesus dear God All bloody Mighty." He had come past mounds of corpses to reach us, and I imagine his own recollection upon opening that door will remain with him for as long as my own memory of him will remain with me.'

'What happened then?'

'He went away. I could barely stand. I wanted to call something out to him in his own language. I wanted to explain to him what he was seeing. I wanted him to know that we were men in there, and not some grunting, shuffling animals he had unexpectedly come across.'

'He wouldn't have thought that.'

'No, but it was how some of us had come to regard ourselves. A man swinging himself down from an upper bunk kicked me in the face.' He opened his mouth wide to reveal the gap which still remained in his teeth. 'By the time I myself reached the doorway ready to explain all this, the man was standing back from the barracks and in the company of several others. They all wore berets, I remember, not helmets, black berets. Our liberator was explaining to these others what he had seen. He was standing with his back to us, and the other men were looking over his shoulder at us. And seeing that they were distracted, he too turned and saw us again. He pointed to us. He was crying as he spoke, and the other men, I noticed, kept their distance from him. Someone shouted for us to go back into the hut, but no one heeded the call. Eventually, I made my way outside and called out to these men in berets. Someone heard me and came to me. As he came, another of the prisoners reached out and touched this man's arm, and he flinched at the contact, struck out and shouted for everyone to stay away from him. I saw that he wore an armband with a red cross on it. He shouted to me from beyond the gathering crowd. He wanted to know if I

299

was English. Needless to say, my answer disappointed him. He called for me to tell the others not to go any distance from the barracks. I told him that there were corpses in there, too, and that few of us had been outdoors in over a week. It was a bright, dry day. Some of the others lowered themselves awkwardly to the ground and sat with their heads in their hands.

'I remember a woman came to us, another prisoner, asking everyone she encountered if they knew of the husband she had not seen for two years. Or if not her husband, then her father, or her brothers, or her sons. She wore a yellow headscarf, I remember, and I remembered that Anna, too, had worn one of the same colour. It was all I could do to stop myself from shouting to ask her where it had come from.'

'Did you see Anna upon her own arrival there?'

'I was fortunate. Everything was in disarray. We were the sweepings, swept one way and then another, each push of the broom leaving so many fewer of us to brush away. I learned of Anna's arrival from a man selling home-made alcohol. He told me where she was and how to find her. There were still guards, of course, but they were not the men they had once been. Most guessed what was coming, and most, I imagine, were just pleased to be far beyond the reach of the Russians. There was even a rumour that the Germans had signed a pact with Churchill and the Americans to fight the Russians when Hitler finally capitulated. When our Scotsman first appeared, the man beside me, a Pole, listened to his impenetrable accent and said, "American? Russian?"'

'I heard the same rumours,' Mercer said.

'I found Anna in the company of some of the women she had known in Auschwitz. They had travelled there together. There were three times more women in

Belsen during those last months than there were men. And among them there were at least a thousand children, most of whom died before the end. There were furnaces for the corpses, but too many corpses for the furnaces, and so the bodies piled up. Someone had decided that the children should not be thrown into piles, but that they should remain clothed and that they should be laid out in lines to await disposal. There were even babies, who must have been born, lived and died using only their bodies' reserves.

'Anna was already sick and weak from the journey, but there was little doubt then in my own mind that this was where we would remain until the war's end, and so I told her to rest and to save her strength, to do whatever was necessary to *persist*. I lied and told her Holland was only twenty miles away. I told her that the English and the Americans would be there within weeks, days even. Month after month I told her this, as though it were all that was needed to keep her alive. I even managed to buy some medicines for her – though God knows what was in the bottles I was given. I told her to eat all she could. I told her where I was, told her how she might contact me. I asked the women who were with her to take care of her and they promised me they would. It was a desperate fool's paradise we inhabited. How could *I* ask anything of *them*? How could they promise me anything in return? All I had left to try and persuade them to help was the fact that we were brother and sister, that this connection still existed between us where so many millions of other similar connections had been so brutally and arbitrarily severed, and where countless thousands now wandered completely alone. Perhaps I thought that by showing them how we two had survived, they might be able to accept or believe the same for themselves.

301

Perhaps somewhere out there, waiting or wandering alone and without hope, was their own brother, or husband, or father. I know it makes little real sense now to think like this, but it made sense then. For almost two years we had lived without any real expectation of surviving, and now here, at last, was the faintest light towards which we might both turn our faces. So much. And even if it was a few more months, and not weeks or days, then surely it was still something we might endure.'

'How long did she survive after her arrival?' There was no other way for Mercer to ask the question. He had not gone to Bail's in anticipation of hearing this tale, merely to determine what had happened concerning Bail's visitors of two days earlier. His concern was unfounded. Nothing in the place had changed, and only Bail and Jacob continued to live there.

'I worked it out afterwards,' Jacob said. 'She survived for thirteen weeks and one day; and four weeks and two days later, the camp was entered.'

'And you were safe.'

'Saved. I was saved. No one waved a wand and brought the dying back among the living. That, too, had seldom been a journey that might be travelled in reverse in the past, but now it was possible.'

'I'm not sure I understand.'

'To stop dying and to start to live again. For a sick man to become healthy and strong again. For some – thousands – it was already too late – they were too ill, too far along that particular road. For some, I think it was the shock of knowing they might survive that killed them. They had lived as nobodies for so long, as those animals, that suddenly to turn back into a somebody again, a human being, with thoughts and feelings for the others around him, was too much for them. I saw one man killed by a bucket of clean water thrown over him by his friend in an effort to revive him. He was barely conscious and the water hit him and the shock of it knocked his head back against the ground, and when the water had finished running from his face, he was dead. He hadn't even seen the men in berets who had come to save him.'

'How soon were you able to go in search—'

'In search of Anna?'

The remark made Mercer cautious. 'I was going to say in search of anyone who had been with her when she died.'

'No — it was Anna I went in search of. Anna. Of course, she no longer existed. I knew that. I knew she had died. I was kept isolated for a further twelve days until my own recovery was secured. I weighed almost three stones less then than I do now.'

Mercer deliberately did not lower his gaze over Jacob's wasted body and limbs.

'Imagine that. A walk of fifty yards and I needed to sit down and rest for an hour. I went in search of Anna's ghost. I went in search of all the places she had ever been in the camp. I sought out the planks upon which she had slept, the chairs upon which she might have sat. I sought out the door handles her hands might have turned, the panes of glass through which she might have once looked. I searched for the plates from which she might have eaten, the cloths that might have bandaged her feet. I sought out all those others who had known her and who had been unable to keep their promise to me. I filled all the empty spaces she had left behind her. I walked upon her ground, I breathed her air.' He fell silent.

'And was there much of her left to find?' Mercer said.

'Plenty,' Jacob said proudly. 'I found everything. Everything I searched for, I found. Only *she* was missing.'

Mercer remained wary of what Jacob was telling him, uncertain where these breathless revelations might lead.

But Jacob had finished talking, and he leaned back where he sat, his eyes closed, a look of contentment on his face. He wiped a hand across his wet mouth.

'I'm pleased there was so much left for you to find,' Mercer said, expecting Jacob merely to nod his acknowledgement and for them both to know that this difficult conversation was at last over. But instead, Jacob sat forward until his head was close to his knees, where he held it in his hands, and began gently to convulse.

Mercer rose. 'I'll leave you,' he said.

' "Oh, my poor bloody boys",' Jacob repeated, this time perfectly mimicking the man's accent, his fingers tightening and growing pale where they gripped his head.

36

Two days later a strong wind blew in from the sea and work on the site became impossible. Clouds of dust and sand enveloped the men and the machinery. Sand covered the road in a perfectly corrugated pattern – the pattern left behind by an ebbing tide; it collected in scalloped mounds against everything in its path. And as the wind rose, it started to rain, lightly at first, but then with a sudden ferocity that had the workers running for cover, and which quickly turned the whole site into a quagmire. A shallow skim of water lay over everything, through which only the mounds of rubble and the supply stacks now rose. This heavy rain lasted several hours, and by the time it slackened and the wind finally dropped, it was too late to resume work.

Waiting until the men had gone – and unwilling to reveal to them his frustration at another day lost – Mercer made a tour of inspection to assess the extent of the flooding.

He was dismayed to see how quickly and completely the rain had filled all the shallow excavations, and how even the deeper ones now held at least a foot of water. He knew how slowly these might empty if left to drain naturally, and how much worse the problem might suddenly become were a high tide to fill those channels surrounding the site. He saw again what a precarious balance was struck there between the water rising from below, the rain and the comings and goings of the sea. In the wider scheme of things, the land was little more than a thin pad of absorbent tissue, never completely dry except in its uppermost inches or where it had been raised, and then only during the height of summer, which was now long past.

He calculated that an additional two days would be needed to pump clear the most vital of the excavations and to allow the ground to dry out around those wall-bases already laid. He saw how considerably less appealing a wall rising from water would look to the men about to build them higher.

Reaching the road and turning back to the tower, he came upon Daniels and another man.

He told them what he was doing, what he had found.

Neither man shared his concern at the flooding.

'Happens every year,' Daniels said. 'You soon learn which drains and dykes fill and which don't. We know, by and large, which ones to keep clear.' He raised the narrow spade he held, its blade balled with tan-coloured clay.

Both men agreed that the first of the early autumn storms did not usually arrive for another month, at the start of October.

'Soon,' the man beside Daniels said, 'the mists will start, and then you'll know that the good days have gone for good. When winter comes here it only knocks once.' He was deadly serious in making this announcement, and Mercer and Daniels exchanged a glance.

'What happens at the houses?' Mercer said.

'Happens?' Daniels said. 'They stand it as best they can. Like rocks having another layer stripped from them. Look at them, they've been neglected for so long now by the Light men, and with the war and everything, another few years of this and they'll fall down of their own accord.' He knew as well as Mercer did that the houses would not survive even that short time and spoke only for the benefit of the other man, whom he introduced to Mercer as Riley.

Mercer wondered if any of these vague and pessimistic predictions had been incorporated into the Trinity House calculations; it would certainly appear to make more sense to demolish buildings already weakened and considered unfit for habitation.

'We could have told you which smaller gutters to keep clear,' Daniels said, indicating the shallow flooding beside which they stood. 'An hour's work and you could have avoided all this.'

'They won't work in the rain,' Mercer said.

'How else are you going to know what's running and what's blocked?' Riley said. Both he and Daniels were saturated from head to foot. Water dripped from their fingers and cuffs, though neither man seemed to notice this.

'I don't think common sense plays much part in their reasoning,' Mercer said.

Daniels told him where the nearby drains had filled and then backed up into the excavations. If they were cleared now, he suggested, then the water would drain away during the night, leaving only that in the deeper holes to be pumped out in the morning.

Mercer wondered if he was offering to do the work. The sun had set by then, but there was still sufficient light to see by. Then Riley said that if all three of them did the work, it would only take an hour. He left them and started hacking at a mound of brambles which had grown over the closest channel.

Mercer and Daniels joined him and began work on clearing the drain.

This was finished in a matter of minutes and they watched as the risen water started to flow swiftly away. Then Daniels kicked down the pipe at the end of a second, shallower channel and the water flowed even faster. He pointed out where several of the flooded excavations were joined to a single drain. They worked together on other courses, and within an hour water flowed from them all. Mercer calculated that half the following day's work had been done.

They stood for a short while longer watching the water flow.

When Riley suggested fetching lanterns and unblocking more of the culverts, Mercer said they had done enough. But it was a natural thing for the men of the place to want to do after a storm, and only when Mercer compromised and told them to show him on his charts which drains to clear the following day, did they finally accede to his entreaties to stop working.

Now all three of them were soaked and caked in mud. Mercer insisted on them accompanying him to the tower, where he could lay out his charts for them, and where he might find something with which to reward their efforts. Neither man had asked for any payment.

The quickest way back was along the road, taking the three of them close to the houses, where some of the others, including Lynch, Mary and her mother, now stood and looked out over the sodden surroundings.

'He'll want to know what we've been doing,' Daniels said in a low voice to Mercer.

As the three of them approached, Lynch left his wife and daughter and came to the road, splashing through the water rather than skirting it.

'We've been unblocking drains,' Daniels said to him. He neither slowed in his step nor turned to acknowledge any of the watching others.

'None of my business what you've been up to,' Lynch said, feigning surprise. He walked alongside them in a half-march, his arm brushing Mercer's.

'We're going to show him the outflow channels on his maps,' Riley said, his voice betraying his concern at this sudden appearance of Lynch.

'So, if you don't mind . . .' Mercer said, his own conviction strengthened by Daniels's presence.

'So if I don't mind what?'

'Leaving us to get on with it.'

' "Us" is it?' Lynch said. 'You working for him now, are you?'

'Leave it, Lynch,' Daniels said loudly. He stopped suddenly and turned to face Lynch, who stopped a step later, his face inches from Daniels's.

Lynch held up his hands. 'Free country,' he said, smiling. 'Been cooped up all day in the rain. Stuck in that poky little box with her and the kids. You telling me now that I can't walk on the road?'

'Please yourself,' Daniels told him. 'Just stop trying to stick your nose in where it's not wanted.' He stood six inches taller than Lynch.

'What, so just the three of you are going back for a spot of supper, are you, all pals together? Going to be washing each other down and drying each other off?'

By then Lynch was playing to the onlookers, his wife and daughter included. Several of the men in the small crowd laughed.

Mary and her mother stood close to their door, unwilling to come out on to the wet ground.

Encouraged by the laughter and the calls of these others, Lynch said, 'Next thing you know, you'll all be sitting round sharing old Army stories, getting all tearful over—'

Unable to restrain himself any longer, Daniels grabbed Lynch by his collar and drew back his fist ready to hit him in the face. Lynch locked his own hands around Daniels's forearm, struggling for breath.

'No,' Mercer shouted.

Beside him, Riley took several paces away.

Daniels stood for several seconds longer before releasing his grip and lowering his fist. He stepped back from Lynch.

Lynch coughed and spat on the ground, leaning forward, his hands on his knees as he regained his breath.

It was clear to both Mercer and Daniels that each of these gestures was exaggerated, and that they were again for the benefit of the watching crowd. But despite one of the women calling out to ask Lynch if he was hurt, no one came to his assistance.

Eventually, Lynch stood upright, sucked in and blew out several times. Seeing that no one had come forward, he called for everyone to stay where they were. His eyes never left Daniels.

'Save your breath,' Daniels said. 'No one's coming.' He leaned forward slightly so that no one else might hear him.

Then Mercer said to Lynch, 'I regret that happening. Not for your sake, but for theirs.' He indicated Elizabeth Lynch and Mary.

'They'll get over it,' Lynch said immediately, his voice a snarl. 'In fact, seeing as how you're so concerned about them, I'll do all I can to *help* them get over it. You'd think they might at least have come to see if I was all right. Three against one – not very fair that, is it?' He spat again, and this time the phlegm hit Mercer's boot. 'Sorry about that.' He rubbed his throat where Daniels's hand had been.

'You had it coming,' Daniels told him.

'Not from you, I didn't.' He turned to Riley. 'You think that, too, do you?'

Riley lowered his head.

'I'm talking to you. Answer me,' Lynch shouted.

'No,' Riley said, his head still down.

'Then you want to be careful who your friends are. You and me are going to be here for a long time yet. Not like some. Besides which' – Lynch paused and turned to those watching – 'you never know what kind of company you might be keeping.'

But few understood the remark, and no one laughed.

'Jerries and Jew-boys he's had in there,' Lynch said. 'Never has none of us in for afternoon tea, but *they* can come and go at all hours as they please. Makes you wonder what this war was all about.'

Some of the onlookers finally warmed to this and there were a few shouted remarks in support of what Lynch said.

'If you've got something to say to me, then say it,' Mercer told him.

'He wants to know if I've got something to say to him,' Lynch shouted.

Mercer saw the impossibility of conducting any discussion under those circumstances: everything that might now be said or done would have considerably more impact on the watching woman and girl than on

311

Lynch himself. It was another of his pointless yet deliberate confrontations, and one from which he, Lynch, had again gained the greatest advantage.

Daniels took a step back towards him.

'Leave him,' Mercer said.

Daniels looked hard at Lynch for a moment and then turned and walked away.

'You'll turn your back on me one time too many,' Lynch said, his voice now little more than a hiss.

'I know,' Daniels said, but without turning. 'And it's the only way you'll be brave enough to do anything about it.' He and Mercer continued walking to the tower.

Riley remained standing at the side of the road.

'Better get running after them,' Lynch said to him.

Mercer turned at this. It was clear by then that Riley had no intention of returning to the tower, and so Mercer said to him, 'There's no need to come. Go home and get cleaned up. Thank you for everything, for your help and advice.'

'See,' Lynch said to the man. 'You're not wanted any more. Surplus to requirements. You've got your hands dirty for him and now he's telling you to bugger off. I hope he paid you enough.'

There was no way Mercer could say anything more to the man without Lynch seizing on it to prolong Riley's anxiety at being so suddenly exposed between the two of them.

Seeing this, Lynch shouted to Mercer, 'What – lost for one of your long, clever words?'

Daniels went back to his companion and spoke to him. They shook hands briefly, and then Riley crossed the road back to his home while Daniels and Mercer stood and watched him go, ensuring that Lynch neither said nor did anything as Riley passed by him.

And then, as suddenly and as unexpectedly as they had started, the night's events were over and the others began to walk back to their homes. Some, Mercer hoped, might now regret their own small and passive part in the proceedings. He watched them return indoors, until only Mary and Elizabeth Lynch stood framed by the light of their doorway. He turned away from them and went back to where Daniels waited for him.

They reached the tower and Mercer unlocked the door.

Inside, they cleaned off the mud and the clay as best they could and sat together.

'I know Mathias and Jacob,' Daniels said. 'Mathias, especially. I've never spoken to Jacob, but I used to see him often enough with Mathias before you came and started work here.'

Mercer poured them both whisky.

'Do you think all this – me being here, all this tearing apart – has anything to do with Lynch's behaviour?'

'I try not to pay too much attention to what he thinks or says. Never did.' It was too obvious a lie, and he drained his glass to wash it from his mouth.

'Hard to ignore him, though, I imagine, especially in a place like this.'

'Show me your charts,' Daniels said, unwilling to speculate any further.

Mercer spread the first of these on the table.

'There have been people living here for four hundred years,' Daniels said. His hand lay over the outline of the houses, as though by this means alone he might deny the harsh reality of the months ahead.

'Does he hit Mary, do you think?' Mercer said, making pencil marks where Daniels indicated on the chart.

'Her mother gets the worst of it. I told her once—' He stopped abruptly.

'Told her what?'

'That she ought to be gone before he got back. He tells everybody that he volunteered for active service once he'd been sentenced, but that they wouldn't have him. Truth is, he knew what they'd say before he asked.'

'And once he knew, he went on asking?'

'So nobody could say he hadn't tried. There isn't a man here – or woman or child, come to that – who hasn't suffered in some way, who hasn't lost something or someone they could ill afford to lose, but to hear him talk, you'd think he was the only one.'

'It's perhaps because he wasn't involved that he feels the need to keep bringing the thing up now,' Mercer suggested.

'While the rest of us are just sick of it all and want to move on.' He paused. 'Except we returned to this backwater and moving on was no longer a serious option.' He held out his glass for Mercer to fill it. 'No, I doubt he hits the girl much. Him and her were always tight.'

'So everyone says. But I wonder what that means with a man like him.'

'It means he thinks first of himself, and of others only insofar as they might be of some use to him.'

'She thinks he's going to leave and take her with him.'

Daniels laughed. 'He'd be lost anywhere else.'

'Where men would stand up to him?'

'Where he'd be forced to see himself for what he really is. He was angry tonight because the bad weather fouled up a little run he'd got planned.'

'What was it?'

'We were supposed to meet a boat out in the Middle

314

Channel. We waited, but nothing came except the wind and the rain.'

'Will he go, do you think? Will he walk out on them?'

'I imagine so. One day.'

Their work on the charts finished, Mercer returned these to a drawer. Daniels inspected the room around him. Mercer invited him to stay longer, but he declined.

Before he left, Mercer said, 'Will you thank Riley again for me.'

'I was going to see him anyway. He lives for this place more than any of them. He'd have been out there digging all night if we'd left him.'

'And knowing what you know . . .'

'About what a waste of time and effort it would all have been for him? Don't worry, I won't say anything. Do you ever read poetry, Mr Mercer?'

The question surprised Mercer. 'Sometimes. Rarely. A long time ago.'

'There's a poem by Hardy which tells of a man who loved the only woman he ever truly loved, the only woman he was ever capable of loving, and who, for the rest of the long life he lived after loving and then losing her, referred to himself as a "dead man walking".'

'And you feel the same about yourself?' Mercer said, immediately regretting the crass remark.

'I imagine it's how we all feel on our bad days. Or perhaps it's only how I *hope* we all feel.'

They descended to the ground floor.

'Thanks again,' Mercer said. 'For Lynch, I mean.'

'If I'm honest, I did it more for Riley than for you or myself,' Daniels said.

He left the tower and walked quickly into the enveloping darkness.

37

The following morning the sky was again pale and cloudless, but despite this, there was a sense that the true summer had finally ended, and that the continuing good days now were the better days of the approaching autumn. Mercer did not envy the men who would come there to labour through the worsening weather ahead, and he could only guess at how much more time might soon be lost to the deteriorating conditions.

He rose early, determined to make a start before the arrival of the others.

It was not yet six when he left the tower, and he walked to where he, Daniels and Riley had worked the night before. Water continued to flow unchecked in the channels and the shallow diggings were already mostly empty. No further rain was forecast.

He dragged one of the wheeled pumps into position, but then wasted almost an hour coaxing it into life. The whole of the engine was caked in thick oil and sand and he cursed aloud the man whose job it had been to maintain it and protect it from the weather. It finally started, sucking up the water in loud gulps and splashing it out over the land above.

He started two more of the machines, and when there was nothing more he could achieve alone, he sat by the road and waited. Smoke rose from several of the houses, and a few other early risers came and went. He watched Elizabeth Lynch's door, but saw nothing.

When the shallowest of the depressions was emptied of all but a few inches of water, he dragged the pump to another hole and repeated the process there.

At eight, he left the centre of the site and went to await the arrival of the others.

A few minutes later, he heard the first of the lorries, and then watched from a bank as they came. But instead of the usual dozen vehicles, only three now approached. He searched further back for the others, but a light mist lay over the wet ground, rising in the warming day, and he could not follow the course of the road as far as usual.

The men from the three lorries climbed down and stood in a group beneath him.

'Where are the others?' he asked one of the drivers.

'Ask him,' the driver said, indicating the only foreman to have arrived.

The man came to Mercer waving an envelope. 'Told me to give you this,' he said, shrugging, though it was clear to Mercer that they were all already aware of the reason for this reduction in their numbers.

Mercer took the envelope and tore it open. It contained a brief message from the contractor who had hired the men – his own employer – saying that Trinity House had contacted him to state that, with the bulk of the excavation work completed, the number of men now required at the site was consequently reduced, and that the appropriate action should be taken. Those men who had shown most commitment to the work – the phrase made Mercer laugh – were to be kept on and returned to the site; the remainder were to be paid off or sent elsewhere.

Mercer read all this with growing disbelief. He looked around him at the men who had been sent. They were not the best workers. The contractor had simply filled the first three lorries and held the rest back. There was no course of appeal, or even reply. The Trinity House men must have known all along that this was what they would do.

He read the notice to the men gathered around him. They expressed their dismay at the dismissal of their companions, and at the growing realization that their own time there was now short-lived and un-certain, that they, too, might soon be treated in this same peremptory manner.

'This is as much of a surprise to me as it is to you,' Mercer said, hoping to forestall any further discussion of what had happened. It was clear by their response that few believed him.

The foreman insisted Mercer was right. He told them to forget those who had gone and to be grateful for the fact that they were still employed. Anyone working there until the completion of the work stood a good chance of being taken on by the construction firms waiting to build the new Station, he said. Mercer considered this unlikely – they would have their own workforce – but he saw how some of them grasped at this and he nodded encouragingly at everything the man said.

As the men dispersed, he took the foreman to one side and told him what needed to be done. He pointed to where the pumps were already working. Where he had anticipated almost a hundred men, he now had fewer than thirty. He had prepared plans for them to follow, but he saw how far beyond the reach of such a depleted workforce this work now was. He would return to the tower and make new preparations. Meanwhile, he announced, they could all continue clearing the sites on which he had already started. He showed the foreman which channels to tackle first.

The man returned to the others and started telling them what to do. Mercer left them, hearing their complaints as he passed through them.

In the tower, he took out a blueprint and began making new marks on it.

He finished revising these plans and went back out. He would relay the changes he had made only to the foreman and avoid all direct contact with the others until their own unfocused anger had settled.

It was after he had given the man his instructions, and as he was returning to the tower along the airfield perimeter, that he saw Mary and Elizabeth Lynch standing at a distance from him and looking out over the same expanse of rapidly disappearing concrete. Heavy tractors had already started ploughing the underlying soil, darkening it, and immediately and dramatically changing the appearance of the place.

He turned away from where they stood, but as he did so, Mary called to him. She waved to him and started running over the uneven ground towards him. Elizabeth Lynch followed slowly behind, keeping her distance from her daughter.

'If it's about last night, I don't want to talk about it,' he said.

Mary stood on the lip of a dry and shallow drain, catching her breath.

'You could have said or done something then,' he added, knowing how unfair the remark was. The woman was still some distance away, still coming slowly towards them.

'He's gone into town,' Mary said, her head down, breathing heavily.

'So?'

'You can imagine what happened after you and Daniels had gone. She reckons she pays for just about everything you say to him.'

'Only because she's the only one he's brave enough to take it out on.'

She said something he didn't hear.

'What?'

'I said "And me".' She raised her face to reveal where her lip had been cut, and where a scab of dried blood still stuck to it.

He looked hard at this for several seconds before meeting her eyes. 'I wish I could say I never imagined it would happen,' he said.

'I know. You'll think I'm still making excuses for him, but it was mostly an accident. He was drunk and angry after what happened outside. He went to open a drawer, but it wouldn't come. He pulled harder at it and it broke and came out and caught me on my mouth. It looks worse than it is.' She tested her lip with the tip of her tongue.

'Or perhaps it's every bit as bad as it looks and you *are* still making excuses for him.'

Elizabeth Lynch had come much closer by then and she stood several feet behind her daughter.

'She's already told me it was an accident,' Mercer called to her, hoping his true understanding of the situation was clear to her.

'It was,' Elizabeth Lynch said quietly, her own

320

abjection complete. She, too, bore the marks of the man's anger. As one small bruise faded, so another appeared. 'She told you he's gone into town?'

'Yes.'

'She tell you what for?'

He looked to Mary, and she looked directly back at him, but without speaking.

'Tell him,' Elizabeth Lynch said.

'Someone told him that they were finally kicking Bail out, that the bank had sold his yard. He said that seeing as how there wasn't any work here for him – *you'd* seen to that – then he'd go and have a look there. Stands to reason, he said. It's a big place, and if they're clearing it of all the junk, they're going to need a lot of men.'

At first, Mercer did not believe her, guessing that Lynch had only said this knowing how he, Mercer, would react. Whatever else Lynch was doing, he had not gone in search of work.

'What time did he go?'

'Before we were up.'

He had seen no one, and he had been out since six. Lynch would not have set off so early.

'He was lying to you,' Mercer said.

Mary shrugged. 'He knows it's where Jacob lives,' she said.

'Someone else who won't fight back.'

She did not respond to this.

'Nothing we could do to stop him,' Elizabeth Lynch said. She stood with her hands balled tightly together.

Mercer looked at the pair of them, the woman and the girl, and he saw what a shift had taken place in the balance between them. When her husband went – as he undoubtedly soon would – then Elizabeth Lynch would stumble, stand again and continue to move slowly forward, just as she had done during his absence. But when her daughter finally went – and that, too, Mercer now considered inevitable – then she would reach out to grab her and hold her and try to pull her back, but the girl would be deftly beyond her reach and the woman would finally lose her balance and fall, unable afterwards ever to rise and stand fully upright again. She, too, it seemed to Mercer, watching her closely over the short distance which separated them, fully understood all that was now going to happen to her. She would be left with her small son, and that would be all. She would be homeless, her past and her future would be gone, and all that would remain would be the boy.

'What did he say last night?' Mercer said to Mary.

'Nothing. He was too busy, remember?' She tilted her cut mouth at him.

'Do you blame *me* for that?'

She shook her head.

He knew that nothing would be achieved by following the man to Bail's Yard. He knew that this was what Lynch wanted. If Bail was finally being evicted, then there would be enough confrontation and confusion in the place for Lynch's presence there to be of no consequence. He knew Bail would take care of Jacob, or that Jacob would be sufficiently forewarned of what was about to happen to avoid Lynch completely.

On the airfield, a siren sounded. The noise startled Elizabeth Lynch, and she turned to look.

'Will you go to Jacob?' Mary said to him.

'Why should I?'

'To make sure he's safe.'

'Safe from what? Safe from the beating your father thinks he deserves simply because he's a Jew?'

'You know what I mean.'

'That's exactly what he wants me to do – run after him. Besides, he was probably lying about Bail's Yard. The bank won't be foreclosing on him so soon.'

'Bail's known it was coming for the past year,' she said. 'Everybody knows about it. It was only ever Bail who closed his eyes to it all. Most people in the town can't wait to get rid of the eyesore. If the beet factory comes, there should be lots of new jobs.'

'Even one for you, perhaps?' he said, knowing even as he said it that it was the cruellest thing he could have said to her.

'I told her to go and ask,' Elizabeth Lynch shouted.

Mary looked hard at Mercer and then turned and walked away from him.

He called for her to wait. He stepped across the drain and went to where she stood with her back to him.

'There's no point me going after him,' he said, his voice lower.

'I know – you said.'

'Even *you* can't truly believe he'll do anything to Jacob.'

'He said the Jew-boy was probably putting ideas into Bail's head, telling him that he could keep the new owners out, stuff about his rights.'

'And as far as everyone else is concerned, the sooner Bail goes, the better?'

'He said that all Bail needed now was someone to help him on his way.'

'I have to get back,' Elizabeth Lynch called to them. 'Peter.' She wanted her daughter to go with her, but Mary gave no indication of complying. The woman waited several minutes and then turned and walked away alone.

'She wanted you to go with her,' Mercer said.

323

'I know. You don't even believe he's gone, do you?'

'Not much I can do about it either way.'

She looked over the site. 'Where are the rest of them?'

'Finished. Gone for good.'

They now stood closer to the airfield perimeter, and over her shoulder he saw the distant figures gathering in groups to eat and rest. Individuals wandered away from the others and stood alone.

She studied him for a moment. 'He picked up Jacob's glass bowl and threatened to smash it,' she said. 'But she told him that if he did then he'd never see her or his children again. He laughed at her and pretended to throw the bowl into the fire. She told him she was serious.'

'And was she?'

She nodded. 'All the time it was in his hand she never took her eyes off it. He told her it was worthless rubbish. He told her that if she wanted to keep it, then he didn't want it anywhere he could see it. He told her the little bubbles in it were probably full of the Jew's breath.'

'What did he do?'

'Just kept it held above his head. He'll wait until you expect him to do one thing, and then do the opposite just to spite you. She said his name.'

'Jacob's?'

'Jacob Haas. She just said it.'

He turned to look in the direction the woman had gone, but she was no longer in sight.

'She said he was an artist and that the bowl was probably the most valuable thing in the house. He laughed at her and said that if that's what she thought, then she ought to take better care of it. He jerked his arm as though he was going to throw it to her, but she didn't move an inch. She just stood there and went on looking at the bowl.'

'What happened?'

'Finally, he just put it back down where it had always been.'

'Beside the photograph.'

'Yes. I expected her to pick it up and take it away or something, but she didn't. She just left it where it was and went on doing whatever it was she'd been doing before he picked it up. He's smashed a thousand things in the past.'

'She knows what Jacob's work means to him,' he said.

'She said he'd seen things the rest of us couldn't even begin to imagine. She said she couldn't even imagine what *one* million men and women looked like. She said they killed children, even babies.'

'Everyone,' Mercer said.

She looked all around them. 'Will it happen again?'

He wanted to deny this. 'Probably,' he said. 'But not here. Somewhere else.'

'It's men, isn't it,' she said.

She came to him and slid her arm through his and they walked to the dunes, where they stood together and looked out over the sea. A distant freighter left its smoky course in the sky and the terns still rose and fell in the calm shallows.

'Will you tell him?' she said. 'Jacob.'

'About what happened, what your mother said about him?'

She nodded.

'I doubt it. It might be too much for him to bear, to know that she understands him so well.'

'It still doesn't make any sense,' she said, and he felt her hand tighten around his arm.

38

Later, he saw Mathias and told him what had happened. He expected him to express some concern about Jacob, but he did not, dismissing Lynch's threats as merely that. He told Mercer that Bail would take care of Jacob, or, failing that, that Jacob would have to look out for himself. Just as Mary's remark had surprised him earlier, so the harshness of this dismissal surprised him now, and he did not pursue the matter other than to ask Mathias when he had last seen Jacob. It was clear to him that Mathias remained preoccupied with his own rejected appeal and the possibility of his imminent repatriation.

Mathias had come to him from the airfield. There were now even fewer restraints placed upon him, he said, and he and the others were allowed – within reason and the demands of their work – to come and go between the airfield and the town as they chose. They were expected to report for work each day, and were still counted upon their arrival, but that was all. He repeated the words 'within reason' as though they were at once both unintelligible and hilarious.

Mercer imagined that there was someone somewhere keeping a watch on the prisoners, but neither Mathias nor the others were aware of anyone. They were all still waiting, Mathias said, and he wondered if this new degree of freedom was not some kind of test.

'To see who runs?' Mercer said.

'Perhaps.' He was unwilling to say more.

Then Mathias confessed that he had seen Jacob earlier that same day. It was true that Bail was finally being evicted, he said, and that the new owners of the yard were eager to clear it and begin their own building there.

They sat on the concrete platform of the new Station. Rusted mesh rose all around them.

From the moment of his arrival, Mercer had sensed that there was something else Mathias was avoiding telling him. He asked him where he thought Jacob might now go.

'The same place we all go,' Mathias said. 'You, him, me, Bail, Lynch – nowhere.'

'You're—' Mercer began.

'I'm what,' Mathias said sharply. 'I'm overreacting? Is that what you want to say? I should just accept the inevitable, however unacceptable it might be?' He shook his head and then rubbed his face. He had been working, and dirt and cement dust still coated his back and arms. He ran a hand through his hair and the dust rose there, too.

'Have you heard anything specific?' Mercer asked him.

Mathias shook his head. 'Three days ago, Roland absconded.'

'Absconded?'

'He couldn't bear the thought of not going home for at least another six months and so he took matters into his own hands.'

'Where will he have gone?'

'He caught a train to London. He was found in the docks there asking about ships leaving soon for the continent. Someone reported him to the Authorities and he was arrested. He believed he had bought himself a berth on a ship to Bremerhaven. He was sitting in a dockside bar, drunk, toasting his good fortune while he waited, and no doubt showing everyone photographs of his children and grandchildren.'

'And speaking in German.'

Mathias laughed. 'What else?'

'Has he been brought back here?'

'Last night. He wept all night. I sat with him and found out everything that had happened. So, you see, we must all live with the dramas and tragedies of our small and pathetic endings. What did we imagine would happen – that the war would end and that the world would tilt back on to its proper axis and slow down sufficiently after all those years for us all to bury our dead, build again our homes and resume our old lives?'

'What will happen to him now?' Mercer said.

Mathias shrugged. 'Contrary to all his own gloomy predictions, not much, I imagine. Who knows, he might even have made himself even *less* desirable by his escape attempt; perhaps they'll send him home sooner rather than later just to be rid of him. One of the Military Policemen who brought him back to us said he was lucky not to be put into prison for what he'd done. It was probably an empty threat, but it made us think. There were a dozen others among us who might have tried the same.'

'But not now?'

Mathias shook his head. 'No, not now.'

Mercer studied the foundations around them.

'Are you happy with the work?' Mathias asked him.

'I would have appreciated more time. Everything's done that needs to be done. How about the airfield?'

'Someone is coming soon for the remains of the aircraft.' Mathias shielded his eyes to look to where the last of the silver fuselages lay piled in the distance.

'Will you go to see if Jacob is still there?' Mercer said.

'Of course. But don't imagine that he himself is not fully aware of what is now about to happen. In all likelihood, he will have a far better grasp of the situation than Bail himself.'

'You think he's known all along that it would come to this?'

'I think he will have known everything. I imagine all this is just another well-planned part of his strategy of withdrawal.'

The remark surprised Mercer and he asked Mathias what he meant by it.

'Don't you see it?' Mathias said. 'Did you think he was going to live like this for ever, in a cold and comfortless room above a warehouse in a scrap-yard, pretending that his pathetic pieces of glass and the forge in which they were made was all he needed, all that fed and sustained him? You and I, I imagine, at least *we* see the dim light of the future glowing distantly ahead of us. All Jacob sees is that same dim light being slowly extinguished behind him. And when it is finally out—' He clapped his hands together.

'What?' Mercer said, already knowing what Mathias would say.

'Then the darkness around him will be complete and he will be invisible at its centre.'

'But someone will know him, who he is, what he does, what he has endured.'

'Who? You? Me? Bail? Who?'

'There must be organizations that—'

Mathias smiled. 'This new world is full of those organizations. It was an organization that took him away from the camp, another organization that brought him here; it was an organization that told him how many of his family had perished, another organization that pretended to know where the remains of his sister were buried, yet another that pretended to him that there was some individual humanity and understanding in the cold, stark details of her death. Everywhere you look, there is an organization. With Bail, at least, living that same isolated and scavenging life, Jacob was briefly beyond the reach of all those organizations.'

'And now he is once again exposed?'

'To their pity, their sympathy, their false hope, yes. All these confused and fading trails all over the Earth. Look around you, here, the airfield, the Levels, the town, everywhere you look. Like ghosts wandering through some half-known world. What difference is there between Jacob and Roland when neither of them has what lies ahead of him within his grasp – one man because he sees nothing ahead of him through that growing darkness, and the other because he sees it all too clearly, and sees, too, how rapidly it recedes ahead of his own exhausted stumbling?'

Mercer understood that he was talking about himself. He considered what he might now say to console the man, but nothing came.

It's men, Mary had said, but he knew it was everyone.

'How will you get back to town?' Mercer asked him.

'Walk.'

'You're welcome to stay.'

'Roland will be expecting me. I am his only ally. The others think he has ruined things for the rest of us and many of them have turned against him.'

'Do you think some of them were about to do what he did?' He was asking the question directly of Mathias, and Mathias understood this.

'Perhaps. Almost certainly. But only in the belief they were doing nothing wrong, thinking only that it was their right so long after the war's end. Why should anyone care any longer? We were each of us beaten men on the day we stuck up our hands. What threat are we now to anyone?'

There was no honest or straightforward answer to any of these questions, and anything Mercer said would have been an evasion.

'I ought to go,' Mathias said finally, and he rose from beside Mercer and held out his hand. 'It has been a great pleasure knowing you,' he said, and Mercer knew then that he intended this as their final parting, that, despite his denials, he possessed a plan for his own disappearance.

There was nothing Mercer could say. He watched as Mathias walked back towards the airfield. It would be dark in an hour, more than enough darkness for them all.

He watched him cross to the bed of broken concrete, then leave this to follow the line of the recently ploughed land.

Mercer rose and walked the perimeter of the raised foundations, and it was as he completed this circuit that he heard someone calling to him, and he looked to where the distant Mathias, now alongside the few remaining buildings, was shouting and waving to him with both hands.

A second figure now stood beside him, and Mercer's first impression was that this was either Roland, who had waited behind for Mathias upon the departure of the others, or that it was Lynch, returning from the town. Whoever it was, Mathias was still calling for him, and Mercer started running towards him.

Only as he reached the end of the runway did he pause to look again. It now appeared to him that the two men were fighting, locked together in a single figure, and he resumed his running.

He was slowed by the freshly ploughed earth, and so he returned to the edge of the broken runway to make better progress, feeling the slabs rock and shift beneath him, leaping from one to another and hearing them slide away behind him. It was only then, as he crossed this final distance to the buildings, that he saw that it was neither Roland nor Lynch with Mathias, but Jacob, and that, rather than fighting, Mathias was struggling to hold him upright.

Leaving the planes, Mercer finally joined them.

It was immediately clear to him that Jacob was barely conscious and that he possessed no strength. He took one of the man's arms over his own shoulders and helped Mathias drag him to a balk of timber, where they were able to lower him into a sitting position with his back propped against a standing post.

'Hold him,' Mathias told Mercer. He ran into a nearby building and emerged with a can of water, which he held to Jacob's lips and poured. Jacob swallowed little of what he was given, and most of the water ran over his chin and his chest, leaving a spreading stain. He could not sit unsupported and his head continually fell forward. Mathias fetched more water, but again Jacob was able to swallow only a little of it.

Mercer took out his handkerchief, soaked it and wiped Jacob's brow. Whatever it was he was suffering from had clearly worsened since he had last seen him several days earlier.

'What's he doing here, so far, in this condition?' he said to Mathias.

'He said Bail was raging at the men picking over his yard. He carried that.' He motioned to the sack of his belongings that Jacob had brought with him to the airfield. It was inconceivable to both of them that he had come so far in such a weakened condition.

'Was he looking for you?' Mercer asked. Coming across the open countryside, the airfield lay between Bail's and the tower.

'If that's what you prefer to believe,' Mathias said.

Beside them, Jacob gave a choking cough and slumped forward. They held him upright. Mathias rubbed his back as he went on coughing. Saliva fell in thick strings from Jacob's mouth, and Mercer wiped this away.

'I think Lynch was there, too,' Mathias said, his voice low. 'He said "Lynch", that's all.'

'And so he ran,' Mercer said.

'I imagine he was more or less ready to leave, not to witness or to add to Bail's final humiliation.'

'Lynch's arrival can't have helped the situation,' Mercer said.

'*If* he was there. You can't blame the man for everything.'

Jacob's coughing subsided and he mumbled something neither of them properly heard. He indicated the can, and this time when Mathias held it to his lips, he was able to drink from it. After that, his exhaustion was complete, and he fell back between them, his eyes closed, his breathing short and laboured.

'We can carry him to the tower,' Mercer suggested.

'Or I could make him a bed here,' Mathias said, indicating the brick shell close by. 'I'll stay with him.'

Mercer looked at the building. Most of its roof was missing and its floor was overgrown with nettles. He insisted they carry Jacob to the tower.

They waited several minutes longer and then explained to Jacob what they were about to attempt. He made no response to this, convincing Mercer further that he needed to be taken indoors and to a proper bed.

They lifted the barely conscious man and worked out how best to carry him.

Mathias retrieved the sack, and they started to walk.

They avoided both the ploughed earth and the broken runway, and went instead along the rim of a bank which curved away from the tower before turning back towards it alongside the road.

It was by then almost dark. The sun had gone, but the horizon was still brightened by it.

It took them an hour to walk along the bank and come close to the tower. They rested every few minutes and spoke reassuringly to Jacob. Sweat continued to form over his face. Both men felt the bones in his arms and in the fingers of the hands they held.

Mercer told Mathias to cross the open ground close to the dunes and to come to the tower out of sight of the houses, where, despite the darkness, someone might see them and come to investigate. In all likelihood, he said, Lynch would already have returned, and would now be anxious to make his presence felt, angry that Jacob had earlier eluded him. Mathias considered this unlikely, but said nothing.

They finally arrived close to the tower and Mercer went ahead alone and unlocked the door. Only when he was certain they were not being watched did he return to help carry Jacob over the remaining short distance.

Once inside, and with the door bolted behind them, both men rested. Jacob sat where they had lowered him. He remained barely conscious, less aware than ever of what was happening to him, or where he now was. He continued to mumble, increasingly agitated by whatever he was saying or by the lack of response to his words, and still they could understand little of what he said.

It would have been impossible to manhandle Jacob up the stairs into the room above without causing him even more pain, and so Mercer brought down his thin mattress and several blankets and they made a bed for him on the floor where he sat. Mathias took off his shoes, beneath which his feet were bare and dirty and bruised.

Waiting beside Jacob until he was asleep, and his breathing more regular, Mercer and Mathias then went upstairs and sat at the table. Still unwilling to attract attention to their presence, Mercer lit no lanterns and they sat together in the darkness.

'I can do this alone if you need to go,' Mercer said. He stood a bottle and glasses on the table.

Mathias acknowledged the opportunity he was being offered, and shook his head.

'First thing in the morning, I'll get a doctor,' Mercer said.

Mathias looked at his watch.

An hour later, when the darkness was complete, and during which time Jacob had remained asleep and his breathing grown calmer, Mathias insisted on taking one of the chairs into the room below and sleeping beside him. 'I'll keep watch over him,' he said.

Mercer offered to share the responsibility, but Mathias refused, promising to wake him if anything happened.

39

Mercer woke with a start several hours later, taking a moment to remember what had happened during the previous day and night. It was three in the morning and the moon cast its cold glow all around him.

Something had woken him, and as he lay in the silence the sound of someone crying rose up to him from below.

He went down to the lower room.

Mathias was on his knees beside the makeshift bed with Jacob's head resting on his thigh, one hand pressed to Jacob's cheek and the other stroking the hair from his brow. He looked up at Mercer's appearance and put a finger to his lips.

Mercer went closer and crouched beside him.

'He started crying in his sleep,' Mathias whispered.

Here, too, the room was illuminated only by the light of the moon.

'What can I do?' Mercer said.

Mathias indicated where the blankets had fallen

from Jacob's legs, and Mercer retrieved these and laid them over him.

Jacob, meanwhile, continued to sob; his breathing slowed and then erupted without rhythm.

'Is he dreaming, do you think?' Mercer asked Mathias.

'I think this happens most nights. I stayed at Bail's once, and the same thing happened then. Bail told me he had seen Jacob wide awake and wandering among his piles of scrap at all hours of the night. I was afraid he might choke.' He spoke without taking his eyes from Jacob's face, his fingers now caressing the side of Jacob's mouth and chin.

'He ought to be in hospital,' Mercer said.

'You can tell him that a thousand times, but it won't put him there. He's beyond all that. And it's beyond us to intervene. The simple and unavoidable fact is, he has taken his life back into his own hands and he will never again relinquish a single moment of it.' He held up his hand for Mercer to see the dark hairs which lay threaded between his fingers.

A louder gasp than usual silenced them both and they sat without speaking until the convulsion subsided and Jacob lay still again.

Eventually, Mathias lowered Jacob's head back to his pillow, turning it so that he might rest on something dry. He picked the last of the hairs from his fingers and threw them down. He rose slowly, rubbed his legs to free them of cramp, and then he and Mercer went to the far side of the room, where they sat beside the window and smoked.

'He told me once that he'd saved a lock of Anna's hair,' Mathias said. 'He even showed it to me. He wouldn't let it out of his grasp. He said it was his most precious possession. More precious even than his glass. A month later, he said he'd burned it in his kiln. I thought at first that this was something symbolic for him – that the burning hair might pattern or colour or become in some way imprinted on a piece of his glass – but he only laughed when I suggested this to him and told me it was none of those things. Then he confessed to me that it had not been Anna's hair he had saved, merely some he had cut from another corpse which in some way resembled Anna – I imagine there were plenty to choose from – and which bore the same colour hair. He'd tried to convince himself that it was her hair, but then, all those months later, he saw what a hopeless and undermining lie he was trying to sustain. He said he was a cripple walking with the aid of rotten, crumbling sticks.'

'He wasn't with her when she died,' Mercer said.

Mathias shook his head. 'She had died in the infirmary several days before he learned of the fact. A woman who swilled the floors there told him she had seen Anna's corpse being removed along with all the others at the end of the previous day. He'd sought the woman out to ask her how well Anna was responding to her treatment and whatever medication she might have been receiving, and the woman had insisted on being paid before telling him what she had seen. He told me that at first he thought she was lying to him, that it was a cruel scheme of hers to get more from him. Apparently, she told him to please himself what he believed; she had plenty more anxious relatives to sell her information to.'

'He believes they killed her,' Mercer said.

'Of course they killed her. That was the whole point.' Mathias had started to shout, but quickly lowered his voice. 'What else do you think was meant to happen? It might have been called an infirmary, but that was all. What mattered more to him, what destroyed every vestige of his belief in himself, what brought him here, to this place, and what has kept him here crying in his sleep every night, is the simple and undeniable understanding that, once beyond his own desperate need to protect her and keep her alive, she herself – his blessed Anna – simply lost the will to live. She had suffered for too long. They were by then the two halves of the same small and blighted world; nothing else existed for either of them. I wonder if you or I can have even the slightest notion of how much he lost when she died.' Mathias paused. 'I'm sorry,' he said. 'You understand all of this as well as I do. I've known him longer, that's all, and, God knows, it took me long enough to work it all out for myself.'

Mercer put his hand on Mathias's shoulder and Mathias nodded. He was close to tears, and this simple gesture drew him back from them.

'In the final March of the war,' Mercer said, 'I was seconded to the US Sixth Armored Division. It's a long story. We drove in half-tracks along an autobahn near a place called Giessen on our way to Berlin.'

'Giessen,' Mathias said. 'I know it.'

'The road was steeply banked, and all along the grass verges, both sides of the road, sat thousands and thousands of surrendered German officers. We knew they were officers by their caps and by the shine of their boots. Thousands of them, all just sitting there in the sun and watching us race past them. You could almost feel the hatred and the contempt being poured down those banks towards us. The Forty-fifth Division had arrived at Dachau only three days earlier, and everybody in that unstoppable convoy at Giessen knew what they'd found there. None of us had seen it, but everybody knew. Nothing stopped in those days. Move, move,

340

move. Your armies were in disarray. We were through and beyond what remained of them even while they were planning their defence strategies. Nothing stopped, nothing stood still to take account of anything. Every mile east was another mile of territory conquered, another minute or an hour or a day closer to the end.'

'Some of those men on those banks will never stop hating you,' Mathias said.

'I think we understood that even then. I never forgot that day. I don't fully understand why, but something about it – its unnatural calm, perhaps; seeing all those men; knowing what I knew – something of it will stay with me for ever.'

'A kind of epiphany,' Mathias said.

'I wouldn't make so grand a claim for it,' Mercer said, but knowing he was close to the truth.

'Only because you have your useless English notions of reserve and decorum to maintain.'

Mercer acknowledged this.

They sat without speaking for several minutes. At the far side of the room, Jacob appeared to have grown calmer. His breathing remained shallow and erratic, but he no longer sobbed. The smoke from their cigarettes settled around them in the night air. Outside, a low mist once again covered the ground.

'I have something similar to tell,' Mathias said. 'Something that I, too, will never forget, and which helped everything make sense to me. Or if not sense, then which at least helped me to understand men and the things of which they are capable. I know that this, too, sounds like a grand notion, but it is something I have never forgotten. I imagine there are others – Roland for instance – who would tell you the same tale.' He paused, as though suddenly uncertain of his ability to say what he was now committed to saying.

'Go on,' Mercer urged him.

'There is a chapel here in the town. A Methodist chapel, at the end of the High Street.'

Mercer closed his eyes and saw the building. 'I know it,' he said.

'In the closing weeks of the war – when you were racing along the autobahns – a much closer guard than usual was kept on us. We were confined to our camp. Even those of us who were already working on farms and in factories were told that we must remain in our huts. You can imagine how deprived we felt. We had all met some good people here, made what we considered to be good friends. We know these people still. We were told by the Camp Administration that the fighting was now taking place in our home towns, that our families and friends in Germany were now in jeopardy – you can imagine how I allowed myself to smile at this after all those years of bombing – and they told us that we were being kept more closely confined because of all those men who might not be able to control or contain their anxiety or anger, and who might do something stupid at whatever bad news they might now receive. They were never any more specific than this, but what could we expect – we were still prisoners.'

'And did anything happen?'

'No. Not like they imagined. And, besides, the war was soon over and all our uncertainty was at an end. The men who were alive then were men who were now going to live into old age. The Authorities were not unsympathetic to those men who lost loved ones. We had our own padres; the Red Cross still visited us; letters were still sent and, occasionally, received.'

'And the chapel?'

'Immediately peace was declared, it was the first of

our privileges to be returned to us. Each Sunday morning, those men who wished to worship – whatever their denomination – were escorted to the chapel. It was where most of our friends worshipped. We knew the ministers, the organists; we knew the men and women who handed out the Bibles and the hymn books, who arranged the flowers, who showed us where to sit, who took us on their outings with them, who had invited us into their homes for Sunday afternoon tea, who had allowed us to play with their children.' He paused. 'You cannot imagine what such trust meant to us, especially to the men with families of their own, and to be deprived of all that, even for those few weeks, was a great loss to us all.'

'It must have been a relief for you to be allowed to return to the chapel and worship again,' Mercer said.

'Yes. We were not allowed to sit among these others, of course – that would have been too great a liberty – but we were given pews at the rear of the building and we shared their prayers and their hymns, and we listened to the kind words of the ministers, who spoke directly to us, whatever our guards told them was or was not permissible. And at the end of each service we were made to stand and wait behind until everyone else had gone. Such glances and smiles we received from most of those people moving slowly past us on their way out. I never saw people move so slowly. Some of the men beside me, especially those who *had* lost someone close to them in those final weeks, stood and wept at the kindness they received in those silent glances. Our guards were ignored and some of the departing men and women spoke briefly to us and pressed their hands into ours.

'And then, after everyone else had gone, the minister would tell the old woman who played the organ to play a hymn while we ourselves filed out of the building. The hymn they always played for us was the one that began "Glorious things of thee are spoken". Do you know it?'

Mercer thought for a moment and then began to hum the tune.

'It is also our national anthem,' Mathias said. 'See?' He, too, hummed the first line of the hymn. 'The minister and the organist sang at the tops of their voices to disguise what they were truly doing. Few of us understood what they sang, but that was not the point. For those few minutes while we stood and waited, and then as we left the chapel, we were being treated as men again, as men with families and with an identity; we were no longer merely prisoners, no longer punished because of what we had done or what we had once been. We were being shown a kindness, a common humanity, in which we could scarcely allow ourselves to believe, and which was far more than we could ever hope to bear in those days. I knew with that hymn, with the old man and the old woman singing it, I knew then that some of us, at least, might be forgiven for all that had been done in our name. You felt that unspoken hatred at Giessen, and I felt its equally unspoken opposite in that chapel.' His voice cracked then, and he motioned to Jacob. 'Where do you imagine *his* redemption lies?'

Mercer looked for several minutes at the sleeping man.

'Is that what you believe it to be – redemption?'

'Of sorts. Perhaps. I don't know.' He rose to look through the window. He remarked on the mist and the features and boundaries it now obscured. 'My father once told me never to confuse my dreams with my longings,' he said, sitting back beside Mercer. 'The best

344

most people can expect of a dream is that it comes true, he said, and he did not yet know of any dream-come-true which had not failed in some way to disappoint the dreamer.'

'But, surely, he himself must have dreamed of creating a perfect or unique rose,' Mercer said.

'I daresay, but it did not stop him grafting and grafting and grafting those tens of thousands of failures and then afterwards destroying them because they all fell short of that dream.'

Mercer indicated Jacob. 'Would they have lived together, do you think, if she'd survived?'

'She would have been mother, sister, wife and daughter to him. Or that's what he would have made her. And that would have been their tragedy. Perhaps she would have been stronger than him, perhaps she would not have shown him sufficient gratitude, perhaps she would have resented his obsessive care of her; perhaps she would never have accepted what he now believed she owed him, what he would have demanded in repayment from her every remaining day of their lives together.'

'A pity, then, that neither of us ever knew her,' Mercer said.

'We know *him*,' Mathias said. 'It's enough. Go back up. I'll make myself comfortable down here. I doubt he'll need watching any longer.'

40

The following morning, Mercer was woken by Mathias, who shook him and told him that the lorries were approaching along the coast road. Mercer remained clothed, and at Mathias's urging he went below to Jacob. The previous night, it had occurred to Mercer that Jacob might easily die in his delirium, and he was surprised and relieved now to see him awake and watching closely as the two men went back down to him. Jacob propped himself on his elbows to listen to what they had to say to him, and Mercer wondered if he hadn't been more aware of the night's events than either he or Mathias had imagined. He remembered all they had said in the sleeping man's presence.

Mathias explained to Jacob that the workers were coming and that it was necessary for him to climb to the room above, where he might continue to remain hidden from them and from anyone else who came to the tower.

'He's right,' Mercer said simply when Mathias had

finished talking, and as Jacob looked to him for his opinion.

It was clear to them both that Jacob was still too weak to climb the open wooden stairs unaided, and so between them they devised a way of half-carrying, half-dragging him to the steps and then of hoisting him up these. It was a painful process for the sick man, but other than his insuppressible groans of pain at each knock and jolt, he made no objection to this man-handling. Mathias did most of the carrying, and then he pulled Jacob up through the trapdoor while Mercer climbed beneath him, his shoulders providing the platform upon which Jacob rested as Mathias hauled him from above.

When this operation was completed, and Jacob lay on the boards panting and coughing, Mercer returned below to carry up the mattress and all other signs that the two men had slept there.

Mathias laid the mattress against the wall opposite the windows and lowered Jacob onto it. When he was settled, and again covered by the blankets, Mercer took Mathias to one side.

'I have to go out, but I'll come back as often as possible,' he said.

'Then I'll stay,' Mathias told him. 'Go to the airfield perimeter and then to the bunker we occupied. Tell one of the others where I am. Tell them I'm ill. Don't mention Jacob. They may not believe you, but it hardly matters, not now. Tell Roland, if you see him; he'll think of something to say.'

The noise of the lorries rose up to them. Mercer went to the window and signalled for the disembarking men to start work.

'You'll have to keep out of sight,' he warned Mathias. The discontented workers, now so close to their own departure, would need only the slightest excuse to disrupt their labour, and the discovery of either the German or the Jew in the tower would be considerably more than that. And whatever the workers discovered, the locals would quickly learn.

'I know,' Mathias said.

'What will you do if he gets worse?' He indicated Jacob, who lay on his side, watching them, and listening intently to everything they said.

'Don't worry, I'll do what I can. I doubt he expects us to cure or save him.' He said these last words loudly and, on his bed, Jacob grinned at them.

Someone tried the door below and then knocked.

'Go to them,' Mathias told Mercer.

Mercer went first back to Jacob, crouched beside him and told him he would return as soon as possible. He would do everything in his power, he said, to get Jacob the care and treatment he needed. Jacob closed his eyes and nodded.

Once outside, Mercer drew the men away from the tower by spreading a chart over a stack of crates and explaining to them what work now needed to be done. Someone commented on his dishevelled appearance and he told them he'd been working late. They laughed disparagingly at this and he said nothing more. There was now a feeling among them that their work there was finished, and this release, this slackening of procedure and routine was only too obvious to Mercer in everything they said and did. He thanked them for their work and commitment over the previous weeks and they stood around him in silent, suspicious assessment for several minutes before finally dispersing.

Alone, he crossed to the airfield, and went to where

the work was starting. He asked the first man he encountered if he knew where Roland was. The man searched around him and then pointed to where a solitary figure stood by the road and looked out over the sea.

Mercer went to him. He knew that Roland spoke little English.

At his approach, Roland looked up, started to swing the pickaxe he held, then recognized Mercer and stopped.

'Mathias hat mir erzählt, was passiert ist,' Mercer said. 'Es tut mir leid.'

Roland nodded, and said, 'Danke.'

It was obvious to Mercer that the man would try again to return home before his release, that there was a desperation and an urgency within him that now governed his every thought. Mercer tried as best he could to explain why Mathias was not coming.

Roland looked up at the word *krank*.

'Wie ich?' he said, tapping his temple.

'Nein,' Mercer said. He mimed coughing and wiped his brow.

Roland said he understood and promised no one would notice Mathias's absence.

As Mercer turned to go, the German grabbed his arm and said, 'Sag ihm, dass ich ihn sehen werde, wenn wir beide wieder zuhause sind. Sag ihm, dass er immer noch bei uns zum essen eingeladen ist. Sag ihm einfach irgendwie, dass ich bei ihm sein werde.'

Mercer understood only half of what he was being told. Something about Mathias and Roland at home together in Germany and sharing a meal. He nodded and said, 'Natürlich,' and Roland released his arm and turned away from him. Mercer saw how unappealing this promise would appear to Mathias, and he knew by the way Roland avoided his eyes as he spoke that he understood this too.

'Ich hoffe, es wird alles klappen für dich,' Mercer said. 'Viel Glück.'

'Ja,' Roland said. 'Good luck.'

Mercer left him and returned to the site.

After the rain, the sun was again bright and full, and its reflection on the sea and the last of the lying water dazzled him. He moved among the men and their machinery, but spoke to no one. Convinced that none of them suspected anything, he returned to the tower.

Someone had started a fire outside the houses, and he paused to look at this. He saw Daniels emerge from his home carrying two chairs, which he threw on to the blaze before returning indoors, reappearing a moment later with a small chest, which he struggled to push through the narrow doorway. This, too, he threw to the flames.

As Mercer was about to leave, Lynch, Mary and her mother emerged from their own home and went to Daniels's open door. Lynch went inside, calling for Daniels. The two men came out, Daniels carrying a roll of carpet. Lynch walked close beside him, shouting at him, and punching Daniels on his arm. Daniels seemed oblivious to the blows, concentrating instead on feeding the fire, which was by then blazing fiercely with all this new fuel. Others emerged to watch, attracted by Lynch's shouting.

It unsettled Mercer to see Daniels burning his furniture like this, but he resisted crossing the road to find out what was happening. Mary saw him watching and stood looking back at him rather than at the small and violent drama close by. Once again, Lynch followed Daniels into his home, but this time came out alone. He returned to his wife and daughter and pushed them both ahead of him towards their own door. He stopped when he finally saw Mercer, looked from him to his wife, and then struck the woman so violently on her back that she almost fell.

Behind him, Daniels struggled out with four heavy drawers, dropping one and then kicking it ahead of him to the blaze. It was not a solidly built fire and its large, unstable pieces fell in flames around its core until it was several fires in one. No one else who stood and watched attempted to approach or to help the man, and it seemed to Mercer, who understood better than most what Daniels was now attempting, that to these others there was something fearful in the violence and the finality of his actions, in this unmistakable act of severance, and although they might again be content to stand and watch, they were careful now to keep their distance from him, afraid that his madness might be contagious and that they too might soon suffer from its touch.

As Mercer watched all this, he saw Lynch draw Mary to him and stand close behind her, his arm firmly across her chest, his hand clasping her shoulder. He leaned forward and kissed the top of her head, his eyes still fixed on Mercer.

Mercer wanted the girl to struggle free of him and stand apart, but she did nothing to resist him. Lynch pressed his face to the side of hers and she tilted her head to avoid his mouth – though whether to accommodate or to avoid him, Mercer could not be certain. Lynch said something to her and Mary raised her arm and waved at Mercer, who, guessing what the man had said to her, turned his back on them and walked away. Even at that distance, he could hear Lynch's forced laughter above the noise of the flames.

In the tower, Mathias waited for him behind the door.

'I saw what was happening,' he said. 'I can watch from down here without being seen.'

Mercer motioned above them. 'How's Jacob?'

'Sleeping better. His breathing remains difficult and he still sweats heavily, but I sense some degree of stability. Perhaps he is recovering from his journey.'

It was something in which neither man could truly believe.

'His limbs shake all the time,' Mathias said. 'Even beneath the blankets.'

Mercer told him he intended going into town – he would find an excuse to be driven – to gather together whatever medicines he was able to buy. He would also visit Bail, find out what had happened at the yard, and let Bail know that Jacob was safe. He still did not know for certain if Lynch had been there, or even if Bail had finally been evicted from his home and his livelihood.

'I saw Roland,' he said. 'He told me to tell you that he'd see you again once you were both safely home.'

'He creates fantasies within fantasies,' Mathias said.

They were interrupted by a sound above them, and went up to find that Jacob, having attempted to push himself up from his pillow, had slipped from the mattress and hit his head on the boards. He had cut himself beneath his eye, and Mercer attended to this as Mathias helped him back into bed. He looked no different to Mercer from when he had left them three hours earlier.

Later, approaching noon, Mercer sought out one of the drivers and told him to take him into town.

41

He visited both the town's chemists. A 'summer cold' was all he told them, feigning casual uncertainty and disbelief, and adding that he thought several of the other workers were also suffering. He did not delude himself that the few unprescribed remedies he was able to buy would reach the cause of Jacob's suffering, but they might at least alleviate his fever and the worst of his physical aches. And even if they only allowed him longer spells of unbroken sleep, he reasoned, then some good might come of them. He convinced himself of all this while he lied to the chemists, rubbing his sore throat and wiping imaginary sweat from his brow.

Arriving at Bail's, he was dismayed to find the gates padlocked and a large sign already in place warning trespassers to keep out. The notice had been posted by the new owners. The building in which Jacob had lodged, and in which Bail had maintained his forge, had already been half-demolished, and the exposed shell now stood derelict and open. He looked to the edge of the yard and saw that the house in which Bail had lived was also being torn down. A bulldozer pushed flat what remained of the walls, and diggers scooped the rubble into the backs of waiting lorries. He had grown accustomed to change over the previous months, but it shocked him to see how quickly and completely it had taken place here.

He walked towards the house and saw Bail standing by the drain at some distance beyond the flattened building. He called to him, but Bail gave no indication of having heard him, and so Mercer went to him, careful to avoid attracting the attention of the men undertaking the demolition work.

Bail stood with his back to him and stared into the water of the drain where Mercer had seen the swan. The surface of the channel was coated with a grey scum which clotted in curves in the stagnant water. A short distance away, a mound of rubble from the house had been shoved over the low bank and into the water.

'Did you know that all this was so close to happening?' Mercer asked him.

Bail nodded, still without turning.

'You must have known for months.'

'So what? So why didn't I do something about it instead of pretending everything was going to be all right? So why didn't I try to make a proper go of the place, pay back the bank and keep everyone out?'

'I didn't mean to criticize.'

'Perhaps because I'm no different from all those tens of thousands of others who thought they were owed something, a breathing space, a chance to take stock and catch up. Perhaps because I believed everything I was told. Get the war out of the way and the future will take care of itself. Well, not here it didn't, not here.' The man's disillusionment and sense of betrayal were complete.

354

'Jacob's safe,' Mercer said eventually. 'He's with me.'

'I guessed as much.'

'He's ill, worse. I know how much you did for him. I know what your trust and friendship meant to him.'

'Yes, well . . .' Bail said, meeting Mercer's eyes for the first time. 'I doubt *he* lives in much hope of anything from anyone else.'

'Mathias is with him.'

'And what's *he* going to do? Wait until you're not looking, get the nod from Jacob and then smother him with a pillow?'

'You surely don't believe that.'

'No, but I can see it's something *you've* not given any thought to.'

This further hostile remark made Mercer even more wary of him, and he made no response to it.

'That bastard Lynch was here,' Bail said. 'Arrived just as this lot got here.' He jabbed his gloved hand over his shoulder, unable to look around him and face what was happening there. 'Waited for them to break open the gates and then came in with them, swearing and cursing and shouting the odds about what he was going to do to the filthy Jew, about what a disgrace he was and what he deserved.'

'But why? He doesn't even know the man,' Mercer said.

Bail looked at him coldly. 'There's always somebody asking, "Why?" Always somebody standing off to one side and asking, "Why?" I don't bloody know why. Why does there have to be a reason? There isn't a reason. The man makes up his own reasons. He was never any different – always looking for someone weaker than himself, someone to blame for everything that was wrong in his own life. Perhaps that's why. Perhaps it's as simple as that. I doubt it's the kind of explanation that would satisfy a man like you, but perhaps it's all there is for the rest of us.'

'And presumably Jacob had already gone.'

'I got him out the back while they were still smashing down the gates and threatening to shoot the dogs. They came early. I was expecting a few more days. I went up there and helped him get his things together. He left a lot of stuff which I boxed up and put in the house.' He looked at the flattened building. 'And then they came for that, so the stuff's out in the yard. Nothing he'll want, nothing valuable. A few books and clothes. He left his crucible and tongs and the other bits and pieces of his glass-making.'

'Are there any of his bowls?'

'Smashed. Every one of them.'

'Does he know?'

Bail laughed. 'Know? He did it. There's me rushing round gathering everything together for him, shouting at him to get out, and what does he do? Goes straight to the cupboard where he keeps them all, takes them out and then smashes them one at a time, piece by piece, smash smash smash.' He made a throwing motion into the water. 'And those that didn't shatter into enough pieces for him, he crushed with his foot.'

'Didn't you try to stop him?'

'Why should I? He would just have done it later. I didn't see this lot look too carefully at everything *they* smashed to pieces. I was born in that house. So, no, I didn't stop him. I just let him get on with it while I grabbed what I could of his other things. They were through the gates by then.'

'And you, no doubt, confronted Lynch while Jacob made his escape,' Mercer said.

'He could scarcely walk, especially with his bag. If he made it as far as you then he must have dumped

356

half of what he set out with. I stopped Lynch at the forge door. He's not so keen when people stand up to him.'

'Especially people cradling iron bars?'

Bail smiled. 'I told him Jacob was long gone and that I had enough on my hands with everything else that was happening to bother with him. They were all over the place by then. They wanted to know who Lynch was and what he was doing there. He took himself off into town after that.'

An oil drum floated beneath them, the sheen of its spilled fuel spreading slowly in its wake.

'Do you have any idea what medicines Jacob was taking?' Mercer said.

'I asked him once, but he wouldn't say. He said they were all useless. I never asked again.'

A bulldozer approached close to where they stood, pushing a mound of bricks and earth ahead of it.

'They shouldn't come so close to the drains,' Bail said. 'They haven't got the first idea.'

Mercer told him that he had to leave. 'I'll tell Jacob I saw you, shall I?' he said.

Bail nodded. 'We sort of fell against each other for support,' he said. 'I lost my brothers and he lost his sister and everyone else. We just fell and leaned together waiting for the first one to move.' He breathed deeply and then blew out his breath.

'I saw a swan here once,' Mercer said.

'They nested further along the drain. They won't be here for too long now, not with all this going on.'

Mercer could think of nothing more to say to him, and so he left him and walked back into the centre of the town and the waiting driver.

42

Upon his return, he saw that the fire outside Daniels's house still burned, though much lower now, and was more ash and charred remains than kindling or flame. Daniels himself stood beside it and several others congregated a short distance from him. Neither Lynch nor Mary nor her mother were among them.

At the site, the workers were preparing to leave. The foreman told him of the day's mixed achievements and delays, and he could imagine how little had been done during his absence. He waited until the last of the lorries had gone before going inside.

Mathias was waiting for him. He stood at the barely open door and watched as the last of the lorries manoeuvred onto the road.

Mercer spread out the medicines he had collected. Mathias watched him, but with little interest or enthusiasm.

'They ought to help,' Mercer said, but he, too, lacked conviction. 'How's he been?'

'Sleeping, mostly. He was woken once or twice. Lynch was here.'

'What did he want?'

'Just to bang on the door, shout for you, and to rant and rave. He was convinced you were inside, hiding from him. I think he'd been looking for you on the site.'

'Did he know either you or Jacob were here?'

'I doubt it. He just wanted to make his presence felt and to put on a show for the others.'

'Others?'

'They've been standing round that fire all day. He had his daughter with him. He shouted up for you to show yourself and to look out at her. He said that if you were too much of a coward to reveal yourself to him, then you could at least be man enough to answer the girl.'

'Did she say anything?'

'Not a word. She came back alone, later. She knocked and called two or three times, and then she left again. I think her father was somewhere on the site with the men.'

'When was this?'

'An hour ago. I considered letting her in, but there were workers nearby and they would have seen. I thought of letting her in to sit with Jacob until you got back. I need to see Roland, to try and talk him out of doing anything stupid.'

You're already too late, Mercer thought.

'From what you told me of your encounter with him this morning . . .'

Mercer held open the door and Mathias went, promising to return as soon as possible.

He climbed to where Jacob lay. The tremor of his limbs was more marked than earlier, and sweat still coated his face and chest. And looking down at him, and knowing that Jacob might not now even be aware of his presence, let alone respond to him, he saw how futile his errand had been, how pointless his absence at such a critical time.

He knelt beside Jacob and told him what he had managed to buy, then told him of his meeting with Bail. But Jacob gave no indication of having heard him. His eyes flickered restlessly beneath their closed lids. Mercer wiped his face and hands and slid a clean pillow beneath his head. Jacob groaned as he did this, and Mercer turned away at the sourness of his breath. He wiped the damp cloth over Jacob's lips.

He sat for an hour at his chart table, uncertain how much of the day's anticipated work had been completed, and he saw again what a clean and ordered fiction the charts represented, how little of the place's true history or geography they revealed. He saw, too, and not for the first time, what necessary deceits he himself had perpetrated at that crucial time in the place's history: he was no longer the man standing at the calm centre of the rising storm, no longer a mere observer, someone detached and apart from the lives and events already meshed and spinning unstoppably towards their conclusion there: he was a part of that storm, and, possibly, in all he was there to demolish and to build anew, its most potent and destructive current.

He fell asleep where he sat, and was woken by someone knocking softly on the tower door. Imagining this to be Mathias, and waiting until he was certain it was not Lynch, he went down.

He opened the door and Mary came quickly in.

By then the sun was much lower, and the inside of the tower was filled with its yellow light.

She stood to one side, waiting for him to close and bolt the door behind her before speaking.

'You and your father were here earlier,' he said, unwilling to listen to her excuses.

'He said you'd go out to him if I was there.'

'And this morning's little performance?'

'He was just angry.'

'He's always angry.'

'He was mad that Daniels was leaving.'

'Why should that matter to him?'

'Because it's Daniels who the others trust. He said that Daniels was abandoning them all, that he'd betrayed them.'

'Did Daniels *say* he was going?'

'He burned everything he owned.'

'What else did your father say?' It was clear to him that Lynch had had no idea that Mathias and Jacob were in the tower when he had come there earlier.

'He said that he was going, too. I told him that I was going with him, and my mother grabbed me and asked me what I was talking about. He waited until I'd told her I was leaving and going with him before telling me he had no intention of taking me with him. He let me say it. He stood and smiled and nodded at her while I said it.'

'Proving another of his points. Letting her know what lies ahead of her.'

'She knows that well enough.'

'You still said what you said to her.'

'And he made sure she heard every word of it. I told him he'd promised me and he told me to go to him. He grabbed me and shook me and shouted in my ear to ask if I was hearing him any better. He laughed at me, at us both. She told him to go back out and to carry on picking a fight with Daniels. She said Daniels was ten times the man he would ever be.'

'And so, presumably, he hit her to prove her wrong.'

She took a deep breath. 'He went on hitting her. Those outside must have heard the noise she made because someone knocked on the door and shouted in to ask if everything was all right. Daniels came, too, and shouted the same. He banged on the door. My mother shouted that she was fine and for everybody to go away and leave her alone. He hit her again, but she didn't make any noise after that. He was hitting just her instead of both of us. He made that much clear to her. He kept asking her if she'd had enough, because he hadn't finished yet. She shouted for me to go upstairs to Peter.'

'And?'

'And I went.'

'Where is he now?'

'He waited until everybody had gone and then he went out. I thought he might have come here again.'

'Do you think he might have done what he's been threatening, and gone for good?'

She shrugged. 'He had nothing with him.'

'Had he been drinking?'

She nodded.

A noise from above distracted them both.

'I have to go back up,' he told her, still unwilling for her to accompany him and see Jacob there.

'Is it Mathias?' she said.

'Yes, Mathias.'

'No, it isn't,' she said. 'I saw him leave earlier. It's Jacob, isn't it?'

A further noise silenced them both.

'He's ill,' Mercer said. 'They were both here earlier when you and your father—'

'I know,' she said. 'I saw the two of you carrying him last night. I watched you from the dunes.'

'I have to go back up to him,' he said. He climbed the stairs and she followed him.

Jacob had again half-fallen from the mattress and Mercer pulled him back onto it.

'What's that smell?' she said.

Jacob had vomited onto his blankets. A clear, viscous pool. She wiped the bulk of this up with newspapers and then soaked a cloth and dabbed at what remained.

'Do you know what's wrong with him?' she asked Mercer, looking hard at Jacob, at the ridges and hollows of his exposed chest.

'No.'

She wrung out the cloth and wiped Jacob's face. He choked at her touch and retched again. 'Sit him up,' she told Mercer, and he held Jacob propped upright as the last of the bile fell from his mouth into the cloth.

Afterwards, his throat clear, his breathing became easier and they laid him back down and left him.

'Is he dying?' she said.

It was beyond him to answer her.

She went back alone to Jacob. She held his hand and whispered close to his ear.

Mercer watched her, surprised and yet inexplicably reassured by what she did. There had been fear in her voice when she had asked him if Jacob was dying.

She remained beside him for several minutes, his hand in hers, her face close to his own. After which, she laid his hand across his chest, rose and came back to Mercer.

'What did you say to him?' he asked her.

'Nothing. I just told him that someone was here, looking after him. It would be awful if he was too sick to know where he was. He might even wake up and

363

think he was back in that place.' She washed her hands, sniffed them and washed them again.

Her grasp of the situation surprised Mercer, and in the absence of Mathias he was grateful for her presence.

'Daniels told him that all the houses were going to be knocked down anyway,' she said. 'And then *he* told *her* that you could have told us all this the minute you arrived. He said you'd known all along, so what did we think of you now?'

'It's true,' he said, wondering what else he might now reveal to her.

'Good,' she said.

'You won't necessarily be re-housed.'

'Meaning we definitely won't be.'

'Where will Daniels go?' he asked her.

'He won't say. What does it matter? Once he reaches the end of the coast road they'll forget he was ever here.'

'Does everyone know about the houses?'

'What do you think?'

Across the room, Jacob resumed gasping for air. Bubbles of saliva formed on his lips, burst and shone on his chin. Mary returned to him with the cloth.

'It'll pass,' Mercer told her, remaining at the table.

Again, she knelt beside Jacob and wiped his face, this time holding her hand to his brow as his gasping eased and he grew calm again. She spoke to reassure him, more noise than words, and again Mercer could hear nothing of what she said.

He took the whisky from the cupboard and poured himself a drink. The sun was close to the horizon and the evening chill could be felt. The mist already blurred the distant boundary between the land and the sea. It would be dark in less than an hour.

She came back to the table and pretended to drink from his glass.

'Perhaps you should be a nurse,' he told her.

'I don't think so,' she said.

'I doubt he even knows we're here.' He drained the glass.

'I felt his hand tighten,' she said. 'Each time.'

'It's something,' he said, uncertain whether he believed her, and she smiled, as though he had paid her a well-earned compliment. 'He knows you were there, in the dunes with him,' he said. 'He was only pretending to be asleep.'

'I know,' she said.

'You knew?'

'I made plenty of noise to let him know I was coming. I saw him moving. When I got to him he was pretending to be asleep.'

'What happened?'

'Nothing. I pretended I believed he was asleep. I told him I was sorry for everything that had happened to him. I told him I wished his sister was still alive and that the two of them were still together. I thought he might suddenly open his eyes and tell me to clear off and leave him alone. But he didn't. He just went on pretending to be asleep.'

'Were you with him for long?'

'Just a few minutes. I couldn't think of anything else to say to him. He knew I knew he wasn't really asleep.'

'How can you be sure?'

'I just knew.'

'Perhaps he was scared of what attention you might attract to the pair of you.' The waiting boats had still been out on the water.

'It wasn't that. He just wanted to lie there and listen to me talking.'

'Talking about his sister.'

She nodded.

'And so you both pretended.'

Neither of them spoke for several minutes.

He told her eventually that he was waiting for Mathias to return. Every few seconds she looked at Jacob, making it clear to Mercer that she would rather be back beside him doing something she considered to be useful instead of sitting at the table and talking.

He was about to suggest that they sorted through the medicines he had bought, when he heard shouting outside, and he immediately recognized Lynch's voice. Mary rose in her seat and he pushed her back down so that she would not be seen by the man below.

'He'll know I'm here,' she said.

Earlier, he had lit one of his lamps, and the light from this would be visible from outside.

Lynch continued shouting, closer now. He called for Mercer to go out to him. And then he shouted up that he knew Mary was there, too. He wanted to know what Mercer was doing with her, why he'd made her go up to him. He wanted to know how long they'd been alone together. His drunkenness was evident in every-thing he said.

Mercer went to the window and looked down.

Lynch stood on the road. He held a piece of timber and swung this from side to side, then beat upon one of the generators with it. In his other hand he held a bottle, which he threw into the air, swung at and struck, shattering the glass all around him. He laughed at what he had done and then resumed his shouting.

'Ignore him,' Mary said. 'He'll go away.'

'Stay where you are,' Mercer told her. 'He doesn't know you're here – not for certain.'

'Where else would I be?' she said.

'Go and sit with Jacob,' he told her. He watched Lynch as he spoke. The man moved back and forth on the road, but did not come onto the rougher ground of the site. It occurred to him that Daniels might go out and confront him, but there was no light from Daniels's home, only the dying glow of the nearby fire. The door to the house stood open, revealing the impenetrable darkness of inside. Pieces of clothing lay scattered on the ground.

Mercer returned to the table, and his disappearance from the window caused Lynch to resume his shouting. This time, his repeated accusations were laced with obscenity. There can have been no one in the houses who did not hear everything he said.

The noise disturbed Jacob, penetrating whatever delirium he endured, and he mumbled to himself and turned his head from side to side as though in search of the shouting man. His hand clawed the air, and Mary went to him and again took it in both her own.

'I'll have to go down,' Mercer told her. 'He mustn't find out he's here.' He stood above her and saw how Jacob's fingers agitated inside the loose restraint of her own soft palms.

43

By the time he reached the road, the others had come out of their homes to investigate. But whereas previously they might have gathered together in a group to discuss what was happening, now they stood scattered, separately or in pairs, and all of them careful to keep their distance from Lynch, who continued to stagger back and forth, swinging his club and shouting.

Mercer knew that he would achieve more in the eyes of these others by confronting Lynch and his accusations directly than by any denials he might have shouted down from the safety of the tower.

'Come to start knocking them down, have you? Now, in the middle of the night when there's no one to see?' Lynch called to him, suddenly much more sober than he had seemed only a few minutes earlier, and Mercer saw how he had again been deceived by the man.

'No one is going to demolish the houses for some considerable time, and certainly not without first consulting everyone who lives here,' he shouted. He knew immediately how evasive and patronizing the remark sounded.

Lynch mimicked his words, gratified by the laughter and the calls of his scattered audience. He kept his eyes on Mercer as he came. A second bottle stood on the ground beside him. 'Thought I was too drunk to do anything about it, did you?' he said, but this time so that only Mercer heard.

Mercer wanted to turn and see if Mary was watching, but the gesture would only have confirmed her presence to Lynch. He could still not be certain that the others were not about to side with Lynch in goading him. Some of them, having heard his remark about their homes, might be prepared to believe anything Lynch now suggested.

And almost as though the man were reading these thoughts, Lynch said, 'Leave her back in your bed, did you?'

'You're being stupid,' Mercer said immediately, knowing he dare not hesitate in his rebuttals. 'She's your daughter, for Christ's sake. She's fifteen.'

'So what?' Lynch said, his eyes now fixed on the tower.

It occurred to Mercer that Lynch was going to run past him and drag Mary out into the open where the others might see her, and then use her presence as evidence of all he said.

He was relieved to hear one of the younger women say, 'Leave the girl out of it, Lynch. She's got nothing to do with the houses. It's him we want answers from.' But Mercer knew that the houses were not Lynch's true concern, and that he would not allow them all to be so easily diverted from his own narrow course.

'Yes, she's there,' Mercer shouted. 'She came an hour ago. She's alone there now, too scared to come out.'

'Too scared?' Lynch said. 'Too scared of what? You trying to tell them she's scared of me?' He turned from the tower back to Mercer.

'Scared she might end up with as many bruises as your wife now has,' Mercer said.

Several of the women began talking among themselves.

Lynch stared hard at Mercer, his eyes narrowing, and it was clear to Mercer that the man had not expected so direct or so blunt an accusation after all his previous diversions.

'Whatever she's said, she's lying,' Lynch shouted, and this vague and unconvincing denial encouraged Mercer even further.

'Simple enough to find out,' Mercer said, his own voice calm and low. The women, he guessed, had long since been aware of Lynch's violence towards his wife, and perhaps they at last felt some shame at not having confronted the man themselves.

'I never once touched the girl, never once,' Lynch shouted. 'Get her out here. Ask her. She'll tell you. If she's hurt, *he* did it.' This second, faltering denial confirmed everything Mercer believed.

'We could always go to your home and ask your wife,' Mercer suggested. But he knew even as he spoke that this would be beyond him – that he would not perpetrate anything so cruel or humiliating on Elizabeth Lynch – and he wondered if Lynch, too, understood this and might now turn it to his own advantage.

But Lynch seemed more uncertain than ever of his own way forward.

'Where is she?' one of the women called to him, meaning his wife.

Lynch started to turn to her, but then swung back to

face Mercer. 'Who cares where she is?' he mouthed silently so that again only Mercer could hear him.

It chilled Mercer to hear the words, and to see what pleasure Lynch took in them.

Elizabeth Lynch's home remained in darkness, but she would hear everything that was happening, and would understand better than any of them the consequences of the night's events. Mercer wished he could go to her, or that she might emerge from her home to confront Lynch directly, but he knew that neither of these courses was likely, and that the darkness within which she now sat was wholly of her own making.

Though already a year dead, the war, or so it seemed to Mercer, still clung to everything it had once touched, having lasted too long and been elsewhere too destructive and all-consuming to leave no frayed edges, no ineradicable stains and no blighted men and women fighting in its wake. They had all, he now understood, confused the dying tremors of that violent past with its lasting reverberations into all their futures. More importantly, and regardless of their tales of sinking ships, of drowned men and crashing aircraft, it was not the lingering presence of that distant war in this isolated place, but its *absence* with which they were all now struggling to come to terms.

The night air was filled with the scent of the smoke, which thickened in the mist, and which filled every dip and hollow in the ground around its dead heart, undisturbed in the stillness. The moon lay unbroken on the surface of the sea. The mist itself had seeped inland, filling the deeper channels and drains as though it were water flowing along them.

Lynch said nothing for several minutes. He picked up the bottle at his feet, drank from it and then offered

371

it to the man standing closest to him, but the man simply shook his head and went on watching him.

Sensing that Lynch no longer possessed the conviction to continue, and relieved that this final confrontation had ended without any further violence, Mercer looked at those around him and called out, 'This isn't the time to talk about the houses.' He took several paces to one side so that Lynch no longer stood directly between him and the others. 'I'll come in the morning and tell you everything I know.'

And it was as he waited for them to acknowledge this offer – to accept it because there was now no other course left open to them – that Mary screamed in the tower behind him and then appeared at the lighted upper window to stand and look down at them all with her hands and face pressed hard against the glass.

44

Lynch was the first to start running, and he collided with Mercer and knocked him to the ground. Mercer fell badly, feeling his arm wrenched beneath him. Others among the onlookers followed Lynch to the tower. No one stopped to help Mercer to his feet. The young woman who had earlier shouted to Lynch paused beside Mercer and looked down at him, and he waited for what she might say to him, which of Lynch's allegations she might repeat, but after a moment of her silent judgement, she turned and walked back to the houses and the dying fire.

Mercer rose and followed the others to the tower. Lynch had already reached the building and gone inside. The others stood around the open door, reluctant to enter, and Mercer pushed through these and scrambled up the stairs to where Lynch, Mary and Jacob now awaited him.

Mary stood at the window where she had revealed herself, and Jacob still lay at the far side of the room, on the floor, his chin pressed to his chest and his arms stretched out ahead of him as though he had dragged himself from his bed in the act of striving for something beyond his reach.

Running back to the tower, it had occurred to Mercer that Jacob might have finally been overcome by his illness and had died in Mary's arms, and that this was what had caused her to scream and to show herself at the window. He looked closely at Jacob and saw that he was still breathing. The fingers of his outstretched hand opened and closed slightly. The cloth with which Mary had wiped his face lay beside him.

Lynch stood with his daughter at the window, and it was clear by the expression on her face that something had happened there, and both men understood this.

Lynch grabbed the girl and shook her, asking her over and over to tell him what had made her scream.

It then occurred to Mercer that perhaps Lynch had not yet seen the man on the floor. He rubbed his wrist where he had fallen. It was discoloured and had started to swell. He attempted to flex his fingers but stopped abruptly at the sudden pain. He cried out at this, and Lynch turned to face him, looking quickly from where he stood at the trapdoor to the man on the floor beside him.

'She was up here alone with *him*?' he shouted disbelievingly. 'You left her up here, alone, with *that*?' He released his grip on his daughter and came towards Mercer, who moved to stand between him and Jacob.

'He's sick,' Mercer said. 'Look at him: he hasn't been able to move for two days. Ask her.'

'She screamed,' Lynch said simply. 'Something must have made her scream.' He moved from side to side to get a better look at Jacob. He screwed up his face. 'He stinks,' he said. 'They all do.' His fists were already tightly bunched at his sides, and he drew back one of his feet ready to kick out.

Mercer appealed silently to Mary to intervene and explain to them what had happened, what had alarmed her, but she avoided his eyes and looked only at the man on the ground. He heard the others in the room below, some of whom now stood at the foot of the stairs and called up to find out what was happening. He hoped one of the men might join them and help him to restrain Lynch, but no one came. His wrist grew even more painful.

On the floor, Jacob groaned and resumed his groping. Mercer knelt beside him and tried to lift his head back onto his pillow, but with only one hand this proved impossible, and painful for them both.

'Help me,' he said to Mary, but she gave no indication of having heard him. He asked her again, and this time she shook her head. 'Then help *him*,' he said. But again she made no move towards him and merely went on staring at where Jacob lay.

By then, Lynch's anger had grown beyond him, and as Mercer tried to rise he pushed him back down.

'You were the one who left her with him,' he said. 'Whatever happened, *you're* the one responsible.' He called through the hatchway that the Jew was there, that he was pretending to be ill, and that he was the cause of all the trouble. He said that Mercer had deliberately left his daughter alone with the man while he had gone out to them to spread the rest of his lies. There was a moment of silence in the room below, followed by the rising murmur of speculation.

'Just tell me what happened,' Mercer said to Mary, knowing that her explanation – her voice even – was now the key to defusing the situation.

Eventually, she looked up from Jacob and seemed as though she was at last about to speak.

'Tell me,' Mercer urged her.

She clasped her hands together. 'I was wiping his face,' she said.

'Wiping his face?' Lynch shouted. 'I've told you not to go anywhere near him.'

Mary continued looking at Mercer as though her father had not spoken, as though he were not even present in the room beside them. 'He opened his eyes,' she said. 'He wanted me to get closer to him. He was trying to tell me something so I put my ear close to his mouth to try and hear what he was saying. It was just his breathing, he couldn't clear his throat. He wanted me to get closer to him. The only way I could do that was by lying down on the floor beside him.'

'Lying down?' Lynch said.

And again she went on talking as though the man had not interrupted her.

'One noise over and over,' she said. 'And then, when I was as close as I could get to him, still trying to understand what he was trying to tell me, he suddenly reached out and grabbed hold of me. He didn't seem capable of it at first, but I was lying propped on my side and there was nothing I could do to avoid him; I fell away from him and the next thing I knew his arm was round my neck.'

'The bastard,' Lynch shouted.

'Let her finish,' Mercer said. 'You can see she hasn't been harmed.'

'He tried to grab hold of her. You heard her.'

'It probably wasn't deliberate,' Mary said. 'His arm was where I fell, and when I landed on it, he folded it round me. He wasn't really hurting me, more holding me. It was as though he just wanted me to lie there, to let him hold me. That was when I screamed. It wasn't hard to push him off once I'd got my balance, and after that I went to the window. He scrambled on the floor for a few seconds and then he started coughing again and seemed to lose all his strength. I heard then what he'd been trying to say to me.'

'He thought you were his sister,' Mercer said.

'Anna,' she said.

It was beyond Mercer to imagine what Jacob must have seen or heard in his barely conscious delirium, or where he now imagined himself to be.

'He woke and thought you were his sister tending to him,' he said.

'He started crying,' she said. 'When he tried to grab hold of me and I pushed him away.' She took several paces back towards where Jacob lay, until Lynch put out his arm to stop her.

'If I'd known . . .' she said to Mercer.

'I know,' he told her. Mercer finally rose to his feet.

'Known what?' Lynch said. 'If she'd known what?'

She tried to reach down to the man on the floor, but again Lynch stopped her, pulling her sharply back to him.

'Let go of her,' Mercer said.

Lynch swung her round so that she stood between them. 'Or else what?'

And at that moment, perhaps because he had been alerted by the voices around him, or perhaps only because he had heard the girl and his sister's name repeated so many times, Jacob, too, said, 'Anna,' and reached out his hand until it connected with Lynch's ankle, which he then feebly attempted to grab.

Lynch cried out at this and released his hold on his daughter. He lifted the foot Jacob had touched and then stamped it down hard on Jacob's fingers.

'Anna,' Jacob said, and again they all heard him clearly. He went on saying the name, forming it over and over until his voice faded to a dry whisper, oblivious to Lynch's foot.

Hearing him speak, Lynch finally stepped away from him, and then, before either Mercer or Mary could intervene, he swung a kick at Jacob which caught his arm and threw it awkwardly back across his face.

Unable to restrain him in any other way, Mercer threw himself against Lynch and knocked him to the floor.

Someone below shouted up again to ask what was happening, and this time Mercer heard Mathias's voice amid the cacophony. He called down for him to come up to them, trying to keep himself between Lynch and Jacob. And while he did this, Mary went back to the mattress and lifted Jacob's head back onto the pillow. She gently picked up the arm Lynch had kicked and laid it by his side. Jacob no longer attempted to speak to her, and his mouth fell slackly open to reveal his teeth.

Mathias climbed through the hatchway and shouted to ask what was happening.

'Help him,' Mercer said, indicating Jacob.

Mathias stood for a few seconds trying to understand what he was seeing, alarmed by the presence of Lynch and his daughter.

And in those few seconds, Lynch finally pushed himself free of Mercer, turned to where Mary knelt beside Jacob, and swung another kick at the man, this time catching him in his side and causing Jacob to groan and then to choke at the pain of the blow.

Mary shouted for her father to stop, and in an effort to protect Jacob, she held herself over his chest and put her arms around his head. Oblivious now to all that was taking place around him, Jacob continued to choke, and every fibre and bone of his head, neck and chest were brought into sharp relief by the effort.

Lynch shouted again for Mary to move away from him, and drew back his foot for a third kick.

But by then Mathias had grasped what was happening and he struck a blow to the side of Lynch's head which caught him by surprise and knocked him to the floor.

Lynch rose quickly and turned to face Mathias, but as he did this, Mathias struck him again, and this time Lynch stumbled backwards, missing his footing and putting one of his feet through the open hatchway. He fell badly, striking his head against the side of the opening, wedged where he had fallen, and from where he now tried to pull himself back to his feet.

Both Mercer and Mathias watched him struggle there for a moment.

'Help him up,' Mercer said eventually.

But instead, Mathias went to where Lynch held out his hand to be pulled up and kicked at his arm and shoulder until he fell through the hatchway and down the steps into the room below. The voices beneath stopped immediately.

Mercer went to the opening and looked down. Lynch lay without moving at the bottom of the steps, his legs above his body, one of his feet caught between the rungs.

'He's landed badly,' he said.

'Good,' Mathias said, and he looked from Mercer to where Mary still knelt with her arms around Jacob's head.

Jacob finally stopped choking and lay calmly in her embrace.

Beneath them, the voices resumed and a woman screamed.

'You ought to go,' Mercer said to Mathias.

But Mathias shook his head. 'No, I ought to stay. I shouldn't have gone in the first place. If I'd stayed with him, none of this would have happened.'

He went to the mattress and knelt at Jacob's feet. At his arrival there, Mary started to rise, but he indicated for her to stay, and she put her hands back to Jacob's face, stretching herself alongside him on the thin mattress. She whispered to him and he grew calmer. He closed his mouth and turned to face her.

Mathias remained kneeling at Jacob's feet, holding them in both his hands and caressing their soles with his thumbs. He started to cry, and then said something through his tears which neither Mercer nor Mary properly heard.

Again, Mercer looked down to where Lynch had fallen, and where he still lay without moving. He lifted the open trapdoor and then lowered it into its space, sealing the four of them off from everyone below.

He went to the window and looked down on the men and women outside, most of them now walking slowly back to their homes. It was brighter there than in the tower, and the moon cast their shadows ahead of them.

Above them, a flock of gulls flew in from the sea, rising and falling in wavering lines, their vividly white outlines flickering and spectral as they passed silently overhead.

The smoke from the fire still clung to the ground, and the men and women passing through it resembled nothing more to Mercer than aimless waders in a shallow sea, uncertain of their destinations or of the hidden depths ahead of them, the disturbed smoke curling and then settling around them as they went.

THE END

THE BOOK OF THE HEATHEN
Robert Edric

'MORE DISTURBING EVEN THAN CONRAD IN HIS DEPICTION
OF THE HEART OF DARKNESS'
Peter Kemp, *Sunday Times*

'RELENTLESS , . . AN IMPRESSIVE AND DISTURBING WORK
OF ART'
Robert Nye, *Literary Review*

1897. In an isolated station in the Belgian Congo, an Englishman
awaits trial for the murder of a native child, while his friend
attempts to discover the circumstances surrounding the charge.
The world around them is rapidly changing: the horrors of
colonial Africa are becoming known and the flow of its once-
fabulous wealth is drying up.

But there is even more than the death of a child at the heart of
this conflict. There is a secret so dark, so unimaginable, that one
man must be willingly destroyed by his possession of it, and the
other must participate in that destruction.

'MANY RESPECTABLE JUDGES WOULD PUT EDRIC IN THE TOP
TEN OF BRITISH NOVELISTS CURRENTLY AT WORK . . . AS A
WRITER, HE SPECIALISES IN THE DELICATE HINT AND THE
GAME NOT GIVEN AWAY'
D.J. Taylor, *Spectator*

'STUNNING . . . EVOCATIVELY BRINGS TO LIFE THE STIFLING
HUMIDITY AND CONSTANT RAINFALL OF THE CONGO'
John Cooper, *The Times*

'A VERY GRIPPING STORY . . . THE READER IS DRAWN IN
INEXORABLY TO DISCOVER WHAT HORROR LIES AT THE
HEART OF IT . . . AN APOCALYPTIC FABLE FOR TODAY'
John Spurling, *The Times Literary Supplement*

'RENDERED IN PROSE WHOSE STEADINESS AND
TRANSPARENCY THROW THE DARK TURBULENCE OF WHAT
IS HAPPENING INTO DAMNING RELIEF. IT WILL BE
SURPRISING IF THIS YEAR SEES A MORE DISTURBING OR
HAUNTING NOVEL'
Peter Kemp, *Sunday Times*

0 552 99925 3

BLACK SWAN

THE SWORD CABINET
Robert Edric

'A KALEIDOSCOPIC MEDITATION ON CELEBRITY,
MUNDANITY AND HORROR'
Mark Sanderson, *Time Out*

Robert Edric's brilliant novel recreates a faded world of seaside
entertainers, stuntmen and illusionists. Mitchell King, failed
impresario, ruined club-owner and embezzler, searches for his
lost mother, the former girl-assistant to Morgan King, escapologist
and chief suspect in an unsolved case of serial killing dating back
to 1950.

'SPECTACULAR . . . EDRIC DARTS BETWEEN INTERLINKED
STORIES, SPINNING THEM LIKE PLATES ON STICKS'
Ruth Scurr, *The Times*

'GLORIOUSLY DISCOMFORTING AND MYSTERIOUS . . . A
PHILOSOPHICAL PUZZLE'
Alison Huntley, *Independent*

'EDRIC'S TECHNIQUE RESTS ON SUBTERFUGE AND
CONCEALMENT . . . A THOROUGHLY ARRESTING
PERFORMANCE'
D. J. Taylor, *Sunday Times*

'THE REWARDS COME FROM THE CLEAR AUSTERITY OF THE
PROSE, THE UTTERLY BELIEVABLE CHARACTERS AND THE
SATISFYING MIXTURE OF REAL AND METAPHORICAL
ILLUSION . . . IMPRESSIVE'
Natasha Cooper, *Sunday Express*

1 862 30066 6

CRADLE SONG
Robert Edric

An imprisoned paedophile and child murderer unexpectedly appeals his conviction. In return for a reduced sentence, he offers to implicate those involved in the crimes who were never caught; to provide evidence of Police corruption at the time of the original investigation; and, most importantly, to reveal where the corpses of several long-sought, but never found teenage girls are buried.

Unhappy at what may be about to happen, but at the same time desperate to locate the body of his own missing daughter, the father of one of these girls approaches Private Investigator Leo Rivers with a plea for help.

Rivers' enquiries stir cold and bitter memories. Long-dead enmities flare suddenly into violence and a succession of new killings. Everyone involved, then and now, and on both sides of the law, is unprepared for the suddenness and ferocity with which these old embers are fanned back into life. As the investigation progresses, it gathers momentum, and now must speed inexorably to the even greater violence and sadness of its conclusion.

The first of a trilogy of contemporary crime novels set in the city of Hull, Robert Edric's new novel is reminiscent of Chandler and Mosley, and yet remains uniquely British. Against the backdrop of Internet pornography, Police corruption and child murder, this dark and intense novel reads like a game of chess where each piece is invested with a deceptive significance.

NOW AVAILABLE FROM DOUBLEDAY

0 385 60574 9